Dear Reader,

Welcome to another exciting month of Duets—romantic stories guaranteed to make you smile!

In Duets #25 Kristin Gabriel's *The Bachelor Trap* is the first book in a new miniseries called CAFÉ ROMEO, about a coffeehouse that also doubles as a dating service. *What better place to find both lattes and love!* Talented Kristin received a RITA Award this year from the Romance Writers of America for her Love & Laughter novel *Monday Man.* Popular Carrie Alexander also kicks off a trilogy, called THE COWGIRL CLUB, about three lifelong female friends who love horses and—what else?—cowboys! You'll have a galloping good time reading Grace's story in *Custom-Built Cowboy.*

In Duets #26 we return to the BEST OF THE WEST with fan favorite Cathie Linz. This time, in *The Lawman Gets Lucky,* charming Reno Best is the sheriff hero who comes undone when he encounters gorgeous new schoolteacher Annie Benton. *The West will never be the same!* New author Isabel Sharpe delivers the sharply funny *Beauty and the Bet,* another book in the MAKEOVER MADNESS miniseries. Beautiful Heather Brannen makes herself over as a plain Jane in order to best ladies' man Jack Fortunato. But she's sure surprised when Jack falls hard for the plain "Marsha," and Heather is jealous of herself!

I hope you enjoy all our books this month and every month!

Happy reading!

Birgit Davis-Todd
Senior Editor, Harlequin Duets

Harlequin Books
225 Duncan Mill Road
Don Mills, Ontario
M3B 3K9 Canada

"Oh, stop with the charm, Reno."

Annie smiled coolly. "All I want is to find my brother."

He grinned as he tipped his Stetson. "And that's my job. Having you walking around town like that—" he frowned at her skimpy shorts and top and teased Big Hair "—isn't about to loosen the tongues of any guys with information. Trust me," he drawled, "the effect will be quite the opposite."

His grin hadn't flustered her before, but now his visual appraisal made her feel hot and bothered. With his boyish good looks, breezy confidence and old-fashioned charm, Reno Best represented trouble and temptation in a way that made a gal want to line up for it.

Annie knew her place in the sexual hierarchy food chain. She was a minnow. Reno was a shark. Even now he was studying her with a hungry look. His hazel eyes made her minnow heart shiver.

Surely she could say no to trouble...and temptation?

For more, turn to page 9

Heather gasped. "Jack! *Here. Now. Omigod.*"

"Can you give me a minute, Jack? I'm just out of the shower."

She dashed to the bathroom. Hands shaking, she popped in the brown contacts, yanked on the padding and frantically coiled her hair to go under the wig, all the while cursing like a sailor.

Another knock came at her door. "Marsha." She did a last check in the mirror, grabbed her glasses and raced for the door.

Jack stepped into the apartment and his brows drew together as he gazed at her. "You look different, Marsha."

"I...haven't put on my makeup yet."

He took another step closer, eyeing her up and down. "Very different, Marsha."

She pushed past him into the middle of the room. "We need to talk, Jack."

"We certainly do, *Marsha*." He caught her arm. "For starters, I'd like to know why your rear end has migrated to the front of your body."

For more, turn to page 197

HARLEQUIN DUETS

ISBN 0-373-44092-8

THE LAWMAN GETS LUCKY
Copyright © 2000 by Cathie Linz

BEAUTY AND THE BET
Copyright © 2000 by Muna Shehadi Sill

Visit us at www.romance.net

Printed in U.S.A.

CATHIE LINZ

The Lawman
Gets Lucky

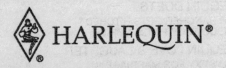

HARLEQUIN®

TORONTO • NEW YORK • LONDON
AMSTERDAM • PARIS • SYDNEY • HAMBURG
STOCKHOLM • ATHENS • TOKYO • MILAN • MADRID
PRAGUE • WARSAW • BUDAPEST • AUCKLAND

Dear Reader,

Mountains. I love them. Some people prefer a hot sandy beach, but my idea of heaven is being surrounded by mountains. And no, I don't ski or mountain climb. I just enjoy the view! And that view is made all the more appealing when my hero Reno Best is around. Reno is the charmer in the family—think Tom Cruise and Matthew McConaughey. I sure did! And what great inspiration they were, indeed. Ah, yes, mountains and great-looking men made writing this book a real joy.

And let's not forget my heroine Annie and her habit of baking when she's stressed out. I confess to having a similar behavior pattern. Chocolate chip are my favorite cookies, but brownies come in a close second. So go ahead, dip into your cookie jar and then curl up with a good romance novel, like this one! I hope you enjoy reading this last book in my BEST OF THE WEST trilogy, where you get to meet the entire Best family again before they ride off into the sunset.

Happy reading!

Cathie Linz

Books by Cathie Linz

HARLEQUIN DUETS

HARLEQUIN LOVE & LAUGHTER

BEST
OF THE
WEST

1

A LITTLE PEACE AND QUIET. That's all Reno Best wanted. And a medium-rare cheeseburger with all the toppings. It didn't seem like much to ask for. Not after working an eighteen-hour shift that had included four barroom brawls and two fender benders, one involving a fully loaded chicken truck.

As the town sheriff for Bliss, Colorado, keeping the peace was his job. It was a job that had gotten increasingly harder to do since word had gotten out last month that there was a fortune in gold buried somewhere around Bliss, hidden over a hundred years ago by western outlaw Cockeyed Curly Mahoney.

Reno still wasn't sure how the secret about Curly's newly discovered treasure map had leaked out. His dad, who had the map locked up in his safe, claimed it hadn't been him. Ditto for his two older brothers and their wives.

All Reno knew was that suddenly hordes of treasure hunters had come crawling out of the woodwork and some days it felt as if he was the only sane one left in Bliss.

He was certainly the only one in the recently opened Golden Treasure Diner, allowing him to eat his cheeseburger in peace and quiet. Or at least it was quiet until *she* stormed into the diner. Ignoring the sanctity of his lunch hour, she slid into his booth without an invitation. "What are you going to do about my brother?"

Reno had seen the new schoolteacher around in town—anyone who hadn't been around when Eisenhower was elected was considered to be "new" in town. It took him a minute to mentally pull up her name…it was something innocent-sounding like Annie. Yes, that was it. Annie Benton. She'd come west from some small town in Iowa and was very popular with the parents hereabouts, but that still didn't give her cause to go interrupting a man's meal.

"Your brother?" he repeated, not having a clue what she was talking about.

"That's right. My brother. The one who's missing. I called the sheriff's office and left a message this morning for you to call me back. You didn't."

"That could be because I didn't get your message." He swiped his mouth with a paper napkin, silently cursing the fact that his regular secretary and dispatcher, Opal, was home with a head cold. She'd sent her daughter in as a replacement, but twenty-year-old Sugar preferred listening to Ricky Martin to writing down phone messages. "If you'd wait until I'm back in my office after lunch, we can discuss this—"

"I'm not waiting another second," Annie angrily declared.

This shouldn't have surprised him. Since the discovery of the treasure map, it seemed as if everyone in town was as impatient as a raging bull in a rodeo pen.

She was cute, if you went for wholesome clean looks and no cleavage. Not that Reno judged a woman by her bra size. No, he liked to think he was more liberated than that. But he did have a weakness for a well-endowed woman like Roxanne over at the Homestead Restaurant who was four-time grand champion of the wet T-shirt contest held each spring at the truck stop. And grand she'd been and still was even though he and Roxanne had amicably broken up several months back. Since then he'd enjoyed playing the field and dating several women. Blondes, red-heads or ponytailed brunettes like the schoolteacher here—he loved them all. And to his eternal gratitude, they seemed to love him right back.

Not that this woman appeared to be thinking too kindly of him, not judging by the way she was glaring at him. She did have the biggest brown eyes he'd ever seen, though, framed with thick lashes. Her button nose added to her cuteness while her generous mouth hinted at a more passionate nature than he'd detected at first glance. And now that he took a closer look at the curves beneath the baby-blue camisole top she was wearing, he revised his earlier estimation regarding cleavage.

He sent her a friendly smile. "You're the new schoolteacher in town, right?"

"I'm hardly new," she frostily informed him. "I've been here almost four years. But that's irrelevant. I'm here because I need your help in finding my brother. He hasn't checked in with me in two days."

Reno knew about Mike Benton—he did part-time ranch work when it was available, or construction work. He'd also been known to enter a rodeo or two. And to place a bet on just about anything, from a Broncos game to the date of the first snowfall in Bliss. Mike was on the road a lot. Reno had seen his type before, drifters who hated being tied down to one place and who always thought there was something better over the next hill. "Two days isn't all that long, ma'am. Not for someone like Mike."

"I think I know my brother better than you do, Sheriff."

"Call me Reno," he invited her. "And yes, I'm sure you do know him better than I do, but I'm just saying that time has a way of getting away from a fellow when he does as much traveling as your brother does. For all of that, maybe he decided to try his hand at finding Cockeyed Curly's gold like half the folks in this town."

"He'd call me," Annie insisted. "He knows I worry about him."

"Has he ever done anything like this before?"

Reno could tell by her hesitation that her brother had. "He promised he wouldn't do it again," she said. "When I called the last place he was staying up in Bozeman, they said he left and didn't say where he was going. His car broke down, he told me he was leaving it there. That was two days ago. He may be hitchhiking. I can't believe you're just sitting there *eating*—" she said the word with utter disdain "—while my brother could be out there someplace needing help."

Her attitude irked him. After not having the time to eat for the past twelve hours, his stomach was just about pinned to his backbone from hunger. And now this schoolmarm had to come storming in, friendly as a diamondback and sore as a boil, to ruin his lunch hour.

He put a hand on his cheeseburger. It was stone-cold. So was her glare. His usual patience went out the window. "I'm sorry, ma'am, but there's no law that says a man has to check in with his sister every day of the week. I suggest you calm down and stop worrying. He'll call you when he's ready.''

ANNIE BENTON WANTED to take the cheeseburger—the one he was clearly more interested in than her story—and shove it down the sheriff's throat. Usually she was a calm, quiet and polite person, but where her younger brother was concerned she was like a fierce lioness protecting her cub. She'd had to be. She'd practically raised her brother herself.

And now this laid-back lawman had the nerve to act as if she was some kind of overbearing hysterical woman.

She'd heard about Sheriff Reno Best and his womanizing ways. It was rumored that he'd dated the past three Miss Colorados—two of them in the same weekend when he'd gone down to Denver for a law enforcement conference. The younger women in town had nicknamed him ''Jerry Maguire in a uniform'' because of his similarity to Tom Cruise in that movie. The older women in town wished they were young enough to chase after him.

She supposed he was handsome. His brown hair was rumpled and he was sporting a sexy stubble on a chin that looked as though it could be intractable. He had the kind of chiseled cheekbones that artists and photographers loved. His hazel eyes looked as if they belonged to a man who found humor in life, judging from the laugh lines at their corners. His hands were gripping his cheeseburger with capable strength, while his mouth...

Okay, so the guy was incredibly sexy. Everyone in town was right.

She didn't care. She only wanted him to find her brother. ''Let me get this clear,'' she said, using her "teacher" voice, the one she reserved for perennially misbehaving third-graders. "You're telling me that you're going to sit there on your posterior and not lift a finger to help my brother?"

"I'm going to sit here on my posterior and eat my lunch," he replied, not looking the least bit repentant.

So much for having the sheriff ride to her rescue. She'd wanted his help, but she wasn't going to get what she wanted. She was used to that. She knew the drill. If she wanted something done right, she had to do it herself.

"Fine. You sit there on your posterior."

His golden-hazel eyes gleamed at her humorously as he drawled, "You seem mighty interested in my posterior, ma'am, if you don't mind my saying so."

"I do mind and I'm not interested in you. What I am is concerned about my brother. But clearly you're too thickheaded to share my concern. Which means I'll have to handle this matter myself."

"Whoa there, ma'am." He reached for her hand, preventing her from sliding out of the booth as abruptly as she'd entered it. "I don't like the sound of that. What do you mean, you'll handle this yourself?"

"I mean that if you won't track down my brother, I will."

He frowned. "I don't think that's a good idea."

"Do I look like I care what you think?"

"You look like a woman about to embark on a wild-goose chase."

"I'm a woman on a mission," she stated, ignoring the flare of awareness his touch had provoked.

He shrugged. "End result is the same. Trouble. And quite frankly, I don't need any more trouble."

"Trouble?" she repeated, yanking her hand away.

"You don't know the meaning of the word, but you'll find out, if anything has happened to my brother!"

"Give it a day or so, and I'll—"

"Forget it. I'm not waiting. And I'm not impressed with your skills as a law enforcement officer," she added for good measure.

"Just with my posterior?" he suggested with a wicked grin.

"It may be the only good thing you have going for you," she retorted. "Trust me, it's *not* enough." With that parting volley, she left the diner as abruptly as she'd entered it.

2

"TELL ME EVERYTHING you know about Annie Benton," Reno instructed Opal the minute she walked in the door the next morning.

"My head cold is much better today, thanks for asking," Opal Skywood mockingly replied as she stashed her purse in her bottom desk drawer. In her mid-fifties, Opal described herself as a late bloomer and hadn't worked outside the home until five years ago. But she'd taken to her job like a duck to water and Reno was at a loss whenever she was gone. She wore her dark hair cropped short with spiky bangs covering a forehead that had its share of wrinkles— most of them caused by her youngest daughter, Sugar, in Reno's opinion.

Married and pregnant at eighteen, Opal had been in her mid-thirties with three kids almost raised when she got pregnant with Sugar. Truly the baby in the family, Sugar had been spoiled from the moment she entered this world. The only reason Reno used her as a temp on the rare occasions when Opal was sick was to do Opal a favor, knowing the family needed the extra income. And folks weren't exactly lining up to hire the capricious and headstrong twenty-year-old.

"Come on," Reno coaxed her with his famous grin. "You already know how relieved I am that you're back to normal."

"I was never normal," Opal said, her grin as wide as his.

"Compared to your daughter Sugar, you are." Reno closed his eyes and shuddered at the memory of the young woman spilling her nail polish over a report he'd spent an hour completing.

"Sugar told me that you yelled at her. She thought it made you look even sexier, for an older man, of course."

Reno shuddered again. "That girl needs a keeper. So does Annie Benton."

"Really? I can't imagine two females more unalike than my Sugar and Annie."

"So tell me what you know about her."

"Sugar?" Opal asked, deliberately misunderstanding him, Reno was sure.

"No. Annie."

"Why the sudden interest?" Opal countered, her curiosity clearly aroused. "What did she do?"

"Interrupted my lunch yesterday."

"Last I heard that wasn't a criminal offense."

Sighing, Reno dropped into the chair in front of her desk and shot her an exasperated look. "Don't give me a hard time, Opal. Just tell me what you know about her."

"As in is she available or not, romantically speaking?"

He paused in his inspection of the stapler he'd swiped from Opal's desk. "You think I couldn't find that out on my own?" he challenged her.

"I'm sure you could." She removed the stapler from him with the possessive firmness of a woman who doesn't like her office supplies messed with. "Which is why I'm surprised that you're asking me for help. This must be a first."

"With a reaction like this you can see *why* I

haven't asked for your help before,'' he grumbled, reaching for a pile of paper clips.

"Now don't go getting all grouchy about it,'' she told him even as she slapped his hand away from her stash of paper clips. "I was just having a little fun with you. Last I heard, Annie wasn't seeing anyone. Although now that it's early June and school is out, I imagine she might have some extra time on her hands.''

Reno propped one booted foot on his knee, his fingers thrumming the chair arm. He'd never been one to sit still. "So what do you know about her?''

"Geraldine is really the one who knows everything about everyone in this town,'' she needlessly reminded him.

"There's no way I'm asking Geraldine. She'd talk the hide off a steer.''

"If I didn't know better, I'd think you were afraid of her.''

"But you do know better.''

"Right. You're the tough lawman, not afraid of anything.''

"Tough, but charming,'' he corrected her with a grin.

"Yeah, right. That's why I work here. 'Cause of your charm. It's certainly not because of the working conditions.'' She gave a pointed glance at the cramped quarters in the double-wide trailer that served as the sheriff's office. To reach the fax machine you had to lean over a file cabinet. And getting to the copying machine required contortions Reno had yet to successfully accomplish. "But getting back to Annie.'' Opal paused to gather her thoughts. "Let's see. If my memory serves me correctly she moved here about three or four years ago from Iowa. Her younger brother joined her shortly thereafter. She's a super teacher and the kids all love her. She adores her brother. Bakes fabulous cookies and makes incredible jams. In fact, she's won the blue ribbon two years in a row for her wild strawberry jam. I'm surprised you haven't sampled her wares before now," she added with a mischievous smile.

Knowing darn well that she wasn't referring to food, Reno gave her a reprimanding look. "I'm a busy man and I'm only asking about her for professional reasons."

"Right."

He looked insulted by her obvious disbelief. "I'm telling the truth. She wanted my help tracking down her brother."

"He's missing?" Opal's concern was immediate.

"I don't think so," Reno replied. "She thinks he's missing because he didn't call yesterday. But there's no law that says a man has to check in with his big sister every forty-eight hours."

"Let me get this straight." Opal fixed Reno with a stare that had him fidgeting in his seat. "Annie fears her brother is missing, but you don't think so?"

"Hey," he said defensively, "I said if she hadn't heard from him by tomorrow I'd take action, but she didn't want to wait that long."

"What does she plan on doing?"

"Tracking him down on her own."

"That doesn't sound like a good idea."

"That's what I told her." He was pleased that Opal agreed with him.

"Of course it *is* all your own fault," she added.

He blinked at her. "Excuse me?"

"Well, if you'd said you'd help find her brother, she wouldn't have had to take any action on her own."

"Maybe she won't do anything foolish." He tried

to sound hopeful. "You know her better than I do. What do you think she'll do?"

Opal shrugged. "There's no telling. Normally she's a very levelheaded young woman, but where her brother's concerned, she does seem to have a blind spot."

"Son of a buck, can't a man get glasses without everyone in town talking about him going blind?" Reno's father demanded from the doorway.

"We weren't talking about you," Reno said.

"Hmmph." Despite the new glasses he wore, the disbelieving expression in Buck Best's blue eyes was still clearly visible. His white hair was as thick as ever and so were his bushy eyebrows, the left one of which he raised at his son with mocking humor. "So, son, you arrested any family members today?"

Reno rolled his eyes at his father's grumbling comment. "I can't believe you're still bellyaching about my arresting you a year ago. I was just doing my job. You and Tad Hughes were totally out of control last summer, fighting in the middle of Troublesome Creek no less."

"We were just having a difference of opinion," Buck self-righteously maintained.

Reno wasn't buying it. "A difference of opinion involving breaking each other's fishing rods. Spending the night in jail brought you both to your senses soon enough."

"Tadpole and I have reached an agreement," Buck acknowledged before leaning closer to confess. "You might even say we've formed a partnership of sorts. Regarding Cockeyed Curly."

Just the sound of the outlaw's name was enough to irritate Reno. Legend had it that his great-great-great grandfather Jedidiah had saved Curly's life in a barfight so Curly had given him the map as a thank you.

There was no record of Jedidiah ever looking for the treasure. The map had gone missing for a century or so until Hailey found it last year while researching some Best family papers in an old trunk up at the homestead where Cord lived. What with Cord's proposal to Hailey in front of the entire town a few days later, the discovery of the treasure map was temporarily put on the back burner. Then the snow had started flying, postponing the treasure hunt until this spring. Since then things had gotten increasingly crazy. "Do you have any idea how much trouble the news about that treasure map of his has caused around here?"

"Whoa, there." Buck held out his hands as if to ward off his son's antagonism. "I already told you I wasn't the one who spilled the beans. And Tad swears it wasn't him neither. I don't know how word got out about the map. I tried to be mighty discreet."

"Which is pretty much like asking a steer not to grow horns." Reno's voice was rueful. He loved his dad but he had no false illusions about him. Buck was loyal and stubborn, and always put his family first, but the man didn't have a discreet bone in his body. Reno didn't doubt his dad's ability to keep a secret, just his ability to monitor what he said at all times. You always knew where you stood with Buck Best, because he'd tell you at the drop of a hat.

"Here's what I don't get," Opal inserted. "If you've got Curly's treasure map, Buck, why don't you just go dig up the gold?"

"Because these things are complicated," Buck said.

"Because they can't read the map," Reno explained.

"No one could," Buck said defensively. "Curly

was mighty clever and he didn't use regular landmarks that would be easy to recognize."

"Maybe you should ask for someone else to help you decipher the map," Opal suggested.

Buck vetoed that idea by shaking his head so violently his glasses almost flew off. "I got enough people offering to help for part of the goods. I don't need that kind of help. My new daughter-in-law is a professor, and she can't figure out the map neither."

"I heard Hailey was busy finishing that book on Colorado outlaws," Opal said.

"She's finished it already," he said proudly. "It's coming out in a few months, with plenty of information about Curly, so it should be a bestseller."

"In my father's eyes, Curly is more important than Wyatt Earp, Billy the Kid and Jesse James all rolled together," Reno inserted wryly.

Buck declared, "None of them could write poetry the way Curly could."

"Thank heavens," Reno muttered.

Pulling up a nearby chair, Buck sat down and said, "Why just listen to this recently uncovered masterpiece...

Cockeyed Curly robbed this bank,
And left a note to say thanks.
I hope you like my verse today,
'Cause it just cost you all a lotta pay."

"Have you considered having Curly's poems published?" The question came from Opal.

Reno shot her a look that said "Don't encourage him" but Opal just blinked at him with phony innocence.

"They're gonna be in Hailey's new book," Buck said. "Another reason it'll be a bestseller."

"Yeah," Reno noted sarcastically, "it'll be right up there with the poetry of Dr. Seuss."

Buck frowned. "Was he that dentist over in Crested Butte?"

"No, Dad. He wrote kids' books like *The Cat in the Hat*. I got the twins a set of his books."

"Son of a buck." He slapped his weathered hand on his knee. "I knew I'd seen his name someplace. That 'Ham and Green Eggs' story is my favorite."

An incoming 9-1-1 call interrupted further conversation. Opal handled it with her customary calm before turning to Reno. "There's a 1020 at 31 Third Street."

"A report of vandalism," Reno translated for his father. "What was damaged?" he asked Opal even as he prepared to go out and handle the case.

"Mrs. Carruthers's garden. Seems someone dug huge holes in it last night."

ANNIE WAS READY to climb the walls. She had to do something. She couldn't just sit around here, hanging over the phone waiting for Mike to call.

She'd already tried contacting the few friends she knew he had, but none of them had heard from him lately. The problem was, with his wandering lifestyle, Mike didn't have many permanent friends. He got along fine with folks while he was with them, then forgot about them when he moved on. Except for her. Mike never forgot to check in with her. Well, not after that one time last year when he'd gone to Nevada and disappeared for a week.

She'd been so frantic then that he'd sworn he'd never do anything like that again. She had her reasons for acting the way she did. After her father's death when she was fourteen and her brother was only seven, she'd become the caretaker in the family. Her mom, a free-spirited hippie from the sixties who never did quite grow up, didn't have a practical bone in her body.

So Annie worried about her brother more than most sisters did. It was a tough job, but someone had to do it. And that someone was her.

And whenever Annie worried, she baked. She'd already made a double batch of chocolate chip cookies this morning in between trying to piece together her brother's possible whereabouts.

Nibbling on a still-warm cookie, she looked at the list she'd written up of local contacts and locations where Mike liked to hang out. Since his car was always breaking down, he frequently hitched his way to wherever his next job might be.

With that thought in mind, she decided to pay a visit to the truck stop over on the interstate, hoping she'd get lucky and find someone who'd seen her brother, maybe even given him a ride.

But first she had to dress for the occasion. It wasn't that she was a fashion plate by any means. Just that she needed to wear something appropriate for a woman on a fact-finding mission. She doubted the truckers would be willing to share much information with a schoolteacher dressed in a denim jumper. No, this assignment called for something more...outrageous. Something one of those spunky female detectives she so enjoyed reading about would wear.

Fifteen minutes later she stared into the mirror with a doubtful expression on her face and very little on her body. The cutoff jeans were too short, which was why she never wore them.

Oh, they didn't show anything they shouldn't, providing she remembered not to bend over. And the truth was that she'd seen shorter shorts on other women.

As for her bubble-gum-pink crop top, she hadn't noticed when she'd ordered it from a catalog that it was designed to display a generous amount of midriff. She thought she'd been ordering a cute sweater set and instead found a skimpy tube top along with a sweater that wouldn't keep very much warm but was intended to raise a few male temperatures.

Since the set wasn't returnable, she'd stashed it in the back of a drawer. This was the first time she'd worn it since trying it on when it had arrived. Eyeing it critically, she tried tugging on the hem, wondering if it had somehow shrunk while in the drawer those months.

"You wanted something daring," she reminded her reflection in the full-length mirror. "You wanted to loosen up the guys at the truck stop and get them to talk. This and a batch of cookies should do it."

The sexy outfit she was wearing was definitely at odds with the cheerful furnishings of her bedroom. The walls were whitewashed while the yellow madras plaid curtains matched the comforter on the bed. She'd added a few whimsical touches, like the metal lawn chair she'd spray-painted yellow and the sunny color-washed pottery vase decorated with blue dragonflies.

It didn't look like the room of a woman comfortable with flaunting her navel.

"It's for a good cause," she reminded herself as she picked up her hairbrush and began teasing her hair. By the time she left the house, she almost didn't recognize herself in the small gilded mirror by the front door.

Throughout the drive in her blue Geo Metro, she reminded herself of the importance of her assignment.

By the time she pulled into the parking lot, she'd finally stopped being startled by her own reflection in the rearview mirror.

The sound of Shania Twain's hit "I Feel Like A Woman!" greeted Annie as she walked into Eddie's Truck Stop. So did the smell of grilled onions and beer. The farther into the room she went, the bluer the air got, both from the cigarette smoke and the language. The tablecloths were plastic and so was the cutlery, for those who bothered to use it.

Since there wasn't an empty booth available, Annie headed for the first empty stool at the counter. A harried young woman, a pencil stuck behind one ear, which had three pierced silver studs in it, came to take her order.

"Can I help you, ma'am... Hey, Ms. Benton. I almost didn't recognize you! I'm Trish Volkman, you had my brother Sam in your class two years ago. He still talks about you being his favorite teacher." Leaning closer, she said, "What are you doing in here?"

"I'm looking for my brother."

"Mike?" Trish's expression brightened at the mention of his name. "I haven't seen him. Wish I had. That brother of yours is an H2L4."

Annie frowned. "A what?"

"A hero to lust for." Trish paused to grab a sponge to wipe the counter clean before giving Annie the kind of pitying look that someone in the know gives to someone who isn't. "You don't get on-line much, do you?"

"On the Internet you mean? Only for work or research. You say you haven't seen my brother lately, but he has been in here in the past, right?"

"Sure," Trish replied. "He knows he can always sweet-talk a meal out of me. And he's gotten rides from some of the truckers when that beat-up car of his doesn't work, which is most of the time.''

"When was the last time you saw him?"

"Um, let me think a minute…it must have been about two weeks ago."

Annie tried not to be disappointed. It would be too much to expect that things would be that easy. But she'd just gotten here, there were plenty of other people to interrogate. "Do you mind if I ask some of the truckers here if they've seen him?"

Trish shrugged. "No, I don't mind. I just work here. But why are you looking for him? Has he gone missing or something?"

"I'm afraid so."

"Oh my gosh!" Trish almost choked on the gum she'd been chomping. "Have you contacted the sheriff?"

"If you mean that sorry excuse for a law enforcement officer, Reno Best, then the answer is yes, I contacted him. And he refused to do a thing." The mere memory of the incident was enough to make her angry all over again.

"Wow." Trish blinked. "I can't imagine Reno doing that."

"Well, he did."

"It's not that I think you're fibbing or anything," Trish assured her. "It's just that Reno is usually a good guy."

"So is my brother and I'm worried sick about him."

"I understand." Trish patted her hand as if she were the adult and Annie the younger one in need of help.

The truth was that Trish probably had more experience with guys than Annie did. Pushing that thought aside, Annie said, "Maybe one of the truckers saw him at another truck stop farther down the interstate. I brought a picture of Mike.''

"I can show it around and ask them for you."

It was tempting, but Annie couldn't let someone else do her work for her. "Thanks, Trish, but I'd rather do it myself."

"Okay, but just be careful with the guys in the back pool room. They've had a few too many brews and are getting a little rowdy."

Now Annie was the one who patted Trish's hand. "Don't worry, after handling a roomful of rowdy third-graders, I can handle anything."

Trish didn't look convinced as she murmured, "If you say so."

"WHO WOULD DO SOMETHING like this?" Mrs. Carruthers demanded with the same sharp tone she'd used to intimidate a generation of high-school English students, including Reno. Retired now, she directed all her attention to her garden. "I'm sure it was that awful Dickens next door!"

"Mr. Dickens next door?" Reno couldn't imagine the retired barber digging in his neighbor's yard, but then who knew what gold fever could do.

"No, not Mr. Dickens himself. I mean that new dog of his. He's named it Dickens. The animal is the size of an elephant and it loves to dig. Just look at what the beast has gone and done to my lovely peony bushes!" Mrs. Carruthers wailed.

"Those holes seem mighty big for some pooch to have dug 'em," her husband, Nolan, observed.

Reno agreed and took a closer look at the undisturbed ground nearby. It had rained last night and there were still muddy patches where the sun hadn't baked the ground dry yet. "It wasn't a dog, unless he wears size ten athletic shoes," Reno said, pointing to the print he'd just found.

Mrs. Carruthers frowned. "What kind of weirdo would dig up my peonies?"

"A weirdo looking for gold," her husband replied.

"It better not have been you," she warned him with a threatening shake of her fist. "You never did appreciate those peonies the way I do."

"I don't even own any of them fancy athletic shoes," Nolan protested even as he quickly backed away. "I'm telling you, it must have been treasure hunters."

"Why would they think Cockeyed Curly buried his treasure under my peony bushes?" Mrs. Carruthers said.

"Your bushes are old, but they're not as old as that treasure," Nolan replied. "Who knows what was here back in those days?"

Mrs. Carruthers fixed her laser-gaze on Reno. "I heard your family has the treasure map, Sheriff. Why don't they just use it to dig up that treasure instead of allowing everyone to go crazy like this?"

"The map isn't exactly specific in details and things have changed since the 1880s—trees are gone, cabins gone. My dad hasn't been able to figure it out yet."

"Well, tell him to get a move on, would you?" Mrs. Carruthers's voice was as tart as a lemon. "I've heard talk that he does know and just doesn't want anyone else to know, so he's playing dumb. I said that Buck can't play dumb, that's the way he always is." Realizing what she'd just said, she hurriedly tried to cover her faux pas. "Not that I think your dad is dumb, that's not what I meant."

"You better quit while you're ahead," her husband advised.

After taking a photograph of the footprint and making a few notes on its size and width, Reno had Mrs. Carruthers sign the complaint that she insisted be filed on behalf of her beloved peonies.

"That didn't take you long," Opal noted when he reported in, using the radio from his patrol car.

"Someone's been digging in Mrs. Carruthers's backyard and they got her peonies."

Opal, bless her heart, didn't laugh, although with the slight static on the channel he couldn't be sure.

"That's the third yard in as many days." Trying to look for the silver lining, he added, "At least it wasn't another fistfight at Floyd's."

"Naw, the call that just came in wasn't from Floyd's. There's a possible disturbance out at Eddie's. Involving a certain schoolteacher."

"HONEST, GUYS," Annie said as she attempted to extricate herself from the mob of rowdy males. "It's not that I don't think you're all wonderful pool players, it's just that I'm not interested in a game right now."

"Think you're too good for us, do you?" the burly man with the most tattoos demanded. He appeared to be the leader of the motley crew gathered around her. His head was shaven and he sported a gold hoop earring in his right ear. His leather vest and about a hundred tattoos were all that covered his chest.

"Doesn't that hurt, getting all those tattoos?" The question slipped from her lips before she could stop it. That happened when she was nervous. The editor between her brain and her mouth disappeared.

"Ah, darlin'," he slurred, "you worried about lil' ole me bein' in pain? Then you just come on over here and sit on my lap to make it all better."

A second later she was on his lap.

Pointing to the largest tattoo on his arm, she said in her best teacher voice, "I would think a man who loves his mother would be better behaved."

"I've never had a woman talk so prissy to me. I like it," he said with a sloppy grin.

"Well, I don't," she said tartly. "Let me go!"

"Give me another cookie first."

"You already ate the entire batch!"

"Then give me a kiss." He unsteadily leaned forward.

She angrily shoved him back. "Listen, you, I've had it with this bad behavior. Stop it right now! Let me go!"

"You heard the lady," she suddenly heard Reno say. Where had he come from? "Let her up." Reno's voice was calm, but something about his stance got through the man's inebriated haze.

The tattooed man immediately released her and put his hands up to prove his good intentions. "Hey, I was just having a little fun. No harm done, Sheriff. I didn't know she was yours."

Annie quickly hopped off his lap and headed straight for Reno. Protectively putting his arm around her, Reno rushed her out the back door to fresh air and safety. "It'll be okay," he murmured soothingly.

"No, it won't," she said in a furious voice. "You ruined everything!"

3

RENO STARED at Annie as if she'd grown two heads. "Excuse me?"

"You heard me." Her voice reflected her anger. "You ruined my investigation."

"What exactly were you investigating on that guy's lap?" Reno retorted. "The size of his—"

"Watch it," she interrupted, her brown eyes daring him to say another word.

"Hey, if you'd warned me that you had a habit of walking into the truck stop looking for trouble, I wouldn't have dared to interfere with your fun. When we got a call that there was a disturbance involving a schoolteacher, somehow I just knew it would be you," he muttered in exasperation.

"I was here investigating my brother's disappearance," she loftily informed him.

"And what, you thought that biker had your brother hidden in his lap?"

She frowned. "I didn't know he was a biker, I thought he was a trucker. Not that I cared about his profession. I just wanted to know if anyone had seen or heard anything about my brother. Things were going fine until that man with all the tattoos got overly friendly."

His expression was stern. "I told you that you'd get into trouble trying to take the law into your own hands."

"I could have handled things."

"*You* were the one being handled," he reminded her.

She glared at him. "I'm very aware of that fact."

"Then you should also be aware that what you did was downright dumb. You need a keeper, lady."

"What I need is a lawman who'll do his job instead of making me do it for him."

Her barb stung but he refused to be drawn into a childish fight with her. Where women were concerned, he'd always preferred making love to making war. In the past, he'd always been able to charm his way into a woman's good graces and talk his way out of a relationship, without having any screaming matches or scenes. But Annie was different. "Look, we seem to have gotten off on the wrong foot here."

"That's putting it mildly."

"Most folks think I'm a reasonably charming fellow," he said with a grin that would have done Tom Cruise proud.

She wasn't impressed. Reno frowned. False modesty aside, most women he came in contact with responded to him favorably. But this woman showed no signs of melting, bending or relenting.

Annie could tell she had him stymied. And a little part of her couldn't help being pleased at that fact—on behalf of quiet, unassuming women everywhere.

She knew she was no beauty. Her mother had been the one who'd easily attracted men, albeit the wrong kind of men, with a mere bat of her eyes. Growing up with such a stunning and eccentric mother, Annie had been a wallflower in comparison, escaping notice. And she'd accepted that. She'd learned to cope with her feelings of inadequacy, learned that the spotlight wasn't for her. If it hadn't been for this situation with her brother, she would never have dreamed of drawing attention to herself.

She'd lived in Bliss for almost four years and Reno had done nothing more than glance at her. She doubted he'd even registered her existence in all that time, this despite the fact that Bliss was a small town where everyone knew everyone else and their personal business.

Which meant she knew all about Reno Best and his charmer ways. The only female in town who hadn't fallen prey to his flirtatious ways was Geraldine Winters, the postmistress, and she wasn't overly fond of anyone, although she did have a way of ferreting out the minutest details of everyone's life.

When Mike hadn't called in, Annie had gone to talk to Geraldine first, even before she'd approached Reno. But the head of Bliss's grapevine hadn't heard a word about Mike's possible whereabouts.

"So most folks think you're charming," she belatedly responded to Reno's earlier comment. "I can't help it if they're hopelessly misinformed."

His grin widened. "Looks like I'll have to convince you that you're the one who's misinformed."

"Oh, stop with the charm already," she said in exasperation. "All I want is for you to find my brother. And I do not need a keeper!"

"Anyone who dresses like that and strolls into a truck stop needs a keeper."

"I'll have you know that I dressed this way deliberately, to loosen the guys up and get them to talk to me."

"Trust me," he drawled, "that outfit doesn't loosen a guy up. Quite the opposite."

His grin hadn't flustered her before, but for some reason his appreciative visual appraisal suddenly made her feel all hot and bothered.

For the first time Annie had personal experience of why this man could be so destructive to a woman's reason and common sense. Powerful stuff. With his boyish good looks, breezy confidence and old-fashioned charm, Reno Best represented trouble and temptation in a way that made you want to line up for it.

Annie had no false illusions about herself. Hunks like Reno simply did not fall for women like her. Ah, but if they did…

She squelched that thought with a quick mental stomp. Sure Reno noticed her now, dressed as skimpily as she was. Most men would. The bandeau top even made *her* look busty, no easy accomplishment. Her hair was teased and piled on top of her head, held there with so much hair spray that she feared it would be glued this way forever and she'd end up going to her grave with Big Hair.

But this, the shorts, the abbreviated top, the wild hair, wasn't her. For the first hour she had this outfit on, she'd had to sit on her hands to stop herself from covering up her belly button. Not the actions of a bold woman.

She knew her place in the sexual hierarchy food chain. She was a minnow. Reno was a shark. Even now, he was studying her with the hungry look of a natural-born predator. His hazel eyes held a gleam that made her minnow heart shiver.

Surely she was strong enough to say no to trouble.

MIKE BENTON KNEW he was in trouble. He also knew it was his own fault that he found himself in his current circumstances.

He'd never planned on things ending up this way. In fact, it had all started out so positively when he'd left Bozeman...he did some mental figuring...had it only been three days ago?

His sister would kill him. But she'd have to stand in line. There were plenty of folks who'd like to hang him out to dry. That's how the whole thing had started. Well, actually the whole thing had started over in Vegas a few months back.

So he did a little gambling. No big deal. So Lady Luck had deserted him. She'd come back with the next roll of the dice. So he was behind in his debts. He'd make it up next time.

Problem was, he'd run out of next times.

Yeah, Annie would kill him for messing up. If his bookie didn't get to him first.

Which is why Mike had done what he had. Desperate situations called for desperate action. And no doubt about it, Mike was a desperate man.

He was also a kidnapped man.

In a rental cabin. In the mountains north of Bliss. With two men holding him captive but feeding and treating him very well.

"You sure you're comfortable?" Hector "the Burrito" Fleishmann asked him. He was a giant of a guy with the deepest voice Mike had ever heard. Hector's thick dark hair and big bushy eyebrows gave him the look of a startled hedgehog. "You want me to put more logs on the fire?"

"Nah, Hector, I'm fine," Mike replied. "Thanks for asking."

Hector wrapped his beefy arms around his middle and shivered. "It sure gets cold up here in the mountains."

"You'll be warm enough when we find the gold," his partner, Roger Midway, replied. He was the boss of the operation. A short stocky guy, he reminded Mike of Danny DeVito. His hair was thinning, and he made it worse by combing one strand across his balding head. Roger prided himself on his clean hands, buffed fingernails and pinkie ring with cubic zirconias in the shape of a dollar sign.

"You're not cold?" Hector asked Roger.

"I'm wearing cashmere. Nobody gets cold wearing cashmere." Roger picked a piece of lint off his sweater, which probably cost more than Mike had made last year. "Fine clothing is the only thing my bloodsucking ex-wife left me. I had a successful business back in Florida, you know. Had me a mobile-home dealership that made everyone back in the old neighborhood in Jersey proud of me. Any of them retired down in Florida, they came to me for their mobile homes. Hector here handled the books for me. Then Gracie divorces me and I have to sell the business to pay back taxes. Taxes that no one would have known about if Gracie hadn't blown the whistle on us with the IRS."

"But our luck's changing now," Hector said, moving closer to Roger as if seeking to share some of the shorter man's body warmth. "Right?"

"Right. When we find Crooked Curly's gold, this ring will have diamonds in it instead of czs," Roger said, buffing the ring on his shirt sleeve.

"Actually, it's Cockeyed Curly," Mike corrected him.

Roger shrugged. "Whatever. I'm not the detail man, I'm the idea man. It was my idea to kidnap you from the parking lot of that bar in Bozeman and I left the details of it to Hector here."

Hector's chest swelled as he proudly threw back his shoulders. "That's right. I'm the detail man. I can make something out of nothing. You got a broken TV? I can fix it. Ice maker not working? No problem. I'm your man. Got automotive troubles? There ain't a car out there I can't make purr like a kitten. And numbers, hey, no one crunches 'em like I do.''

"A man of many talents," Mike congratulated him.

Yeah, Mike was a desperate man. And he wasn't the only one. Hector and Roger were also desperate men. And they had a mission. To find Cockeyed Curly's gold. Mike's mission was to stay alive long enough to see his next birthday in a few weeks. Which was why he'd come up with this plan, wild though it might seem now that he was sober.

As long as he was with Hector and Roger, Mike was safe from his bookie. And even more importantly, he was out of the dangerous clutches of Sven, the Vegas loan shark who was Mike's bookie's boss. Hector and Roger were men with a dream, if not a lot of brains. As long as they thought Mike could help them fulfill that dream—of finding Curly's lost treasure—he'd be fine.

So, for the time being, he was a most content captive.

A part of Mike felt badly that his sister might be worrying about him, but he couldn't afford to let her know where he was. Sven was sure to be looking for him by now. The loan shark would never hurt Annie. He had a reputation for going after only those who owed him money, but innocent family members were off limits. And no one was more innocent than Annie.

Which meant that things should work out for the best. At least it would give him some breathing room to come up with an alternative plan.

"Yes siree, it was an extremely clever move on your parts when you two decided to kidnap me," Mike said cheerfully. "So, guys, anyone in the mood for a hand of poker?"

"THANKS FOR THE RIDE," Annie told Reno, still feeling like a fool after her little blue Geo Metro had refused to budge from the truck-stop parking lot, threatening to leave her stranded.

"No problem. Al from the service station will tow it into his place and check it out."

"I don't know what could have gone wrong. I just had it serviced a few months ago." How could the normally dependable car have let her down this way? She couldn't help the twinge of automotive betrayal she was experiencing. Big Bertha, as she'd affectionately named her compact, had always been there for her. Blizzards didn't faze her car. Mud didn't stop her. But Reno shows up and the car stuttered and stammered before going coyly silent.

Annie could relate. Sitting in the patrol vehicle with Reno, the darkness surrounding them as they traveled the lonely stretch of highway back to Bliss, was like being cocooned in a sensual world of tripping heartbeats and hidden meanings. Had he meant for his thigh to brush against hers as he shifted in his seat or for his arm to brush against her body as he leaned forward to adjust the air vents? Had he deliberately brushed her bare knee when reaching for the radio to report his position?

His position had been, and still was, entirely too close to her. Were those accidental touches no accident at all? Were they instead standard Reno operating procedure—flirt first, seduce later? Or was she overreacting? Could he tell he was getting to her?

"I'd better go," she said, hurriedly reaching for the car door latch the second he pulled in front of her house.

His hand on her arm stopped her. "Hold on a second."

Her eyes shot to his, trying to ascertain if he felt the same jolt of electricity she just had. Despite his outward charm, he wasn't an easy man to read. He wasn't giving any secrets away. But she could see warmth and humor in his expression, as if he knew she was curious about him. Knew it and was pleased by it.

That alone should have been enough to make her pull back. But there was something else there, some curiosity of his own. About her.

Her breath caught. Was there more to Reno than what met the eye? Not that what met the eye wasn't downright striking. He had the kind of face you could stare at for hours. A lean strong jawline. Angular features. Rumpled brown hair. A smile that didn't just knock your socks off, it threatened to do away with the rest of your underwear as well. And the kind of eyes you could simply lose yourself in.

"Hey, Ms. Benton, are you under arrest?" Timmy Raimerez, one of her students from last year shouted as he rode by on his bike. "What'd they get you for?"

"Insanity," she muttered, shifting away from Reno and putting some much-needed distance between them. She had to be insane to be allowing herself to fall under Reno's spell this way.

He was doing it deliberately, probably to teach her a lesson. She remembered the intrigued look he'd given her when she'd refused to be impressed by his charm.

Intrigued was not a good thing where hunks were concerned. She'd learned that in high school where she'd been ridiculed because of her mother's unconventional lifestyle. Rumors that she was as easy as her mom had followed her down the hallways and showed up in suggestive notes taped to the front of her locker. So she'd held herself aloof, not dating even thought a part of her had desperately wanted to fit in and be like the other girls.

Then in her senior year, football quarterback Heath Landon, whom she'd had a crush on and shared an English class with, had asked her to the prom. When she'd turned him down, he'd been intrigued and he'd asked her again, every day for a week. He'd seemed so sincere. For the first time in four years it felt as if someone saw her. It wasn't until she was drinking punch at the prom that she overheard Heath collecting the money for the bet his buddies had placed on him being able to get her to go out with him.

She hadn't cared much for hunks, football, or gambling since then.

The men she usually dated were just regular guys, definitely leaning toward the conservative side. Some might even describe them as nerds. She thought of them as safe.

There was nothing safe about Reno.

Was that why she was attracted to him? Because he represented some forbidden fantasy to her? Maybe it was the uniform, such as it was—a long-sleeved denim shirt and jeans. Or maybe it was the badge. Was she looking for an authority figure?

She was looking entirely too much. Tugging her gaze away from him, she again made a move to exit the car.

"Wait a second," Reno repeated. "Before you go, I want your promise that you won't be pulling any more stunts like you did tonight."

Foolish? Bingo! He hit it on the head. She was being foolish. Over him. It had to stop. "I try never to repeat myself," she informed him sweetly before scooting out of the car.

4

"I KNOW HE'S your brother-in-law and everything,"
Annie was telling her friend Tracy over the phone the
next morning, "but really, don't you think that Reno
should have taken my brother's disappearance more
seriously than he did?"

Annie had bonded with Tracy when the other
woman had first come to Bliss as Zane Best's housekeeper and, as a judge at the Fourth of July Women's
Auxiliary festivities, had chosen Annie's wild-
strawberry jam. Annie hadn't just felt the connection
with Tracy because she'd chosen Annie's jam over
the others, but because Tracy had had the courage to
say so, despite the pressure for her to award the prize
to Mrs. Battle's sister-in-law, who had won the event
for decades.

In Annie's eyes, the incident was an example of
Tracy's courage and forthrightness. It couldn't have
been easy for Tracy to leave behind her life in Chicago as a big advertising executive and come out to
Colorado to start all over again. Annie had only
moved to Bliss after visiting the small town before-
hand during a driving vacation in Colorado. She'd
seen the mountains here and fallen in love with the
view. The deep connection she'd felt with Bliss had
been immediate and intense. Even then, she'd rented
a house for a year and been a substitute teacher before
committing to purchasing her small home and signing

a teaching contract. She wasn't the type to jump into anything without researching it first. Caution and control. They were so important to her because of the chaotic environment she'd grown up in, where the only thing she could count on was upheaval and change.

She felt more secure when she had things under control. And acting cautiously made her feel more in control. Which is why she'd taken her time that first year before deciding to stay in Bliss.

The small-town atmosphere appealed to her, making her feel as if she were part of a community, as if she weren't alone. And after having felt like an outsider for all those years in Iowa, it was nice to be somewhere where she wasn't known as the daughter of "that wild woman." Here in Bliss, Annie was only known for her own achievements.

"You asked me if Reno should have taken your brother's disappearance more seriously, but Reno rarely does what I think he should," Tracy was saying. "I thought he should have taken the modeling job for a major jean ad campaign—we're only talking a few days to shoot it—but he just grinned and said he'd rather go fishing in his free time."

"That doesn't surprise me," Annie muttered as she swung her bare legs over the arm of her comfy denim couch. The only other pieces of furniture in the room were a pine armoire, which held her stereo and TV, and the rectangular pine chest used as a coffee table. She stored her books inside the chest, allowing a rustic faded blue coffeepot as the only decoration on top of the chest. Annie hated clutter. Clutter meant lack of control. "The man is driving me crazy."

"I can tell. You've always been so calm and down-to-earth before. But going to that truck stop wasn't

your brightest moment.'' Tracy paused a beat before
adding, ''You should have had me come with you.''

Annie laughed. ''Right. Your husband would have
loved that.''

''The Best brothers do tend to be a little old-
fashioned in their thinking, but they come around in
the end. Right after you've just about given up hope,''
Tracy noted dryly. ''And then they make this grand
gesture that simply melts your heart.''

Annie remembered how furniture maker Cord Best
had dropped to his knees in front of the entire town
at the Founders' Day celebrations last year and declared his love for Hailey Hughes, the girl next door.
And Tracy had told her how Zane had climbed a huge
cottonwood tree to reach Tracy and tell her he loved
her after she'd locked him out of his own ranch house.
But Tracy was a gorgeous blonde and Hailey was full
of fire and passion. Both women were powers to be
reckoned with. Annie didn't see herself that way.

Instead she saw herself as a woman who'd blend
into a crowd, someone who was most often described
as ''nice.'' She believed that a lot of men never saw
her at all, but those who did notice her would also
often describe her as ''nice.'' Many of them would
say they enjoyed their date with her and then not call
her back. Not the track record of a woman who was
a power to be reckoned with.

Unless she was in a classroom. Then she felt as if
she knew what she was doing. But even there the kids
didn't consider her to be a powerhouse. They obeyed
her rules because they liked her. Most people liked
her. She was a likable person. Just not a noticeable
one.

And that had always been fine with her. Until now.

"Do you want me to talk to Reno?" Tracy asked her.

"Do you think it would do any good?" Annie countered.

"I doubt it," Tracy cheerfully acknowledged. "But I'm willing to give it a go if you want me to."

"No." Annie sighed before streching full-length on the couch, jiggling the phone between her jaw and her shoulder while using her free hand to tuck a yellow gingham pillow beneath her head. "I should handle this problem myself."

"Everyone could use some help now and again. There must be something I can do."

"Just talking to me helps."

"You and your brother are very close, aren't you?" Tracy said.

"I practically raised him," Annie admitted.

"You've never talked about your life before you came to Bliss, or your parents," Tracy astutely noted. "Did they pass away when you were young the way mine did?"

"My dad passed away when I was fourteen and my brother was seven." Annie's voice was quiet. "He was a teacher. High school. American history. After he died, someone had to take over being the responsible one in the family. That someone was me."

"What about your mother?"

"I love her, but she never grew up. She was definitely a child of the sixties. She's always been...um..." Annie paused, trying to come up with a suitable description. "Flamboyantly eccentric. A free spirit. Dances to the beat of a different drummer and all that. Which is all good and fine, but it won't pay the bills or put food on the table." Annie closed

her eyes at the memories of times when she and her
brother had gone to bed hungry until Annie had gotten a part-time job at the local hamburger place. "My
mother gave away most of my dad's life insurance
payments to her favorite causes. She tried to start up
an artist's commune and then didn't have the heart to
collect rent. She took up with a guy, a painter who
was twenty years her junior, and decided we should
call her SeaSprite. When she tried changing my
brother's name to Moonchild, he refused to speak to
her for a month. My mom loves flaunting her unconventional lifestyle, which didn't go down every very
well with the folks back in Cedar Rapids."

"When was the last time you saw her?"

"It's been years. But she usually drops us a post-
card once or twice a year. The last one I got was from
somewhere in Tibet. She went there with her latest
love, her yoga instructor, Mario."

"You don't think your brother might have traveled
there to see her, do you?"

"It would be highly unlikely," Annie's voice was
terse. "Besides, Mike doesn't even have a passport."

"It was just a thought."

"I know. And I didn't mean to snap your head
off," Annie said apologetically. "I really appreciate
you listening to my family problems. I didn't mean
to ramble on like that."

"You didn't ramble and besides, you sure helped
me when I was floundering in the kitchen. And you
were such a sweetie about it, too, not making me feel
like an idiot because I could barely boil water without
burning it."

"You just didn't have much experience in that
area."

"You made it fun," Tracy said. "That's why

you're such a great teacher. Because you make learning an adventure. The twins tell me that you're still their favorite teacher.''

Rusty Best and his twin sister Lucky had had a reputation in Bliss for raising Cain. Shopkeepers actually put up the Closed sign when the two hellions showed up in town. But Tracy had seen beyond their wild ways to the lonely kids beneath the surface. And after marrying their father, she'd taken her responsibilities of mom very seriously, making frequent trips to school to consult with Annie about the twins' progress, doing whatever she could to help them.

"Yes, well, I have a special place in my heart for those two as well," Annie confessed.

"So when are you going to come out and see them?" Tracy demanded. "Why not come for dinner tomorrow night?"

"I don't know..."

"Are you worried about running into Reno?" Tracy astutely guessed. "Are you going to let him keep you away from your friends?"

"No way."

"Good. I'll see you tomorrow night then."

After hanging up the phone, Tracy turned to her husband and triumphantly said, "I think the last Best Bachelor is about to bite the dust!"

WHEN HER FRONT doorbell rang, Annie was expecting Al from the service station. He'd called a few minutes ago to say that her car was ready and that he'd drive it over if she'd give him a lift back to the station. When she'd asked him what was wrong with it, he'd muttered something about a few loose wires and hoses but that there'd be no charge.

She'd just had the car tuned up a month ago.

Maybe they hadn't reconnected something properly by mistake. At least it worked now.

Quickly removing the brownies she was baking from the oven, she hurried from the kitchen through the living room.

Opening the front door, she said, "Thanks, Al—"

But it wasn't Al who stood on her covered porch. This man made Al, who stood over six feet and weighed two hundred and eighty, look like a skinny weakling. The stranger had long blond hair and looked as if he should be wrestling on TV, although at the moment he was wearing an expensive, stylish suit that fit him to perfection.

"Can I help you?" she said, certain he must be lost.

"I am looking for Mike," the man replied with a slight Scandinavian accent.

"And you are?"

"A friend of his," he countered smoothly before looking behind her with interest. "Is your brother here?"

Sensing trouble, Annie immediately swung the wide-open door almost closed, blocking his view into her home. "How did you know I'm his sister?"

"He told me all about his beautiful sister."

Okay, right off the bat she knew the guy was a liar. Mike never called her beautiful. He called her smart or bossy but never beautiful.

"My brother isn't here," Annie said, her feelings of distrust now on full alert.

"When do you expect him back? It is most urgent that I speak with him."

Instead of answering, Annie asked a question of her own. "Where did you say you met my brother?"

"We met through mutual friends. I was driving

through and thought I would drop by to visit Mike while in this area.''

Yeah right, she silently scoffed. *If I believe that, you've got a bridge to sell me.* ''And you're from where?''

Instead of answering, the man who had yet to identify himself, simply said, ''Tell your brother I am looking for him. I will leave you my card. If you hear from Mike, please do me the courtesy of calling me. It would be better for everyone concerned.'' Handing her the card, the man turned on his heel and moved away with a swiftness surprising in a man of his size.

''Hey, you...'' She glanced down at the card he'd given her. On it was his first name and a phone number. ''Sven, wait a minute! Why are you looking for my brother?''

''Just tell him what I said. And tell him that time is running out,'' he added ominously.

Annie didn't like the sound of that at all. Automatically making note of the license-plate number on the black BMW, Annie closed the front door and raced into her bedroom for her shoes. She cursed her bad habit of going barefoot at home as she scrambled for her car keys on the hook in the kitchen before realizing Al hadn't returned her car yet.

Another knock at the door. This time it had to be Al. ''I'm so glad you're here,'' she said breathlessly. Only it wasn't Al. It was Reno.

''*You* glad to see *me*?'' he noted in a teasing voice. ''That's a nice change. Mmm, something smells good.'' He leaned forward to sniff appreciatively. ''Are you baking something?''

Looking past Reno, she saw the shining blue hood of Big Bertha in her driveway. He was dangling her key from his index finger.

"I brought your car for you," he said with a smile that was more than just friendly. "Al got backed up at the station so I volunteered to drive it over for him. If you were to pay me with a bit of whatever that is you baked, I sure wouldn't object."

She didn't even bother asking why the sheriff was moonlighting as a grease monkey. She just grabbed the keys and raced down the steps.

"Hey!" Reno shouted after her. "Where are you off to in such a hurry?"

If she'd been smart, or thinking clearly, she would have made up something clever instead of simply blurting out the truth. "I'm going after a guy who just came looking for my brother."

"Whoa, there." Reno's hand on her arm stopped Annie in her tracks. This was getting to be a habit of his. And not a good one in her opinion.

"Out of my way!" she ordered him, not bothering with pleasantries. "The guy is getting away."

He didn't budge. "What guy?"

"None of your business." Only the fact that she'd scribbled down Sven's license-plate number kept her from mowing over Reno and hopping into her car no matter what he said.

"Let me get this straight—some guy came here looking for your brother and you plan on tailing him?"

"He was up to no good."

"All the more reason for you to steer clear of him," Reno said.

She glared at him. Once again he'd gotten in her way. Annie wasn't stupid, she didn't plan on confronting Sven. She just planned on following him for a while, to see where he was headed. But Reno had put the kibosh on that plan. She'd never catch up with Sven now. Too much time had gone by.

"Great! You've ruined things—yet again," she said, stomping back up her front steps.

Reno stomped right after her, clear into her living room. "Have you forgotten what happened that last time you tried to take the law into your own hands and play amateur sleuth? Do you have any idea how vulnerable a woman can be? If not, allow me to show you."

Without further ado, he came up from behind her and grabbed her.

She reacted instinctively, using a maneuver she'd seen on *Oprah* that involved shoving his fingers backward in a way that was guaranteed to bring any attacker to his knees.

But the minute she thought she was hurting Reno, she let him go.

"Big mistake," he growled, yanking her into his arms. "You've got too soft a heart to be in this line of work." Holding her pressed against his body, he intended to teach her a lesson by showing her how dangerous her actions were. Instead Reno found himself in danger of giving in to the hot attraction sizzling between them. The storminess of their argument created a sexual tension that was all-powerful.

With her startled face turned up to his, her lips were too close to resist. Annie barely had time to react to him tugging her into his arms before he was kissing her.

Despite the anger in his voice, there was no anger in his kiss. Instead, there was plenty of passion as the kiss went on and on, moving from warm and whispery persuasion to hot and sexy entrapment. And she was a willing victim to his seduction. Victim, ha! She was an eager and quick learner as, for once in her life, the teacher became the pupil.

He coaxed her to part her lips, convincing her that there were untold pleasures to be had if she complied. And for once he was right. Heavens, the man knew how to kiss! Knew when to press his advantage, knew when to pull back with a teasing swipe of his tongue.

He was imprisoning her in a growing web of enchantment. A distant part of her brain warned her that she was foolish to give in to Reno, that a hunk like him would only kiss a woman like her to prove a point. But that internal voice was soon drowned out by the overwhelming waves of pleasure crashing over her. She'd never been kissed with so much finesse, so much skill, so much *everything!* She moaned with pleasure, the blood rushing to her head, as he erotically nibbled on her bottom lip.

There was rightness in the way he touched her, an inevitableness in the way his hand moved to the hollow of her throat to undo the top button of her shirt. The brush of his fingers against her breast created such a powerful response that she gasped and pulled away. Her heart was pumping, her pulse pounding in places she didn't even know it was supposed to.

His brown hair was even more rumpled than usual, made that way by her own fingers combing through the strands. She'd acted like a wild wanton. Her hands shook as she raised them to her lips, as if testing to make sure they were still on her face and not permanently affixed to his.

What had she been thinking? She'd responded to him like a love-starved fool, longing for him the way she'd longed for hunky Heath the quarterback back in high school. How dumb could she get? She should know better. How many times did she have to get hit over the head to learn this lesson? She was not the kind of woman to capture let alone keep this kind of a man's attention.

He'd been angry with her, that's all. Not attracted to her.

Her eyes sought out his. She was surprised to find a look of stunned surprise there amidst the lingering desire. His golden-hazel eyes were ablaze, making him even sexier than usual.

"I'm sorry." His voice was low and rough. "I shouldn't have done that."

"Darn right you shouldn't have done that!" she shot back, embarrassed that he'd just proved her right. He was clearly already regretting his actions.

"You didn't seem to be disliking it all that much," he said bluntly.

Neither did you, she wanted to retort but lacked the courage. Being the sexual minnow she was, all she could come up with was, "You caught me by surprise." She winced at the lameness of her excuse, but she'd been unprepared for his frankness, the same way she'd been unprepared for him to haul her into his arms and kiss her senseless.

"Next time I'll give you more advance warning," he huskily promised, his slow grin making her weak in the knees and confusing her. Was this flirting a knee-jerk reaction from him, or was he saying he really did want to kiss her again?

Saying there wouldn't be a next time seemed like a remnant of Victorian outrage, so instead she briskly said, "You do that. And next time don't stand in my way when I'm trying to get information about my brother."

"Listen, if I promise to help you find your brother,

will you promise not to do any more running around on your own?''

"But—"

He placed his index finger on her lips. "No buts about it. I want your promise.''

"Didn't your mother ever tell you that you don't always get what you want?''

"I don't remember my mother,'' he said matter-of-factly. "She died when I was a little kid.''

Annie knew that, but she hadn't been thinking clearly, a problem she seemed to develop whenever he was around. Stepping away from him, she reminded herself that the bottom line here was finding her brother.

"Do I have your promise?'' he asked again.

"All right. I promise.'' She deliberately made her voice very crisp and businesslike, as far away as possible from the breathless wanton who'd kissed him.

"Good.'' To her relief, he replied in kind, his voice lacking the teasing warmth of a few minutes ago. Now he sounded like a lawman. "Now, what have you found out so far?''

"Well, I've mapped out my brother's locations over the past month. Come on, I'll show you.'' Grabbing him by the hand, she hauled him over to show him what she'd done. Her dining room had been transformed into a command center that would have done any TV cop show proud. She had two large easels set up, one with the map she'd talked about, another with a flowchart of people she'd interviewed and the time and date of their last contact with her brother. There were also several piles of papers on the table exploring various possible scenarios.

Seeing his stunned yet impressed look, she modestly shrugged and said, "I read a lot of mysteries.''

"Maybe I should hire you instead of Barnie to be my deputy," he noted dryly.

"I thought you said I didn't have the heart for this line of work."

"Oh, you've got heart all right," he murmured with a meaningful look at her lips. "I've got no doubts about that."

Well *she* had plenty of doubts, like what she was getting into here. It was one thing turning the matter over to Reno, quite another to be working with him. Spending time with him, a man with the ability to get past her defenses and tempt her.

So he could make her kneecaps melt with just one kiss. She refused to panic. She'd just have to be extra cautious around him. He'd soon grow bored with flirting with her and move on to easier and prettier prey. She could do this, she *would* do this. For her brother. She'd do just about anything to help Mike. Even rubbing shoulders with a sexy charmer like Reno.

"I also got Sven's license-plate number," she said, holding up the scrap on paper she still held clutched in her hand, really crumpled thanks to her fisthold on it while he'd kissed her.

He took the paper from her, smoothing it out so he could read it. "And who is Sven?"

"I don't know. But he came here looking for my brother. He said it would be better for everyone if Mike called him and that time was running out. I didn't think that sounded very good."

"You thought right."

"That's why I was trying to follow him."

"That's where you made your first mistake."

"I thought my first mistake was going to the truck stop yesterday," she retorted mockingly. "That's what you told me then."

"I'm just glad I was able to stop you from going after him. A wiser move is for me to track down this license with the DMV and see what I can dig up about this Sven guy."

"He left me his business card, but it only lists his name—first name only—and phone number."

"Then give me the card, too." Reno held out his hand for it.

Annie hesitated. It was one thing handing over the license number, because she had no access to tracing information from that. But the mysterious Sven's phone number was another thing entirely. Maybe she could call him and finagle some more information out of him.

It wasn't as if she wasn't an able interrogator. After all, anyone who could get eight-year-old Timmy Raimerez to confess that he'd been the one who'd freed the class hamster had a way of finagling information out of people. Granted, she wasn't as good as Geraldine in the post office yet. But she was no slouch when it came to grilling suspects. She'd certainly read enough about it. Whether the heroine was a down-on-her-luck bondswoman on the trail of bail jumpers or a smart female private investigator after some no-good felon, the women she read about always got their man. On their own.

So instead of handing over Sven's card, she merely read Reno the phone number. He didn't look pleased but he wrote down the information.

Yes, the women she read about always got their man. She simply needed to remind herself that Reno wasn't the man for her. She needed someone steady and reliable, not a wildly sexy charmer who moved from woman to woman. She refused to be like her mother, blinded by a man's handsome face and flirtatious ways to his unsteady nature and inability to commit.

Annie knew better, she knew what she wanted. Stability and control. She couldn't afford to lose track of those goals now.

WHEN ANNIE ARRIVED at the Best ranch the next evening the place was in an uproar. But it was the sort of controlled uproar that Annie experienced in her classroom throughout the school year. Buck was out barbecuing ribs on the grill, and that smell alone was enough to make her mouth water. Add the whiff of homemade cherry pie as Tracy's sister-in-law, Hailey, walked by and waved it under her nose and Annie's stomach actually started growling.

"I brought some peanut butter cookies and a salad with some of the vegetables from my garden. Where do you want me to put everything?" Annie asked Tracy.

"Wherever there's an empty place on the counter," Tracy replied. Pausing to peek over Annie's shoulder, she added, "Did you use those delicious golden tomatoes that I love so much in your salad?"

"I sure did," Annie replied.

A tugging on the long skirt of her sleeveless turquoise-blue dress made Annie look down to see both Rusty and Lucky gazing up at her with smiles on their faces. "We snapped the green beans," Rusty said, his boyish voice bursting with pride.

"Did they snap you back?" Annie asked with a grin.

The twins laughed before racing off to help their grandfather at the grill.

Watching them through the kitchen window, Tracy's voice was reflective as she noted, "You know, sometimes I still find it hard to believe that I'm really a rancher's wife, and other times it seems like my life back in Chicago belonged to another woman.''

"Do you miss your life back in Chicago?" Annie asked.

"No." Tracy shook her head, her long blond hair gathered up in a ponytail. Even though she was dressed in a short jean skirt and pink T-shirt, she still managed to look elegant. "I still do some freelance ad work when time allows, but work doesn't define my entire life anymore. That's Zane's job now," she added with a grin at her husband.

"What's my job?" Zane asked, pausing on his way through the kitchen to slip an arm around his wife's shoulders.

"Defining my life." Tracy's teasing reply was accompanied by a smile bright enough to light Denver.

"Ditto," Zane murmured.

"The man is such a sweet-talker," Tracy said, patting his cheek with affection.

Taking her hand in his and kissing it, Zane said, "My baby brother Reno is the sweet-talker in the family."

"Cord gave Reno a run for his money at last year's Founders' Day event," Hailey loyally defended her husband, who'd just entered the room. "I still get teary-eyed when I think of what Cord did, getting on his knees in front of the entire town and proposing that way."

"Makes me teary-eyed, too," Cord growled. "With terror."

"Crowds are not Cord's thing," Hailey admitted.

"Neither is sappy stuff." Cord belied his words by

kissing his wife with so much loving passion that Annie blushed and felt the heat half a room away.

A second later Annie realized the heat was coming from the burning pot of potatoes on the stove she was standing beside.

"Carbon alert!" Zane said, grabbing the pot's handle with the well-practiced ease of someone accustomed to dealing with culinary disasters.

"Son of a buck!" Tracy exclaimed. "I can't believe I forgot to turn off the potatoes. Geez, you'd think I'd just arrived from the big city and never cooked before."

"It's our fault," Hailey said. "We were distracting you. What can I do to help?"

"Take Annie's salad out to the dining room table before I ruin that too," Tracy said.

"Food's on!" Buck shouted as he marched through the kitchen with a huge platter filled with ribs dripping with his tangy barbecue sauce. The twins trailed behind him, chanting the mantra, "Come and get it."

"Looks like I arrived just in time," Reno announced from the back door.

Tracy shot him a startled look before quickly sending Annie a visual message that said *I didn't know he was coming tonight.* "What are you doing here, Reno?" Tracy asked him.

"Eating dinner. No thanks to you I might add." He paused to give his sister-in-law a reprimanding look. "Geraldine was the one who told me Dad was cooking up a batch of ribs tonight."

"I swear that woman knows everything," Buck muttered.

"She doesn't know where my brother is," Annie said quietly.

5

DINNER WASN'T as stressful as Annie thought it might be. Reno went out of his way to be charming. Or maybe he was just that way naturally. The man had a gift.

Tonight he was casually dressed. The black T-shirt made his unusual green-gold eyes—*hazel* was too common a word for them—stand out. He must have inherited them from his mother, since his dad and older brothers all had blue eyes. Both his denim jacket and jeans had been well-washed and conformed to his body with age-old familiarity.

Watching him interacting with his brothers, she didn't pay attention to the words as much as to the attitude. Zane, the oldest, was firmly sticking to his guns, while middle brother Cord was intensely pitching an opposing opinion. And then there was Reno, moving between the two points of view like a skillful dancer.

"Come on, guys," Tracy inserted as the discussion heated up. "It's not as if you're talking about the fate of the world here. You're just talking about the fate of the Denver Broncos."

Every set of male eyes at the table turned to view her with horror.

"The fate of the Broncos is more important than the fate of the world," Zane solemnly informed his wife.

"I believe they even teach that philosophy in grade school these days," Reno noted, his voice tinged with humor. "Isn't that right, Annie?"

How did Reno do that? Invite her into some inner secret circle comprised of just the two of them by doing nothing more than talking to her. Surely it was a God-given talent. And surely he'd used it on more women than she could count.

"I don't care about football," she said.

Now the sets of horror-filled male eyes were focused on her. "Well, I don't," Annie said defensively.

"And she seemed like such a nice gal," Buck noted with a sorrowful shake of his head.

"I don't like football neither," Lucky said in defense of her teacher, reaching out to pat Annie's hand reassuringly.

"Not my cup of tea, either," Hailey added.

"I suppose us girls should stick together," Tracy said. "Despite the guilty pleasure I feel at watching tight ends on the field, I'll stand by my sisterhood here. I can honestly say that the fate of the Broncos is not the most important thing on the face of the earth." She waited a beat before adding, "The fate of the Chicago Bulls is."

A heated discussion ensued regarding the merits of football versus basketball, with a touch of fly-fishing philosophy tossed in by Buck from time to time. Annie couldn't help noticing how much the family seemed to enjoy the back-and-forth comments, which were delivered with much laughter.

Her own family situation was so far removed from the one she was watching. With her mother living in her own world, it was difficult for Annie to have a conversation with her that didn't sooner or later spin into the twilight zone. Which is why she and her brother stuck together as much as they did.

"Time out," Reno declared, his eyes on Annie's face as if sensing that her thoughts were becoming consumed by her brother and his disappearance. "We should have a more intellectual discussion in honor of our guest. What would a schoolteacher be interested in?"

"The capitals of the states," Rusty suggested. "And I want to go first. Alabama."

"Montgomery," his sister, Lucky, instantly replied.

"No fair!" Rusty protested. "I'm supposed to give the answer."

"That's not the way we do it in school," his twin sister said. "The person asking doesn't answer. Those are the rules."

"You make your students memorize all fifty capital cities, Annie?" Reno's eyebrow lifted, giving him a quizzical expression that made him look downright adorable. It was the first time he'd ever actually said her name and he made it sound better than it was.

"Your niece and nephew happen to excel at geography and have an interest in it," Annie replied.

"We can read maps and everything," Rusty proudly boasted. "That's why when we saw Curly's map—" Rusty clapped his hand over his mouth as he belatedly realized what he'd just revealed.

"When did you two see Curly's map?" Buck asked suspiciously.

"You showed us, Grandpa," Lucky said with an innocent bat of her eyelashes that would no doubt break male hearts in another ten years. At the moment it gained her no ground with Buck, however.

"I did no such thing," he denied. "I may be gettin' old but I ain't senile yet."

"You shouldn't use ain't, Grandpa," Lucky primly reprimanded him. "Not in front of our teacher."

"I'm too old to be watching my grammar, but I should have been watching you two closer. When did you see the map?" Buck repeated in a voice that meant business.

"We were watching you through the office window using that new telescope we got for Christmas," Lucky confessed.

"It made the map look real big," Rusty said. "Almost as big as the bumps on the moon."

"You didn't happen to tell any of your friends at school about seeing the map, did you?" Reno asked in a friendly voice that had Rusty answering before thinking.

"Only Timmy Raimerez," the little boy replied. "And he promised he wouldn't tell no one."

"Anyone," Reno corrected Rusty. Looking at Zane, he said, "Well, that answers my question about how the news about the map got out. At first I thought Dad or Tad Hughes must have let something slip."

Buck snorted. "I told you I didn't spill the beans."

"But Timmy said he wouldn't tell," Rusty said.

"Timmy's teenage brother has been selling his own version of the map. It's a total fake," Reno assured his dad. "But it sure helped stir things up."

"Males can't be trusted," Lucky stated with a regretful shake of her head.

Zane shot his young daughter a startled look. Seeing it, the little girl added, "That's what Mom says whenever you guys do something bad like walk over the kitchen floor she just washed."

"Nice going," Zane told Tracy.

"Hey, I wasn't the one who got them a telescope," Tracy retorted.

"It's no use pointing fingers at this late date," Reno said.

"Besides, pointing is rude," Lucky said.

"You're such a...girl!" Rusty said in disgust.

"And you're a buttwipe," Lucky hotly retorted.

"*You're* the buttwipe!" Rusty returned.

"You're *both* a pair of buttwipes for bringing up a word like that at the dinner table," Buck reprimanded them before Zane could.

Lucky blinked at him. "But you taught it to us, Grandpa."

"That so, Pa?" Zane asked.

"Isn't it time for dessert?" Buck said with a desperate look around the table.

Apparently taking pity on his predicament, Hailey said, "We've got peanut butter cookies and cherry pie. Anybody interested?"

A half-dozen hands shot into the air. It wasn't until after the last crumb of pie had been eaten, the plateful of cookies just a memory, and the table cleared that Reno approached Annie. "We need to talk. In private." Placing his hand on the small of her back, he guided her outside onto the large front porch.

Leaning against an upright support beam, Annie wrapped her hands around her middle as the chilly night air hit her. She'd brought a sweater but it was inside the house.

"Here." Reno removed his denim jacket and draped it around her shoulders. The warmth of his body surrounded her, retained by the material.

"Thanks." Her fingers curled around the edges of the jacket as she held it in place. Looking up at the darkening sky, she said, "I love looking at the stars.

When I was a little girl my father used to tell me that each star was an angel's candle, flickering in the night so I'd never be afraid of the dark. When I got older, he'd point out the constellations. The Big Dipper. The Lazy W."

"I wanted the ranch to be called the Lazy W but my dad didn't think it was a good idea. That was during my rebellious period."

"Which ended, what, a month ago?"

He grinned. "Who said it's ended? You mean I don't seem like a rebel to you?"

"It's not enough that you're a charmer, you have to be a rebel too?" she countered.

"I guess Cord is more of a rebel than I am," Reno admitted. "He didn't go to college the way Zane and I did. And he's determined to go his own way on his own terms."

"You don't exactly seem like a follower to me," she noted.

"It's true that I prefer giving orders to following them."

"And is that the appeal of law enforcement for you?"

"Is it the appeal of teaching for you?" he countered.

"No."

"Same here," he maintained. "You might say that I enjoy keeping the order."

Annie knew all about order. It was right up there with control, something she valued highly. Granted, she couldn't obtain it in the classroom all the time. But in her own home she made up for that. After all those chaotic years with her mom, it was reassuring to Annie to have her surroundings be as orderly as possible. The minimalist furnishings ensured that everything was in its place at all times. She might not totally have her act together yet, but by God her underwear drawer was always as neat as a pin.

Thinking about her underwear in Reno's presence, even if it was in an innocent context, made her blush like a teenager. The collar of his borrowed denim jacket brushed against her heated cheek as she inhaled the scent of him. It wasn't aftershave. It was pure male, pure Reno. Part fresh air, part tangy citrus soap.

"I got some info back on the trace on that Nevada license-plate number you gave me yesterday." His quiet voice was more serious than usual.

"You did?"

He nodded before giving her a warning look. "I don't think you're going to like what I found."

"Just spit it out," she said in exasperation, his words only making her more nervous.

"The car is registered to Sven Erickson of Las Vegas, Nevada. His occupation is listed as financial adviser but the authorities in Vegas tell me that he's a loan shark. He makes his money through a series of bookies who work for him, placing bets for their customers on everything from basketball games to horse races."

"Gambling?" Annie repeated, her heart dropping to her shoes. Mike had promised her that he wouldn't get involved in that world again, not after she'd bailed him out the last time.

"Does your brother have a gambling problem?" Reno bluntly asked.

"He had a slight problem several years ago." Her voice was defensive. "But he's been clean since then." Now her tone was emphatic.

"Or so he told you."

Reno's words hit her hard. Was this why Mike had

gone missing? Because he'd gotten in trouble with a gambling debt and was afraid to face her? Was she that bad a sister? Tears welled in her eyes as she sank onto the cushions of a nearby porch bench. "He's in trouble and he didn't feel he could come to me."

Normally Reno was not one of those men who, like his brothers, freaked at the sight of a woman's tears. Not that he liked to see women cry, but he did seem to have a way with comforting them. However, the sight of this woman's tears hit him in a way that nothing else ever had.

Words, always at the ready on the tip of his tongue, simply evaporated, leaving him feeling as helpless as a newborn calf.

What was it about this woman that hit him this way? The other day he'd acted like a caveman, grabbing her and kissing her without his usual teasing build-up. That wasn't like him at all. And now this—her tears brought a lump to his throat. Something weird was going on here. The need to comfort her was greater than his need to figure things out so he sat beside her, and was about to put his arms around her when a lasso flew over his head.

"What the—" Reno turned to find his young nephew glaring at him accusingly.

"You made her cry!" Rusty said.

"I did not. Tell him," Reno turned to order Annie.

"Give me the rope, Rusty," Annie said instead. She stood and held out her hand.

Hesitating a moment, Rusty reluctantly scooted up the porch steps to hand over the rope.

"Thank you," Annie said. "Now, you go on inside. I've got things under control here."

The boy did as she requested. Muttering under his breath, Reno went to lift the rope from his arms only to have Annie tighten the rope's hold on him. "Hold on there a minute, cowboy," she drawled. "You and I aren't finished yet."

"Hey, there's no reason to kill the messenger," Reno reminded her, not trusting the sudden gleam in her brown eyes.

"I told you that my brother was in trouble, but would you believe me? No." She tightened the rope again. "You waited another two days before helping me."

"If you'd told me that your brother had gambling problems I might have moved a little faster," he retorted.

"You're the one with the problem. You already know what you think and you don't like being confused with facts."

Leaning back, he reached up to yank the rope she held, thereby tumbling her down onto his lap. "I don't like being confused by a woman who seems intent on driving me crazy."

Sprawled across his thighs, with his seductive mouth so close to hers, Annie couldn't think straight. She could feel his warm breath on her cheek as he bent down until his lips hovered over hers. Then he licked the corner of her mouth in a move that had her shuddering with excitement.

Her small gasp was enough of an inducement for him to repeat the caress as he made his way from one side of her now-parted lips to the other. By the time his mouth settled on hers, she was about to explode. Their kiss took off like a rocket, complete with sizzling thrust.

Because his arms were still restricted by the rope, he devoted all his attention to the kiss, accomplishing incredible feats with a flick of his tongue or an erotic nibble of his white teeth.

Her arms were free to encircle his neck and tug him even closer. Her murmur of pleasure was cut short by the sound of a young girl's voice tinged with irritation. "Mom, Uncle Reno is making out on the front porch again!"

Annie jumped to her feet and stumbled back a few steps to put some distance between her and Reno.

It wasn't until she heard a thump that she realized she was still holding on to the rope and that she'd just dragged Reno from the comfy wooden bench onto the porch floor.

When Tracy strolled through the front door to find Reno at Annie's feet, she couldn't resist chuckling. "How like you, Reno, to try and outdo your brother. Instead of going down on your knees the way Cord did, you just fall at the poor girl's feet."

"She hog-tied me," Reno said indignantly while yanking off the rope and irritably tossing it aside as he leaped to his feet.

Tracy gave her friend a look of appreciation. "I have to tell you, Annie, you're the first woman who's thought to actually tie the guy up, although many have been tempted, I'm sure."

"I didn't tie him up," Annie modestly denied. "Rusty did. Or rather, he lassoed him. I was just trying to talk some sense into Reno."

"Really?" Tracy appeared intrigued if not convinced. "And did it work? Talking some sense into him, I mean?"

"I doubt it. Maybe you should ask him."

"Okay, I will." Tracy turned to him.

But Reno held out his hand, forestalling the question. "I'm not the kind of guy who kisses and tells."

"He's just the kind of guy who kisses a lot on the front porch," Annie tartly retorted.

"It's not my favorite location," he said with dry humor.

"Much as I'd love to stay and learn more about your favorite make-out locations, I've got to be going," Annie said, her aggravation with him apparent. Actually she was just as aggravated with herself. She knew better. But it didn't seem to matter what her brain said; where Reno was concerned, her hormones just took over. Here she was, about to turn twenty-eight and regressing into puberty.

Forbidden fruit always tasted sweeter. Maybe it was time she stopped fighting Reno and instead investigated the physical chemistry between them. The rebel thought stole into her mind with breathtaking swiftness.

"What do you aim on doing?" Reno asked, making her wonder for a moment if mind reading was another of his talents along with awesome kissing abilities.

"Doing?" she unsteadily repeated.

"About your brother? You're not going to head off on another harebrained scheme, are you?"

She supposed that entertaining the idea of making love with Reno qualified as a harebrained scheme if anything did. "You don't think I should do anything foolish?"

"Not unless you're doing it with me," he replied.

Whoa, this was getting spooky! Her startled gaze met his. There was no way he could have known what she was contemplating...could he? Sure, the guy knew women, but even so...

"I won't make anything foolish tonight," she promised before making a hasty departure.

All the way home she kept reviewing the idea of exploring the physical attraction she felt for Reno. It was an important decision, one she shouldn't make lightly. She fully understood that. Just as she fully understood, better than most women given her mother's checkered romantic track record, the dangers of giving in to physical attraction.

But was that all she felt for him? Could it be that she was already on the brink of losing her heart to him? Or was this just sexual infatuation?

How should she respond to this weakness she had where he was concerned? He kissed her and she went up in flames.

Looking out her car window at a stand of charred fir trees along the road, it suddenly hit her. They cut down on forest fires by having controlled burns. That's what making love with Reno would be like. A controlled burn. *She'd* make the decision, not be seduced into it in a weak moment and risk being consumed by the flames of a passion out of control.

The plan did have its good points. Sleeping with him and getting it over with seemed like a logical approach—given the way he had of disarming her defenses anyway.

On the other hand, there were risks, too. The risk that she'd fall for him, that she'd like making love with him so much she'd never want to stop and would become his love slave. Yeah, right. Or how about the risk that she wouldn't be any good at it at all. Much more likely.

But Reno was probably so good at it that he'd make it good for anyone. Just look at what he'd done to her merely by kissing her—made her think about going to bed with him. And that was no small feat in her book. In fact, it was a very big deal.

Maybe the stress of her brother's disappearance was warping her decision-making process. It was certainly true that she wasn't at her best. And while she was very worried about her brother, she wasn't panicked yet, because some inner core told her that he was still okay, wherever he was. For now.

But it couldn't be good that Sven was looking for him. Maybe she should don her truck-stop outfit again and see if it would work on getting information out of Sven.

But what could he tell her? That her brother owed him money? She'd figured that much out for herself.

The bottom line was that Sven had no more of a clue about Mike's whereabouts than she did.

So Annie didn't have a clue where her brother was and she didn't have a clue what she should do about Reno, only what she was *tempted* to do.

6

SEVERAL DAYS LATER, Annie was still no closer to locating her brother or deciding what to do about Reno. Each time she heard Reno's voice on the phone, her heart leaped. The first few times it happened, she told herself it was because she hoped he'd have news of her brother. Then her honesty kicked in, and she admitted that it was also because she liked the sound of his voice.

His low-pitched, slightly husky voice was very expressive and often filled with humor as he related the goings-on in Bliss. It was clear to her that he loved this town and his job, even if there were times it drove him crazy.

His sexy drawl drove her crazy.

"Yoo-hoo, Annie, you're holding up the line!" The comment came from Geraldine Winters, the vivacious postmistress who was the town gossip.

Blinking, Annie pulled her thoughts together and realized she'd been staring off into space instead of paying attention to her surroundings in the post office. Looking around, she realized she was indeed next in line. Thankfully, she was also the *only* one in line. "Sorry," she hurriedly apologized, stepping forward. "I was just thinking...uh...anyway I need a sheet of stamps."

"Kiss and make out! Kiss and make out!" Geraldine's colorful and chatty parrot shrieked in the background.

Geez, were her thoughts regarding Reno posted all over her face, for cripe's sake? Could the bird read minds now, too?

"Hush, Dispatch," Geraldine chastised her pet. Turning to Annie, she added, "Ever since those stories about Hailey and Cord were going around town last year, Dispatch has picked up some new phrases and he just won't stop using them. He used to say only postal phrases, you know. I wanted those *Guinness World Record* folks to come on out and see him, but they never did reply. No manners, that's the problem with folks these days. Did you know that Tex Jackson's daughter-in-law didn't even send him a birthday card? And then there's Rhonda, who used to work at the Cut'N'Curl. But wait, did you hear that they're going to rename the beauty parlor Curly's in honor of Cockeyed Curly? This whole town is going cockeyed if you ask me. I can't tell you how many strangers are in town these days, picking up their mail General Delivery here. And I don't have a single empty post-office box. They're all rented. To people I don't even know," she added as if this were a criminal offense. "And packages. I've got packages coming out the wazoo. Lots of them are from a company in California. I looked them up on the Internet and you know what they sell? Metal detectors for treasure hunters. And you heard what they did to Mrs. Carruthers's poor peonies, didn't you? Those flowers have been blooming for decades and they just dug them up. The garden club has decided to hire Barnie during his off-hours from the sheriff's department, and he's got plenty of them, to patrol and protect the gardens of Bliss. Anybody tries any funny stuff and they'll be in a heap of trouble for sure." Infamous for her long rambling monologues, Geraldine finally paused to draw breath. Her dark, birdlike eyes flitted over Annie's face with avid curiosity. "So what were you so deep in thought about? That poor brother of yours?"

Annie nodded, trying not to feel guilty that she'd been fantasizing about Reno instead of focusing on Mike. "Have you heard anything about his possible whereabouts?"

Geraldine shook her head. Her short hair was dyed Lucille Ball–red in a special color that Luanne over at the beauty parlor whipped up just for her. "I've been keeping my head to the ground. Or is the phrase supposed to be keeping my ears to the ground? I can't recall now. But I've been on the lookout for anything suspicious. But with all this gold fever going around, everyone and everything seems suspicious. Except for you." Geraldine patted Annie's hand. "You're such a nice innocent young lady."

Annie wondered if the postmistress would still think so if she knew about Annie's thoughts regarding Reno.

"I hear you accosted Reno the other day," Geraldine noted, her dark eyes alight with curiosity.

How had the postmistress already heard what had happened on the Best ranch front porch last night? Had the twins tattled on her? After all, they had talked about the treasure map even though they knew they weren't supposed to.

"Yes, well, you know how these things are exaggerated," Annie said with a vague wave of her hand.

"I heard this directly from Eve over at the Golden Treasure Diner."

"Oh, right. At the diner."

Geraldine immediately picked up on the relief in her voice. "Why?" She frowned suspiciously. "Did you accost Reno someplace else, too?"

"Of course not. And I didn't accost him at the diner, I just wanted his help finding my brother. In a professional capacity."

"I also heard you've been baking up a storm."

"Guilty as charged." Annie slid her backpack off and brought out a plastic container of cookies. "As always, I made too many so I brought some for you."

"What did you make this time?" Geraldine's expression was one of anticipation.

"Oatmeal scotchies."

"Mmm." Geraldine was already eating one. "Since that brother of yours went missing, we've all been eating real good."

"I can't help it." Annie shrugged. "When I get upset, I bake."

"We're not complaining, believe me. And you know, if you want to talk to me about things, I'm a good listener," Geraldine assured her. "Folks are eager to talk to me on account of my people skills."

That, and the fact that Geraldine put the Spanish Inquisition to shame. The woman knew everything there was to know about everything and everyone. Not that she got it right each time, but she was usually pretty darn close.

Which is why Annie had no intention of even mentioning Reno's name in her presence.

As it had turned out, Geraldine had brought him up anyway. "Roxanne over at The Homestead Restaurant was talking to me about Reno the other day. Did you know she won the wet T-shirt contest four years in a row? Reno was one of the judges. Anyway, she was telling me how Reno chased after a customer of hers that walked out without paying. She and Reno used to be an item a few months back you know. But then Reno and just about every woman in this town have been an item at one time or another.'' She cackled, before fixing her birdlike gaze on Annie. "Except for you. I sure hope that Reno has mended his ways and is doing his best for you.''

Mended his ways? Annie thought. About what? Dating every woman in Bliss or believing her brother was truly missing? What could a man who went with a woman who won wet T-shirt contests possibly see in her? There was no way she'd "measure up." And why should she even want to? What did she see in a man who judged wet T-shirt contests anyway?

"Would you like me to give him a talking to about helping you find that missing brother of yours?" Geraldine asked. "If he's not helping you…"

"He's been fine," Annie hastily assured her.

"He sure is *fine*," Geraldine agreed with a wicked gleam in her eyes. "A fine and dandy example of male pulchritude. Ah, if only I were a few years younger or he was a few years older.''

"Bad bird, bad bird!" Dispatch shrieked.

"Not that I'm one to be swayed by a handsome face and a charming manner," Geraldine said while breaking off a bit of cookie for her parrot. "But that boy knows how to handle a public-address system, and I tell you, that's hard to find these days. Why, at the Founders Day celebration last year, Reno saved the day by fixing that hum in the microphone before I spoke. Yes, a talent like that is hard to find. A wise woman would snap him up.''

Geez, every female in Bliss adored Reno, even Geraldine.

"A wise woman would know that Reno isn't catchable," Annie replied.

"A wise woman wouldn't have to catch him," Geraldine retorted. "She'd just slow down enough to let *him* catch her."

"I'VE GOT A NEW JOB," Barnie proudly declared. Scarecrow-thin, the deputy did his namesake from the classic *Andy Griffith Show* proud. His mom still bragged to this day that she'd named him Barnie because she knew someday he'd grow up to be a deputy just like Don Knotts. "I'm going to be doing some moonlighting on the side."

"You're not going to play your accordion on amateur night over at the Bliss Bar again, are you?" Reno absently asked, his attention on the stack of messages Opal had just handed him.

"No," Barnie replied. "I still have a lump on my forehead from the last time I played there and someone threw peanuts at me."

"Gee, you must bruise easy if a peanut will give you a lump," Opal said.

"The peanuts were still in the bowl at the time," Reno inserted.

"Some folks just don't appreciate the beauty of a good polka." Barnie shook his head regretfully.

"They're just philistines," Reno said.

"I don't think they were from out of town," Barnie said. "Which gets me back to my original topic, my new job." Proudly sticking out his thin chest, Barnie said, "I'll have you know that you're looking at the new garden club guard."

Reno frowned. "And what exactly are you guarding?"

"Gardens. Peonies, petunias, roses, rhododendrons."

"You know what any of those look like?"

Barnie shook his head. "Geraldine gave me a book though. With pictures of the flowers and everything. The main thing I'll be doing is keeping on the lookout for any trespassers. They've even promised me a guard dog."

"Great," Reno muttered. "That's all I need. The citizens of Bliss hiring their own vigilantes."

Barnie's eyes brightened. "Hey, I never thought of myself that way, but I suppose you could consider me to be a sort of hired gun right out of those old stories from the Old West Buck Best is always talking about."

"Except those hired guns were protecting sheep or cattle," Opal pointed out.

"Animals, flowers, it makes no never mind to me," Barnie replied with a wave of his hand.

"Did Annie Benton call in?" Reno asked, quickly thumbing through the rest of the messages.

"No," Opal replied. "Have you gotten any leads on her missing brother yet?" Opal asked.

"I've informed the authorities in Nevada in case he shows up there trying to recoup his losses."

"If he's a gambler, he could have gone anywhere. These days he could even access the Internet and gamble there," Opal said before adding, "Ask me how I know this."

"How do you know that?" Barnie obediently said.

"Because my daughter Sugar racked up several hundred dollars' worth of debt that way."

"I didn't know she was into gambling."

"She's not particularly. She did the same thing with a 900 psychic-hotline last year. She just likes turning her mother's hair white, that's all. She's back on-line now, a smarter if poorer person. I really do believe she's learned her lesson since it took her almost a year to pay me back.''

"Maybe we should hire her here more often," Barnie suggested with a glance in Reno's direction.

"Forget it." Reno's voice was emphatic. "No offense, Opal, but I'm still peeling nail polish off my paperwork. As a temp, she's fine."

"Because you know she won't be here long. I get it." Barnie nodded.

"I'd be upset with you two if I didn't happen to agree with you. By the way, I heard a rumor about you, Reno."

"It's probably true," Barnie said.

"Gee, thanks," Reno said irritably.

Opal's eyes gleamed with anticipation as she said, "This rumor had Annie hog-tying you on the front porch of the Best ranch like a calf during spring roundup."

Barnie chortled. "Is that little gal planning on putting her brand on you, Reno?"

"Don't believe everything you hear," he retorted. "Me, branded? Yeah, that'll be the day. Now let's get back to work. The taxpayers aren't paying you to sit around and speculate about my love life."

"Now you tell me," Opal said with a mocking grin.

THE NEXT DAY dawned with gray skies that looked as if they might begin to drizzle at any moment. The thought of Mike being out there somewhere in the damp and cold made Annie sick with worry. She was determined to focus her attention on locating her brother.

Focusing wasn't hard to do when the first call she got was from Sven. "Has there been any word from your brother?"

"I haven't heard a word from him," she said honestly. "I think he might have gone on a long trip, maybe visiting my mom overseas." This was a lie, to throw Sven off the track.

It worked, somewhat. "Does your brother often take off like this?" Sven demanded.

"He's rather footloose and fancy-free that way," she replied.

"In the end, he will have to pay his debts. Everyone does." Sven's voice was rock-hard. "You tell him that."

"But I haven't spoken to him…"

"Just tell him," Sven ordered before hanging up.

"I will," she muttered to herself. "I'll tell him right after I give him heck for scaring me this way. But first I've got to find him." After calling the sheriff's office and leaving a message for Reno that she'd heard from Sven again, she placed several calls to friends of Mike's she had yet to speak to directly, leaving more messages on their answering machines or with their friends and family members.

When frustration set in, Annie whipped up a batch of butterscotch brownies before deciding to go through the boxes Mike had stored in her basement. She felt guilty going through his things, but if it would help her find him and keep him safe, then she'd deal with the guilt later.

She opened one cardboard box to find all kinds of stuff inside, everything from a catcher's mitt to an old report card of his from the fifth grade. Sitting on the bottom basement step, she wiped away the tears as she saw his class picture from the same year.

"Just come home," she whispered to his photo. "We'll work things out. Together. Just like we always have. Just come home."

Wiping away her tears, she set to work on the next box, which held more recent material. Rodeo magazines. Swimsuit issues of a major sports magazine. A small black address book. The light wasn't the best down here. Picking up the box, she brought it upstairs where she could get a better look at its contents.

She hadn't realized she'd be lugging boxes upstairs when she'd put on her jean skirt that morning. She'd teamed an oversize red knit cardigan with it, the sleeves of which kept falling over the backs of her hands as she struggled with the box, which was heavier than she'd at first thought. Moving cautiously, she made her way through the door at the top of the steps.

Only as she turned the corner did she realize she was no longer alone. Her startled shriek was automatic.

"I knocked, but you must not have heard me," Reno said apologetically. "You shouldn't leave your door unlocked," he chastised her, taking the box from her and setting it on the large pine box she used as a coffee table.

Turning to face her, Reno almost bumped into her, not realizing she was right behind him. The moment he put his hands out to steady her, she felt the familiar chemistry race through her system. Here was the one man who could make her lose control. Why oh why did she have to be tempted by this particular lawman, one who broke all the rules about what she wanted in a relationship. Her lips parted, her breathing rapid, as was her heartbeat. His mouth was so close to hers. So close…was almost touching, almost kissing.

The tiny distance between them was filled with

electricity, humming with awareness. In contrast to his previous moves of grabbing her and kissing her before she could prepare, this time the awareness was building, burning, towering, quivering. Anticipation was increasing the input from her senses—the sound of her own breathing mixed with his, the clean natural smell that was uniquely his, the sight of his eyes so close to her own she could see the ring of navy-blue around the gold-and-green-flecked iris.

His mouth was hovering just above hers, so close she could feel it, almost brushing hers when they were abruptly interrupted by the ringing of the phone.

Startled once again, she jumped.

"Um, I'd better get that," she said. "I left several messages with friends of Mike's again this morning and it might be one of them calling back."

Sure enough, it was. Calling collect from Bozeman, which is what she'd instructed him to do. "This is Bryan Patch. I heard you were looking for me."

"Thanks so much for getting back to me. I'm looking for my brother."

"So I heard."

"Do you have any idea where he could be?" she asked, her fingers crossed for good luck.

"Not really."

She tried not to be disappointed. Still, there was something about the way Bryan said the words that made her think he knew more than he was saying. "When was the last time you saw him?"

"At a bar in Bozeman a while back."

"How long a while?" she persisted. "A month?"

"Two weeks ago."

Her heart lifted. This was the most recent sighting of Mike.

"Listen," Bryan said, "I wouldn't worry about

Mike if I was you. He's got his reasons for laying low."

"Because of Sven?"

Bryan sounded surprised. "You know about Sven?"

"I know Mike owes him money."

"Then you know why Mike has to lay low for a while. He told me he had a plan."

"What kind of plan?" she desperately asked.

"I don't know. He didn't say. Listen, I've got to go, someone else wants to use the pay phone."

"No, wait!"

All she got was a dial tone.

"What's wrong?" Reno asked.

"That was a friend of Mike's. He says he saw Mike two weeks ago at a bar in Bozeman. He didn't say which bar, just a bar. And that Mike told him then that he had a plan and would be laying low."

"That makes sense."

"None of this makes sense!" she denied. "My brother should have come to me if he was in trouble."

"You can't live his life for him."

"I'm not trying to do that. I just...I just want to know he's safe, that's all."

"I've alerted the authorities in Nevada just in case he shows up there to try and recoup his losses. But I suspect he's headed for the hills until things cool off."

"What if Sven has already found him?"

"Didn't you leave me a message saying Sven called you this morning?" Reno asked.

"Yes."

"Well, he wouldn't still be looking for Mike if he'd found him. Like his friend told you, Mike is laying low somewhere. If I were a betting man, I'd be willing to bet on that."

"Are you telling me you're not a betting man?" she said.

He smiled, the laugh lines fanning out from the corner of his eyes. "I'm a man who goes after what he wants rather than waiting around placing bets on what might happen."

"A man of action, hmm?"

"That's right. Do you have a problem with that?" he asked, tucking a loose strand of hair behind her ear.

"No," she whispered. "No problem."

She'd made her decision. It was time. Time to let her desire for Reno loose instead of always trying to slam the door on it. Time for this little minnow to ride the powerful current and swim with the shark. Something that felt so incredibly right couldn't be wrong, could it? Not when every cell in her body called out for her to do this.

"So you wouldn't have a problem with me taking action now, by, say, taking down your hair?" Without waiting for an answer, he removed the denim scrunchy she'd wrapped around her hair to pile it on top of her head. As her long silky brown hair came tumbling down, he threaded his fingers through the loose strands. "I like it better down this way," he murmured.

"You do?" Was that unsteady voice hers?

He nodded. "You look less like a schoolmarm and more like..."

"Like?"

"A woman who knows what she wants."

"I do know what I want."

"I know." He nodded solemnly. "You want me to find your brother."

"That's right. And…"

"And?" he prompted her, seductively brushing his thumb across her lower lip.

"And I want you," she said huskily.

"Thank God," he whispered before kissing her.

The earlier anticipation had laid the foundation for the fire. Now it flared to life, consuming her. He wanted her, she could tell by the way he held her, as if he couldn't get enough of her.

Was it so wrong to want him in return? She knew there was no future in this, but she didn't care. His desire for her here and now was enough. Wrapping her arms around his neck, she blocked out any lingering doubts and instead gave herself over to the pleasure coursing through her body. He did things to her with just a kiss that left her breathless.

She made no protest when he gently lowered her to the denim couch. In fact, she welcomed him with open arms. He pressed closer, moving against her as one kiss blended into another. The pace was slow and seductive as he showed her the pleasure to be had.

When his lips left hers they moved on to nibble her earlobe. Annie shivered with delight as he went on to caress the ridge of her collarbone displayed by the open V-neckline of her cardigan. His mouth was finding all sorts of erotically sensitive areas along her neck and throat while his hands were dedicated to undoing the buttons and revealing her white bra beneath.

She should have felt self-conscious about her plain-Jane lingerie, she hadn't anticipated ending up making out with him on her couch. But he gazed at her with such heated appreciation and then caressed her with such sexy tenderness that there was no room in her mind for awkwardness. Everything he did was done smoothly, with her pleasure in mind.

He could have unfastened her bra and hurried her, but he didn't. Instead he kept the pace in line with her response. He lapped his way down the valley between her breasts. His index finger slid beneath the practical white cotton of her bra to gently stroke the underside of her breast.

In the end, she was the one who helped him undo the front fastening of her bra. By the time he lowered his head to tease her nipples with the wet point of his tongue, she was burning up inside.

His hands slid over her hip and down to the back of her knee. She thought she was already utterly steeped in passion, but when his magical hands slid beneath her skirt to gently rub against the juncture of her thighs, the world slipped away entirely.

An aching heat throbbed deep within her in a way that was both humbling and exhilarating. He waited for her nonverbal permission before moving farther, and she granted it to him with the way she arched against his hand. Shivers of pleasure danced over her bare skin as he continued his gentle assault on her breasts with his mouth, toying with one peak before feathering the crest with his tongue, taking his time until she writhed against him. That's when he slipped his hand beyond the prim elastic of her white cotton underwear to greet her in the most intimate of caresses, his fingers sliding into her with evocative skill.

When he feathered his thumb against the heart of her femininity, she soon spiraled out of control, the sharp pulses of pleasure and subsequent rush of release catching her by surprise.

She dug her fingers into his back and held on when

the aftershocks continued to rock her body as she shivered and shattered in his arms.

"I didn't know…" she murmured huskily. "I never dreamed…I've never felt…"

"You mean the men in your life haven't…?"

"Made me feel like this? Never," she said with a dreamy smile.

He frowned. "But you have…I mean, you have…you're not a virgin or anything, are you?" He laughed, as if embarrassed to even be asking.

She blinked up at him. "Why, yes, I am."

7

"YOU'RE A VIRGIN?" Reno repeated in an astonished voice as he abruptly sat up. "How did that happen?"

"It's more what *hasn't* happened, isn't it?" Annie said irritably, missing his body warmth, missing him, period. "And I'd appreciate it if you'd stop looking at me as if I were some kind of freak."

For once his customary charm seemed to desert him as his words stumbled into one another. "You're not…it's just…a virgin…I haven't—"

"I know you haven't," she quickly interrupted him. "You stopped. And I'm wondering why."

"And I'm wondering why you'd decide that I should be your first lover," he said bluntly.

"Trust me, at this moment I'm wondering the same thing myself," she tartly replied, jumping from the couch to stand a few feet away, her trembling fingers refastening her bra before attempting to refasten the tiny buttons on her cardigan. How had he managed to get so many of them undone so quickly and with so little trouble?

Experience. That's how. He had plenty of experience. Something she lacked and he wasn't about to give her. What on earth had made her think this might be a good idea?

She'd thought she could maintain her control. She'd thought that it was okay to trust her heart instead of her head. She'd thought that she and Reno had shared something special. Instead it seemed that he'd wanted a willing female body, and any female would do. Except for her, a virgin female.

Shame at her lack of control rushed through her, staining her soul. Because instead of gazing at her with desire, he was staring at her with panic in those damned sexy eyes of his.

"I think maybe you should think this through a little more," he said in a serious voice, even as his eyes drifted to the door as if he was planning his escape. "We probably both should."

"I agree. And I think you should leave."

He nodded and couldn't seem to get out of the house fast enough.

Which only proved to Annie that Reno hadn't really been interested in her, he'd simply been playing one of his macho games with her. Maybe he'd wanted to complete his sexual scoresheet by bedding the one woman in Bliss he had yet to bag.

The smell of something burning sent her racing into the kitchen, where she pulled the burnt brownies from the oven.

Ruined. They were ruined. Completely singed.

She knew exactly how the poor pathetic brownies felt.

Sinking onto a pine kitchen chair, her knees shaking, she put her hands to her face as memories of her past came back to her—of another teacher she'd worked with who'd played mind games with her. Their so-called romance had ended up being a humiliating replay of her high-school experiences.

It felt like that all over again. Just like before, Annie had been a challenge to a man by not falling for his charm right off. Which meant that he had something to prove.

But her being a virgin was too much of a challenge for Reno. The women in his past had no doubt been experienced lovers able to meet him on an equal basis. Sexy women with erotic tricks up their sleeve. Not a woman like her. Not a "nice" woman who wore a 34A bra and valued order in her life.

This was doomed from the start. Back at the truck stop, when she'd flaunted her navel and Big Hair, that disguise hadn't changed her place in the sexual-hierarchy food chain. She was a minnow. Reno was a shark, a natural-born predator. And it felt like he'd just bitten a huge chunk out of her heart.

A VIRGIN? Reno wiped the beads of nervous sweat from his forehead. Geez, he might have some faults, but going around deflowering virgins wasn't one of them.

Which only went to hit home his first impression of Annie, the wholesome, clean-cut schoolmarm. She wasn't the kind of woman you fooled around with. Her heated response to his kisses had temporarily blinded him to the reality of that fact. Annie was the type of woman you gave your heart to, the type you settled down with to raise a bunch of kids. Hell, she even baked. He'd never known a woman who baked. He'd never known a woman like Annie, period.

That alone should have raised a red flag with him right there. He'd known a lot of women, some he'd had sex with, many he hadn't. But none of them had prepared him for Annie.

He was doing her a favor by walking away. She deserved someone ready to settle down.

He wasn't ready for that yet. Reno ran his damp palms over his jeans. Just the thought of it was enough to strike terror in his heart. And there wasn't much that scared him. But sticking with just one woman for the rest of his life scared him spitless. Because maybe she'd see beneath his charm and discover what he'd always feared. That there wasn't much there.

Reno had always known that he lacked the depth his brothers possessed. Zane had a rocklike stubbornness that had seen him through some incredibly tough times—his wife running out on him, having to raise two toddlers on his own. Zane had even handled his ex-wife's death with his usual resoluteness. There was no room for failure in Zane's book.

And then there was Cord. Deep and dark. Half the time Reno didn't know what his middle brother was thinking, and he'd known him all his life. Cord felt things so intensely that he'd hidden himself behind a fortress, like the ones he'd built out of logs when they were kids.

It figured that Zane and Cord would find women who saw beneath their surface to the rich core inside. But no woman had ever seen more to Reno.

He knew what women thought, they told him often enough. He was a ladies' man, a man who got by on his charm. A man who stayed friendly with the women in his past, but never let one get her hooks so deeply into him that he couldn't walk away. He'd always known when to call it quits before either he or the woman in his life got in too deep.

But Annie wasn't the kind of woman you could walk away from. Not the kind you could forget. And not the kind to be blinded by surface charm for long. He'd done the right thing to walk away when he had. Before she'd seen that beneath his smiles and jokes and winning ways was a desperate fear that he was missing something essential at his core, that there was nothing there but a bottomless hole.

He reminded himself that he liked being shallow. It sure beat feeling things so intensely that they broke you. He preferred things light and lively. He was a pro at flirtatious foreplay and sexual friendship, but incapable of bone-deep intimacy. Yeah, he'd definitely done the right thing walking out on Annie when he had, before either one of them made a huge mistake.

"YOU WANT TO DO WHAT?" Luanne Jackson at the beauty parlor formerly known as the Cut'N'Curl exclaimed in dismay.

Tugging on the ends of her long brown hair, Annie said, "I want you cut it all off. Short. Real short."

"Now, hon—" Luanne patted her shoulder "—I don't think you really want to do that."

"Sure I do. Want some chocolate cookies?" Annie tugged a plastic container out of her backpack. Popping off the airtight lid, she waved it enticingly beneath Luanne's nose. "They've got peanut-butter bits in them, just the way you like them."

Luanne took a cookie but refused to change her mind.

"No man is worth cutting your hair for," Luanne said. "If you still want your hair cut in a week, I'll do it then. I'll even make the appointment for you now. I'd just hate to see you making a sudden decision you might regret."

"What makes you think this has anything to do with a man?" Annie demanded indignantly.

"Hon, I've been doing hair for thirty years now. I know that look in a woman's eyes when I see it."

"What look?"

"That *I'll show you* look. The best thing you can do to forget a man is to get back up on another horse and find another man. You know that supermarket manager over in Kendall would love to go out with you. And my nephew Bobby is always asking after you."

"I'm not feeling very kindly toward the male of the species right now," Annie said.

"All the more reason to go out with a nice one, to make sure you don't tar 'em all with the same brush. Wouldn't be fair now, would it?"

Annie shrugged. "I'll think about it."

"You do that. Meanwhile, tell me what you think of our new sign out front."

"I didn't notice it," Annie confessed.

"Come see." Dragging her outside the shop, Luanne pointed up. "See, it says Curly's. All in gold script. Think folks will make the connection?"

"I suppose. I didn't think there was anything wrong with your old sign."

"Gotta flow with the times. Yesterday I had three guys in here getting their hair styled. They'd been up in the mountains searching for Curly's gold. Said they were from California. And the day before that, another guy came in for a wash-and-dry. Said he was from Florida and he seemed real impressed with that hair-thickening conditioner that I make up. So you can see that I couldn't keep calling the place a beauty parlor. It's a styling salon now. Here..." Luanne dragged her back inside. "See, my new business cards say styling salon. Opal's daughter Sugar did them up for me on her computer."

"I didn't know Sugar was interested in computers."

"There's more to Sugar than most folks think, including her own mom. Now I'm not saying that she isn't scatterbrained. But she's a real creative person with plenty of big ideas.''

"Maybe I should have *her* cut my hair," Annie noted teasingly.

Luanne grinned. "You'd run the risk of her dying it green."

"Never mind." Annie shuddered.

Luanne patted her shoulder. "Like I said, if you still feel you want it cut by next week, I'll do it. But hon, you were meant for long hair. It's in such super condition, naturally thick and soft. I know women who'd kill for your hair. So just wait. And try my advice about distracting yourself with another guy. Like I said before, my nephew Bobby is in town for the summer and I know he would ask you out in an instant."

"I'll think about it," was all Annie would say.

As she walked down Main Street, Annie noticed other changes in town aside from Luanne's new sign. For one thing, there was more traffic. Bliss had no traffic signals at the two intersections—First and Second Avenues—because stop signs had always sufficed. But today there was actually a line of folks waiting at the stop sign, and several of the vehicles had out-of-state plates. A sign in the window of one store proudly announced that they had shovels and picks in stock, for a price that seemed inordinately high to her.

Change. She wasn't a big fan of it. Change made control more difficult, and heaven knew she liked having things under control.

By the time Annie had walked the two blocks from the beauty…uh, styling salon…back to where she'd left her car, Luanne had somehow managed to flex her matchmaking muscles. Because there, standing by Annie's blue Geo Metro, was Luanne's nephew, Bobby Phenton.

Annie recognized him immediately. He'd moved down to Denver last year. She didn't remember why, to get a better job she thought.

"Why, Annie, how lovely you're looking today," he said.

Looking at his nice smile and slicked-back blond hair, Annie couldn't help wondering why her heart couldn't have gone into overdrive by someone like Bobby. Someone stable. Normal.

"The Homestead Restaurant is doing their 'All You Can Eat' catfish special tomorrow and I thought you might like to accompany me there," Bobby said in a hopeful voice.

He looked so incredibly eager and sincere that she found she didn't have the heart to say no and stomp on his heart the way Reno had stomped on hers. "That sounds nice," she said.

So what if her voice lacked conviction. Bobby didn't seem to care, he was too busy making plans on when to pick her up at her place.

Maybe Luanne was right. Maybe going out with someone else was the best thing she could do to get her mind off Reno. Surely it couldn't hurt.

"GUESS YOU HEARD the news," Opal told Reno the minute he walked into the office Tuesday morning.

"What news would that be?" he said wearily. He hadn't gotten much sleep last night. A certain seductive schoolmarm had filled his dreams. She'd leaned over him, her long silky hair trailing over his naked body as she drove him to the edge. He'd woken up soaked in sweat and as hard as a fence post. No matter how he tried to push thoughts of her away, those erotic images wouldn't get out of his mind. "Did anyone dig up any more peonies?"

"No, but I hear that over at Drigel's Market, the price of shovels and picks has doubled. And they're completely sold out of them in Kendall. In every store."

"Great." Reno slumped into the chair in front of her desk. "Just the kind of news I wanted to hear." He reached for the letter opener stuck in the mug she used to hold her pens and pencils.

Opal smacked his hand away while continuing, "And there are reports that someone is trespassing up on Bear Tooth Mountain."

"Which only covers about a thousand acres of wilderness. Any other good news?" Reno inquired sarcastically, getting up to head for his own cubbyhole of an office.

Opal smiled. "Well, there is the fact that Annie is going out to the Homestead Restaurant with Bobby Phenton tonight."

Reno paused in his tracks.

"Not that you'd care," Opal added. "After all, you did tell me two weeks ago that your interest in her was purely professional. Isn't that right?" Opal blinked at him innocently.

"Sure."

"There hasn't been any word on her missing brother yet?" Opal's expression was more serious now.

Reno shook his head. "Not yet."

"Then I'm glad Bobby is around to comfort her in her time of need."

What about *his* time of need? Reno wondered irritably. The memory of her shattering in his arms and the dazed heated look in her big brown eyes had stuck with him like a burr to a saddle blanket. Not to mention that hot dream about her last night.

The woman was driving him crazy. He couldn't give in. She was a virgin, one who had the keen eyesight to see clear to his soul and discover how empty he really was inside. He didn't need that. He didn't need her.

"Aren't you glad that Bobby can comfort Annie?" Opal pressed.

"Oh yeah, I'm just tickled pink," Reno growled.

"But wait, there's more," Opal said. "Mrs. Battle is over at the Bliss Bar."

"Nothing illegal about that, although I'm not sure the Women's Auxiliary would approve of their president hanging out in a bar."

"Especially not when she's got a red boa around her neck and is calling herself Miss Kitty and crooning to the bar patrons."

"She's what?" Reno couldn't believe he'd heard Opal correctly. "But why would she do something like that? I mean, well, she's in her eighties."

"So is Floyd and he wants you to go there and get her to stop, she's driving away business. Oh, and someone has parked their RV on the edge of town and posted a sign saying they're declaring that land as theirs and any claim jumpers will be severely punished. And your dad called earlier to say that prospectors were trying to pan for gold in Troublesome Creek, and were scaring away the trout. But that you didn't have to worry about that because he and Tad were going to take care of the varmints was the way I believe he put it."

Reno groaned.

"Let's see, I think that's about it. Unless you count

the fact that my daughter Sugar wants to know if you're free to go to your dad's early birthday barbecue this weekend. I told her your rheumatism was acting up and you weren't sure you'd make it to the party without your Ben-Gay.''

''Thanks.''

''No problem. I'm sure she'll get over you shortly. She did seem interested in Annie's brother, Mike, but with him taking off the way he did, she's at loose ends.''

''Then why doesn't she go after Bobby Phenton?'' Reno suggested.

''Trying to get Sugar to take your competition off the market, hmm? Smart move,'' Opal said in an impressed tone of voice.

''I was just kidding.''

''Yeah, right,'' she scoffed.

''I don't have time for this. I'd better head over to the bar and see what possessed Mrs. Battle to go off the deep end.''

''Maybe she was trying to get Floyd's attention,'' Opal suggested.

''I suspect she's gotten it,'' Reno noted wryly.

He arrived at the bar in time to hear Mrs. Battle warbling the final verse of ''Smoke Gets in Your Eyes.''

''Take her away,'' Floyd pleaded with Reno from his position behind the bar. Floyd had been both bartender and bar owner for as long as Reno could remember. In all those years, he'd never seen the older man more agitated. Not even the time Reno's dad and Tad had almost had a fistfight in the middle of the bar last year.

The saloon's dim and smoky interior couldn't disguise the fact that Mrs. Battle had plastered enough makeup on her face to practically make her glow in the dark. Upon closer inspection, Reno realized she was glowing because she had a klieg light aimed at herself.

"Uh, Mrs. Battle," Reno began.

"Call me Miss Kitty," she replied, flipping her red boa around her neck with a flair he wouldn't have expected from her.

"Okay then, Miss Kitty. I think it's time for the show to end now. You don't want to ruin that lovely singing voice of yours, now, do you?" He reached out his hand.

Instead of replying, she smacked his hand with what looked like a colorful *Sesame Street* microphone she'd apparently been singing into. "You stay away from me. Police brutality. Floyd, you've got to save me!"

"Hey, now, there's no need to use force," Floyd protested, coming out from behind the bar. "That's no way to treat a lady."

"I didn't touch her," Reno retorted in exasperation. "If you think you can do better, then *you* handle her."

"Oh, the both of you stop looking at me as if I've lost my mind," Mrs. Battle replied in her normal tone of voice. "I was trying to make a point here."

"The point being?" Reno inquired.

"That Floyd was acting like a crazy man, all wrapped up with this legend of Cockeyed Curly's gold, spending his free time digging out back behind the bar."

"Not you, too," Reno said with a disapproving look at Floyd.

The bartender shrugged defensively. "Hey, Curly might have buried it on my property. Who knows?"

Returning his attention to Mrs. Battle, Reno said, "I still don't see why Floyd's treasure hunting led you to…uh…"

"Make a fool of myself," Mrs. Battle supplied. "I wanted Floyd to see me, *really* see me. And I knew he wouldn't do that unless I did something outrageous."

"Aw, Millie, y'mean you did all this for me?" Floyd asked with a sappy look on his wrinkled face.

Millie? Reno hadn't known Mrs. Battle's first name, no one had ever used it as far as he knew.

"That's right, you old coot," Millie Battle replied, dabbing her feather boa at the corner of her tearing eyes. "Don't you know how I feel about you?"

"Aw, Millie," Floyd said gruffly.

Seeing them in each other's arms, Reno decided his presence was no longer needed. One crisis dealt with, three more to go.

The next item on his "to do" list was the RV parked on the edge of town. Reno stopped his patrol car right in front of the decoratively painted sign that said "We declare this land belongs to Ralph and Audrey Oberhausen. Any claim jumpers will be severely punished." Someone had gone to the trouble of posting four corner sticks some thirty or forty feet out from the RV and running a rope around the perimeter.

Upon closer inspection he discovered that the RV had a bumper sticker that proclaimed "We're blowing our kids' inheritance!" and Arizona license plates. He ran the license number through the computer he had in his patrol car and discovered they did indeed belong to Ralph and Audrey Oberhausen of Sun City, Arizona. Both were aged eighty. The RV had not been listed as stolen.

What was it with these senior citizens? Reno wondered. Was there a full moon or something that made normally practical people go wacky?

"Hello there, Sheriff," a friendly-faced woman with wispy white hair greeted him as she peered out from behind the RV's screen door. "What can we do for you today?"

Reno was tempted to tell her she could go away, but he didn't. "Ma'am, you can't leave your RV parked here."

"We're not parking here," she calmly replied, opening the door and coming outside. "We're living here. On our claim. My husband is calling it the Lucky Seven Mine."

"Ma'am, there's no mine here."

"Well, not now, but there will be once we start working our claim."

Reno held on to his patience as he said, "Ma'am, you're trespassing."

"We're doing no such thing," she vehemently denied. "Ralph, you come on out and tell this lawman that we're not trespassing."

Her husband looked like a nice enough guy, dressed in a Hawaiian-print shirt and plaid shorts. "What's the problem?"

Audrey fluttered her hands. "This man says we're trespassing."

"Impossible," Ralph replied. "No one owns this land. That's why I've staked a claim on it. Look here, I've got a map. Come inside and I'll show you."

"Why don't you bring the map outside," Reno suggested.

"Fine, I'll do that."

"Would you care for some chicken and dumplings while you're here?" Audrey politely asked him. "I just cooked up a big pot of it and you're welcome to have dinner with us."

"Thank you, ma'am, but I'm on duty."

"I understand." She patted his arm. "I'll just go put some in a plastic container for you to take with you."

"That's okay, I don't..." But Audrey had already gone back inside the RV, passing her husband who was coming out with several rolled-up maps tucked beneath his arms.

"Here you go." Ralph rolled them out on the hood of Reno's patrol car. "If you look right here—" he stabbed the map with his thick index finger "—you'll see that this quarter-acre area is between two other properties and that it's never been claimed."

"That's because it's in a floodplain. This may look okay now, but it's a dry creek bed, and when it rains heavily this entire area is filled with runoff water."

"And that runoff water will remove the surface soil and allow us to find the gold beneath." Ralph smiled, clearly pleased with himself. "Don't you see, we're letting the water do the work for us."

"And don't you see that if this area has a flash flood, that runoff water won't just remove the surface soil, it'll remove your RV as well. It only takes six inches of fast-moving water to knock someone off their feet. Just a few feet will turn over a vehicle. I've seen it happen before. I don't think you appreciate how much of a risk you're taking by stopping here."

"And I don't think you appreciate how much we're willing to risk to protect our claim. See, here," the older man waved a sheaf of papers at him. "We've filed papers and hired an attorney."

"Fine. Then leave your sign here and just move your RV to a safer location," Reno said, his tone of voice coaxing. "I'll tell you what, you can temporarily park it in Bliss Park behind the sheriff's office." That way he could keep an eye on them.

"Here you are, son," Audrey said. "Here's your chicken and dumplings. I also included a slice of my carrot cake in some tinfoil for you. I hope you don't think I'm bragging when I say that I make the best carrot cake this side of the Mississippi."

"Ma'am, I was just telling your husband here that you've got your RV parked in a floodplain and that it isn't safe staying here."

"Why, how sweet of you to worry about us old folks." Audrey patted his arm again. "You're a nice boy. Isn't he, Ralph?"

Ralph nodded as he rolled his maps back up.

"So will you move your RV?" Reno asked.

"We'll take it under consideration," Ralph said.

"Thanks for visiting the Lucky Seven Mine. You come on back any time." Audrey waved.

As he left, big black clouds were boiling up in the southwest and lightning flashed on the distant horizon. It looked as if the past two days' worth of dry, sunny weather was coming to an end and a humdinger of a storm was on its way. Great. What else could go wrong today?

WHAT ELSE could go wrong today? Annie wondered as she gazed down at the nail she'd just broken down to the quick. She'd already blown up her hair dryer and poked herself in the eye with her mascara. If not for Bobby and not wanting to hurt his feelings, she would have canceled tonight's date an hour ago.

The distant sound of thunder rattled her windows and her composure. There had been something in the air all day, an unsettling sense of building anticipation. For what, she wasn't sure. It certainly wasn't for her date with Bobby.

Not that he wasn't a nice enough guy. He just didn't do a thing for her.

Which brought her thoughts back to Reno and his horrified expression when he'd found out she was a virgin. Well, maybe horrified was a tad strong. Stunned would be more accurate.

She had her reasons for staying celibate. Aside from the issue of AIDS, there was also the fact that she hadn't met anyone who'd truly tempted her, someone she could see herself spending the rest of her life with. Oh, she'd been tempted a time or two or three. And had come close. But something had always held her back.

Perhaps she feared real passion because of her mother's history or maybe she was simply rebelling against her mother's free-wheeling lifestyle and numerous lovers. The bottom line was that she'd tried to steer clear of men she had a strong response to and had instead chosen guys who were stable, who didn't make demands on her. Except for Ben, that teacher back in Iowa. He'd been a close call and he'd put the final nail in the casket labeled SEX.

She'd stoically accepted her role as the responsible one in the family. She wasn't about to jump into bed with some guy on a whim. She wasn't about to become her reckless mother's wild and wanton daughter.

None of which she'd discussed with Reno. Her reasons were her own business. At one time she would have talked to him about them, but not now. Not when he'd made her feel like a dinosaur.

Logically she knew she wasn't the only twenty-eight-year-old virgin on the planet. In fact, recent studies showed that more and more people in their twenties were choosing to stay celibate before marriage. No, she wasn't alone. She was just feeling lonely.

Where was her brother? Plopping down on the corner of her bed, she tried to keep the anxiety about his well-being from taking over. What kind of sister was she to even be spending one iota of time worrying about Reno when all her thoughts should be consumed with finding her brother? Bobby had told her he had some friends in Bozeman that he'd check with to see if anyone had seen Mike.

Since she didn't consider this evening to be a date, she wasn't sure what she should wear. Jeans and a T-shirt seemed too casual for the Homestead. So she'd worn a dress. A casual one with pretty shell buttons cascading down the front and precisely placed tucks on the bodice. The color matched the delicate handmade earrings of natural turquoise dangling from her ears and the light flowing silver-and-turquoise necklace around her neck.

As for her shoes…she stared in the full-length mirror, turning this way and that with some doubt. Tracy had assured her that chunky-heeled sandals were all the rage and convinced Annie to buy a pair during a shopping trip into Steamboat Springs right after the school year had finished.

As she twisted her hair and pinned it in place, she remembered Reno's sexy voice telling her he liked her hair down. Her face flushed at the memory of his fingers threading through her hair. Muttering under her breath, she jabbed another hairpin in place, the whimsical dragonfly hairpin at odds with her dark mood.

Bobby arrived right on time. The storm had yet to

arrive, but the distant rumble of thunder warned of its leisurely approach.

"You look real nice," Bobby said, reaching around his back to hand her a corsage with a lovely white rose surrounded by baby's breath.

She didn't have the heart to tell him she was allergic to roses. "Thank you, Bobby." Leaning forward, she kissed him on the cheek. As she did so, she was enveloped in a cloud of strong aftershave. "It's too lovely to wear. I'm going to put it in some water here." Grabbing a crystal bowl amidst the files on her brother from the sideboard in the dining room, she slipped into the kitchen to turn on the tap. The corsage looked lonely floating in the water, adrift much the way she was.

RENO WATCHED the big raindrops plop on his patrol car's windshield with a sense of inevitability. The weather service was predicting strong thunderstorms with heavy rain as a front moved through.

After dealing with a domestic dispute, he'd swung back by the Oberhausens' RV to see if they'd taken his advice and moved their RV. Of course, they hadn't. No one seemed to be listening to him these days.

Muttering under his breath, Reno watched the rain increase from a few splattering drops to a more consistent rainfall that blocked out the surrounding mountains. Yanking his rain slicker from the seat beside him, he tugged it on and went to bang on the RV's door.

"Why, Sheriff, how nice of you to come calling," Audrey said. "Now you come on in here out of the rain. It's coming down cats and dogs out there."

"Yes, ma'am. That's why I need you to move the RV."

She blinked at him. "Why, you must have ESP, Sheriff. That's just what we were about to do."

Reno sighed in relief. He really wasn't relishing them putting up a fight. "I'll just wait outside to make sure you make the move with no trouble."

And so it was that he was standing in the rain, untying the surrounding rope to let the RV through and then refastening it under Ralph's watchful eye. It took him another hour to get the Oberhausens settled at the edge of Bliss Park.

By then he was wet, cold and not in the best of moods. Barnie was taking over this evening, which looked as if it would be quiet, thanks to the rain.

He wasn't exactly sure how he ended up at the Homestead Restaurant. A man had to eat, didn't he? And this place had the best steak on the Western Slope. So what if Annie was going to be there?

He saw her the minute he entered the front door. It was hard to miss her. She was laughing at something Bobby said to her and she had her hair piled up on her head again. Her big brown eyes stood out more than usual, thanks to the makeup she wore.

She'd never worn makeup like that for him. Oh, it wasn't laid on with a trowel like Mrs. Battle's was in the bar. No, it was subtle. So was the lipstick on her generous mouth.

She looked good enough to kiss.

Refusing to give in to her temptation, Reno strolled across the dining room to a free table, where he proceeded to flirt outrageously with Roxanne, who waitressed there.

"Hey, gorgeous," he drawled, "How are things doing?"

"*Things*—" Roxanne deliberately aimed her impressive breasts right at him "—are doing just fine."

"I can see that."

"Just say the word and you can see lots more," she purred.

Even as Reno smiled at her and tossed out compliments left and right, his heart just wasn't in it. And that panicked him. Had he lost his touch? Had Annie messed up his mind that much? Hell, he was worse off than he thought.

Watching him, Annie wasn't surprised by his behavior. She was surprised to feel more than a twinge of jealousy as she watched him flirt with the infamous Roxanne of wet T-shirt fame. Even from across the room she could see his eyes twinkling with naughty mischief. The man was up to no good, she felt it in every bone in her body.

That feeling was confirmed when, a moment later, he slid a darkly brooding look in her direction.

She refused to even look in his direction after that. Instead, she enjoyed her catfish dinner and even had dessert afterward.

After dinner, Bobby asked her if she'd care to take in a movie at the Roxy Movie Theater, but by then she had the beginnings of a headache, so she begged off.

The ride home was quiet until they were half a block from her house. Then the flashing red lights of a patrol car bounced around the interior of Bobby's green pickup truck. Turning around in disbelief, she saw that a black Bronco with a portable emergency light on the roof had pulled to a stop right behind them. And out stepped Reno, looking like the devil himself.

8

BEING THE GOOD CITIZEN he was, Bobby immediately pulled over to the curb.

She actually heard him gulp as Reno approached the driver's side of the vehicle. "Is there some problem?" Bobby nervously asked.

"I clocked you speeding." Reno's voice was filled with authority, meant to intimidate.

"Speeding?" Annie repeated in disbelief. Mr. Dickens's dog had been running along the sidewalk faster than they'd been driving.

"That's right, ma'am."

"Don't you *ma'am* me," she said, her voice reflecting her increasing anger. "There's no way Bobby was speeding."

"I got you on radar," Reno said.

"And how fast to you think we were going?" she demanded.

"Too fast."

"How fast exactly?" she persisted.

"You were doing twenty-nine in a twenty-five-mile-an-hour zone," he stated in a curt cop voice.

Four measly miles an hour? He was going to ticket poor Bobby for four measly miles? Hadn't she read somewhere that police departments' radar systems had a five-mile-an-hour margin of error?

"I need to see your license and registration," Reno said briskly.

"This is ridiculous!" Furious, Annie jumped out of the pickup truck and marched around the front of the vehicle to confront Reno.

"What do you think you're doing?" she demanded angrily.

"Writing out a ticket," he calmly replied.

"Your radar system isn't accurate to within four miles. And since when do you have a radar in your own vehicle?"

"I have various pieces of backup equipment in the vehicle should I need it."

"Ha! This isn't about speeding," she said, angrily jabbing him in the chest with her finger. "This is about you being jealous that I went out with poor Bobby here."

Poor Bobby gulped again.

"That's ridiculous," Reno scoffed.

"You're the one who's ridiculous," she told him hotly. "How dare you use your position as the sheriff to harass us."

"That's not what I'm doing," Reno replied just as hotly. "You can go out with every guy in the state of Colorado for all I care."

"And do you plan on giving each of them a ticket, too?" she retorted.

"Only if you're going too fast."

"A turtle goes faster than we were going!"

"What's the matter, Annie?" Reno taunted her. "You don't care to be called fast?"

"Not unless I deserve it and I don't."

"I wouldn't say that. Tempting one man and then turning around and running around town with another guy sounds pretty fast to me."

"I was not running around town. I was having a

nice dinner. Or at least it was nice until you showed up and started shooting daggers at me.''

"Daggers? Where'd you get a phrase like that?" he scoffed. "From those mysteries you read?"

"Uh, would it be okay if I left now?" Bobby interrupted them to hesitantly ask.

"Yes," both Reno and Annie said in unison.

Clearly eager to avoid a ticket, Bobby took off.

"I can't believe your nerve," Annie told Reno, her face flushed with anger.

"And I can't believe the way you think the world revolves around you."

"You were stalking us at the restaurant."

"I was not. I was eating dinner. It's been a long day and I was hungry."

"You mean you're not even on duty now? And you have the audacity to stand there and pretend this isn't about your being threatened by my going out? Agh." Unable to say another word, she pivoted and marched off toward her house.

Reno marched right after her. "As if I'd feel threatened by Bobby Phenton."

"He kisses better than you do." Annie didn't know what made her say that, it certainly wasn't experience since she had yet to kiss Bobby other than on the cheek.

"Yeah, right."

"He does."

They were interrupted by the sound of a call coming over the radio in Reno's Bronco. It was Barnie. "Uh, I've got a report of a disturbance on First Street. The thing is, it involves someone who looks like you. The call came in from Mrs. Carruthers, and her eyesight isn't the best, but she swears it's you. I was just wondering, should I come out there?"

Grabbing the microphone, Reno said, "Negative. I have things under control."

"Because if you need backup, I'm there for you." Barnie sounded excited at the prospect.

"That's not necessary."

"You sure?"

"I'm positive."

"Well, heck, then. Okay, never mind."

Locking his Bronco, Reno hurried to catch up with Annie, who by now was on her front porch, rapidly approaching the front door.

Sensing his presence, she angrily turned to confront him, catching him off guard.

"You're the one who walked away," she reminded him, jabbing his chest with her finger again.

"Maybe I'm regretting that," he said quietly.

"Then just say so, don't terrorize poor Bobby the way you did."

He surprised her by smiling ruefully and saying, "Think you'll ever refer to me as poor Reno in that tone of voice?"

"You don't need looking after," she scoffed.

"Don't I?" His voice sounded almost melancholy. She shook her head.

"Maybe I do," he said huskily. "By the right woman."

"And am I the right woman?"

"I only know that I don't want anyone else being your first lover."

Her heart stopped. Staring into his eyes, there was no mistaking the raw honesty of his words. It was there for her to see, no longer hidden behind a sexy drawl or a seductive look. It was as if he was finally baring his soul to her.

"I don't want anyone else," she whispered back.

Empowered by his ragged confession, she framed his face with her hands and kissed him.

Reno was surprised for a moment. Then he returned her kiss with heartfelt passion before abruptly pulling back. "Anyone can see us out here," he muttered, resting his forehead on hers. "And while that doesn't bother me, I don't want your reputation to suffer. Maybe we should continue this inside."

"Sounds like a good idea to me." She opened her door, and stepped inside, looking around to make sure that the room was in order. That need of hers to have everything under control, especially her surroundings, always increased whenever she was nervous.

As if able to read her jittery thoughts, Reno reached out to cup her cheek. "This is a very special occasion."

"Mmm, yes." While her body hummed with pleasure from even this simple caress by Reno, her mind was racing ahead. Should she take another shower? She'd taken one before going out to dinner. If she did shower again, then what? Should she come out in a towel? Did she even own any sexy nightgowns?

"…Friday night."

Realizing she wasn't paying attention to what Reno had just said, she felt chagrin. Here she was, putting the cart before the horse. "I'm sorry, what did you just say?"

"I said we could make a date for Friday night."

"Friday night?" she repeated blankly.

"Yes. That way we can do it properly."

She frowned. "You can only do it properly on a Friday night?"

He grinned. "Sweetpea, I can do it properly any day of the week. But this is a special occasion for you, like I said before, and I just thought that rather than rush things, we should do it up special, with roses and—''

''I'm allergic to roses,'' she interrupted him. ''And I don't want to wait until Friday.''

He quirked an eyebrow at her, giving him that endearing look she found so irresistible. ''Afraid you'll get cold feet?''

''Afraid I won't be able to wait,'' she murmured with unabashed honesty.

He rewarded her confession with a swooping kiss that stole her breath away. Their tongues tangled in a sweet reunion as his fingers stole up to undo her hair clips. When her hair came tumbling down, he showed his appreciation by tangling both his hands in the silky mass.

''Where's your bedroom?'' he whispered against her lips, threading his fingers through her long hair.

''This way,'' she mumbled, not wanted to remove her mouth from his. She back-stepped her way down the short hall leading to her large bedroom. Seconds later, Reno was lowering her onto the bed.

The first thing he did was spread out her hair. First thing she did was remove his denim shirt. The shoulders were still damp.

''I was out in the rain earlier,'' he explained.

Remembering the fierce storm that had blown through town, she sent him a worried look. ''You don't know enough to come in out of the rain?'' she scolded him.

He zeroed in for another kiss, his lips warm and erotically clever. The same adjectives applied to his fingers, which were besieging the pretty shell buttons on the front of her dress with impressive speed. He stopped at her waist and spread the silky rayon material apart to leisurely caress her. He was tantalizingly slow with his approach.

She was practically ripping off his shirt in comparison. She was making inroads on the button-fly front of his jeans, the backs of her fingers brushing against the hard ridge of his arousal when Reno abruptly broke off the kiss and came up for air with a groan.

"We have…to…stop. I don't have any condoms with me," he unsteadily confessed, his face flushed, the hunger in his awesome eyes apparent.

"We don't have to stop." She raised her hand to his face. "I have a box of condoms." She opened the drawer to her nightstand and showed him several different types, textures and sizes. "You can order anything over the Internet. I had no idea, but I ran into Sugar the other day and we got to talking about e-commerce."

"Sugar suggested ordering condoms over the Internet?"

"No, of course not. Tracy suggested that."

"You and Tracy talk about condoms?"

"A man of your experience shouldn't sound so surprised."

"I just wasn't expecting you to have a stockpile of condoms in your drawer."

"I may be inexperienced, but I'm not stupid. And I only ordered this many because I wasn't familiar with the product, so I didn't know whether extra-strength textured were better than ultrafit sensitive. They had a hundred different condoms for sale at this on-line drugstore website. I had no idea."

A different idea just occurred to him. "Did you get these mailed to you? Does Geraldine know you ordered condoms?"

"Only if she has X-ray vision."

"Which wouldn't surprise me one bit," he said.

"Of course," Annie added thoughtfully, "the Condoms R Us return label may have given her a clue about the contents."

Reno almost choked.

She had no idea teasing him would be so much fun.

Growling, he tugged her down to him.

Kissing him was even more fun. And taking off his jeans felt downright decadent.

Placing her hand on the front of his light-blue boxer shorts, he gave her a wicked grin and said, "Feel free to familiarize yourself with the product and size up the situation."

She hadn't expected this—well, she'd expected that he'd feel as good as he looked. But she hadn't expected this humor and sense of play to be a part of making love.

"This is my first day on the job so I don't know how well I'll be able to...size up the situation," she murmured with a wicked grin of her own. "But I am well-read."

"Yeah. Mysteries."

"And the occasional romance as well as some non-fiction research thrown in as well."

He gasped as her fingers closed over him with gentle wantonness. "You...learned that...in a book?"

"Am I measuring up to the job?" She couldn't believe how sultry her voice sounded, how sexy she felt, how hot and hard he felt!

"That's something I should ask you." His husky laugh reflected his delight at her unexpected sauciness.

"Mmm, yes," she purred. "You measure up."

"Ah, but we're just beginning." He undid the fastening of her bra and peeled it away from her.

He caught her self-conscious glance down at her breasts, which weren't generous.

"You measure up, too," he assured her, cupping her breasts with his hands and brushing his thumbs over her taut nipples.

When his mouth surrounded her, the pleasure was unbelievable as his lips closed around her breast. Embedding her fingers in his thick hair, she shut her eyes and held him close.

The pressure of desire was building within her when his fingers returned to the remaining buttons on her dress. Once they were all undone, he unwrapped her as if she were a precious present. He removed the few items of their remaining clothing with quick dispatch.

Opening her arms, she welcomed him to her. Now there was nothing between them. His hands spread their heated message over her bare body, from her collarbone down the valley between her breasts to swirl around her navel to the juncture of her thighs. There he began a butterfly-like probing with his fingers that sent slick pulses of pleasure surging through her.

Rolling away from her, he quickly donned a condom and returned to resume where he'd left off, bringing her joy and utilizing all his skills as a lover to make her first time as good as it could get.

And it got incredibly good. She expected the tightness when he finally slid into her. And the brief surge of sweet pain. She hadn't expected the ultimate delight as she closed around him. With iron control, he kept the rhythm easy and smooth as he rocked against her, guiding her movements as she quickly picked up the cadence.

He murmured against her ear as they moved as one, his hands threading through her hair as he nibbled at her lips. When he slid one hand down to brush his thumb against her with intimate knowledge, she cried his name as an ecstasy that went beyond sensation pulsed through her, each wave increasing and merging with the next.

THINGS WERE GOING BETTER than Mike had expected. But he was starting to worry about running out of excuses and clues.

Excuses why they hadn't found Curly's treasure yet and clues as to where it was. When he'd first devised this scheme, he'd bragged at the bar to Hector and Roger about having seen the treasure map and having a photographic memory about such things.

Mike had been tipsy at the time, but he'd been able to tell that the two men weren't dangerous—they were two tenderfoots from Florida who were more familiar with a six-pack than a backpack and who had big dreams of tracking down an outlaw's hidden stash of gold.

Then several days ago Roger had dropped the name of a famous treasure hunter who worked off the coast of Florida, saying the man had come and bought a deluxe mobile home from him. Which had given Mike a few nervous moments wondering if these guys were smarter than he'd given them credit. But then Hector had admitted that Roger didn't actually know the treasure hunter, he'd just wanted to impress Mike.

The next bump in Mike's scheme had occurred two days ago when Roger had come back with two bags of groceries...and a metal detector.

Roger had caressed the portable piece of machinery with the kind of loving admiration most guys reserved for their girlfriends, horses or Harleys. "This baby has a variable operating frequency and selectable signal boost," Roger had said.

"Nice," Mike had replied, his heart in his throat as Roger began running that metal detector over every square inch of the area Mike had suggested might be Curly's hiding place.

Mike had finally disabled the metal detector yesterday when Roger was out getting more balsamic vinegar he needed for a recipe and Hector had fallen asleep in front of *Wheel of Fortune* on TV. Roger had immediately called to order a new one, but they were on back order with the manufacturer due to a recent run on metal detectors.

Mike had heaved a sigh of relief. He'd been given a reprieve.

"When I was in town, I saw your poster up in the post office," Roger told Mike. "It wasn't a very good likeness."

"Is he a wanted man?" Hector asked in a worried voice.

"Only by his family," Roger assured him.

Hector appeared concerned by this news. "Maybe we should return him."

"What am I, a package?" Mike demanded. "You can't return me. Not until we find the gold."

"But if the law is looking for you..."

"There isn't much law in this area," Mike quickly assured them. "There's only one sheriff and his deputy, who doesn't even really count. And with all those gold hunters down in Bliss, they won't have time to come up here to the mountains to look for me."

Hector asked, "What makes you think Curly buried his treasure up here and not in town?"

"I told you. I saw the map," Mike lied. "What outlaw is gonna bury his treasure in the middle of a town?"

Roger nodded. "That makes sense."

"What about your family?" Hector said. "I feel bad about causing them trouble."

"They'll understand." Mike felt badly about not being able to contact his sister, but he was afraid she'd blow his cover. The less she knew the better. She was no good at telling lies, her face was like an open book. She couldn't play poker because a two-year-old could read her expression.

Besides, he was a grown man, able to look after himself. He shouldn't have to check in with his sister like a baby. It wasn't as if he couldn't take care of himself. Heck, he'd done pretty darn good so far.

"So, what's for dinner, guys?" Mike cheerfully asked his captors.

IN THE END, Annie got the shower she'd considered taking earlier. Only this time she took it with Reno. By jasmine-scented candlelight. It was incredibly romantic. And visually challenging since she only owned two candles and they didn't provide much illumination.

"All the more reason for me to feel my way," Reno said when she voiced her concern about the lack of light.

"If we slip in here..."

"You won't have to dial 9-1-1 for emergency assistance because you've got the sheriff right here beside you. Now stop worrying and just lean back and enjoy."

She did.

When they were cuddled in her bed once more, Reno's expression turned serious as he propped himself up on one elbow to gaze down at her. "I acted like an idiot."

Her stomach sank. "You regret what we did?"

"No, I don't regret making love with you." He smoothed her hair away from her face to study her closely. "Do you?"

"No." Her voice was firm and decisive. "What did you mean when you said you were an idiot?"

He looked a tad sheepish. "I meant going to the restaurant and later pulling Bobby over the way I did."

"I was right." She triumphantly smacked her open palm against his bare shoulder. "You *were* jealous."

"Which is weird for me," he ruefully admitted. "Ask anyone. They'll tell you I'm not the jealous kind."

"I can see why. After all, you are the handsomest guy in Bliss."

"My sisters-in-law wouldn't agree with that."

She nodded. "You do have good-looking brothers, I'll grant you that."

He felt a twinge of envy—his good-looking brothers were also deep and complicated. Intelligent women like Annie admired that. She'd made no mention of loving him. She'd said she wanted him. But not even in the throes of passion had she ever said she loved him.

One corner of his mind couldn't help wondering if she'd chosen him to be her first lover because of his experience with women. But now that that hurdle was out of the way, would she stay with him? Or move on to another man?

He couldn't cope with that idea. He hadn't said he loved her, either. He didn't know how he felt about her. And being the shallow charmer he was, he noted bitterly, he sure as heck didn't want to examine his feelings too closely. Not when there were better things to do, like caress her in a way that made her big brown eyes widen with a blink of surprise.

Before he could do that, she gave him a solemn look as she confessed, "Usually, I'm not the kind of woman to do things on the spur of the moment."

He didn't need her to explain that by "things" she meant making love with him.

"Funny thing about spurs," he murmured. "They can get you going faster than you want to go if you're not careful."

"I've always been careful. And look where it's gotten me."

"In bed with me," he drawled with a wicked grin.

MIKE COULDN'T BELIEVE what a difference a day made. Yesterday he'd felt he had things completely under control. This morning the cow dung had hit the fan.

It had started out when Hector had presented Roger with a statement of their expenses so far.

"You guys don't have to keep feeding me these gourmet meals," Mike said, looking down at the Belgian waffles with fresh raspberries he'd just devoured.

"We don't have to keep feeding you at all," Roger growled. "All this money out of pocket and I have yet to see anything concrete."

The mention of concrete made Mike uncomfortable, reminding him of Sven's threat of fitting clients who were late in making their payment with concrete overshoes. Sven was a fan of old gangster movies. Mike was afraid Sven viewed them as training tapes.

"We're close," Mike told his captors. "I can feel it."

"Close is not good enough," Roger retorted, angrily pulling up the sleeves of his cashmere sweater. "We've been looking two weeks now. And still nothing. Zip. Nada. I think we should call the whole thing off."

"You mean let him go free?" Hector asked.

"That's right. You got a problem with that?" Roger demanded.

"*I've* got a problem with that," Mike interrupted.

When both men stared at him suspiciously, Mike realized he was treading on thin ice here.

"Whoever heard of a captive not wanting to be set free?" The words came from Roger but they were mirrored on Hector's face.

"It's not that I don't want to be set free," Mike lied.

"I'm starting to think you might not know as much about this treasure as you claim." Now Roger looked downright angry, and Mike knew enough to know that antagonizing your kidnappers, however cordial they might appear to be, was not the brightest of ideas.

"Haven't I been working real hard for you guys?" Mike pointed to the fake maps he'd drawn. "If the treasure was that easy to find, somebody would have gotten to it already. But I think I'm on to something now."

"Yeah," Roger noted sarcastically. "It's called a free meal ticket."

"I'm talking about an abandoned gold mine." Mike jabbed a spot on his map. "I think Curly buried his treasure there."

"Then take us there right now," Roger ordered him. "And I'm warning you right now, if we don't find something... Well, let's just say I wouldn't want to be in your shoes."

Shoes. Concrete shoes, Mike thought with a sense of uneasiness.

9

SATURDAY WAS A BIG DAY in Bliss. Bigger than Founders' Day. Bigger than the Fourth of July. Or so declared Buck Best. Because Saturday was his big birthday barbecue bash.

It was a big day for Annie as well because it was the first time she was going out in public with Reno. As his date.

She'd tried on four outfits before settling on what to wear. Since she only owned four nonwork dresses, six skirts and six slacks, her choices were somewhat limited. Where before the smallness of her wardrobe had appealed to her dislike of a jammed closet, now she wished she had more choices. None of the jumpers she wore for school would do, but she didn't count them among her dresses. Maybe a dress or skirt was too fancy for a barbecue anyway. She wasn't sure.

Choosing her jewelry was much easier. Again, she didn't have much of it. She wore the same turquoise necklace and earrings she'd worn when Reno had pulled her over and they'd ended up making love for the first time. With them she'd finally settled on a pair of jeans and a navy blue T-shirt with a lacy edge along the neckline.

Since the day was sunny but on the cool side, she'd added her red cardigan—the one she'd been wearing when she'd told Reno she was a virgin. She'd left her hair down specifically to please him, pinning a few strands away from her face with her silver dragonfly hairpin. She'd also taken extra care with what little makeup she wore. She didn't want to stand out as looking totally different, even though she felt totally different.

Looking at herself in the gilded mirror near her front door, she wondered whether anyone could tell by looking at her that she was no longer a virgin, that she and Reno had "done the deed." She knew it was silly, but Reno made her feel that way—silly and giddy. And worried. Worried that by getting involved with him she was following in her mother's footsteps.

Speaking to her reflection in the mirror, she said, "You made love with a man you don't even know well enough to know what kind of music he likes or even where exactly he lives in Bliss. How cautious is that? And now he's taking you out to the family ranch. Tracy is bound to ask questions and demand answers. What are you going to tell her, missy?" She gave herself a reprimanding look before breaking into an uncontrollable grin. Thinking about Reno had that effect on her, prevented her from thinking clearly, from giving in to the nagging worries at the back of her mind, and instead had her breaking into stupid smiles.

This really wasn't like her at all.

A knock on the front door stopped her from giving herself any more lectures.

Reno looked as good as always dressed in his usual attire of a long-sleeved denim shirt and jeans. Today those jeans were faded more than usual and clung to his body. The white cowboy hat he wore perched on his head was the same kind that any one of the men in Bliss, or the state of Colorado for that matter, might wear. Including Bobby Phenton. But Reno wore the hat with the rakish air of a man who knew his own worth.

"Have I got shaving cream on my chin or something?" he asked her with a teasing solemnness.

"I was just admiring the view," she replied with a newfound boldness.

His grin told her that he noticed and appreciated her sauciness.

"Why, I was just doing the same thing, ma'am." Using his thumb to tip back his hat, he gave her a visual once-over that was hot enough to scorch a stone.

She had yet to find a good description of his eyes. His two brothers and his father had blue eyes, which were very nice. But Reno's eyes were unlike anything she'd ever seen before.

And they had the power to make her weak at the knees with a mere glance. The dedicated stare he was giving her now, accompanied as it was by a delicious smile, was enough to make her take him by the hand and pull him into her house. The minute the door was closed he was kissing her.

She had her arms up around his neck and had just smoothed back his rumpled hair when she caught sight of her watch. "We're going to be late," she exclaimed, pulling out of his arms and searching the hardwood floor for the dragonfly hairpin he'd removed from her hair. Picking it up, she hurriedly stood in front of the mirror to put it back in place.

When Reno came to stand behind her and nibble on her neck, she almost gave in. The image of them was evocative. Until a tiny voice pointed out how much better-looking he was than she was, how much more experienced, how much more everything.

"If we're going to go, we'd better go now," Reno said as he reluctantly stepped away from her.

"What do you mean if we're going to go? Of course, we're going. It's your father's birthday celebration."

"Actually my dad's birthday is in December, but he decided that this year he wanted to celebrate it in late June. So he picked today's date and sent out the word. He claims that if the queen of England can have an Official Birthday and a real one, so can he," Reno noted ruefully.

"The members of the Best family certainly don't suffer from lack of self-esteem or confidence," Annie noted wryly.

If only she knew, Reno thought to himself.

"'NO TRESPASSING and no metal detectors allowed.'" Annie read the sign aloud as they crossed over the grated entrance to the Best ranch. "I hadn't actually considered bringing a metal detector to a barbecue. All I brought is a golden-tomato salad and a batch of butterscotch cookies."

"Never underestimate the power of your... cookies," Reno noted with a naughty grin in her direction.

Why hadn't she noticed the flash of a dimple until now? Here she was, sleeping with the man, and she didn't even know he had a dimple? What kind of woman was she? A woman like her mother, a woman who was irresponsible? The dark thought popped into her head without any warning.

"Hey, that was a joke," Reno noted in a gentle voice.

Great, he must have read something in her face. She wondered which fear was the most powerful.

That she was like her mother? Or that Reno would leave her and invariably move on to another woman? Or that she'd fallen in love with him? Or that he'd break her heart?

Oh yes, there are an abundance of things to be afraid of, but she refused to give in to them today. Instead she made the conscious choice to plunge ahead despite her truckload of worries and try something new for her—trust her instincts. And trusting Reno.

Wanting to restart the conversation, she said, "Why did that sign mention metal detectors? Where do they come into the picture?"

"Treasure hunters use them to locate anything from coins to..."

"Cockeyed Curly's treasure." She completed his sentence for him. "I get it now."

"After catching several trespassers on the property, my dad wanted to make it clear that the treasure hunting ends where our ranch begins. Most of the ranchers hereabouts have taken to posting No Trespassing signs."

"If Buck thinks the treasure is buried out here on the ranch, then why is everyone in Bliss digging all over town? Have you noticed the series of holes in people's yards? It's worse than a prairie-dog village."

"Yeah, the Garden Club hired Barnie to act as a guard for them. The Garden Club put notices all over town saying that anyone caught digging or trespassing on private property would 'suffer severe consequences.' But those holes you saw were dug by the residents who don't care about their lawns or gardens, not by prowlers. Barnie and Fang have kept the Garden Club members' peonies and pansies safe."

"Who's Fang?" she asked, trying not to get distracted by the way the wind through the open windows of his black Bronco tossed his hair beneath the brim of his hat.

"Fang is the guard dog the Garden Club provided for Barnie."

"Sounds like a vicious guard-dog name," she noted.

"Yeah, it is. For a Chihuahua."

"Fang is a Chihuahua?"

"Fang Dang is his full name, or so Mrs. Battle informs me."

Annie nodded, trying not to get distracted by the sight of a ray of sunlight shining in on Reno's lean fingers curled around the steering wheel, fingers that possessed a wicked ability to make a woman melt and shiver at the same time. "I heard about her performance at the Bliss Bar."

"I was there for the occasion and I still have nightmares." He rolled his eyes with exaggerated fear.

"Is she going to be at the barbecue?"

"Everyone from Bliss will be there."

Reno was right. As they pulled up in front of the ranch house, the side yard was already filled with parked pickup trucks and other vehicles. Walking around the house, Annie paused to appreciate the lines of the graceful old building, although she doubted Buck or the rest of his macho brothers would appreciate her use of that adjective. But it did have a sort of grace to it.

It was painted white and had a wraparound porch that had recently been repaired and no longer sagged. And it exuded a warmth and sense of welcome that reflected the people who lived there.

As she walked around the back corner, it suddenly struck her that from this vantage point the two-story

home was reminiscent of the farmhouse on the out-
skirts of Cedar Rapids where her mother had set up
her artists' commune. But that house in Iowa had
never been cared for, or been a home. It had, in fact,
been falling down around their heads due to a lack of
maintenance, and with her mother's friends constantly
coming and going, felt like a motel.

Her mother again. She momentarily closed her eyes
and ordered her thoughts to go in another direction.

"What have you done to the poor girl, making her
go all squinty-eyed like that?" Buck demanded of
Reno.

"I had her taste some of your 'Rip-snortin' Hot'
brand of barbecue sauce," Reno drawled.

Buck's chortle could be heard across the yard,
which was laid out with goodies from one end to the
other. They might have been in northwestern Colorado but the culinary spread was Texas-size, with
doors set up on sawhorses and being used as buffet
tables. The red-and-white-checked tableclothes added
a cheerful note to the festivities. Annie recognized
Hailey's pink potato salad and her famous cherry pie
as well as Tracy's sour mango slaw. The double
brownies, which won first prize each year, had to be
from Hailey's Aunt Alicia and the pecan pie had Mrs.
Battle's name written on it—literally.

Among those foods she recognized were plenty she
didn't, but looked forward to sampling. Before she
got the chance, Buck had handed the food she'd
brought to Reno with instructions to add it to the rest
of the "fixings," as Buck put it. Meanwhile, the older
man was leading her over to the grill to join a crowd
already gathered there, including Floyd from the Bliss
Bar and Mrs. Battle. Reno had told her that the
woman's first name was Millie, but Annie still

thought of her as Mrs. Battle. The name just suit her too well not to use it. Also there was Luanne from the Cut'N'Curl, now known as Curly's. And Geraldine, sans Dispatch, was there, as well, along with Hailey's dad, Tad Hughes, and his sister, Alicia.

"Okay," Buck said. "Now as I was telling you folks, my number-one rule for grilling is—"

"A clean grill is a happy grill," Floyd inserted. "You already told us. Ten times."

Buck continued, "And the biggest mistake is—"

"Hasty basting," Floyd again interrupted. "You told us that, too. Listen, boy, I'm gettin' older by the minute here. Are we gonna eat any time soon?"

At eighty-something, Floyd was one of the few in town who could refer to Buck as a boy.

"These old folks," Buck retorted with a shake of his head, his thick white hair falling over his forehead. "Always in a hurry."

"This from a man wearing a Women Want Me, Fish Fear Me T-shirt," Floyd scoffed.

"Don't forget the grilling apron." Buck proudly held it away from his body so everyone could read what it said.

Floyd snorted. "Aprons are for sissies."

"Not when they say Master of the Grilling World," Buck retorted.

"Having fun?" Reno asked Annie over her shoulder. "I brought you a glass of lemonade."

"Minus the soap bubbles," Tracy said as she came forward to give Annie a big hug. "I'll never forget the first time I made the twins lemonade. I hadn't rinsed the glass pitcher well enough after washing it and it still had a residue of soap in it."

"There's probably been a time or two when the twins could have used their mouths washed out with soap,'' Zane noted as he joined them along with his kids.

Lucky and Rusty both wrinkled their noses at their dad's comment.

Surrounded by friends, Annie had no trouble letting go of her worries and enjoying the beauty of the day. Sitting on a picnic bench with Reno at her side and a plate of delicious food in front of her, she had a front-row view of the mountains. They were one of the things she liked best about Colorado. Coming from the relatively flat topography of Iowa, she felt a special affinity for these mountains with their peaks sharply silhouetted against a sky so blue it almost hurt your eyes to look at it.

Seated at the family table along with Zane and Tracy and Cord and Hailey, as well as Buck, and Hailey's aunt Alicia, the conversation naturally turned to the subject of Cockeyed Curly and his missing treasure.

''One thing I want to know is this—if Cockeyed Curly gave the map to our great-great-great grandfather Jedidiah as a thank-you for saving his hide in that barroom brawl in Leadville, why didn't old Jedidiah go dig up the treasure there and then?'' Cord was saying.

''That's why it's a legend,'' Buck replied, shoving his glasses up the bridge of his nose. ''Because we don't exactly know all the details, like if Jedidiah did dig up the treasure and didn't tell anyone.''

''And we also don't know if Jedidiah knew that Curly was instrumental in Jedidiah's sister Rebecca eloping with Rafael Hughes when the county was on the verge of a range war between the sheepherders and the cattlemen,'' Hailey said.

Buck nodded his agreement before adding, ''We

don't even know how much gold was buried there. Best estimates are that it was over a year after Curly's biggest heist that he had that fight in Leadville where Jedidiah helped him out."

Annie knew that the amount of that heist was sixty thousand dollars because Reno had mentioned that to her once. She certainly hoped Buck wasn't going to toss that figure around, because as far as she knew, it wasn't generally known exactly what the amount was. And Reno wanted it to stay that way. And while they were seated at a family table, the rest of the population of Bliss wasn't far away and could easily overhear anything being said if they had a mind to.

"I don't know why everyone is making such a hullabaloo over this," Alicia said in a voice that was unusually sharp for the normally soft-spoken and shy woman. "I for one am tired of hearing nothing but Curly-this and Curly-that. As Floyd mentioned earlier, none of us is getting any younger. Maybe I should spend my time with someone who sees me, really sees *me*, instead of someone who is totally wrapped up with a treasure that may or may not exist."

"Don't know who that would be," Buck made the mistake of saying. "Everyone in these parts is pretty much consumed with Curly's gold."

"Not everyone," Alicia maintained. "Murph isn't interested in treasure hunting."

"Murph?" Buck repeated in disbelief. "You mean that son of a buck has been working here since Zane was knee-high to a grasshopper? He's not interested in anything," Buck retorted.

"That's not true," Alicia angrily retorted. "He's interested in *me*." With that announcement, she grabbed her empty plate and headed off, leaving a stunned Buck behind.

"I don't believe this," Buck muttered. "What a thing to spring on me on my birthday."

"Alicia knows your birthday is really in December," Zane pointed out. "What?" he demanded when Tracy smacked his hand. "What'd I say?"

"Did you know about this, Hailey?" Buck demanded.

Hailey shook her head. "She hasn't said a word to me."

"Maybe she was just funnin' me," Buck said. "Yeah, that must be it." He looked over his shoulder where Murph was standing with his buddy Earl.

Annie knew the two ranch hands were bashful and usually preferred the company of cattle to that of people. Even now the two men stood together off to the side of the crowd, Murph nervously rolling the brim of his hat as he greeted Alicia with an awkward shyness that was visible clear across the yard.

Buck made no more reference to the incident as he blew out the candles on a chocolate cake that Tracy had baked just for him. "First time it's turned out," she proudly stated, leaning down to give her father-in-law a kiss on the cheek.

"Mom—" Rusty tugged on Tracy's black broomstick skirt "—can we have two birthdays like Grandpa?"

"Not until you're your grandfather's age," Tracy replied.

The boy was clearly disappointed by her answer. "Aw, by then we'll be *old*."

"Thanks," Buck retorted. "I may be old but I can still beat you two pups at a game of horseshoes."

Annie warned Reno that she couldn't toss a horseshoe, but he didn't believe her, until she narrowly missed knocking out the passenger window of his parked Bronco. Then he quickly agreed that it would be best for public safety that she not play any longer. He didn't let her off the hook as easily for touch football, however.

"I already told you, I don't like football."

"This isn't plain football, it's touch football. Much more fun to play," Reno assured her with a wicked grin and a flash of that newly discovered dimple of his. "First off, we'll need to do a little one-on-one work."

"Where are we going to be one-on-one in this crowd?" she demanded, hands on hips.

"I know a place."

He took her out behind the barn, beyond the meadow, until the people at the barbecue were out of sight. He'd paused in the barn long enough to pick up the football he now held with both hands.

"Okay," Reno said. "I've got the ball. Your job is to get it from me. How are you going to stop me from running in a touchdown?"

"How about this?" She pulled up her T-shirt and flashed her black sports bra at him.

Sure enough, he dropped the ball.

"Why, you little hussy!" He sounded both surprised and impressed.

Quickly lowering her navy blue T-shirt, she said, "Hey, watch who and what you're calling *little*, buster."

"Sweetpea, the best things come in small packages," he assured her in a sexy drawl.

"Yes, well, I wish these small packages were a little better," she noted, gazing down at her chest with self-deprecating humor.

"Want to know what I wish?" Coming closer, he nuzzled her neck. "That we were alone."

"Stop that," she gently scolded him. "Someone might see us. My students are at this barbecue. Past, present and future. So are their parents."

"And it wouldn't do for the schoolmarm to be seen making out with the laid-back lawman, huh?"

Was there a new edge to his voice or was she just imagining things? "How did you know I once called you a laid-back lawman?"

Reno shrugged. "Nothing anyone says in this town stays a secret for long."

"Do you realize that I don't even know where you live?" The question may have seemed as if it came out of the blue, but it had been on her mind most of the day. She knew Reno didn't live here on the ranch any longer.

He frowned at her. "I live in Bliss."

"I mean where specifically in Bliss."

He shrugged again. "I would have thought that Geraldine would have filled you in on all the details of my life."

"I'm not that plugged into the grapevine." Was he deliberately avoiding her question? It sure was starting to feel that way.

"I'm rehabbing an old place on the edge of town," he finally replied.

"The one with the red shutters?"

"That's the one. According to the historical society, it was rumored to have been a bordello at one time."

"I see. And is that why it appealed to you?" she inquired with studied innocence.

Reno shook his head, his hair tumbling over his forehead. He'd removed his hat before they'd begun their football game. "I liked the woodworking and the crown molding. No one does workmanship like that anymore."

"Now you sound like your brother Cord."

"I'm not like Cord," Reno scoffed. "Cord would have finished this project years ago. My brother is very dedicated, and once he starts a project he always finishes it. Me, I'm more of a dabbler."

She wondered if Reno was a dabbler with women, too. He didn't have a track record of sticking around long enough to see something completed where his previous romantic relationships were concerned. Not that any of the women in his past had anything bad to say about him. They all seemed to agree that he was just a footloose and fancy-free kind of guy, not the kind of guy to grow up and commit.

Which was okay with her, wasn't it? She didn't want to marry Reno or anything. Did she? Did she love him? Was that the explanation for the rush of tenderness she felt today when she'd watched him teasing his family? Is that what this feeling was? Love? And what about Reno and his feelings for her? Rubbing her forehead as the beginnings of a headache took hold, she wished she had a few answers to all these questions running around in her head. But they remained elusively out of reach.

"Hey, Ms. Benton!" Rusty shouted as he raced to join them. "They're starting up the wheelbarrow races. Want to be on my team?"

"Sure thing."

"What, you prefer wheelbarrow races to touch football?" Reno demanded in pretend outrage.

"You can be on Lucky's team," Rusty told his uncle before taking Annie by the hand and dragging her back into the thick of the crowd.

"You don't have to do this," Reno said as he joined her at the starting line.

"Afraid I'll beat you?" she taunted him with a sexy wiggle of her hips from her position in the row next to him where she was holding the handles of the wheelbarrow containing a grinning Rusty.

"Your distracting feminine wiles aren't going to prevent me from winning this race," he stated with stoic pride.

He was right. Her wiles didn't prevent him from winning. A loose wheel on his wheelbarrow did, sending him into Annie's lane and in her way. She managed to avoid a crash and still win the race, much to Rusty's delight.

Needing a tall lemonade to cool down after all that exertion, Annie headed over to the refreshment and snack table where Luanne was sipping a beer and Sugar was reaching for a soda from a metal tub filled with ice.

"I'm so glad you took my advice about not cutting your hair," Luanne told Annie.

"I decided to wait, like you said." Pulling a scrunchy from her pocket, Annie pulled her hair off her neck and up into a ponytail. "At least when it's this long I can get it out of my way when I get hot."

"Reno would make anyone get hot," Sugar said in a dreamy voice.

Trying not to smile, Annie said, "I saw the business card you did for Luanne. You did a super job with the design of that, using a treasure chest and everything."

Sugar shrugged. "That was nothing. You should see what I've done with the Bliss website."

"You've done a website for the mayor?" Hailey said, having just wandered over.

"Oh, the mayor doesn't know anything about it. I don't think he even knows what a computer is. I did the site myself. Something to put us on the map."

"I believe Reno thinks we're already too much on the map," Tracy noted as she joined them.

"Which is why I played up the Cockeyed Curly angle," Sugar stated. "I've even got a link in there to Hailey's new book about the famous outlaw. And to Buck's Barbecue Sauce's website. Which reminds me, Tracy, you really do need to update that website. It's pretty lame."

Instead of being upset by this comment, Tracy looked impressed. "I've been meaning to do that. Would you be interested in doing up something for me? Final design subject to my approval, of course. I'd pay you the going rate."

"Sure," Sugar agreed with a big smile. "You need to have customers be able to place orders directly from your site and you need to have their transactions secured."

Fifteen minutes later, after giving them an enthusiastic minilesson on the merits of e-commerce, Sugar moved on.

Tracy gave the young woman's departing figure an admiring look. "Man, that's me ten years ago."

"You were a size 4 ten years ago?" Hailey said. "I knew there was a reason I hated you."

Tracy laughed. "No, I was never a size 4. I mean her enthusiasm, her eye for the pitch. She'd do great in advertising."

"Her mom thinks she advertises too much as it is, if you get my drift," Luanne said. "But I think the kid has potential. Providing she'll let me do her hair and get that awful orange dye out of it."

Alicia Hughes drifted over with Murph at her side.

"My, it is getting warm this afternoon, isn't it? It's such a lovely party, Tracy. Isn't it lovely, Hailey?" she asked her niece.

"Mmm," Hailey agreed, sipping her iced tea. "Although I'm not sure Buck would agree with that."

"He and my brother Tad are poring over plans to dig up the treasure," Alicia retorted. "I doubt he's thought of anything else all day."

"I wouldn't be too sure of that," Hailey murmured.

"Oh my, I can't seem to get this open." Alicia struggled with a new package of pretzels.

"Here, I'll cut it for you." Murph removed a small knife from his pocket.

Annie stared at the knife. It couldn't be...

"Hey, what are you all doing over here?" Reno demanded. "Do you know I was nearly grievously injured by that wheelbarrow? And did anyone come check me out, I ask you? No. Not a soul."

"Would you mind if I took a look at that knife?" Annie asked Murph.

"No, ma'am." Murph handed it over to her.

"What's the matter, Annie?" Reno said, his expression going from teasing to serious the moment he saw her white face.

"This is my brother's knife!" Annie said in a shaky voice. "He never goes anywhere without it."

10

"WHERE DID YOU find this?" Annie asked the ranch hand in a shaken voice.

"I found it yesterday up on Bear Tooth Mountain near an abandoned old gold mine," Murph quietly replied, a reserved expression on his weather-beaten face.

"You're sure this belongs to Mike?" Reno asked Annie.

"Yes, I'm sure. I gave it to him for his birthday last year."

"There are lots of Swiss Army knives..."

"Not with a scrape on it shaped like a question mark." She showed him. "What if he's lost up in the mountains? Or fell in that mine?"

"Your brother isn't a tenderfoot."

"Maybe not, but he's not a mountain man, either. What if he's hurt up there someplace?" Tears came to her eyes.

Using his thumbs, Reno brushed them away while gently scolding her. "Hey now, none of that. Don't panic, we'll find him. I'll gather up a search party, there are enough volunteers right here at the barbecue to do that, and we'll head up the mountain while it's still light. I'll get the Search and Rescue authorities involved, too."

"I feel so guilty. I should have done more instead of allowing myself to be distracted..."

"By me," Reno quietly finished for her.

"I'm coming with you," Annie declared.

"No, you're not. You're too upset and not thinking clearly."

"I haven't been thinking clearly since I met you," she muttered.

He tried not to be upset by her words. "Besides you're not an experienced tracker or climber."

"But I..."

"You're not coming with us and that's final." Looking over Annie's head to Tracy, he said, "Look after her, will you?"

"Sure thing." Tracy put her arm around Annie. "You go on ahead, Reno. And good luck."

MURPH HAD GIVEN Reno specific directions about the location of the abandoned mine. Reno was familiar with it, as were his brothers, who'd joined him in the search.

Before he left, Sugar had tugged him aside. "There's something I've been meaning to tell you but you never take the time to listen to me."

He'd almost brushed her aside, but she'd been insistent. "It's about Annie and that hunky Scandinavian guy. The one nosing around Annie's car at the truck stop a few weeks ago. I thought you should know that he was there. I didn't see him actually mess with the car, but he was there."

Which left Reno wondering if Sven was the one who'd grabbed Mike while he was hiding out on the mountain. In his Bronco, Reno kept a backpack filled with emergency gear. That backpack was now on his back as he scrambled up the narrow serpentine footpath that wound up the side of Bear Tooth Mountain. Zane and Cord wore smaller backpacks of their own. This path was too steep for the horses, so they'd tethered them down below.

They'd already hiked over a tumbling stream on their way up the pine-covered ridge. All the while, the stark outline of Bear Tooth Mountain jutted boldly into the sky, as if mocking their smallness in comparison to the majestic power of nature.

When Reno paused to take a drink of water from the bottle he'd tugged from his backpack, Zane said, "I hear your Bronco was parked overnight on Annie's street a few nights back."

"I had engine trouble," Reno said over his shoulder, the footpath only wide enough to go single file.

"So your engine conked out half a block from the schoolteacher's house, huh?"

"Yeah, so what?" Reno said defensively, turning to glare at him.

"So, I hope that's all that conked out," Zane noted with the grin of an older brother accustomed to taunting his younger siblings.

"Listen, I don't need any grief from you." Reno's voice reflected his aggravation.

"Uh-oh," Zane said with a shake of his head.

"Uh-oh what?" Looking at the ground around them, Reno said, "What's wrong? Do you see something?"

"Yeah," Zane replied. "I see the face of a man in love."

Reno immediately said, "Then clearly you need glasses, just like our dad."

In love? Reno grappled with the concept for a second before skittering away from it like a nervous filly.

Cord leaned around Zane's back. "Why did you stop? What's the problem here?"

"Reno's got it bad," Zane replied.

"Got what?" Cord asked.

"The love bug," Zane drawled.

"I don't have time for this," Reno growled. "We are on an official search-and-rescue mission here in case you've forgotten."

"You're the one who stopped walking," Cord, ever the practical one, pointed out.

Doing an about-face, Reno continued marching up the path, muttering under his breath, "Love bug, hah!"

"Oh yeah, he's got it bad," Cord agreed. "I recognize the signs."

Reno's voice was curt. "The two of you low-down gizzard-sucking coyotes would do more good looking for signs of Annie's brother."

"He's even using Pa's insults," Zane noted.

"He must lack the brainpower to come up with his own," Cord said.

"Loving a woman will do that to you. Sap your brain cells. It's a little-known medical fact," Zane maintained.

"I'll give you a little-known fact. Killing my brothers is legal if they get in the sheriff's way of accomplishing official business," Reno warned them.

"You can't kill us now," Zane retorted, clearly not intimidated. "You need us to help you find Mike."

"For all the good you're doing, I might as well be up here alone," Reno grumbled. "I'm telling you, the next person who mentions love will get a hundred-dollar fine!"

They reached the mine half an hour later without any further harassing on his brother's parts. Reno had set such a hard pace so no one would have enough breath left for idle talking. A quick search of the area showed that it was deserted, but that it had been visited recently.

"Three different sets of prints," Reno noted as he knelt down to survey the dusty area in front of the mine opening. "And they were here recently, today."

"Where do you think they are now?" The question came from Zane.

"There are only two cabins up in these parts," Reno said. "One about a mile to the east and one a little closer to the north."

Handing Zane a two-way radio, Reno said, "It's time we split up. You two you take the cabin to the east and I'll take the closer one to the north. No heroics here, just a fact-finding mission. Check the place out and see if there's any sign of habitation. Keep in radio contact. Any questions? Okay then, let's go."

"WHERE ARE YOU GOING?" Sugar asked as Annie prepared to saddle a horse in the Best barn.

Annie turned, knowing full well she looked as guilty as a thief stealing off with the family silverware. She'd felt badly deceiving Tracy by telling her that she needed some time alone. Tracy had led her to the housekeeper's quarters at the back of the house where Tracy had stayed when she'd first come to the Best ranch. "No one will bother you here," Tracy had assured her. "Maybe you should lie down and see if you can get some rest for a while. I'll let you know the minute we hear anything."

Annie had waited ten minutes before sneaking out. She'd managed to make it to the barn without anyone seeing her, thanks to a row of bushes running out from the house and shielding her from view of those still gathered in the yard. And now here she was, "borrowing" one of the Best's horses. Something that would have gotten her hung in Cockeyed Curly's time.

"Where are you going?" Sugar repeated.

"I'm going after my brother," Annie stated with unshakable firmness.

"I know a shortcut to the mine."

"Really?" It was the first good news Annie had heard since seeing her brother's scuffed-up knife. "That would be great. Tell me."

"You don't need a horse," Sugar replied. "The path goes from the road to town."

"Even better." Annie wasn't the best horsewoman on the face of the earth. Replacing the saddle where she'd found it, she turned to Sugar, waiting for the directions.

"My Jeep will take us most of the way," Sugar said.

Annie frowned. "I don't think it's a good idea that you come with me."

"It's not a good idea that either one of us goes, but that's not stopping you."

"He's my brother."

"And he was my date to this barbecue," Sugar angrily retorted. "He asked me three months ago. So are we going to waste time standing around here arguing and risk getting caught, or are we leaving?"

To which Annie simply said, "Let's go."

"WE BELIEVE in the golden rule," Roger said solemnly.

"Yeah, whoever has the gold rules!" Hector shouted.

"We're rich!" Roger crowed gleefully.

"There's gold in them there hills," Hector drawled, sounding like John Wayne. "I've always wanted to say that," he added in his own low-pitched voice.

"I told you I'd come through for you guys," Mike said, thanking his lucky stars that these Easterners had never seen fool's gold before. The abandoned mine he'd taken them to had numerous veins of the stuff, if you knew where to look, and never failed to impress outsiders.

"A gold mine of our own. You're sure the place hasn't been claimed?" Roger turned to ask Mike.

"You have to actively work it, and that place hasn't seen any action in decades," he replied.

"Then first thing tomorrow we're filing papers on that mine," Roger said.

"What kind of papers?" Hector asked.

Roger shrugged. "I don't know. We'll find out. Or you can." He pointed at Hector. "You're the detail man."

"That's right. I'm the detail man," Hector said proudly.

"I don't mind telling you, I had my doubts when it took you two days to find the chamber in that cave," Roger told Mike.

"It's a mine," Hector reminded Roger. "Not a cave."

"Well, it looked like a cave from the outside," Roger replied with an impatient wave of the hand, the CZ ring on his little finger shining in the sunlight pouring in through the cabin's uncurtained window. "A cave with danger signs pasted on old two-by-fours held in place by rusty nails all across the opening. And then when that rusty old nail caught my favorite cashmere sweater, I was sure it was a bad sign."

"Roger believes in signs," Hector told Mike.

"But finding that gold was a good sign, huh?" Mike said.

Roger nodded. "Even better than finding Curly's gold."

"I still think he hid it somewhere near that cave," Mike maintained.

"Which means we could have ourselves not only a gold mine but the treasure, too. Wait till my ex-wife hears about this," Roger said. "Boy, will she regret dumping me."

"So how are we going to celebrate?" Hector asked.

"How about a friendly game of cards?" Mike suggested, shuffling the deck with the hands of a pro.

RENO COULDN'T BELIEVE what he'd heard through the open window of the cabin. Far from being in trouble, or being held captive, Mike was in cahoots with these two bozos in some gold-mining scam.

Who were they? Gambling buddies? He didn't recognize the two older men—one a heavyset snazzy dresser and one built like a wrestler with a voice deeper than the mine they'd just claimed.

Moving away from the cabin until he was out of hearing range, he radioed his brothers that he'd located Annie's brother and then returned to confront the no-good son of a buck, Mike. Much as Reno wanted to bust down the door and storm in, he bided his time, making sure that he hadn't somehow misinterpreted what he'd heard earlier.

But there was no misinterpreting the friendly game of poker Reno was observing through the back window, away from the trio's line of vision. Just as there was no way of mistaking the fact that Mike was methodically cheating.

"I'm telling you," the one called Roger said, "my ex is gonna be so sorry that she treated me the way she did."

Reno had heard enough. Testing the back door, he wasn't surprised to find it unlocked.

Walking in, he angrily barked, "Police. Nobody move! Stand up and put your hands where I can see them. On top of your heads. And while you do that, I'll tell you who's gonna be sorry. All of you."

When Roger and the tall guy tried to take off, Reno knew something more was going on than a friendly game of poker. Luckily he was able to put out a foot to trip the big guy, who landed on Roger like a felled redwood tree.

"Bad move," Reno advised them even as he whipped out two sets of handcuffs and clamped them around the two men's wrists and the cabin's support beam, effectively pinning them in place.

Pointing to the badge he had displayed on the right pocket of his denim shirt, Reno said, "Now you've got me wondering why two law-abiding citizens like you would take off at the sight of a lawman."

"We didn't kidnap him!" Roger wailed.

After patting them down to make sure they weren't carrying any weapons, Reno turned his attention toward Mike who looked as guilty as hell.

"Aside from cheating these two guys at poker and running out on your gambling debt and leaving your sister to cope with your loan shark, Sven, who quite possibly tampered with her car, would you care to explain to me what the hell is going on here?" Reno demanded in a dangerous voice. "You've scared your sister half to death with this disappearing act of yours."

When Mike made no reply, Reno grabbed him by the T-shirt. "Answer me!"

"Get your hands off my brother!"

Swiveling his head, Reno was stunned to see Annie standing in the front doorway of the cabin.

"I said, get your hands off my brother!" she repeated in a furious voice.

"Thank God you're here, Annie," Mike practically sobbed, tearing himself from Reno's angry grip and heading for his sister with the desperation of a man who knows when he's in hot water and knows how to play to the audience. His earlier expression of guilt was replaced by a look of boyish desperation. "It's been awful. I was kidnapped by those two guys." He pointed to the men Reno had handcuffed.

Kidnapped? Yeah, right. Reno shook his head in disbelief. It would be the first kidnapping on record where the captors played a friendly game of poker with their cheating captive.

Clearly, a con was taking place here, and Reno had a hunch that Mike was the one doing the conning, not the two poor handcuffed bozos on the floor.

"And then this guy," Mike jabbed a thumb at Reno over his shoulder, "grabs me and tries to punch me."

Hugging her brother, Annie fixed Reno with a fiercely furious glare. "What were you thinking? Is that the way you treat the victim of a crime?"

"He's no victim," Reno retorted, about to defend himself when Annie interrupted him.

"Don't you dare try and pin this on my brother!" Her voice shook with the force of her emotions. "I know you've been angry at him since I first asked you to help me find him. You didn't want to be bothered with this case in the first place. Well, fine, you don't have to be bothered any longer. Instead of yelling at my brother, you should be arresting those two kidnappers and taking them into custody."

Stung by her tone of voice, Reno knew there was no point in telling her the truth right now. She wasn't about to believe him even if he did have the heart to tell her that her brother had, and was continuing to, con her.

So he didn't bother to defend himself against her angry words. She already knew what she thought and didn't want to be confused with facts.

What surprised him was how much it hurt, Annie taking her brother's side over his. This was why he'd stayed away from love. Because it hurt too damn much.

Ignoring her completely, and her brother's Oscar-award–worthy performance, Reno gathered up the visibly shaken men he'd handcuffed and led them out to the rental pickup truck he'd spotted earlier. All the while refusing to give in or even acknowledge the aching stab of pain at Annie's clear indication of where he stood in her life.

Clearly his job was done as far as she was concerned. She'd only needed him to find her brother, and now that he'd done that, she had no further need of him.

11

"ARE YOU SURE you're okay?" Annie asked her brother, holding on to his arm as if still unable to believe she had him back with her again.

"I'm fine," Mike said.

"You stood me up." Sugar spoke for the first time and her words were directed to Mike. Up to this point she'd stayed out on the porch. She and Annie had driven part of the way and then ended up hiking the rest of the way.

This cabin had been on the way to the mine, or so Sugar had said. Hearing Reno's raised voice, Annie had come closer to the cabin, close enough to see Reno grabbing Mike through the uncurtained picture window in front.

That's when she'd burst into the cabin, probably not the brightest thing she'd ever done in her life. But by then she was running on sheer adrenaline.

Now she was trying to put the pieces back together. And some of the pieces weren't fitting.

"How did you know about this cabin, Sugar?" Annie asked.

"When that old ranch hand talked about finding Mike's knife up by this mine, I remembered the time Mike brought me up here and showed me the fool's gold in the mine. Mike cut the path up here himself."

Mike had brought Sugar up here? When had that happened? Annie didn't even know the two had been an item. "Did you know Mike was being held captive here?" Annie demanded point-blank.

"Of course not," Sugar vehemently denied before adding, "not that it wouldn't have served him right to be held captive."

"What did I do?" Mike asked in the universal blank voice of a male being unjustly accused by a female.

"You stood me up," Sugar repeated, her orange-hued hair even brighter in the sunlight.

"He was kidnapped," Annie reminded the younger woman. "It's not like he did it on purpose."

"Didn't he?" Sugar's tone was both cynical and skeptical.

Annie stared at her in surprise. "What are you saying? That he deliberately had himself kidnapped?"

"I wouldn't put it past him," Sugar retorted.

"Just to avoid a date with you?"

"No, not just that. But you had other reasons, didn't you, Mike?" Sugar's look was a direct challenge.

Something clicked into place for Annie. Sugar knew about Mike's problems. "Sven. You know about Sven and the gambling debt."

"I didn't know the guy's name, but I knew about the debt, yes. Mike tried to borrow money from me but he still hadn't paid me back from the last time."

"You borrowed money from Sugar?" Annie stared at her brother as if seeing him for the first time.

He shrugged, obviously uncomfortable at being in the hot seat.

She'd deal with him in a minute. Returning her attention to Sugar, Annie said, "If you knew my brother was in trouble, why didn't you tell me when

I went running all over town desperate to find anyone who knew what had happened to him?''

"Because I didn't *know* what had happened to him. I just had my suspicions.''

"It didn't occur to you that Sven could have hurt Mike?''

"Mike has a way of landing on his feet,'' Sugar said.

"I don't believe this,'' Annie muttered.

Her words fired Sugar's temper. "Just like Reno didn't believe me at first when I told him about the Scandinavian hunk I saw hanging around your car at the truck stop a few weeks ago. But he believed me when he finally bothered to listen.''

"My car?'' Annie struggled to keep up with all these revelations. "You mean Sven tampered with Big Bertha?''

Sugar shrugged. "I didn't actually see him doing anything.''

"Sven would never have hurt you,'' Mike quickly assured Annie. "Otherwise, I would never have planned—'' He broke off as he realized what he'd just revealed.

"I knew it!'' Sugar said triumphantly. "I knew you planned this. There was never any kidnapping, was there? Talk about a lame story, Mike. You conned those two guys into staying up here with you in the mountains, that way you could avoid Sven. And I'll bet you even got the idea from that O. Henry short story I read you.''

"Wait a minute.'' Annie sank onto a nearby chair, unable to believe what she was hearing. She turned to face her brother. "You weren't really kidnapped?''

"Think about it, Annie,'' Sugar said. "Who'd pay to have this guy back?''

Annie read the answer on Mike's face. It was written there in big guilty capital letters. "But why?"

"I'm sorry, sis." Sinking onto his knees beside her, Mike looked remorseful, just the way he had when he'd broken her radio and lied about it when they were kids. "I was drinking at a bar in Bozeman, and after a few drinks it seemed like a good idea. I heard these two guys talking about a rumor of gold and I made it appear that I had inside information about the location of Cockeyed Curly's gold."

Annie frowned. "How would you get that?"

"I pretended that I'd seen the map, making sure that Roger and Hector overheard me. They took me from the parking lot and brought me up here, which is where I told them Curly had buried the gold. I figured Sven wouldn't be able to find me if someone else, someone who wasn't dangerous, had already kidnapped me."

"He's dangerous but you just told your sister that Sven would never hurt her," Sugar said.

"He wouldn't. He prides himself on not attacking the families of his clients, unlike some other loan sharks. Instead, he goes after the bad debtor with a vengeance."

"Why didn't you come to me, tell me you were in trouble?" Annie demanded. "I would have helped you."

"I knew you wouldn't approve of me gambling again."

Anger surged through her. Mike had lied to her. Not once but numerous times, about his not gambling, about the debt, about the kidnapping.

"That's why Reno grabbed you, isn't it?" Sugar was saying. "Because he figured out you were pulling a con."

"I should have let him hit you," Annie said, even angrier at her brother than she had been at Reno a few minutes ago.

"I'll do it," Sugar said, stepping forward to smack Mike between the shoulder blades and send him toppling forward onto the floor.

"Hey, help me out here," Mike called to his sister as Sugar smacked him again.

But Annie was already racing back down the mountain, intent on returning to Bliss and making it up to Reno.

It wasn't that easy. For one thing, she wasn't familiar with Sugar's Jeep and it took her about half an hour to turn it around. At least she'd been able to locate the extra key Sugar had told her earlier she kept hidden in an envelope under the passenger seat. By the time she got to the double-wide trailer that housed the sheriff's department, Reno had an hour and a half lead on her. She knew that because Opal told her so the minute Annie walked in.

"I have to see Reno." Annie's voice was breathless.

"Sorry, honey." Opal gave her a regretful look. "He's busy processing the two kidnappers."

"But they didn't really kidnap Mike. Well, I guess they did, but only because he lured them into it. Well, maybe lured is a little strong, they still had the choice not to do anything and just walk away. Anyway, I have to talk to him."

"I'll tell him you're here." Opal returned a short while later. "Barnie here is going to take down your statement. Where is your brother now?"

"Zane Best is bringing him in. I passed Zane and Cord as I left the cabin. They said they'd bring Mike in along with Sugar."

Hearing her daughter's name, Opal shot her a startled look. "What's my daughter got to do with this? She wasn't in on this scheme, was she?"

"No, I don't think so. But she knew a shortcut up to the cabin where the supposed kidnappers and Mike have been hiding out."

"I'm not even going to ask how she knew about that cabin being up there," Opal decided. "I know she was upset at Mike disappearing like that."

"The way she looked at it, he stood her up. They had a date set up months ago to go to Buck's barbecue party today."

Opal nodded understandingly. "Ah, well, no one stands up a female member of my family. We've got a long memory about things like that."

And what about Reno? Annie wondered with an increasing sense of doom. Did he also have a long memory about things? Like holding a grudge? Or would he forgive her? Would he understand her dueling loyalties between her brother and Reno? Or had she ruined their relationship with her lack of trust and faith in his judgement?

Four hours later, she had her answer. Reno was too busy to see her. No, it wouldn't help to call later. No, he didn't know when it would be a good time.

"I'm sorry, hon," Opal said regretfully.

"Me, too," Annie whispered.

"I BLEW IT," Annie morosely informed Tracy and Hailey early the next morning. Taking out her frustration on the bowl of butter and sugar, she fiercely stirred the ingredients with a wooden spoon.

"So you made a mistake," Hailey said, patting her on the shoulder. "You're only human. We all make mistakes."

"You two don't," Annie noted.

"Excuse me?" Hailey said in disbelief. "You are looking at someone who couldn't get within one foot of Cord without doing him bodily harm. Talk about being clumsy."

Annie stopped beating the cookie dough long enough to stare at Hailey in surprise. "But you seem so together."

"No way. I was chubby as a kid and I never had the self-confidence I needed."

"What changed you?" Annie asked. "You seem very confident now."

"Because I know what I'm good at," Hailey replied. "I found something I have a passion for—the history of the Old West. And I found someone I have a passion for—Cord."

"You're just as passionate about teaching," Tracy told Annie. "And it seems you found someone you have a passion for. Now you just have to go after what you want."

Tracy made it sound so easy but Annie wasn't so sure. "The last time I went after Reno, I made a mess of it by not trusting his judgment," she said, reddening at the memory of how she'd jumped to the conclusion that Reno had sized up the situation with Mike all wrong—when he'd gotten it all too right!

"Yes, but this time it will be different," Tracy assured her.

"How can you be sure of that?"

"Because this time you've got Hailey and me advising you," Tracy replied with an impish smile. "And we're nothing if not experts on the Best men."

"Well, 'experts' may be a tad strong," Hailey noted ruefully.

Tracy waved her words away. "Bah."

"Now you're sounding just like Buck," Hailey said with a grin. "You know, I've heard that if you've been married long enough, you start sounding like your father-in-law."

"Hey, he's *your* father-in-law, too," Tracy reminded Hailey.

"Yeah, but you don't hear me saying bah," Hailey pointed out.

While the other two women were talking, Annie added the flour mixture and chocolate chips to the dough. Wiping away a streak of flour from her cheek, Annie told Tracy, "I'm not as gutsy as you are. You were a successful ad executive. You've got plenty of chutzpah."

"Oh, please," Tracy scoffed, picking up a tablespoon and dropping chunks of dough onto a cookie sheet. "You are looking at a cowardly woman. Why do you think I ran away from Chicago?"

"Because you were looking for a new life in Colorado," Annie replied.

"Because I caught my then-fiancé in bed with another woman," Tracy said. "I didn't even bother canceling the wedding myself. I just tossed my stuff in my Miata and came out here."

Despite this news, Annie still had a hard time seeing Tracy as a coward. "You drive a snazzy red sports car. I drive Big Bertha."

"We are not what we drive," Tracy said, popping the filled cookie sheet into the oven. "Trust me, I'm as scared as the next woman."

"If you say so." Annie didn't sound very convinced.

"I do say so." Tracy washed her hands and dried them before turning her full attention back on Annie.

"I also say that the trick to getting Reno back is sexy underwear."

Annie frowned. "I'm sure he'd look great in sexy underwear, black boxer shorts maybe, but I fail to see how that helps—"

"Not underwear for him," Tracy said in exasperation. "I'm talking about sexy underwear for *you.*"

Annie laughed. "Surely you jest. Look at me." She pointed at her chest. "I'm hardly a sexy pinup type."

"Hey, those bra engineers are working miracles these days," Tracy said. "All you need is a push-up bra and maybe a merry widow."

"A what?" Annie inquired blankly.

Tracy rolled her eyes heavenward. "Haven't you ever looked at a Victoria's Secret catalog?"

Annie shook her head.

"They name their bras," Hailey told her. "Like the Patricia bra."

"I doubt they've got a bra with my name on it. Annie isn't the kind of name you'd put on a bra unless it was a staid white cotton one."

"There's nothing staid about you," Tracy maintained. "You lassoed Reno on my front porch for heaven's sake. Those are not the actions of a staid woman."

"I didn't lasso him," Annie corrected her. "Rusty did."

"A technicality." Tracy waved her hand. "You brought Reno to his knees."

A stickler for accuracy, Annie said, "Actually, he was flat on your porch floor."

"There you go."

"But only because I'd knocked him off his feet," Annie added.

"And that's what you'll do again." Tracy's eyes sparkled. "In sexy underwear. Black, I think."

"Wait a minute," Annie protested. "I don't want to get Reno back using cheap sexual tricks."

"That's not how you'll get him back," Tracy said. "That's how you'll get his attention."

"There is a difference," Hailey added.

"Did you ever do anything like that with Cord?" Annie asked her.

"Well, I did dress to try and get his attention, yes. I confess it. But that's not why he fell for me. Actually, sometimes I'm still not sure why he fell for me," Hailey said with a laugh, "I'm just glad he did."

"He fell for you because he's the smart one in the family," Tracy told Hailey.

"And what does that make Zane?" Annie countered.

"The stubborn one," Tracy replied. "And Reno is the charmer."

"Yeah, I figured as much," Annie said.

"Which is why it's only fair that a little of that charm be turned back on him," Tracy firmly stated.

Annie shook her head. "I don't think you two realize how angry he is with me. He's avoiding me. And I'm sorry, but I can't just pull a Mrs. Battle and start singing in a red boa at the Bliss Bar to get his attention."

"Of course not," Tracy said in a reassuring tone of voice. "Besides, that's already been done. No, this entire maneuver will happen in the privacy of your own home."

Annie couldn't get over how easy Tracy made it sound. "And how do you propose I get Reno over to my house?"

Tracy blinked at her ingenuously. "He's a law enforcement officer. He'll go where he's needed."

"Oh, no." Annie put out her hands as if warding off the devil. "No, I couldn't possibly. I'm sure it's illegal or something."

"Depends what you aim on doing with him once you've got him," Tracy said with a grin.

"SON OF A BUCK, can't a man visit his son without having sawdust dumped on him?" Buck demanded from the bottom of the stairway in Reno's house.

"Sorry about that. I didn't see you down there."

"Cord doesn't even have this much sawdust up at his place and he works with wood for a living."

"Yeah, well, I'm not Cord," Reno noted bitterly. "He would have had this place finished years ago."

"I doubt that. You know what a perfectionist he is. He'd still be working on the parlor."

"Better a perfectionist than a dabbler," Reno muttered under his breath. He was determined to get the remaining doors up here hung on their hinges today. Maybe it would make him feel less unhinged himself.

Cautiously climbing the stairs, Buck said, "I wanted to talk to you about that naked little runt with the bow and arrow."

Reno frowned. "Is somebody doing illegal hunting up on Bear Tooth Mountain again?"

"Heck no, the naked little runt I'm talking about is Cupid. I came to you for some she-folk advice."

"Then you came to the wrong guy," Reno said, returning his attention to the door he was sanding.

Buck stared at him in confusion. "But you're the charmer in the family. What Zane and Cord know about she-folks would fit in the ear of a gnat, but you...you've always been the expert on the ladies."

"Not anymore."

"Well, son of a buck!" his dad growled. "This is one heck of a bad time to stop being an expert."

Reno shrugged. "Sorry."

Buck gave him a long contemplative look. "What caused this turnaround?"

"Nothing caused it."

"Bah," Buck scoffed. "It was Annie. A nice little gal despite the fact she doesn't like football. I bet you could get her to change her mind about that."

"Dad, I'm telling you that Annie and I are history." Reno's voice expressed his impatience.

"History is your sister-in-law Hailey's specialty. Mine, too," Buck added modestly.

"You're not hearing me."

"Because you're not saying anything that makes any sense."

"That's because I'm not deep like Zane and Cord," Reno retorted.

"Son of a buck, they don't make sense most of the time neither. And what's this about you not being deep? What kind of talk is that?" Buck demanded.

"It's the truth. I've always gotten by on my charm."

"And your courage. Two highly prized traits in the old days, my boy. In those days charm was called cheerfulness and it was valued. A cowman laughed at hardships when laughing was hard. And they never complained because complaining was like quitting. That's you, boy."

"I'm always quitting relationships with women."

"You were just waiting for the right one, the one that has a smile you'd go to hell for and never regret it," Buck said quietly.

"Well, the right one doesn't appear to think I'm the right one for her."

"That's the same problem I'm having myself," Buck acknowledged.

"Want a beer?"

"Sounds good," Buck replied.

The kitchen wasn't much more finished than the upstairs was. He had the major appliances hooked up, and a table set in the middle of the room. But the walls hadn't been painted and still had spackle on them where he'd tried to smooth out the bumps. He tried to imagine Annie baking her cookies in this room and couldn't. Her house was never up for grabs. There was nothing on her countertops besides a canister set. You couldn't even see his countertop for the tools, cans and junk mail. Besides, he planned on replacing the countertop. Someday. There hadn't seemed to be any reason to hurry before.

Grabbing a chair and turning it backwards so he could straddle it, Reno took a long sip of his beer and reminded himself that there wasn't any reason to hurry the renovations now, either. Annie wasn't for him.

"So why did you stop by?" Reno asked his dad.

"I told you. For she-folk advice. You were at the barbecue. You heard Alicia. She was about as friendly as a diamondback—"

"—and sore as a boil," Reno completed, having learned that phrase at his dad's knee.

"I haven't seen her that riled up since you tossed Tad and me in the hoosegow last year."

"Clearly she was feeling neglected."

"Because you put us in the hoosegow?"

"I meant at the barbecue. She felt that you weren't

paying enough attention to her. That you were spending all your time and energy on Curly's treasure.''

''So what do you recommend?''

''That you do some old-fashioned courting.''

''Courting?'' Buck repeated, a horrified expression on his face. ''You mean flowers and the like? Why, I haven't done any courting since I met your mother. I never had to court Alicia up till now. I just asked her if she wanted to go to the Homestead for a meal or to the movie theater to see a picture and she says yes. You really think she wants some courting?''

''Afraid so. Don't you think she's worth it?''

'''Course she is,'' Buck said in an outraged voice. ''It's just that...well, truth be told, I'm not much better at that sort of thing than your brothers.''

''I must have gotten my charm from someplace,'' Reno retorted.

''Ah, your mama, she had a way with people. A gift, it was. You've got that gift, son.''

''Not everyone thinks it's a gift.''

''What does Annie think?''

Reno shrugged. ''She's too serious for me,'' he said. ''I'm not ready to settle down.''

Buck's blue eyes shone with the wisdom and empathy of a man who'd been there and done that. ''Who are you trying to convince, son? Me or yourself?''

ANNIE CLUTCHED the package that had finally arrived by an express delivery service ten minutes ago. The lecture Tracy and Hailey had given her two days ago still rang in her ears and replayed itself through her mind. It had taken her forty-eight hours to screw up her courage and get her act together.

She'd meant to spend her morning tidying up because usually clutter upset her when she was nervous. But today she could feel herself rebelling against the tight confines of her existence. So what if she wanted to spread her books out on top of the pine chest instead of hiding them inside it? Or put them on a bookcase where everyone could see them?

So what if she got a little rowdy and ordered bras-with-names from a lingerie catalog? That didn't mean she was her mother. She was her mother's daughter, but she was her own person.

By remaining in the small little box she'd built for herself, she was denying herself the rest of the world. She was letting her past rule her future. And it was about time that stopped.

She didn't have to be the responsible one all the time. The realization had finally hit her with the force of a freight train. And with that realization came a tremendous sense of relief.

There were times when Mike was responsible for his own actions. She belatedly realized she hadn't been doing him any favors by not making him accountable. So she'd confronted him yesterday.

"Things are going to be different from now on," she'd told him.

"You don't have to tell me that," Mike had replied. "Sugar has knocked some sense into me. I've already arranged to work at the Bliss Bar for a few weeks to pay back Sven. Floyd is going to be sending the checks directly to Sven. And Sugar has gotten some information from the Internet on Gamblers Anonymous for me. I don't think I'll need it, I think this last episode has cured me, but if I think I'm having a relapse I know where to get help. And Sugar will be nearby keeping me on the straight and narrow."

"You should be keeping yourself on the straight and narrow."

"I know. And I'll try. But the bottom line is that you don't have to look after me anymore, sis. I'm gonna be okay. It's time you looked after yourself."

Which is pretty much what Tracy had told her, as well. Well, she was finally getting the message. It was finally sinking in. Mike was right. Tracy was right. It was time for Annie to go after what she wanted. Time for Annie to do what was right for Annie. Time, in fact, for Annie to get downright rowdy.

Picking up the phone, she made a few calls.

RENO GOT THE CALL right after lunch. "Robbery in progress." Opal's voice came over the radio loud and clear.

Despite all the craziness in the hunt for Curly's gold, the last actual robbery call in Bliss had been a year ago when someone had stolen Curly's portrait from the historical society. A few days later they'd tracked down the teenage vandals and returned the portrait unharmed to its rightful place. Since then, a security system had been installed at the historical society.

But the address Opal listed wasn't for the historical society. It was Annie's address.

Reno's blood went cold. Annie. Angered by her lack of trust in him, he'd been avoiding her, trying to convince himself that she was the wrong woman for him and that he was the wrong man for her. After his dad's visit the other day, he'd even been avoiding anyone who would talk about her. Tracy, Hailey, Geraldine at the post office.

Even as the rest of him went on automatic pilot and reported back to Opal that he was en route, memories flashed through his mind at the speed of light. Memories of Annie. Her storming into the Golden Treasure Diner and invading the sanctity of his lunch hour. The way she'd teased her hair and shown her navel when she'd gone to the truck stop. The way her big brown eyes had gazed up at him with dazed passion.

He arrived at her front porch with his gun drawn. The front door was wide open but there was no sign of a forced entrance. Had she remembered to lock her door the way he'd told her to?

The living room, dining room and kitchen were empty. Where was she? And the burglar? Was he armed? Was he holding Annie hostage? Where *was* she?

Turning the corner and going down the hallway toward her bedroom, he had his answer.

Annie was in bed, wearing a slinky black bra and panties and little else. He felt like an idiot storming into her bedroom with his gun drawn.

Eyeing the weapon warily, she said in a sultry voice, "You won't be needing that weapon, Officer."

12

"ARE YOU CRAZY?" Reno roared in disbelief. "I could have you arrested for filing a false police report."

"It wasn't false," Annie calmly replied. "I did have something stolen."

"Yeah, right," he scoffed. "What? Your sanity?"

"My heart. And I can help you identify the thief."

"To prove it was stolen, it would have to have been given unwillingly."

"Well, it was at first. And after that I was too blind to see what was happening. I'm not blind anymore."

Instead of coming to her and taking her in his arms, Reno still stood half a room away and she was feeling increasingly silly with her bare navel showing, not to mention the rest of her body. The Patricia bra hadn't looked that outrageous in the glossy pages of the catalog. But once she put it on...

She snuck a quick glance down at her breasts to make sure they were still covered. She almost didn't recognize them as being hers. What a difference a bra could make. It really was amazing.

"I can't believe you pulled a stunt like this," Reno growled.

Frankly, she couldn't believe it either. Not at the moment. Not when it wasn't going very well.

"Do you have any idea how dangerous this was? I could have walked in here and shot you." Holstering his weapon, he continued his ranting and raving. "You've pulled some pretty stupid stunts in your time, like walking into that truck stop dressed up like a Vegas showgirl, or trying to take off after Sven's car, or disobeying my orders to wait at the ranch and instead following me up the mountain and barging into that cabin. You had no idea what you were getting into. It could have been a dangerous situation. Those kidnappers could have been real."

"I'm sorry for misjudging you by thinking you were going to hurt my brother." Her apology was quiet but sincere.

"I *was* going to hurt him. He acted like an idiot." Reno's comments were loud and furious.

"You're right, he did. I'm sorry for the trouble Mike caused by staging his own kidnapping."

"He didn't press charges against the guys who took him, you know. Last I heard, they were headed back to Florida. But that doesn't change the fact that you didn't know what was going on in the cabin when you burst through that door."

"I saw you through the window—"

He cut off her explanation with a wave of his hand. "I don't want to hear it."

"I know you don't want to hear it," Annie shouted back, fed up with his attitude. Didn't he know how difficult this was for her? The least he could do was not make her feel stupider than necessary. "That's why I had to pull a stunt like this. Because you wouldn't talk to me, wouldn't return my calls."

Glaring at her, Reno growled, "You need a keeper, lady."

Kneeling on the bed, she glared right back at him. "If that's what you think, you should apply for the job permanently."

Staring at her all riled up the way she was, her big brown eyes shooting fire at him, Reno surrendered to the truth he'd known deep inside but hadn't wanted to confront. His brothers had been right. He did have it bad. She made him want to give her things he never thought he'd want to give anyone.

"I don't know about permanently," he said, his expression solemn.

Her heart sank to her toes. That was it then. She'd risked all this for nothing. He didn't love her.

"I can only promise you seventy years or so," he drawled, his mouth twitching in a wicked smile.

She'd kill him. The laid-back lawman was a dead man. Grabbing a pillow, she launched it at him. He ducked just in the nick of time.

"Hey, is that any way to respond to a marriage proposal?" he demanded in pretended outrage.

"You did that on purpose," she accused him.

"What? Propose to you? I should hope I'd do that on purpose."

"Are you telling me that's the best a ladies' man sweet-talker like you can do with a marriage proposal?"

"That's right." His voice was husky, his gaze heated. "I can't sweet-talk you because you quite simply take my breath away."

"It's the bra," she said demurely.

"It's you. I love you. I love your big brown eyes, your courage, your loyalty, your long hair, your... cookies."

Only then did she notice the uncertainty in his golden hazel eyes. She'd seen the smiling charmer, the angry lawman, the passionate lover. But she'd never seen Reno unsure of himself, never seen him vulnerable.

"I love you, too," she whispered, opening her arms to him.

A minute later he'd undone his gunbelt, set it atop her dresser, and joined her on the bed, tumbling her back onto the yellow and blue comforter.

"You move fast for a laid-back lawman," she whispered against his lips before he consumed her in a kiss that inched over her mouth with delicious enjoyment.

Her heart swelled with joy and a newfound recognition that this man was the one for her, the one she'd waited all her life for, the one who held the key to her heart. She'd heard of the term soulmates, but had never believed in it until now. How else could she explain this deep-seated sense of rightness at being with him? They might not have known each other long in this lifetime but they must have been lovers in another lifetime.

For the first time she could understand her mother's belief in reincarnation. And for the first time she no longer felt scared of following in her mother's footsteps.

Reno had not given her the courage to face her past. Because something given could then be taken away. No, instead he'd seen her in a way no one else had, thereby making her look at herself in a new way. The courage came from within her. So did the love she felt for this man. A hundred decades wouldn't be long enough for her to express it.

Undoing his shirt, she kissed her way across his bare chest while tugging the shirttails from the waistband of his jeans. A sense of urgency took hold, as if she could already feel the sands of time slipping away. No, a hundred decades wouldn't be long enough to discover everything about him.

Threading his fingers through her long hair, Reno turned her face up for another kiss. This time their tongues conducted a plunging game of hide-and-seek mimicked by his fingers seeking out her innermost secrets. Somehow he'd removed her sexy underwear without her knowing it, although the Patricia bra remained in place.

Their close contact left her in no doubt as to the urgency of his needs. Lifting his hips, he undid his jeans and shoved his underwear out of the way. Unable to wait a second longer, he rolled onto his back so that she sat perched atop him, her bent knees resting on either side of him.

Annie blinked at the sudden change of position. Looking down into his face, her nervousness evaporated the instant she saw the way he looked at her. Propping her hands on his bare chest, she followed his husky instructions and rejoiced in his gasp of raw pleasure as he slid home, filling her with his hardness.

Intimately joined as they were, she was acutely aware of every breath he took, of every move he made. And what moves they were. When she added a few of her own, the pleasure became even more powerful.

She couldn't control the passion running rampant through her body. Sliding friction. Prolonged strokes. One final pelvic tilt combined with one powerful last thrust...and the result was incredible. He sought, she found, and together they experienced the ultimate joy.

So sharply sweet.

So powerfully fine.

Completion.

"NOW I KNOW HOW this town got its name," she murmured. "Bliss." She rubbed her palm over his nipple, enjoying the beat of his heart against her hand. "I could get addicted to this."

"I've created a sex addict." His grin held more pride than a man had any right to, but she couldn't seem to muster up the energy to be upset about it.

"I can't believe I just made love to a man with his boots still on."

"In that case, we'll just have to do it again and again until you do believe," he drawled, placing soft kisses in a random pattern from her jaw to her temple, intermittently returning to the inviting delectability of her mouth.

They were interrupted by the sound of someone pounding on the front door.

Annie froze. "Did you close the door when you came in the house?"

Reno shook his head.

"You two decent?" Buck called out.

Now it was Reno who froze before scrambling off the bed. Annie couldn't help it. She started laughing at Reno's panicked expression even as she grabbed a cotton dress from the yellow aluminum chair beside the bed. Sliding it over her head, she yanked on a pair of white cotton underwear before calling out, "We'll be right there, Buck. Go on in the living room and sit down a minute."

"He's going to know what we were doing in here," Reno warned her.

"At least he won't have to take a shotgun to you to make an honest woman of me," she noted with a saucy grin before sashaying out of the bedroom and down the hallway.

"I've got exciting news," Buck announced the moment he caught sight of her.

"I've got exciting news, too," Reno said, coming

to stand behind Annie and slide his arms around her waist.

"They've found Curly's treasure! And you'll never believe where we found it. Buried behind the old jail-house. Can you beat that?"

"Sure can," Reno replied. "I'm holding all the treasure I want right here."

Buck gave him a narrow-eyed look. "In that case I sure hope you asked the lady to marry you."

"I did. But it occurs to me that she never did give me an answer."

"You distracted me," she said before turning to face Reno, cupping his face with her hand. "My answer is yes."

"Son of a buck! What a great day this is!" Buck chortled, slapping his hand on his denim-clad knee. "Not only do we find Curly's missing treasure, but I get to have me another new daughter-in-law." Buck gathered Annie up in a bear hug before slapping Reno on the back with enough force to make him wince. "Come on, let's go tell the others. Did you tell Annie about your courting plans?"

"Dad…"

"What courting plans?" Annie asked.

"I was trying to figure out how to court you, what would impress you… Stop that," he muttered, seeing the way her eyes slid over his body.

"By golly, you made my boy blush." Buck sounded stunned. "I told you she'd be worth painting the kitchen for," he told Reno.

Annie was confused. "What kitchen?"

"I painted my kitchen, finished the walls, even got a new countertop finally installed. Had everyone over to help me. Both my brothers and their wives, even Murph 'n Earl. And my dad, of course."

"Hope you like blue and yellow," Buck said.

Annie felt as if her heart was too big for her body. "I love blue and yellow."

"You might not like my house," Reno was saying. "It's bigger than yours and it's still torn up in parts—"

She put her fingers to his lips. "We'll fix it up together."

"Come on, you two, get a move on," Buck said impatiently. "They're waiting on us."

By the time they reached the old jailhouse on the edge of Bliss Park, it seemed as if the entire town had gathered there. The Oberhausens' RV was still parked nearby and they'd set out tables and chairs to watch the proceedings and offer refreshments at the same time.

"Leave it to Curly to have buried his treasure within spitting distance of the jail," Hailey noted with a shake of her head. "He'd based his map from one center point without saying what that point was. And then there's the poem." She recited it, clearly having memorized it.

All the loot that Curly took
He stashed in a secret nook.
This here map will tell you how,
To find that place, right now.
Start out careful like, take your gun,
And git your directions from the sun.
Count out the paces real real clost,
And follow the marks on trees and post.
X marks the spot where the treasure's hid,
Dig five feet down, you should hit the lid.
Break open the box and there you'll see,
A king's ransom robbed by old Curly.

"You needed to start out 'careful like' because you were digging right behind the jailhouse," Hailey added. "The trees and posts were leveled at the turn of the century to make this park."

"How do you know it's here?" Reno asked.

"Because Tad and I found the strongbox after digging five feet down," Buck replied. "It's buried beneath a big rock so we're still digging to get it out. Or Cord is digging. Claims Tad and I are too old. Bah!"

"What made you dig here?" Annie asked.

"I wondered where the last place Curly would put his treasure. This seemed likely."

"Here it is. Watch out, it's heavy," Cord said, hauling the strongbox out of the hole and handing it to Zane, who set it at his dad's feet.

"Seems only fitting that you should do the honors," Zane said.

Buck stared at the strongbox as if unable to believe it was real.

"You gonna open it or just sit there?" Floyd called out. "I'm not—"

"Getting any younger. Yeah, I know," Buck replied. "None of us are. But before I open this box, there's something I want to say. Reno here and Annie are getting hitched."

A cheer went up.

"Yeah, those are my feelings on the matter too," Buck said. "But there's something else I want to say. As you know, this here treasure has meant a lot to me. But it doesn't mean half as much as a certain lady does." Holding out his hand, he looked directly at Alicia. "If I was half as good a poet as Curly, I'd be able to write you romantic literature. So I sent you chocolate and flowers. But I don't know if that's enough. So I want you to have this." He pointed down at the strongbox. "Maybe then you'll see how important you are to me."

"Oh my," Alicia gasped, tears coming to her eyes as she joined Buck and hugged him.

"So open the box already," Floyd said.

Buck helped Alicia with the rusty clasp. It took several attempts before the lid flew open.

Annie viewed the proceedings from the comfort of Reno's arms as he stood behind her, his clasped hands resting beneath her breasts, his chin resting on top of her head.

"What's inside?" Geraldine demanded.

"Rocks," Buck said. "Big rocks."

"And a note," Alicia added, handing it to him. "It's from Curly."

"Well, go ahead and read it," Floyd impatiently ordered.

"I can't." Buck handed the letter to Hailey.

No more rhymes.
I ain't got time.
I may be Curly the robbin' poet
But by now you all know it.
The law is on my tail. No time to be fancy. I took the money, Jed, and used it on folks who needed it more than you. I know you helped me out in Leadville and I feel real bad about it, but these folks on the wagon train lost everything in a flash flood last night. Like I said, Jed, they need the gold more than you.

"It's dated a week after the fight in Leadville," Hailey added.

"There's also a journal here," Alicia said, handing it over to Hailey.

After carefully looking through it, Hailey said, "It's a journal filled with the accounts of Cockeyed Curly's eventful life."

"Son of a buck," Buck exclaimed with a rueful shake of his head. "I guess the only treasure you can really count on is family after all."

"There is something else you can count on," Reno said.

"Love," said Tracy, Hailey and Annie in unison—sharing the secret smile of women who'd claimed the hearts of the Best men in the West.

Epilogue

One year later

"ARE YOU SURE you're not going to have the baby right here?" Annie asked Tracy with a concerned look.

"As if I'd miss your wedding for anything. I love this dress even if I do look like a whale in it," Tracy grumbled, staring at herself sideways in the full-length mirror.

"You look pregnant," Hailey said matter-of-factly, adjusting the veil on Annie's head around her long hair. Smiling at Annie in the mirror, she added, "And you, well, you look gorgeous."

"I thought looking gorgeous was Reno's job," Annie retorted with a grin.

"You'll both be gorgeous," Hailey stated. "I've got to tell you, planning this wedding has been so much fun it almost makes me wish that Cord and I hadn't eloped."

"Even more surprising was Buck and your aunt Alicia eloping before Christmas," Annie noted.

"I know," Hailey said. "My aunt was always the one who had her feet on the ground."

"Sounds like me," Annie said.

"But she got swept off her feet by a Best man."

Annie nodded. "I know how that feels. It feels

pretty darn good.'' She couldn't seem to stop smiling today.

"Hold on. You've tilted your veil." Hailey adjusted it again.

"I'm so glad we've got good weather today," Tracy said.

Annie looked out at the mountains, awe-inspiring witnesses to her nuptials, which were taking place at the edge of the meadow where Reno had taught her touch football.

Even though Annie couldn't see the area from the housekeeper's quarters of the ranch house, she'd checked things out at first light. "Thank Cord again for making the beautiful pergola for us."

"He enjoyed doing it."

The rustic archway was fashioned out of cottonwood saplings covered with climbing yellow honeysuckle and would be the perfect avenue for the wedding processional. Baskets of wildflowers—white and yellow with splashes of blue cornflowers—lined the aisle leading to the open-air altar.

Yes, everything was going to be just perfect.

"Luanne transformed that silk material your mother sent you from India into a beautiful dress, didn't she?"

"She sure did." Annie smoothed her hand down the luscious snow-white silk that was layered with organza. She'd combined an antique crocheted bodice from Reno's grandmother with the new silk skirt to make the perfect wedding dress, as far as Annie was concerned. "I had no idea she was such a talented seamstress as well as a hairstylist."

"It was funny how your mom had a feeling you

were getting married and sent you the material for your wedding dress,'' Tracy noted.

''My mom's like that.'' Annie was now able to think about her mother without any regrets.

''It's too bad she couldn't be here.''

''She's here with me in spirit. And trust me, my mother's got plenty of spirit,'' Annie added wryly.

''So does her daughter,'' Hailey noted.

''It's time, girls,'' Tracy announced with a glance at her watch. ''We wouldn't want to leave Reno waiting, not to mention Lucky and Rusty. Lucky is just thrilled to bits to be your flower girl. And okay, so Rusty is not so thrilled to be the ring bearer, but hey, a guy's gotta do what a guy's gotta do.''

''At least he doesn't have to wear a tuxedo,'' Hailey pointed out.

''The Best men just look too good in jeans not to have them all wearing them at this special occasion,'' Annie said with a wicked grin. ''Add a white shirt and dark jacket, maybe a string tie or two, and you've got—''

''—a bunch of hunks, out standing in their field,'' Tracy noted.

Annie laughed and hugged her two sisters-in-law-to-be. ''You guys are the best.''

''And in a few minutes you'll be a Best, too,'' Hailey said.

''All right, no tears,'' Tracy scolded even as she wiped her own damp eyes with a care not to mess her makeup. ''Are we set?''

Annie nodded as Hailey handed her the wedding bouquet, filled with daisies, delphinium and white lilac.

''Sugar is recording the event with her digital camera for the Bliss website," Tracy reminded them. "I can't believe how popular that site has become."

"That's thanks to Hailey's success as a writer," Annie proudly declared.

Hailey's book, *Colorado Outlaws,* had been published to great reviews, but it was her more recent book focusing on the love story of Rebecca Best and Rafael Hughes, as well as the life and times of Cockeyed Curly Mahoney, that had become a huge success. Based on Rebecca's and Curly's individual journals, it had spent the past month on the bestseller lists and garnered the attention of a prominent Hollywood producer as well as interest from the Academy Award–winning actor who'd just commissioned Cord to make the furniture for his new ranch in Montana.

"No bride ever had better bridesmaids than I've got," Annie stated.

"Okay, enough of this mutual admiration society," Tracy said briskly. "Let's get a move on, girls."

Grabbing her hand, Annie said, "What if Reno isn't there?"

"Then we'll send Rusty out to lasso him. Come on, the guy loves you to bits. He's probably camped out there overnight. Now, let's go before I do have this baby."

Seeing Annie's worried look, Hailey hastily assured her, "Tracy would never do anything as gauche as go into labor at your wedding."

"Providing you get married today and not next week," Tracy said.

"I'm ready." Annie held up the long hem of her wedding dress, displaying her tooled cowboy boots beneath. "Let's go."

Reno was indeed waiting for her. She saw him as

soon as she passed around the back of the barn. Mike was waiting to give her away. He'd worked off his debt to Sven and was no longer gambling. He and Sugar had been dating for a year now.

"You look beautiful, sis," Mike told her, the surprised tone of his voice letting her know that his comment was sincere.

But Annie's attention was on Reno, who did look incredibly good as he proudly stood with his brothers at the other end of the flower-strewn aisle. A scattering of chairs had been set out for the guests and covered with yellow-gingham covers tied with blue ribbons. Everyone from Bliss was there.

As Mike handed her over to Reno, Annie's fingers trembled, the sunlight flashing on her sapphire engagement ring.

"You okay, sweetpea?" His voice held tender concern.

"No, I'm not okay," she softly replied. She shot him a wicked grin before adding, "I'm *spectacular*."

"You little devil."

"Hey," she whispered, "I've warned you before to watch who and what you call little, buster."

"Oh, I'm watching all right," he assured her in a husky undertone. "And I'm loving what I'm seeing."

The minister clearing his throat made Annie realize she'd missed her cue by talking with Reno. "Uh, could you repeat that?"

"You're supposed to pay attention," Rusty called out and everyone laughed as the wedding ceremony proceeded without any further hitches. When the minister told Reno, "You may now kiss your bride," he did so with a loving tenderness that almost made her cry.

On the other side of the barn, a spacious peaked tent had been set up with luncheon tables for the wedding reception. The tent was open-sided, allowing Annie to drink in the mountain views.

"I'd like to make a toast," Buck stated. Holding his glass up, he began. "As many of you know, Buck's Barbecue Sauce is being carried in supermarkets across the United States."

"What is this, a commercial?" Floyd shouted, heckling him from a table right in front.

Buck ignored him, focusing his attention on the newlyweds instead as he gazed at them with paternal pride. "And now we've got Reno and Annie married. The first time I saw the two of them together I could tell that Reno took to her like honeysuckle to a porch. So here's to Reno and Annie!"

"Did your dad just liken me to a porch?" Annie whispered to Reno with a laugh after sipping her champagne.

"What are you worried about?" Reno retorted. "He just likened *me* to a honeysuckle. Not exactly a macho western lawman image."

As Buck sat down, Annie patted Reno's cheek with teasing commiseration. "Poor baby."

Tracy stood up next. "Baby!" she cried out with a gasp. "Baby. Coming now!"

"What kind of toast is that?" Floyd demanded. "The two just get married and already she's demanding they have a baby."

"Not the bride," Geraldine replied, smacking Floyd with a rolled up wedding program. "Tracy. She's in labor!"

"WELL, THAT WAS an incredible wedding night," Reno told Annie, kissing her forehead.

"It sure was," Annie agreed, resting her cheek against his shoulder.

"Ever think you'd spend it in a hospital waiting room?" he ruefully inquired.

Lifting her head, she surveyed her surroundings. County Hospital, Kendall, Colorado. Dawn was just breaking through the window across from her, mirroring the orange and yellow theme of the walls where childish drawings were on display showing families bringing home their new baby. The normal medicinal smell of a hospital wasn't as strong here in the maternity ward, which had a warm and fuzzy feel to it. Or maybe she was just feeling warm and fuzzy after everything that had happened.

"Can't say that I did," she replied, her hand clasped in his. "But then I've learned to expect the unexpected when I'm with you."

"And is that okay with you?" he asked her.

She heard the concern tinging his voice and knew it came from his knowledge of her background. She'd told Reno about those years of upheaval as well as her need for stability and he'd been more understanding than she could have dreamed.

"Yeah, it *is* okay," she softly assured him. "And our new niece is more than okay. She's downright awesome. Did you see how perfect she is, right down to her little fingernails?"

"Sure did. Almost makes you want to have one or two of your own."

"You'd make a great dad," she told him.

"You think so?" He sounded a bit uncertain, as if he needed some reassurance.

"Absolutely," she said with utter conviction. They'd talked about having kids before, but it had never seemed real until that moment when she'd held little Olivia in her arms and gazed down at her. She'd seen a similar expression of awe on Reno's face when he'd held the tiny baby as well.

"You two still here?" Zane said when he entered the waiting area. "I thought you'd be off on your honeymoon by now."

Tugging back the cuff of his sleeve to look at his watch, Reno said, "The flight to Jackson Hole leaves in a few hours."

Cord had arranged for them to use a gorgeous cabin belonging to one of his wealthy clients. Annie had changed from her wedding gown into her traveling outfit so that they'd be able to proceed to the airport directly from the hospital. Their bags were already in the Bronco.

Zane's voice was gruff as he said, "You didn't have to stay all night, but I'm really glad you did. For a while there I thought Tracy was going to strangle me when her contractions got bad."

"Personally I thought some of her colorful comments were particularly inventive," Reno noted with a grin.

"You would," Zane retorted, elbowing his brother in the stomach before turning to Annie. "Tracy felt guilty ruining your wedding reception."

"So she told me. About twenty times. And I told her that she did no such thing. Nothing was ruined. I still tossed my bouquet on our way out and everyone threw birdseed at us for good luck as we jumped into Reno's Bronco and drove off with a trail of tin cans behind us."

"Pretty impressive how Mrs. Battle wrestled all those younger women to get that bouquet for herself," Reno acknowledged as he stood and stretched his kinked muscles.

"Never stand in the way of a determined woman," Zane noted. "My wife has taught me that much."

"Glad to hear you admit you needed some educating," Buck said as he walked into the waiting room with the rest of the family gathered around him—Cord and Hailey along with the twins Lucky and Rusty as well as Alicia.

"When do we get to see the baby?" Lucky excitedly asked.

"You can come see her now," Zane said, taking his son and daughter by the hand as he walked them down the hall toward the nursery. "She's so lucky to have a big brother and sister like you two."

"I'm the one who's lucky," Reno said with a meaningful look in Annie's direction.

"We're all lucky," Buck declared. "I'd say that life is pretty doggone good for the Best of the West. Now get on with the two of you," he added, thumping Reno on the back. "You've got a honeymoon to take care of."

In the past Annie had always been the one to take care of things. But now she had a new family who cared about her. Her heart was filled with love and because of that fact, she no longer needed to be wedded to structure and control. Her security lay in Reno and in their love for each other.

And that's when a crazy idea hit her. She didn't need a huge fancy place in Jackson Hole for a honeymoon. She had everything she needed right here in Bliss. "Are those airline tickets to Jackson Hole re-

fundable?'' she asked Reno as they left the hospital
and headed for his Bronco.

"Yeah, they are. Why?"

"Because I just had this crazy idea..."

An hour later, he carried her over the threshold of
the same cabin where her brother Mike had suppos-
edly been held captive.

"Are you sure about this?" Reno asked, still holding her in his arms. "We can go back..."

"We're not going back," she told him, tugging on
his shoulder as he moved as if to walk back out with
her. "We're going forward even if we are returning
to the scene of the crime, so to speak."

Gently lowering her to her feet, Reno said, "I
wasn't sure if this rental cabin would be available."

"It's not exactly on the beaten path," Annie
pointed out. The last time she'd been here she hadn't
bothered to notice the decor much, other than it had
seemed typical—lots of natural wood and rustic furnishings.

A door was open to the bedroom where a huge
four-poster bed with a denim comforter took up most
of the space.

"This is the perfect place to correct something,"
Annie said. "I want you to know how sorry I am that
I doubted you when I burst in here a year ago and
found you reprimanding my brother."

"I was about to slug him," Reno corrected her.

"He deserved it," she readily admitted.

"Yeah, well, he seems to have straightened up
since then. Sugar made sure of that."

"And while I can't promise that things will always
be easy, that it won't take work on both our parts, or

that I will never in this lifetime question your judgement again—''

''You can't?'' he said with pretended outrage.

''I can promise you that I'll love you to the end of
my days.'' She cupped his face with her hands and
looked him straight in those awesome eyes of his,
crinkled laugh lines and all. ''Because I see you for
what you are, Reno Best.''

He arched an eyebrow at her. ''A sexy charmer?''

''No. Much more than that. A man who is something pretty special. A man who has a good heart.''
She placed her right hand on his chest, right over his
heart.

Her reward was an uncharacteristic loss of words
on his part, but he communicated his feelings more
eloquently in his kiss. His embrace was equally elo-
quent and tender as he swept her off her feet and took
her to bed.

Her pale-blue dress was rumpled and they were
both tired after a mostly sleepless night spent at the
hospital, but it didn't matter. Their coming together
was a celebration of beating the odds against them—
his doubts about his ability to settle down, her need
for security.

So when he undid the buttons running down the
front of her dress, she felt the love he had for her.
And when she peeled off his favorite denim shirt, she
did so with love for him. For the real Reno. The man
he was finally allowing her to see.

The scent of the jasmine-scented candles she'd
brought with her permeated the air and reminded her
of the first time they'd made love. And when he slid
into her, it was as if he'd come home, filling her with

his love and with his body as she welcomed him with her entire being.

The completion was absolute, the rippling grip of pleasure all the more powerful because of their shared commitment. They moved as one as he undulated his hips in a slow, driving rhythm that Annie matched, drawing him deep within her. The look on his face as he whispered his love for her filled her with wondrous joy that she'd found this man—the only one for her.

Later, with her head pillowed on his shoulder, his fingers threading through her hair, the candles flickering against the cabin walls, she felt a sense of fulfillment that she was incapable of expressing.

She left it to Reno to do so. "Y'know, my dad was right. Life *is* good for the Best of the West," Reno declared with the satisfaction of a man who'd finally found true happiness.

ISABEL
SHARPE

Beauty and
the Bet

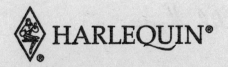

TORONTO • NEW YORK • LONDON
AMSTERDAM • PARIS • SYDNEY • HAMBURG
STOCKHOLM • ATHENS • TOKYO • MILAN • MADRID
PRAGUE • WARSAW • BUDAPEST • AUCKLAND

Dear Reader,

I got the idea for *Beauty and the Bet* from two episodes that occurred within a week of each other. I heard on the radio about a beautiful twenty-something woman who agreed to participate in an experiment. She went into the same establishments on two separate occasions to ask for help, once dressed to the nines, once disguised as a dowdy mess.

The second episode occurred at a mall where I was waiting for a friend. A stunning teenage girl walked in alone; twenty minutes later, she walked out trailing five teenage boys—not guys she knew.

Both these events got the writer's wheel turning in my head. What would it be like to have the same people interact with you completely differently based solely on how you look? What would it be like to be so gorgeous you couldn't do anything without attracting attention?

From there, Heather and Jack's tale was born, a makeover story in reverse. I hope you enjoy it! Online readers can write to me at IsaSharpe@aol.com and let me know!

Sincerely,

Isabel Sharpe

To my brother and best friend Charlie,
who liked this story so much.

1

"BUT OF COURSE size matters!" François made a sound of disgust. "You women say no, but you are always wanting men with the big ones."

Heather Brannen accepted her glass of seltzer from the waiter and took a long sip to avoid blurting out what she really wanted to say. "I just meant that, if the shape is good, it doesn't have to be large. Marco had just what we—"

"Marco!" The old man pulled his ascot up and to the side as if to hang himself. "Marco's is like a small boy's."

"Bryan, then. His was much bigger."

"Hah! He quivers like a nervous teenager."

"Ricky—embarrassingly large."

"Rick, he is a flabby pig."

"Ed, then."

"*Non! Absolument non.* Ed is like an old man. Old! I tell you I have no time for limp fools."

Heather scrunched up her mouth to keep from erupting in total, very loud frustration, and glared at her boss. A gust of hot wind blew across the sidewalk café tables as if agreeing with her current opinion of him.

"We are seeking more than a mere body part!" François threw his signature black beret on the table between them. "We are seeking the pure essence of

manhood. I get perfection, or I don't photograph! No!
Nothing!''

Heather inhaled deeply. *In. Out.* François had to
back down. This shoot would finally get her enough
money to open her own photography studio on the
Connecticut coast. Finally allow her to escape the dirt
and crowds of New York. Finally give her the chance
to define herself, to start putting down her life's roots.

Equally as important, the assignment would put
François's name before the industry again, where his
name deserved to be. Heather had to remember how
much he'd done for her, how much his work inspired
her own development. And forget he tended to behave
like a horse's hind region.

Relax. Be patient.

''Look, we've gone through every male model who
can still breathe without mechanical help. This assignment is a gift from the gods. You can't afford
to—''

''I can't afford to compromise my art. I must
have—how do you say?—a male's male. Who from
every pore shouts, 'I am Man. I conquer Eve. I build
nations. I slay armies. I scratch and don't care who
is looking.''' He flung one leg over the other and
stared at her defiantly. ''You did not show me this
man. Where is he?''

''Right behind you, baby.'' A smug, breathy tenor
voice interrupted them. Heather turned around and
shuddered. Beefcake dimwit from all appearances.
Face too handsome, build over-pumped, blond Fabio
hairstyle—he might as well wear a button saying, ''I
love me—you should too.''

The man took off his sunglasses with an over-
rehearsed gesture, and smiled an orthodontically cor-

rect smile. "I heard what you was talkin' about. My name's Rod." He leaned toward Heather with a suggestive smirk. "I got whatcha need all right. And I'm always ready to audition, if you know what I mean."

François made a rude sound of contempt. "You? Hah! Yours is *petit,* like a baby, round and soft. *Non! Pas du tout!* The worst chin I ever saw."

"Chin?" Rod's dull eyes clouded further in confusion. His buddies erupted into jeering laughter behind him.

A giggle exploded from behind Heather's hand. He'd strutted right into that one.

Rod shrugged in a vain effort to recover his machismo and sidled up closer, bringing with him the odor of dried gym sweat. "The offer stands, beautiful. How about you and me ditch the geezer and go find somewhere cool to work up a thirst? A knockout like you must be lookin' for some real action."

Heather's laughter died, replaced by mild nausea. *Here we go again.* It wasn't her fault she was born looking this way. Men could not seem to understand that a normal human inhabited her body. They seemed to think she wanted nothing out of life but immediate casual sex with whomever happened by. In cold weather she used coats, hats and scarves to camouflage her face and figure, but summer was just too damn hot. Even in a shapeless dress, minimal makeup, and a careless mess of a hairstyle, they found her. She sighed. At least she had developed a surefire way to get rid of the unwanted offers.

Cue evasive maneuver number four-hundred and seventeen.

She smiled brilliantly at the no doubt aptly named Rod. "Would you like to join me? I was just about to go slug-hunting in Central Park. I'm hoping to add the noble Black Corelian slug to my collection. They're amazing creatures—so graceful, so exquisite, but so misunderstood.'' She pretended to dab at a tear. ''Why, I can't wait to tell you everything I've learned from my six-volume *Encyclopedia of Invertebrates*.''

Rod's oily charm slid off his face. ''You're kidding, right?''

''Kidding?'' She opened her eyes super-sincerely wide and clutched her heart. ''Of course not. Our boneless brethren are my joy, my life, my inspi—''

''I, uh, have to get going.'' He backed away and tripped over a metal table leg, arms flailing. Heather kept the smile off her face, though his pals obviously thought he invented comedy.

''You are too nice to these men with your stories, Heather. You should tell them where they can take their foolish lust. *Imbécile!*'' François rolled his eyes and made a gagging motion. ''He dared to think his silly child's chin could even approach the perfection I require! *Oh, la la.*''

Heather turned from dealing with *imbécile numero un* to the second one on her docket. She had to find some way to get her boss to pick a model soon. Holden House had recently launched *Diablo,* its first venture into men's cologne. ''Give us Your Body Parts'' ads had been plastered all over the city for weeks, starting with shots of male feet, and working up. Chins were next. If François waited too long to choose, he could flush the opportunity, along with her studio, right down *la toilette.* ''François, this chance is huge for us. If you do this right, without making trouble, we could—''

''Do this right? Do this right? I am *trying* to do

this right. *You* are the one who is making the trouble.'' He slammed his palm down on the table. ''François will photograph the chin as the chin has never been photographed before. But only the chin of chins, one worthy of my art.''

Heather gritted her teeth and squinted up at the hazy sky, down at the cracked filthy sidewalk, out at the perspiring pedestrians dragging past. Anywhere but at the small, aging, brilliant, sometimes endearing, mostly exasperating man opposite her. Anywhere until she could control her temper, inflamed further by the humid oppression of city air in July.

The studio closing was scheduled for the end of the month; her apartment lease expired at the same time; Holden House wouldn't wait forever—everything hinged on cooperation from this French mule. Small wonder François's once-fantastic career had ground to a halt. You could annoy some of the people some of the time, but once you annoyed all of the people all of the time, you were history, no matter how gifted.

''Let's face the facts here, François. The only reason you got this job is because Holden House didn't like the way Boris filmed rear ends.'' She wouldn't bother adding that when she heard Boris had been fired, she'd worn out her kneecaps grovelling to a friend in Holden's marketing department until they gave François the chance to come back from his recent obscurity. François had taken a chance hiring a no-name like Heather, and taught her invaluable lessons in spite of the demeaning work he got these days. If she could put him back on the professional pedestal he deserved before she blissfully emigrated to Connecticut, she'd have returned at least part of the favor.

"Boris?" François spit delicately on the sidewalk. "He doesn't know the camera from his own *derrière*."

"Well, you can throw yourself out on yours to save Holden House the trouble if you don't choose a chin soon."

"François does not compromise." He leaned forward and fixed her with a dark, intense gaze that shot out from his pale wrinkled face. "You will find me the chin of a lifetime, Heather. Or we do nothing on this. No! Nothing!"

"How am I ever going to find a chin perfect enough to satisfy that small irritant I work for?" Heather reached for a fig from the bowl on her best friend Stephanie's coffee table.

"Don't you dare touch that fig!" Stephanie smacked her hand away. "Took me all afternoon to position the darn thing perfectly. All morning to determine its good side. *Gourmand* magazine is doing an article on high-fiber gourmet."

"Sorry, sorry. I've got chin for brains at the moment." Heather flopped down onto Stephanie's beat-up couch, limbs splayed. "This shoot was supposed to be my ticket out of here, and François's ticket back into the spotlight. Now it's more like a ticket to Hades."

Stephanie squinted critically at her still-life arrangement. "Maybe I shouldn't have the prunes next to the apricots. Prunes always look sort of wistful. I'm trying for 'elegant' here. What do you think?"

"They're elegant, they're elegant. Prince Charming

could take one to the ball.'' Heather gestured exasperatedly toward her friend. ''You've lived next door to Mr. Eiffel Tower for years, you must know some way to get to him.''

Stephanie put her hands on her hips in mock anger. ''I don't think you're taking my prunes very seriously.''

''Sorry, sorry—again sorry.'' Heather grinned and rolled her eyes. ''Your prunes are vital to heaven, earth, and my grandmother. If they had perfect chins, you could add me to the list.''

Stephanie picked up a blueberry, rotated it a quarter turn, and replaced it with infinite care. ''All you have to do is walk down the street in a tight outfit. Every man in the universe will throw himself at you, and you can pick the best one.'' She moved her lean body behind her tripod and squinted into the camera on top.

''Ha, ha. This is serious. I'm so close to making the down payment on my studio in Southport, I can taste the plaster. The only thing that stands in the way of wild success and eternal happiness is some guy's jawbone.'' Heather shook her blond hair out of its haphazard arrangement of clips and scrubbed the waves into a frustrated mane about her face. Why didn't she have normal problems like everyone else? A sweet little leaky faucet, or a happy bout with bunions?

''So men foul everything up, what else is new?'' Stephanie's face appeared from behind her camera to glare at an artful cascade of dried beans. ''Are the beans too much? Maybe I should put them in another shot.''

''The beans are stupendous. Keep the beans. Beans move people deeply.'' Heather dropped her head back on the couch and threw her arm over her eyes. "Maybe I should rob a bank and forget this whole assignment."

"Hmm, doesn't sound like you. How about painting an unflattering portrait of François to get the rage out of your system? That's more your speed. You could call it 'Small Irritant with Pears.'" Stephanie's shutter clicked a few times. "Speaking of which, do you think I should add a few more Bartletts to this basket?"

Heather peered out from beneath her arm. Painting. An excellent suggestion. Her favorite method of working out problems: to drape herself in black, turn up classical music as loud as her neighbors could stand it, and paint her way to exhaustion and peace. "Not a bad idea."

"The pears?"

"The portrait."

"Listen, I'm happy to lend you the money if you want. Heck, I'll give it to you. God knows I have no use for the stuff. Just keeps piling up without my permission." Stephanie jumped for the table. "Oh Lord, another lentil avalanche."

Heather dropped her arm back to her side and stared at the ceiling, considering the cobwebs and her friend's offer. The amount she needed equaled bubble gum money to Stephanie, though Steph made a point of living primarily on what she made photographing food for cooking magazines. Still, Heather couldn't quite bring herself to accept a handout, not when she'd struggled so hard to get this far.

She shook her head. "No, thanks. I really need to do this on my own."

"Good for you." Stephanie interrupted her absorption with high fiber to toss Heather a warm smile. "That's how I feel, too. That's why I started the Chrissman Foundation with my parents' trillions. Might as well give it away and screw up other people's lives." She collapsed on the sofa next to Heather. "Why don't you put an ad in the paper?"

"For the money?"

"For the chin."

"I thought of that, though I can imagine what kind of wackos would answer. Guess I'll try haunting gyms and health clubs first to see if I can spot someone." Heather sighed. She'd hoped it wouldn't come to that. Hanging around a bunch of bicep worshippers did not make her list of top ten favorite activities.

"Mmm. Buildings full of pumped, sweaty men. Sounds like more than you can handle. Need an assistant?" Stephanie threw her a teasing glance and rose to return to her display. "Although next to you, I'd be invisible."

"Ha! Not by a long shot." Heather smiled at her friend. Stephanie had the kind of beauty that stole up on you gradually. Sleek, heavy, shoulder-length blond hair and pale narrow features. She radiated chic seductive calm, like a forties movie star.

Except when she got frantic over fruit.

"I swear those strawberries sneak around on their pointy little bottoms when I'm not looking. I couldn't have put that one there—it's an abomination." Stephanie repositioned the offending berry and lifted her head to look at the antique clock on her mantle. "Roger's coming over any minute to take me to lunch and I have to change. Want to join us? He's bringing his older brother along."

"Wow, meeting the family. 'Sounds like things are

getting serious, young lady!'" Heather did her best
nasal imitation of Stephanie's Aunt Doris, trying not
to feel envious. She'd never been able to apply the
phrase 'getting serious' to any relationship. "Are you
going to tell him you're actually a Chrissman and not
a starving *artiste* soon? Or are you going to wait until
the wedding?"

"I won't tell him a thing until he proves himself
worthy." Stephanie's scowl barely hid her dreamy
smile. She stepped out of her well-worn jeans. "Are
you coming?"

"To your wedding?"

"To lunch. His brother is supposed to be a real
studmuffin. Roger worships him, though he'd never
admit it." Her face emerged from the neckline of a
blue sundress that matched her eyes. "You never
know, you might like the guy."

Heather's hackles rose. "*Et tu,* Stephanie? I
thought I could count on one person in the country
not to try and marry me off."

"A thousand pardons. It slipped out."

"You have no real perspective. You don't realize
Roger is the only normal nice guy in existence."
Heather shoved her hair up and jabbed in clips until
the mess stayed put. "The rest of them are either
gorgeous macho jerks, or insecure nerds who wish
they were gorgeous macho jerks."

Stephanie tsk-tsked. "You're like François, insist-
ing on perfection. A flawless man is like a unicorn—
tantalizing enough to keep everyone searching, but he
simply doesn't exist."

"Not perfection." Heather shook her head in exasperation. No matter how often she explained herself, everyone still thought her a childish idealist.

"Someone capable of sensitivity, of empathy. Someone who can analyze and discuss his feelings and needs. Someone who is independent enough to want a true partner, not a nursemaid. Most importantly, someone who can keep his pants zipped long enough to find out if I can carry on a conversation." She kept her voice determinedly light to hide the shaking. After years of experimental dating, she'd all but accepted her future as a single woman. Thank goodness she had a career waiting to fulfill her—if she could just find a cooperative chin.

"I hear you." Stephanie laughed. "Your looks are like my money, only you can't hide yours as easily."

"Perhaps a stylish paper bag?"

"I think you're better off braving the male assaults. Change your mind about joining us?"

"No, I better get started on the hunt."

"For a unicorn?"

"For a chin." Heather pushed herself off the couch and headed for the door. The sooner she found the guy, the sooner the promising next chapter of her life could begin. "Thanks for letting me emote, Steph. I do feel better."

"Nothing keeps my Heather down for long. How do I look?"

Heather turned back and smiled. A woman in love with a terrific guy. How else could she look? "You look beautiful. Elegant. Like a prune."

2

JACK FORTUNATO stamped hard on an imaginary brake from the passenger seat of his brother's squeaky old car. Driving in New York defied death. Driving with Roger invited it. Driving with Roger when he was edgy and distracted: outright suicide.

A taxi narrowly avoided an intimate relationship with their front bumper, horn blaring. Jack winced. "Did I mention there are only two lanes on this street?"

"Several times." Roger swore at a motorcycle attempting to cut them off. "But the wild and free spirit of Roger Fortunato is not contained by something as mundane as lanes."

"Ah." Jack clutched his knees, anticipating the burning feel of the airbag any second. His normally cheerful and gentle brother became Demon Avenger of the Streets when he got behind the wheel of a car.

Roger screeched to a stop at a red light and punched Jack on the shoulder with a beefy fist. "Stewing over that call from Martinson this morning?"

"I guess." Jack managed a tight smile. "I can't believe they pulled their grant for 'City Kids in Camp' this late. I have to come up with camp tuition for fifty kids already enrolled to start next month. The restaurant is doing well, but we can't go beyond the money we've already put into the program because of the remodelling.''

Roger nodded sympathetically and jammed down the accelerator to shoot the car forward, seconds before the light turned green. ''Grandpa Fortunato must be turning in his grave. Twenty-five years ago he started the program for peanuts. Now, we need—Hey! Outta Lucky Roger's way, you daughter of a warthog!'' He leaned on his horn.

Jack groaned. ''Has Stephanie had the pleasure of your company in a car yet? I think she better experience this side of you before she commits to anything.''

''I'm waiting 'til I'm sure of her.'' Roger grinned over at him. ''You nervous going to meet your future sister-in-law if I ever get up the nerve to ask her?''

''I'm more nervous about going to meet my maker. Could you spare an occasional glance for the road?'' Jack leaned away from an approaching delivery truck, as if the force of his body could help steer the car safely past.

''Sorry, bro. I guess *I'm* nervous. Every woman I've ever been involved with has dumped me the minute she laid eyes on you. I feel in my heart this one's different, but I'm a wreck, I admit it.''

Jack shot him a wry look. ''I never would have known. And you're exaggerating wildly about the women.''

He wished it were true. His looks had been nothing but trouble since first grade, when he unknowingly caused a playground riot over which girl got to kiss him first. His genes hadn't even had the decency to go through a pimply awkward stage during adolescence. He sighed. Anyone who could envy the freakish combination of DNA that made him look the way he did hadn't lived the reality themselves.

The car swerved to the side and screeched to a halt. Jack thrust out his hands to grab the dashboard. "What the—"

"Parking spot! In front of her building. Must be a good luck omen." Roger backed up half a foot, jammed on the brake and gestured obscenely through the rear windshield. "Hey, buddy, outta my territory." He yanked up the parking brake and jumped out of the car to argue with the driver trying to nose into the space behind him.

Jack sighed. From the moment he awoke to the call from Martinson, Inc., one thing after another had gone wrong. The wrong color tiles had been delivered for the floor of his family's restaurant, *La Cucina del Cor*. The plumber hadn't shown up to install the toilets. The new tables might not be ready for the restaurant's re-opening at the end of the month. Now his brother courted road rage in SoHo. If only Jack were near a kitchen, he could indulge in his favorite form of stress relief by cooking up a storm.

He slumped back into his seat and let his head loll to the side, listening to the shouting behind him, wondering if he remembered enough from his Aikido classes to help his younger brother, in case the other driver attempted to remove any of his limbs. Probably not.

The door to Stephanie's building opened and a blond woman emerged, wearing a faded rose-colored sundress. Jack's slump instantly fell victim to a surge of electric attraction.

"Wow." He watched her walk closer, watched the graceful swing of her body move the loose-fitting folds of her dress. She glanced toward the apoplectic men without seeming to register their presence, as if her mind were consumed by thought, or merely numbed by city living. Her features were alluringly constructed, delicately arranged, her eyes large and intelligent, skin flawless, mouth full and tempting. She was beyond beautiful—she was perfect.

He leaned closer, trying unsuccessfully to catch her scent through the still-open door. Her quick light steps brought her even with the car—and past. Jack groaned in protest, and turned to follow the sway of her hips down the block.

"Wow."

He shook himself, realizing he'd been repeating the word over and over like a hypnotized idiot. Been a while since he succumbed to lust on sight. Powerful stuff. Good thing he knew from experience women like that never lived up to their promise. He'd saved himself another disappointment.

Roger jumped back into the car and slammed the door. "Another victory for The Fearless Fortunatos." He swung the car into the parking place and exchanged one last obscenity with the losing driver who pulled away, tires squealing.

"You ready?" Roger narrowed his eyes and stared at Jack. "Hey, whatsa matta you? You had a vision or something?"

Jack managed to grin at his brother, the woman's image still glued to his somewhat rattled consciousness. "You might say that."

"Oh, ho! *That* kind of vision." Roger slapped him on the back. "Glad to hear it. I was beginning to think you were leading up to a lifetime vow of chastity."

"Just wised up, is all."

"Hah. More like got a megadose of stupid. Why don't you go after her? Today's the perfect day for an adventure—get you out of the doldrums."

Jack shook his head. "Not this time."

"Oh no?" Roger leaned toward him, mouth turned up in a wicked smile, one eye mischievously half-closed. "I dare you."

For a few seconds the old reflex kicked in, tightened Jack's stomach and set his heart to pounding. He almost gave in. Then sanity returned; the pumping adrenaline diminished. He grinned at his brother. "You almost had me. Once upon a time I'd have been halfway down the block by now. But I'm afraid maturity calls."

"Sadder words were never spoken." Roger shook his head and pushed open his door. "To think I'd see the day my brother won't take a dare. The guy who once powdered our dog pink, put a tutu on him and let him loose at Stellie's dance recital."

"Give me a break." Jack chuckled. "I'm not sixteen anymore."

"You know what?" Roger got out of the car and poked his head back in, still smiling. "That's the root of your trouble. Let's go." He almost danced over the sidewalk to the front door of Stephanie's fashionably run-down building.

Jack followed, trying not to be envious. He failed. He'd never seen his brother so smitten. Stephanie must be the only normal, nice member of her gender left. He couldn't see Roger falling for any other type. The man had too much sense.

"Yeeess?" A low, rich female voice answered Roger's fevered attack on the doorbell through the foyer intercom.

Roger put his hand to his heart and burst into an off-key Italian love song.

"I'll be right down, Romeo." A buzzer went off, unlocking the building's inner door. Jack followed his brother into the dim hallway.

"We'll wait here." Roger winked and gave a thumbs-up sign. Neither gesture could disguise his advanced state of panic.

"Relax, Roger." Jack stepped on Roger's tapping foot. "She won't even notice me."

Roger mopped his brow. "I'll believe it when I see it."

The elevator doors opened to reveal a tall, striking woman in a light-blue dress. Jack's envy increased exponentially when he saw the way she glowed at the sight of his short, stubbornly pudgy brother.

"Mi amore." Roger grabbed her out of the elevator and dipped her into a kiss. She finally emerged, flustered and blushing, to look in Jack's direction. He braced himself.

Stephanie's eyes opened wide; her jaw dropped. "Gracious, Roger. You told me he was good-looking. You didn't say he could stop traffic fleeing a volcano."

Roger looked like he'd been force-fed a lemon. Stephanie continued to stare. Jack's heart sank; he smiled uneasily. Her gaze seemed to be fixed somewhere below his mouth—maybe she was too shy to meet his eyes. Something strangely speculative lurked in her expression, too, as if she were about to ask how much he cost.

He searched for some inanity to break the tension. "Roger's told me a lot about you. I didn't realize human perfection had actually been accomplished."

His words seemed to break through Stephanie's trance. She laughed, turned to beam at Roger, and planted a kiss on his cheek. "The man is clearly in denial. Don't ever change him."

Roger relaxed visibly; Jack grinned, able to breathe again. "Before you wish that, make sure he drives you somewhere. You might find—"

"Hold! Do not move the muscle. No! Nothing!" The heavily-accented shout came from behind him. Jack turned to see an absurd little man in a black beret, black turtleneck and black pants step through the lobby door, looking as if he'd just seen his own salvation. He approached slowly, his breathing shallow, eyes unnaturally wide and fixed on Jack's face. A curious odor hung off him, like a mixture of wine and film developer.

Jack exchanged glances with Roger. Clearly the man had checked his mental health at the gate. Best to humor him. "Good afternoon. What can I—"

The man jumped forward and caught Jack's arm with surprising strength. "I *must* have you. I must!"

Jack groaned inwardly. Being good-looking in New York meant you attracted a fair number of gay men as well as women, though the men weren't usually this aggressive. "Look, I'm sorry. I'm flattered, but I'm also straight."

"No, no. I must have your *chin*." He shot out his hand, grabbed Jack's jaw, and peered intently. "*Oui. Oui!* Perfection!" He cackled delightedly.

Jack grabbed the man's hand off his face, trying not to show his revulsion and inflame the little weirdo further. He'd heard of foot fetishists, but chins? Sexual deviance wasn't his thing anyway, even with women. "Look, little man, I—"

"Perhaps now would be the best time for introductions." Stephanie slid her way gracefully between them. "Jack Fortunato, meet François, no last name. François is the photographer for the *Diablo* cologne 'Give us Your Body Parts' ads, have you seen them?"

Jack nodded, comprehension finally making its way into his somewhat shocked brain. The guy wanted him to model his chin for some ad campaign. "Yes, I've seen them. But I'm sorry. I'm not a model." Nor bloody likely to be. He'd spent his life alternately hounded and isolated by his looks; the last thing he wanted was to draw more attention to them.

"It is no matter. No! You are perfect. I am so happy to find you." François grabbed his hand and pumped it, beaming. "Jack Fortunato. It is I who am *fortunato*. Yes!"

Jack shook his head, feeling like the star of some French surrealist picture. "You don't understand. I don't—"

"I am in a frenzy to have my camera on you." The little man practically pirouetted down the hallway and back. "When can you start?"

Jack took a deep breath. "Read my chin. I am *not* going to pose for you. Not. Ever. Pose. For you. No."

François sent him a gleeful smile. "But *Monsieur*. I am a man who gets what he wants always, *toujours*." He drew himself up to his full non-height and raised his arm in a dramatic gesture, as if to command the attention of an enormous crowd. "François, he will now become great again! This moment will be—"

"Perhaps a small pill *du* chill, François." Stephanie put her arm around his shoulders and escorted him down the hall. At the elevator, she whispered something that made the old man chuckle and kiss her on both cheeks.

"She's sure got a way with the old guy, eh?" Roger's expression had become decidedly gooey.

Stephanie came back toward them, rolling her eyes. "Sorry about that. He's a little out of orbit occasionally."

Jack nodded. "As long as he doesn't keep trying to change my mind."

"Oh, he won't."

"Really?" Jack looked at her suspiciously. "He doesn't seem the type to give up so easily."

"Let's go. There's a great café nearby, Café Boom." Stephanie gave a Mona Lisa smile that put up every guard Jack had. Women smiled like that for only one reason: they intended to get their way if they had to kill to do it.

"After you." He bowed and gestured for her and Roger to precede him out of the building. Just let her try.

The hot wind whipped dust and litter around their feet as they walked on Spring Street toward the restaurant. Stephanie maneuvered herself between the brothers, linked arms with Roger, and turned to Jack. He increased his guard. Incoming: Stephanie's first attempt.

"Anyone in your life these days, Jack?" Her low musical tone reeked of carefully casual conversation. He couldn't help a smattering of admiration. A classy lady. Lucky Roger had earned his nickname.

"Not these days."

"But he saw one just before we came in who rang

his chimes loud enough to deafen him temporarily.'' Roger chuckled ruefully. "I'm sorry I missed her.''

Stephanie came to an abrupt halt, making Roger rear back like a horse refusing a jump. "You saw her *just* before you came in?''

Jack nodded. So did Stephanie. Only his was a simple nod of affirmation. Hers appeared to have an entire United Nations of strategy and conjecture behind it. "Is that significant?''

"Of course not. Here's the place.'' Stephanie led the way and sat at one of the tables arranged on the sidewalk. "Did you speak to her?''

"No, he didn't.'' Roger gave a dramatic sigh and sat next to Stephanie, edging his chair closer. "I tried to get him to go after her, but he's a dull boy these days. Says women are either sexpot manipulators or wallflowers who wish they were sexpot manipulators.''

Stephanie appeared to be stifling a burst of laughter. "Now why does that sound familiar?''

Jack bristled. "I swore off the entire gender years ago.''

His brother coughed meaningfully.

"Okay, months ago.'' Jack rolled his eyes and sat opposite them.

"What about that woman last—''

"Weeks, okay, weeks. But I'm not putting myself through that misery again.'' Until he figured out what everyone else saw in the experience. There had to be something more to the man-woman thing than the usual sequence he encountered: attraction, action, reaction, dissatisfaction.

"You know what your trouble is?'' Roger shook

his finger. "You only go out with brain-dead super-model types."

"That's not tr—" Jack closed his mouth. It *was* true. They found him in droves.

"Why don't you go after a nice, normal, intelligent, fun woman?" Roger put his arm around Stephanie's shoulder and squeezed.

"Because there aren't any." Jack inclined his head toward Stephanie. "Except for—"

"Don't bother." She smiled warmly. "I've heard the line before. You're wrong, you know. There are millions of them. All of whom avoid gorgeous men on the assumption they're self-absorbed jerks."

His jaw clenched. "Isn't that discrimination?"

"I have friends who would swear it's pure fact." Stephanie accepted a menu from the waiter and bent over the choices.

Jack grimaced at the top of her head. Just when he thought he'd accepted his life sentence of shallow bachelor relationships, another little episode like this would re-activate the pain. Someday, somewhere, he'd find a lawyer and sue his own genes for mental trauma.

Stephanie suddenly jerked her head up and met his eyes, Mona Lisa firmly in charge of her mouth. He might as well have seen the light bulb go off over her head.

"I have an idea."

"Oh-oh." Roger leaned away from Stephanie as if she might be contagious. "If you value your sanity, run for the burbs."

"Let's make a bet, Jack." Stephanie slapped her menu shut, eyes alight. "I'll bet that you can't seduce a normal, nice, intelligent, not-so-attractive woman."

"What?" Jack and Roger spoke together, then exchanged she's-finally-flipped glances.

"Just what I said." Stephanie sat back triumphantly. "I bet you can't."

Jack stared at her, intrigued. She appeared to be deadly serious. This had to be tied up somehow with the chin thing; he could see no other possible motivation. "What are the stakes?"

"If you win, I'll get you the money Roger said you need for your City Kids in Camp program."

"You?" Roger and Jack spoke together again and glared at each other.

"I have a close friend at the Chrissman Foundation. I can put in a word and the money's as good as yours."

Roger's mouth dropped open in astonishment. "Just like that?"

"She's a very good friend." Stephanie gave a rather smug smile.

"And if I fail?" Jack knew the answer before she opened her mouth.

"Your chin will be plastered all over the city."

Jack chuckled and shook his head. She was damn clever. Start with a challenge to the male ego, find something he really cared about to spice up the bait, and bingo. She gets a shot at what she's after.

He thought of all those kids who'd be disappointed if he couldn't come up with the cash. All those kids who'd spend August on the streets instead, preyed on by gangs and drug traffickers before they were old enough to shave. He thought of the thank-you letter one teacher had written, saying some of her students had only seen trees ringed with asphalt, only been swimming in hydrant spray, only seen horses ridden by policemen.

"Where would this woman come from?" He at least owed it to the kids to hear her out.

"I'll find her." Stephanie folded her hands on the table and nodded firmly. "But she won't know about the bet, I promise."

Jack considered the offer with one half of his brain and yelled at himself to stop with the other. He couldn't really be thinking of accepting her challenge. The idea was sheer lunacy.

"How long would I get?"

"Ha!" Roger shook his head. "Make him really work for it. At least twenty minutes."

"Let's see." Stephanie drew down her brows. "End of the month, that's one, two...three weeks."

"Are you kidding?" Roger looked at Stephanie as if she needed psychological assistance. "He could do the entire state in three weeks. I say make it a half hour, tops."

"Shut up, Roger," Stephanie said calmly. Her gaze was fixed on Jack, as if she were trying to persuade him by some form of mental telepathy.

Three weeks. Jack tapped his fingers against his chin. Seemed ample time. But could he afford the risk if he lost? He couldn't even count the number of times he'd been offered modelling jobs. His refusals had become firm to the point of rudeness. He'd spent his entire life wanting people to realize he was worth more than his looks. Even if he alone knew the poster chin belonged to him, he was one person too many.

"I'm not sure..."

Stephanie leaned forward, eyes lit with mischief. "I dare you."

For an endless minute Jack fought the surge of excitement that responded to her words. He could do it. Of course he could do it. What woman had ever resisted his approach? Sometimes he even acted like a jerk on purpose, hoping they'd show some integrity and tell him to go to hell, but they still fell all over him. Bunch of lemmings. Surely a less attractive woman would fit the same mold. The cash would be in his pocket, the kids off the streets, and he'd only have to lift his—

"I dare you, Jack."

This time her challenge swept a superdose of traitorous testosterone through his body, cleansing him of his last shred of common sense. He put out his hand, brimming with confidence. "You're on, lady."

"Hurray." Stephanie smiled sweetly and shook his hand with an iron grip. "And may the best chin win."

"I CAN'T BELIEVE I let you talk me into this." Heather turned sideways to the mirror in her tiny apartment to view the extra padding around her waist. Several inches past voluptuous. "Do you think the large rear is too much? That dress we bought is pretty awful by itself."

"Hmm." Stephanie eyed her critically. "No, I think the extra seating room adds character. The elastic's a little loose. I'll fasten the form to your dress with safety pins. God forbid your buns fall off during dinner. Where do you keep them?"

"My buns?"

"Your pins."

"On my desk, under the pile of papers with the hairbrush on top." Heather pulled the dress from its bag and shook it out. Brown. Brown dress. Brown long sleeves, brown elasticized waist, brown high neck. Not rich, reddish brown, flat dull brown. She hated brown clothes. François had better appreciate what she was doing for him. Dressing like a wallflower and fending off advances from some arrogant stud for the rest of the month definitely did not fit her job description. Thank goodness Stephanie had set a three-week limit on the bet. "What if he sees through the disguise?"

"I can't imagine how he could. You'll look authentically horrendous. And you did all that acting in high school and college. You told me your own roommate didn't recognize you until halfway through one performance." Stephanie returned with the pins and shuddered at the dress. "Why they'd even bother making a garment that drab is beyond me."

"Drab suits my purpose." Heather pulled the dress over her head and began buttoning the front. "I am curious, however, Ms. Chrissman. Why didn't you just tell him he could have his moola if he did the *Diablo* shoot, and leave the seduction thing out of it?"

"Where's the fun in that?" Stephanie frowned at Heather's legs. "Maybe you should wear brown support hose."

"In this heat? Have mercy. The long sleeves and unnatural fibers of this dress will kill me as it is. I'll wear knee-highs instead. The tops will peek out from under the hem when I sit down and titillate him tremendously."

"Perfect. I imagine you know where to get some."

"There's a clean pair in the closet, under the white nightgown on the floor in the far right corner." Heather pulled the dress's brown fabric belt to fit snugly on her newly thick waist and buttoned the brown buttons on the cuffs. Three weeks. She just had to avoid this guy's moves for three weeks, and the shoot would be on; she'd get the studio downpayment in under the wire, and be out of this city and on to a new life.

If she could survive the stress.

"Your idea of 'fun' is going to cause me a month of heartburn, Steph. I still wish you'd done a direct trade: chin for cash." Heather pulled on the knee-highs and studied her reflection. "Should I stuff my bra to look more matronly?"

"Definitely not. The wildly out-of-proportion pear shape is to die for. I bet you'll have the time of your life doing this. Here's your chance to see how people react to mere mortals." Stephanie flipped up Heather's skirt and pinned the form to the dress. "My only worry is that once you lay an eyeball on Jack Fortunato, you'll want to lose the bet on the first date. The man is gorgeous."

Heather twisted slightly and gave her enlarged hips an affectionate pat. "So what?"

"No, I mean he's *really* gorgeous."

"I've seen gorgeous. Gorgeous does nothing for me."

"No, you don't understand. This guy is really, *really* gor—"

"Stephanie, love, your point has been made. How do I look?" Heather opened her arms and made a deliberately clumsy attempt at a curtsy.

"Boy, is that dress *brown*. Yeesh." Stephanie walked around her. "But oh, how divinely it matches the clonky old-lady shoes."

"We low-fashion babes have our chic moments,

too." Heather grabbed a drugstore bag, lying on her dresser amid a jumble of paint tubes and costume jewelry boxes. "Now for the final transformation into Marsha Gouber—looks like 'Goober,' is pronounced 'Gou-*bear*'—orange-y foundation, brown contacts, heavy eyebrow pencil, thick tortoiseshell glasses, and the *pièce de resistance*," she reached into the bag and pulled out a mop of mousey-brown hair, "the Seventies Wig of Horror."

"Ugh. I'll wait out here." Stephanie walked across Heather's cluttered living area. "Any place you recommend I sit?"

"Let's see." Heather contemplated her beloved disorder. "You can move the magazines off that chair and onto the floor near the futon so I'll know where they are."

"You know where everything is—it defies comprehension. Let me know if you need help."

Half an hour later, Heather emerged triumphantly from the bathroom. She'd never looked this bad and she knew it. "Ta-daaaa." She pitched her voice down into a booming Marsha sound and adopted a New York accent. "Mah-sha Gou-*beah*, glee-yad tuh meet ya. What do you think?"

"Wow." Stephanie's features expanded into shock. "Wow. You are...I mean I would never, in a million...wow. You're in the wrong profession, kiddo. You should be on the stage. You even move differently. Truly horrifying."

"Thank you." Heather turned back to the full-length mirror. Even after having put on the disguise herself, looking at her transformation provoked an eery shiver of excitement. Heather Brannen had simply disappeared. In her place, the winner of this year's

Plain Pageant, Marsha Gouber. Spurned and disdained by sports fans everywhere. She grinned at her reflection.

"Don't do too much of that." Stephanie came to stand behind her. "Your smile is still the same one that knocks men to their knees."

"Stephanie, this is so amazing. I can't *wait* to walk down the street like this. Think of it!" She stared at herself, enraptured. "People might even ignore me."

"I'm not so sure of that, but they certainly won't be thinking the thoughts you're used to." Stephanie looked at her watch. "He's due any minute. Let's watch for him out the window."

Heather crouched over the back of the couch next to her friend, eyes scanning the sidewalk, mind spinning over the task ahead of her. Part of her wished she were going on a normal series of dates as "Marsha," to see how men treated women they actually wanted for their personality. Jack would only be trying to worm his macho way into her bedroom. The same old scenario. Luckily, unlike poor Marsha, Heather did have years of experience keeping men out of that particular room. Jack didn't stand a yuppie's chance in a biker bar.

A red sportscar drove up and took over a parking space just vacated by a minivan. Heather gave a cynical snort. "Stud in a sportscar, what a surprise."

A portly middle-aged woman squeezed herself out from behind the wheel. Heather's mouth dropped open. Stephanie laughed. "Serves you right for stereotyping. You should give people the benefit of—" She grabbed Heather's arm and pointed to the opposite sidewalk. "There he is. That's Jack."

Heather caught her breath. A dark, tall, nicely-put-together man crossed the street toward her building. He moved with grace and assurance, one foot confidently set in front of the other, head high, jacket slung over one shoulder. He stood out from the other pedestrians: radiated cool in the hot summer air, projected controlled calm in the noisy chaos of the street. He turned his head to check out a scantily dressed, jiggly breasted woman passing by, then stopped suddenly, inspected the bottom of his shoe, and wiped it exasperatedly on the curb.

Heather dissolved into giggles. "New York dogs: one. Stud: zero."

The man reached the sidewalk and looked up toward Heather's third floor apartment as if he'd heard them. The women ducked instinctively, then slowly rose together, still giggling, to peek over the sill. Heather's giggles turned into a gasp. He still stared up at the building, now minus his sunglasses. A tingling cascade of electricity skittered down her body and came to rest in the pit of her stomach. "Oh. My. Gosh. The man is gorgeous."

"What did I tell you?" Stephanie reared up slightly to watch him walk into the building.

"No, I mean he's *really* gorgeous."

"That's what I—"

"No, you don't understand. That guy is really, *really*—" Her buzzer rang. "*Oh* gosh. He's here. Okay. Fine. How do I—"

"Calm down. Look at me." Stephanie grabbed her arm. "Don't tell me a mere male has rattled you."

Heather shook her arm free. "Nonsense. He's just a man, in for a very frustrating attempt at seduction. Poor thing." She smoothed the tacky dress over her monster hips and buzzed Jack Fortunato in, barely registering an inner desire to be dressed in a to-die-for minidress instead.

"Aha. Well, I'll sneak down the stairs. I promised you wouldn't know about the bet, which of course you didn't—until I told you. Good luck, and keep your legs crossed." Stephanie blew Heather a kiss and let herself out.

For a few endless minutes, sounds in the apartment became sharply defined. A siren. Shouting teenagers. Car horns in the dense traffic. The nervous rattling of every cell in Heather's body. Then a knock at the door.

"Okay." Heather took a deep breath and reached for the knob. "Here we go."

3

HELLO, I'M JACK. Nice to meet you. You look very nice this evening. And what a nice evening it is. Nice, nice nice; first dates were the pits. Jack watched the door swing open into Marsha's apartment, half-eager, half-terrified to see who lurked on the other side. He couldn't claim to have loved all the women who'd visited his bed, but he'd certainly desired them. Would there be any chemistry at all between him and Ms. Gou-*ber?* About a dozen kids' August and his chin depended on the answer.

The open door revealed his date for the next three weeks. Jack's stomach dropped below sea level. By sheer muscular force, he kept the smile plastered to his face.

No chemistry. None. Zip. Zilch. Nada. *Help.*

"Hello, I'm Jack. Nice to meet you. You look very—" His mind screamed *brown.* He ignored it. "nice this morn—evening." He chuckled, his composure completely shattered. Jack Fortunato's next lover could be the poster child for America's fashion-challenged. How could he even bring himself to kiss her? He'd need a sandblaster to remove the layers of makeup first. He glanced around the apartment to escape the chilling sight, registering impressions of the room's contents. Stuff everywhere: an easel set up in the corner; books and magazines in piles on every surface; camera equipment; a *mirror,* for god's sake—she looked that way on purpose?

"Hi Jack. It's nice to meet you, too."

Jack winced. Her masculine, native–New Yorker voice could cut through a hurricane.

"Come on in." She smiled, and for a moment he forgot what she looked like otherwise. She did have a great smile. He could focus on that. It was a beginning, a slight toehold on what would be a long, grueling climb.

"Would you like a drink before we go to dinner?"

"Drink's fine." He definitely, definitely wanted a drink.

"There's a clear chair over there or I can get some of this stuff off the sofa if you'd—"

"Chair. Chair's fine." He needed to ease into the idea of sitting next to her, gradually condition his mind to accept that he'd have to pretend to crave her proximity.

Her extraordinarily large rear waddled its way into the kitchenette. He shuddered. "Need help?"

"You could get the wine glasses. There's one next to the computer, behind the dictionary, the other's on the white bookshelf next to the silk azalea. I was drying them and on the phone at the same time. I pace on the phone."

He retrieved the glasses, still somewhat shell-shocked, and found a few square inches of clear space on the coffee table. Marsha emerged from the kitchen and deposited a tray on a pile of old newspapers near the glasses. A bottle of French wine, bowls of Greek olives and roasted cashews, a plate of baby carrots— apparently she had more taste in food than clothing.

"Wine?"

"Wine's fine." Several gallons might dull the pain. Might even make him able to bring forth a complete sentence.

She poured the wine, handed him a glass, swept a pile of sketch pads off the sofa and sat, looking at him expectantly. He could have sworn something was amusing her. Probably him. He'd been acting like a complete nerd. Time to take charge.

He summoned his meager acting skills, clinked his glass to hers and made himself gaze into her heavily green-shadowed eyes. "Here's to the promise of a lovely evening, Marsha." He tipped his glass and poured half of it down his throat.

"You're a lot better-looking than I expected; I imagine I was something of a shock."

The half glass of wine leaped down the wrong pipe; Jack responded with a spluttering coughing fit that lasted a full minute, much to his relief. He needed every second to formulate a response. How the hell did one answer that kind of directness? "Well, I...I..." He grimaced, thumped his chest, and resorted to another coughing fit.

"Breathe, Jack. Don't forget to breathe." Marsha rose and pounded him on the back. "Dropping dead on a first date is so tacky."

He managed a grin between the subsiding spasms. The pounding on his back gentled. Her scent escaped its brown imprisonment and reached him. Floral and fresh, innocent but with a kick, like lavender and baby powder with a salty splash of sea air. Pleasant. Arousing even. Totally unexpected.

He recovered, hoping the statute of limitations had expired on her earlier comment about her looks and he wouldn't need to respond.

Marsha sat again and stared at him with interest. Not the kind of interest he was used to. Not the stare of woman to man. More like scientist to lab rat.

"What do you do?" she thundered.

Her sudden question startled him. She had him off balance again; a first for him where women were concerned. "I run our family's restaurant, *La Cucina del Cor.* It means roughly 'Cooking from the heart.'"

"Before that?"

"There is no before that. I started washing dishes after college and moved up. My dad doesn't believe in nepotism. If I hadn't turned out to be qualified, he would have hired someone else."

"I see." She nodded and examined a carrot with considerably more interest than she showed in him.

Jack took another gulp of wine. He felt as if he were bombing at a job interview. She smiled pleasantly, but asked the polite questions without the slightest hint of attraction to him. He laughed inwardly. Exactly what he'd craved for so long, and now he hadn't the slightest idea how to handle himself. He had to seduce this woman in the space of three weeks and he could barely string a sentence together. *Come on, Jack.* He looked around to regain his conversational bearing.

"Are you an artist?" He gestured to the easel, genuinely curious. He wasn't sure if he'd ever laid eyes on someone who looked less creative.

"Photographer. But painting is my passion. It clears my head, works the gremlins out of my soul." She took a sip of wine. "What's your passion, Jack?"

He smiled. Finally, familiar ground. Except he couldn't make sensual eye contact and answer, 'beautiful women like you.' Something else then. Something to make her eyes soften; her lips part; a blush stain her...never mind the blush. Nothing would show through that orange cement she'd trowelled onto her face.

He leaned toward her, making the eye contact through her thick glasses as sensual as he could stand. "My passion? Walking hand in hand on a sandy beach at sunset, baring souls in the twilight, making love under a starry tropical sky." He finished with his voice as low and husky as hers, sent over his sexiest smile, and waited for Marsha to melt.

Marsha showed no signs of melting. Marsha stared back as if he just told her he'd eaten contaminated shellfish and would spend the rest of the evening vomiting in her bathroom.

His smile drooped and disappeared. This would undoubtedly be the longest three weeks of his life. He drained his glass of wine and glanced at his watch. The sooner they got the evening over with, the better. "I think we should—"

"Time to go?" She put her half-empty glass down and jumped up with an ease that surprised him, given her bulk. "I'll get my purse."

"I made reservations at *La Côte Basque*." He bolstered his smile back up. The restaurant had a reputation as one of the most elegant and romantic spots in the city. She couldn't help being impressed by that.

"Oh." She retrieved her purse from behind one of the sofa pillows. "Sounds fine."

Desperation seeped into Jack's mood. He might as well have told her he was taking her to his dental appointment. What was wrong with her? Or, more to the point, what did she think was wrong with him? Faced with the least attractive date in his extensive history, he was striking out big time barely an hour into their meeting.

"Let me get my keys." Marsha squatted next to a large oak desk and started rooting through a wastebasket. "I missed yesterday when I tried to toss them on the desk. Aha, here they are." She held them up and rose easily to her feet. "All set."

They took the elevator down and emerged from the building into the oppressive heat. Jack gave a gallant bow to his date, stepped into the street and lifted his arm to hail a passing cab.

Ten minutes later, he still stood there, sweat beading his face and trickling ungallantly down his back, as every cab in the city of New York sped past, completely uninterested in his taxi needs. He sensed Marsha getting restless behind him and sent her a nervous grin. "Guess they're all pretty busy tonight."

She stepped forward. "May I?"

He put his arm down, slightly irritated. Exactly what did she think she could do that he couldn't? "Is there a technique I'm missing?"

"No, just an attitude." She positioned herself dangerously near the speeding traffic, jabbed her finger directly at an oncoming cab, and yelled, "Yo, Cab-*bie*," in a voice that probably carried to New Jersey.

The cab screeched to a stop in front of them. Marsha turned and shrugged apologetically. "Could be a coincidence."

Jack followed her into the cab and gave the name of the restaurant to the cab driver. The driver turned around and eyed Jack suspiciously. "Never heard of it. You gotta address or what?"

"Never heard..." Jack patted his jacket pockets, knowing he'd left the address at home in Connecticut.

He closed his eyes wearily. "I think it's somewhere around—"

"Fifty-fifth street, between Fifth and Sixth Avenue," Marsha bellowed.

He tried to smile gratefully, but had a feeling his intense desire to go home and crawl into bed showed in his eyes.

The cabbie drove in a style that would put Roger to shame, narrowly missing several opportunities to reduce the city's overcrowding problem. They arrived outside the restaurant with a screech of brakes that bounced Jack's head off the back seat and nearly into the front one on the rebound. He turned to Marsha, intending to send her a glad-that-nightmare's-over grimace. She returned his look calmly, seemingly unperturbed by their myriad brushes with death, and unruffled by the earthquake jolt that announced their arrival. All that ballast must have anchored her firmly to the seat.

He quickly changed his look to one of supreme nonchalance, pulled out his wallet and froze in horror. No cash. Not a single dollar. He'd intended to pay for his train ticket by credit card, but he'd been running behind and had to pay cash on board. He'd intended to visit an ATM on the way to Marsha's, but he'd been late and hadn't wanted to make a bad impression. His lips twisted ironically. He'd intended to be a cross between Romeo and Errol Flynn, but he'd been more like Inspector Clouseau and Big Bird.

Marsha handed the cab driver the fare. "Keep the change."

"Thanks, lady. Good thing he gots you to take care of him."

Jack followed Marsha out onto the sidewalk. "Sorry about that. I'm usually more—"

"Where do you live?" Her tone implied the insult all New Yorkers managed to inject into the question when they knew they weren't dealing with a fellow city dweller.

He sighed. "You mean which planet did my spaceship originate from?"

Her mud-colored eyes widened in surprise, then almost disappeared as she burst into a booming cascade of laughter. Jack grinned. The sound was rich, joyous, and totally contagious. Maybe the evening could be salvaged somewhat. He escorted her into *La Côte Basque* and gave his name to the maître d'.

"Jack who? Fortunato?" The maître d' stared down his large nose with an expression of disdain that reminded Jack of a llama he'd seen at the Bronx zoo. "I'm sorry, sir, we have no reservation in your name."

Jack gaped. Apparently the evening wouldn't be salvaged, even somewhat. "But I made the—"

"As you can see," the llama waved a hoof haughtily toward the crowded dining room, "we're completely booked this evening or I'd try to fit you in somewhere."

"There's got to be a mistake. I called last week and spoke to—"

"You can wait at the bar for a table if you wish, but I can't guarantee one will open any time soon." He closed the reservation book and folded his arms primly.

Heat rose into Jack's face. A man could only stand so much mortification on one date. "Listen, buddy, I—"

"There's a deli right over on Seventh Avenue, the Carnegie, where we can get a mean pastrami sandwich." Marsha tugged gently on his sleeve. "Not so romantic maybe, but really good."

Jack turned around and met her eyes, brimming with amusement, no doubt at his expense. He stared at the ceiling until his urge to take out the evening's frustrations on a nearby llama nose subsided. Maybe it was time to cut his losses. "Do they take credit cards?"

She shook her head, and treated him to another smile. "But there's a cash machine on the way. And they've got great strawberry cheesecake for dessert."

He sighed. Brown Woman to the rescue again. "Okay, Marsha. You're on."

The Carnegie was nearby as she said; customers wolfing down huge meaty sandwiches at tiny tables, walls covered with pictures of celebrity diners. After the formal intimacy of *La Côte Basque,* Jack found the atmosphere infinitely more appealing. Especially when his date did not inspire particularly intimate thoughts. They found a table in a relatively quiet corner and ordered their meals.

"I'm glad you thought of this place." Jack folded his arms on the table and leaned forward, his tension falling victim to the lively atmosphere. Marsha even looked a little less brown. "Do you come here often?"

She raised a thick eyebrow. "Was that a pick-up line?"

He could have cheered. After a fall, get back on the horse. "What would you say if it was?"

"I'd say, 'Yes, I do come here often. Because the food is good and I'm not harrassed by space aliens.'"

He grinned. "Has that been a problem for you?"

"Not tonight." She raised her iced tea. "Tonight I am free to be the real me, Marsha Gou-*ber,* woman unhampered by visitors from other planets. It feels great."

He watched her smile the dazzling smile that seemed so out of place in that horribly orange-tinged face, and tip up the tea for a big gulp. Her movements were carefree and confident, as if they belonged to someone comfortable being herself. Her neck rose above the high collar of her beyond-ghastly dress, showing glimpses of smooth, non-orange skin; her nose was straight and well-formed. Her eyes might even be pretty without all the surrounding gunk. Her mouth, isolated from its surroundings, was positively sexy. He itched to run her through a car wash to see what came out the other side.

The waiter brought their sandwiches and left behind the awkward pause after food arrives, before the rhythm of eating and conversation is established.

"You asked about my passion in life." Jack spoke impulsively. The urge to redeem himself in her eyes had taken him by surprise.

"Yes." Marsha paused with the sandwich midway to her mouth. "Are you going to tell me now, for real? No more macho bull—"

"I promise." He chuckled. She was nothing if not direct. "Not too many people know about my real passion. I love to cook."

The sandwich landed back on Marsha's plate. She sat back in her seat and folded her hands in her lap. "Now that is a surprise. I expected you to say you collect women's underwear—with the women still in it."

"Why?"

"Because men who look like you generally do."

He could only stare. He knew people made this assumption, but had never heard the theory quite so openly expressed. Here was an unremarkable looking woman who took it for granted, merely from the placement of his features, that he played the field for all he could get. Indignation stiffened his spine until he realized the unremarkable woman was remarkably correct. He had spent a tremendous amount of horizontal panting time with women who expected nothing less, and for the most part, nothing more. The arrangement had suited him for a while. Only recently had the thrill given way to longing for something other than dinner and sheet-mussing.

Marsha leaned forward again and resumed eating. She ate with relish, a refreshing change from the starvation habits of the women he usually dated. One more half-finished garden salad and sparkling water would have sent him screaming to a monastery.

She glanced up and caught him watching her. She met his gaze calmly, without signs of embarrassment. Her eyes had depth, and intelligence. Except for their flat, peculiar color, they'd be fairly—

"What kinds of stuff do you like to cook?"

He smacked his brain back into focus. Cooking. "Cooking for me is like painting for you—an emotional outlet. I do whatever appeals to me when the urge hits. If I feel over-challenged, I try something hot and spicy, maybe Thai or Mexican, if I'm working out a problem, something more delicate, maybe Japanese. If I'm depressed, I go for the mega-lasagna every time."

"If you're sad and you know it, say, 'beef stew?'"

Jack laughed. He'd forgotten women could have a sense of humor. How many times had he been faced with a beautiful-but-blank stare over the dinner table after a particular comment, and had to explain he'd been joking?

The waiter took their dessert order and reappeared minutes later bearing enormous slices of strawberry-topped cheesecake.

Marsha turned the plate around, examining the dessert. "Do you have any other siblings besides Roger?"

"One sister, Stellie." He was getting used to her abrupt questions. "We're a close family. Mom still summons us to Sunday dinner every week, though we can't always make it. She's a great cook. She started the restaurant with her dad thirty years ago—it was his retirement project. She married the head waiter, and I came along to help wash dishes." He grinned, wondering why he'd given her his entire family history in response to a simple question. "How about you?"

"I'm an only child. I think my parents were so horrified by what they'd wrought, they stopped after me." She took a bite of cheesecake and made an ecstatic face. "Delicious."

"Why do you say that?"

"Because it tastes good."

"I meant—"

"I know." She grinned and shrugged. "I think they wanted a plain, sensible, hard-working Puritan who'd become a doctor and take care of their old-age aches. Instead, they got a free-spirited, artsy, beaut—" Her mouth snapped shut, as if she'd caught it admitting something naughty.

"A beaut?"

Her eyes widened in panic. "A beaut...ician." She ducked down over her dessert.

Jack tamped down his shock, trying not to imagine what sort of female would come to Marsha for cosmetic advice. She must have lied about being a professional photographer. To impress him? A good sign after all. Showed she wasn't quite as immune to him as she pretended. He could try out his next move soon.

"Listen, we all have to make a living somehow. I'm sure you'll be a photographer someday if that's what you want."

She nodded rapidly and dug into her cheesecake as if it deserved every ounce of her attention. Her mouth twisted in an embarrassed, sad sort of scowl, like the kid who has to sit at an otherwise empty table in the school lunchroom. The strangest urge shot through his system: to hug her close and make her feel safe and happy. He glanced down at the rich cake on his plate. Must be sugar shock. Maybe he could make her laugh instead.

"I always wanted to be a TV chef when I was a kid. Kind of a male, Italian Julia Child, basting roasts in front of adoring millions." He bowed his head as if humbly receiving tremendous applause. "Either that or a champion calf roper."

"And?" Her smile erased the scowl.

"I froze in front of cameras, and my brother never stayed still long enough for me to practice."

"Basting?"

"Roping. Though I did polish off a few of Mom's lamps."

Marsha smiled and pushed her plate away with a

sigh of pleasure. A small blob of cream remained on her lips. Her tongue stole out, felt for the moisture, and dragged across the corner of her mouth and her upper lip, wiping away the stain. At the same time, her scent reached him across the table, as if from a time-release air freshener, sweet, sensual—comforting and exciting all at once.

Unexpectedly, his body responded to the pudgy drab vision in brown across the table. He reached out and took her hand, intending to put into words how much more satisfying the evening was than so many he'd had, when it hit him exactly what he was here for. To get those kids off the street and keep his chin private property. Forget the sincerity; he had to get going on the romance.

"That was very sexy."

She looked up at him without lifting her head. "What?"

He took her other hand. "When you licked the cheesecake off your—"

She jerked her hands out of his, and knocked over a glass of ice water. The liquid streamed down into his lap, beating his reflexive jump back. He gasped. His private anatomy made a hasty retreat to warmer climes. Cold. Very cold.

"Oh, gosh, I'm sorry." Marsha jumped up, reached to blot his pants with her napkin, and snatched her hand back. "What am I doing?"

"Don't let me stop you."

She tossed the napkin on the table and gave him a look that made the ice water seem scalding.

"Shall we go?" He stood up, determined to recapture his advantage. Thank goodness he'd worn black; the wetness hardly showed. He just had to force himself to walk normally. A goose waddle didn't quite cut it for his intended seduction.

Once outside, he moved closer to Marsha so their hands would brush together occasionally. She moved slightly away. He tried again with the same result. By the time they reached the corner, she was practically making love to the storefronts on their left. Circumstances called for a more direct approach.

"Would you like to go dancing?" He could hold her close and nuzzle her orange-free zones.

"I'm not much of a dancer."

"How about a movie?" Romance on the screen, a little more in the seats...

"I have to get up early for work."

"A short walk?"

"I should go home."

He put his arm around her, and bent close to her ear. "I don't want the evening to end just yet, Marsh—"

The rest of her name disappeared in a whoosh of expelled breath. A mailbox had appeared out of nowhere and clipped him in the solar plexus.

Marsha gasped. "Oh gosh, I'm sorry! I should have warned you."

Jack remained doubled over until his diaphragm agreed to resume normal functioning. "No, no. 'S okay—" He wheezed in another breath. "—no problem. I'll get a cab." Better try again another night. The Date Gods had clearly deserted him this evening.

He hailed a cab, and got one on about the fourteenth try this time. During the ride to Marsha's apartment, he considered his options. Sex tonight was out of the question. At this point, he didn't even dare invite himself up to her apartment. The elevator cables would snap, or he'd fall out her window. So it would all come down to the old-fashioned kiss in the doorway. Infamous Romeo, Jack Fortunato, would have to be satisfied with that.

He gave the city traffic a wry smile. As much as he didn't want to lose the bet, as much as his ego had been temporarily bruised, Marsha's reticence pleased him. If she kept this up in the face of his determined efforts, he might regain a morsel of respect for the female gender.

The cab pulled up in front of Marsha's building. He paid the driver and escorted Marsha to her doorway. "I had a really nice time, Marsha."

"Mmm, yeah, me too. Where are my keys?" She bent her head down and rifled through her purse.

He frowned. She seemed to know where every speck of dust was located in her apartment. Why the confusion now? Was she delaying? Maybe even hoping he'd kiss her? Some women were champions of mixed signals after all. He smiled. Maybe the rest of the evening had been an elaborate way of signaling she wasn't going down without a fight. Maybe she didn't really think he'd slunk out of a sewer, or crashed his spaceship in Central Park.

He moved a step closer. Her searching became more frantic.

"Marsha." The top of her head, with its horrible out-of-style hair, seemed suddenly endearing. He moved closer to press his first kiss to a particularly inviting spot.

"Here they are!" Marsha jerked her fist up. The view of the top of her head was replaced by the sight of her knuckles an instant before they punched him in the face. Marsha gasped. He reeled back, putting one hand to his nose, the other out to steady himself.

"Oh gosh, I'm sorry! Do you want to come up and put ice on it?" Her eyes widened; she clapped her hand to her mouth. Apparently the implication of her invitation hit her with the same force as her punch.

"It's dothing. Dot a probleb." He attempted a pleasant smile and wished he hadn't when his throbbing nose protested. "Baybe sub oder dight."

"You want ice on it some other night?"

Jack sighed. "I'll just go hobe ad put sub steak on it. Good dight. Thags a lot for the eveding."

He limped away a few steps in his wet pants and turned back to wave. Marsha stood, watching him. For a second he thought he saw a glimmer of triumph in her eyes. He blinked and realized his mistake. She smiled at him sweetly, a little anxiously even, a touch of tender concern just possibly.

He gave her the thumbs-up sign and continued on toward the subway, gingerly testing the bone in his nose for signs it had shattered. The evening had been a disaster from the moment he rang her doorbell. His cool had been non-existent, his clumsy advances expertly rebuffed.

He rolled his shoulders back and stretched carefully, hoping he hadn't cracked any ribs on the mailbox. No doubt about it. For the first time in his recent dating history, Jack Fortunato was intrigued.

4

JACK SCANNED the contents of his refrigerator. "Steak, steak...no steak. Ham slice, turkey breast, mortadella, chicken wings, tofu, pork chop, leg of lamb...Hmm." He shrugged and heaved the lamb onto his counter. "Closest I have to steak, I'll give it a shot."

He got a glass of water, arranged himself in his favorite chair, and attempted to apply the six-pound leg of lamb to his eye, already swelling shut. A few minutes later, with the weight threatening to implode his head, he put the lamb on an end table and applied his eye to the meat instead, turning every once in a while to gulp water, like a swimmer coming up for air.

All the while his thoughts kept going over the evening with Marsha. Something bothered him besides his clumsiness and uncharacteristic ineptitude. Faced with a female who didn't instantly send his body into mating readiness, he'd been unable to function normally, felt completely out of his element.

Had he forgotten how to approach women as people instead of physical specimens? Had years facing expectations of his behavior based on his looks caused him to fulfill their prophecy? Could he, Jack Fortunato, staunch advocate of women's rights, be a total sexist oinker?

He'd dreamed about that woman outside Stephanie's apartment the previous night, an erotic physical odyssey that would have exhausted an Olympic athlete. He'd woken up sweating, panting, and hard as granite—with no reason to become fixated on her except for the way she looked.

He might as well confess his championing of the stronger sex occurred mainly on the intellectual level. Physically, he'd been out there oppressing with the worst of his gender.

The turmoil in his mind and the smell of the lamb began to churn together to bring on the old familiar impulses. Roasted, with garlic and rosemary, sliced and grilled with mint jelly, butterflied and stuffed with goat cheese and herbs... He glanced at the clock. Nearly nine. He probably better—

The phone rang. He reached out and groped for the receiver, careful not to break contact between his eye and the meat.

"Hey, Jack, it's Roger. What are you doing home so early? Things didn't go so well? Or is she there with you?"

"No, no, they went fine. She's..." His mind was so full of words to describe her, he blanked completely. Marsha was a complicated mixture of every female experience he'd had. His mother's strength and practicality. His sister Stellie's directness and sense of humor. The scent and smile of the sexiest women he'd known. The face, body, and fashion sense of Mother Potter, much-dreaded lord and mistress of his Catholic high school. He considered himself, somewhat immodestly, to be an expert on the topic of females, and this example didn't fit any of his tidy categories. Jack frowned. He liked things tidy. "She's…"

"A real bow wow?"

For some reason, Roger's trademark callous humor irritated him. "She's not so bad. I had an okay time."

"Any action?"

Again, irritation prickled through him. He didn't like the idea of discussing what had happened, between them—or not happened, in this case—in such coarse terms. He rolled his eyes. Marsha must bring out the gentleman in him. "I'm taking things slowly."

"Oh ho! There's a first. Well don't take it too slow. You only have—"

"I know, three weeks." He jerked his head in annoyance and whacked his tender nose on the lamb bone. Ouch.

"What's with you? You sound sorta discombobulated. This gonna be a tougher trip that you thought?"

"I guess you could say that."

"Well I gotta idea. Invite her over to Mom's tomorrow or next Sunday. Lots of people, lots of food, lots of noise. Unthreatening family evening with nice Italian boy, Jack Fortunato. Then you drive her home, her defenses are down, you go up for coffee, and bango, you got her."

Jack winced. "Bango" didn't exactly describe his ideas on making love, even to Marsha. "I don't know, taking her to meet Mom and Dad could give her the wrong idea. She might think I'm serious about the relationship and expect more from me." Or completely the opposite: thinking he was serious might induce her to leave the country.

"Whadya think, they'll sit her down and ask what

her intentions are toward their son? Relax. She'll be another face in the crowd.''

"I'm not sure.'' He adjusted his eye on the meat. "Maybe…'' The rich smell of the lamb permeated his nostrils. Curry? Stew? Something Middle Eastern? "I can't quite…''

"You're about to cook, aren't you? I can hear it in your voice. Okay, never mind. Call me back when you decide.'' Roger hung up the phone.

Jack hauled the leg into the kitchen, one eye on the clock. Nine-thirty. Better keep the recipe basic. A roast, with a simple sauce of pan juices and red wine, while he tried to decide what to do about Marsha Gouber.

Half an hour later, the roast in the oven, the dishes washed, dried and put away, he dialed his parents' home in Brooklyn. Saturday night, they'd still be up, watching old movies. Since their semi-retirement from the restaurant, after so many working weekends, they always spent Saturday nights at home.

On the third ring, he snuck the phone back in its cradle. Calling them was a mistake. He couldn't bring Marsha to his parents' house as if he intended to make her part of the family. If they all loved each other, it would be a disaster. Three weeks from now he'd be out of her life. He couldn't do that to her. He couldn't do that to any woman.

He poured scouring powder over the spotless sink and scrubbed vigorously. On the other hand, his body and ego couldn't take another evening like the one they'd had tonight. Maybe Roger was right. Maybe a less formal, less intimate occasion would help melt Marsha faster.

He gave the sink a final rinse and dialed again. One

ring. Two rings. He slammed the receiver down. The plan wouldn't work. What if she hated his family and the entire occasion? What if she didn't fit in at all? She'd want even less to do with him than she already did. How could he hope to get his kids into camp and his chin out of the spotlight then?

He wiped down the already-clean counters and put the sponge in the dishwasher to sterilize it. The scent of garlic and rosemary started to fill the apartment; he inhaled deeply. So what then for their next date? A trip to a museum? He knew nothing about art; she'd find him boorish. A trip to the zoo? Cute and fun, but with his luck he'd fall into the bear pit, or she'd turn out to be fatally allergic to kangaroos.

He cast a final eye around his immaculate kitchen for anything dirty or out of place, then picked up the phone, and dialed a third time. This time no retreat. "Mom, Jack."

"Giacomo! Mary, Mother of God, thank goodness it's you. Some nut keeps calling and hanging up before we can answer."

"I wanted to ask if I could—"

"What? Justa minute. Hey! Vinnie! Turn down that TV, *e Giacomo.*"

Jack pulled the phone away from his ear. His mother's shout could deafen heavy metal fans. She and Marsha had that much in common at least.

"Now, what did you want to ask your Mama?"

"I want to bring someone to Sunday dinner tomorrow. I know it's last minute, but—"

"Ha! At my table there is always enough food and enough room. Is she a nice girl or another of your bimbo women? Why don't you meet a nice girl, Giacomo? Someone like your sister, someone like your cousin Violetta? Why always the gorgeous ones with brains like salami?''

''This one's different.'' He closed his eyes, waiting for the deluge of questions.

''Different? Different how? Hey, Vinnie, he says this one's different...Your Papa says, 'Thank God for that.' You like this girl? You want me to cook my special *osso bucco?* Impress her?''

''She's just a friend, mom.''

''The best way to start. Your father and I knew each other since we were kids. Friends first, then later *l'amore.* Good for you. We almost gave up hope. Does she like to eat, this girl? I'll make *osso bucco,* you think she likes *osso bucco?*''

Jack grinned. No one could be in his mother's company for more than ten minutes without loving her. No one could be in his mother's company for more than four hours without wanting to strangle her. His worries were misplaced. Marsha would both love and hate the occasion. Roger's plan was brilliant. ''I'm sure she'll like whatever you cook, Mom. I'll call her right away.''

''WELL?''

''Well what?'' Heather slashed a bold stripe of Alizarin Crimson through the center of her canvas, phone clenched between her cheek and shoulder, Mozart's *Jupiter* Symphony blaring in the background. Her date with Jack ended barely an hour ago and Stephanie had called already. Heather hadn't had time to sort out her tumultuous feelings.

''I just talked to Roger who just talked to Jack. Would you care to hear his report?''

Heather put down the brush and turned off the Mozart. "What did he say?"

"He thought you were 'not so bad.' Apparently you made out all right—in that you didn't make out at all."

Heather grabbed the brush again and jabbed into the black paint. For some reason, Jack's "no-kiss-and-tell" policy annoyed her. Ridiculous, given the real nature of their association. He had no reason to keep the non-intimate details to himself. "That's right. Little Jacky never made it to first base."

"I'm settled in with a cup of tea and a blanket. Tell me everything."

Heather splatted the black paint on one over-bright corner with sharp jerks of her wrist. How could she even begin to explain the evening? From the minute Jack Fortunato's incredible presence had darkened her doorway, Heather had been caught in a guerrilla war between her feelings and the ones Marsha should be having. Sharing any piece of the conflict before a victor had emerged might plunge her further into bewilderment. "He's 'not so bad,' either."

"Oh come on, Heather, give. Did he try anything?"

Heather sighed. On the other hand, Stephanie's sense of entitlement to every aspect of Jack and Marsha's evening was justified. Steph had engineered the whole setup after all. Heather's reluctance to share details would only fuel suspicion that Jack had had some effect on her. Nonsense of course. He had no more effect on her than a typhoon on a village of twig huts.

"Yes, he tried everything. I was merciless—you

would have been proud. By the end of the evening I felt sorry for the poor guy.''

''Well don't feel too sorry. François has been knocking on my door every ten minutes, wanting to know when his *le chin* will be available. You have to stay strong for the next date.''

''I sincerely doubt there'll be a next date.'' A particularly vicious splat sent black paint shooting across the entire canvas. ''By the time I punched him in the nose he seemed pretty disenchanted.''

''By the time you *what?*''

''I pretended I couldn't find my keys. Then when he bent down to kiss me, I let him have it.'' Heather loaded the brush with cadmium yellow and surveyed her work critically. ''I didn't think it would come to that. I thought he'd quit much sooner. I figured if the dress and makeup didn't get him, the ice water in his lap would. When he even survived my walking him into a mailbox, I knew I had to take drastic measures.''

She smiled and smeared the yellow into a vaguely triangular blob. Talking about the date this way helped. A comical farce, by Heather Brannen. She wouldn't mention that appearing disinterested in the face of the Eighth Wonder of the World had been the hardest thing she'd done in recent memory. Nor would she let slip that having her fist stop the approach of that incredible mouth at the end of the evening almost cost her her sanity. Without painting to steady herself, she'd be sitting on the floor right now, mumbling nursery rhymes and bouncing her head off the sofa.

''My lord, Heather, now *I* feel sorry for him. So

what's he like? Besides sexy and unbearably gorgeous.''

Heather paused, her brush suspended inches from the canvas. What was Jack Fortunato like? Everything she expected, and nothing she expected. The smooth stud looks, the smooth stud lines, the smooth stud moves...and clumsiness, and awkwardness, and humor and an endearing vulnerability at odds with his perfect build and perfect face. As if he'd been trapped by his looks into a personality that didn't fit him.

"He's not what I thought he'd be."

"Aha. Now we appear to be getting somewhere. You like him and you're surprised."

"I never said such a thing. And we're getting nowhere, as you remember."

"I don't know, Heather, I have this feeling—oh, Lord, it's François again. Hang on, I'll let him talk to you."

Heather's body stiffened. The last thing she needed was another unstable mind to connect with. "No, Stephanie, I don't—"

"*Allo?* Tell me you have not given in to your silly feminine desires."

"No, François." Heather covered the yellow triangle with a dull brown swath. "No need for *le* belt *du* chastity after all."

"Ah! *Bon.* When will you again see the man blessed with the chin of *Diablo?*"

"Most likely never after tonight." The brown swath grew larger, longer, threatened to take over half the painting.

"*Zut, alors,* I hear sadness in your voice. You have no real likings for this man, yes?"

Heather put her brown tirade on pause and frowned

in confusion. *Yes? No?* She couldn't even figure out how to respond to his convoluted syntax, let alone analyze her feelings. She wanted to be left alone. "I'm tired. I want to paint."

"Paint! *Mon, dieu,* Stephanie, she is painting. This is a *désastre*. She will never last three weeks. Never! She is in love already with my chin. The bet will not—"

"Sorry about that, Heather." Stephanie's exasperated voice came back on the line. "Get back to your painting. I'll apply a French sedative and call you tomorrow."

Heather hung up the phone and stared at her canvas. The sight of so much brown made her a little queasy after a whole evening living it. She smeared her brush in the crimson again. Time to become reacquainted with reality. She wouldn't fall victim to some guy for his pretty face, even if he made Mr. Universe look like Frankenstein. The evening had been an assignment, not a date; Marsha had done her work well. Unless Jack Fortunato enjoyed self-abuse, he wouldn't look forward to seeing her again any time soon anyway. From now on, his seduction attempts would be half-hearted and tempered with fear for his bodily safety. Just as well. A tiny and rather annoying instinct warned her he would be tough to resist if his efforts were ever sincere.

She spread a warm crimson glow across the painted surface, intensified the edges of the color with orange and yellow accents, then added touches of maroon to deepen the center. Her emotional balance began to restore itself. Everything would work out fine. The little studio in Connecticut might as well have "Brannen" on the door already.

The phone rang. She groped for the receiver, concentrating on adding tiny flecks of white to brighten and define the perimeter of the shape. Just a tiny spot there, in just the perfect—

"Hi, it's Jack. Am I calling too late?"

Her entire body jerked; the brush squashed a large white blotch onto the canvas.

"Marsha?...Are you there?"

"Yes, yes." Heather pitched her voice down to Marsha's gravelly bellow. "I just...yes. I'm here." She put the brush down and started pacing the apartment, occasionally hopping over piles of books and paper. Why was he calling? Had he decided to sue for assault and battery? Or had he just left something in her apartment? She scanned the clutter distractedly. Nothing looked out of place.

"I wanted to see if you were free tomorrow evening to come to dinner at my parents' house."

Heather froze with one foot lifted to leap over a stack of magazines. He wanted her to meet his *parents?* After all she'd put him through? He should be home licking his wounds and thinking his chin might look nice on subway walls after all. What kind of masochistic weirdo would risk the company of Marsha twice?

"...my whole family has early dinner together every Sunday..." He spoke into the silence, obviously prompting her for some kind of response.

Heather's outstretched leg began to shake from holding it up so long. He planned to try and seduce her in front of his entire family?

"...and my mother's a really good cook..."

Of course. Heather let her leg drop. A clever ploy. Nice safe family dinner to lull her into thinking his intentions toward her were honorable. Then just as Marsha began to relax—wham! Into the sack. What kind of slimeball would use his family that way? Not to mention poor Marsha. Heather slumped into a clear corner of the sofa, irritatingly aware of her traitorous disappointment. Call her an *ad nauseam* optimist, but she'd really hoped he was different from other males of the species.

"...so, I was wondering if you'd like to, uh, join me. There. Tomorrow, that is."

She owed him an answer. She could easily win the bet by refusing all his invitations. But what lesson would that teach him? Wouldn't she be doing womankind a service by continuing to see him and demonstrating further that females were worthy of respect? Honor? Worship even?

She looked down at her bunny-slippered feet and made them wiggle. In the process she'd like to satisfy her curiosity completely. Which impression touched closest to who he was—ruthless macho stud or sweet bumbling soul? This call tipped her toward the former, but what better opportunity to find out than among the people who knew him best?

"...unless...you know, you're busy...or something."

Plus, in all honesty, she wasn't ready to give Marsha up just yet. What a thrill to walk invisibly through an entire evening. To enjoy a sense of privacy and personal space, unfettered by the leering interest of passing males—Jack's leering interest being completely feigned. Marsha's disguise let Heather explore sides of herself she wouldn't otherwise discover.

Heather stood and gave a firm nod. Done. "I'd love to go, thank you, Jack."

"Okay, great." He practically gasped out his relief. "I'll come into the city and pick you up around three."

"What should I wear?" Heather grinned at the brown dress hanging on the bathroom doorknob.

"Uh, Mom's kind of old-fashioned about Sunday dinner, so…" He cleared his throat. "I guess something like what you, uh…" He cleared his throat again.

Heather put her hand over her mouth to stifle a giggle. Apparently brown was not his color. "Something nice, like what I had on tonight?"

"Uh…yes. Nice. Nice is good. Okay. See you tomorrow."

"Tomorrow, Jack." She replaced the receiver and sped to the side of the closet where Marsha's meager wardrobe awaited, excitement rising through her system. Another evening not just like any other. Another challenge. A bit daunting to perform in front of so many people, but Roger would be there if she needed help. Somehow Stephanie had made him agree to the bogus bet.

Heather passed a trifle wistfully over a little black nothing she'd bought on a whim and never worn, trying not to imagine Jack's reaction if he saw Heather in it, and selected a shapeless orange pantsuit from the "Marsha boutique." *Ghastly.* The shade would match her foundation to perfection. His family would spend the entire evening wondering how he could stand being around her. She held the suit under her chin and sent her eyebrows into a Groucho wiggle. With a little luck, Jack would, too.

SUNDAY AFTERNOON AT 3:03, Heather's doorbell rang. She buzzed Jack in then rushed to the mirror

for one last look to make sure no part of Heather
survived the transition to Ms. Gouber. Marsha stared
back, muddy brown eyes wide with nerves. An entire
evening on the stage, playing to various audience
members. Roger, who knew Heather, but hadn't met
Marsha; Jack, who knew Marsha but not Heather; and
a whole family of strangers who didn't know either.
Not your average Sunday in the park.

Jack's knock sounded; Heather ran her hands down
the rough orange poly-blend and opened the door,
feeling like a mutant pumpkin.

"Hello, Jack. How are—" She gasped and clapped
her hand to her mouth. He looked like a stunt man
for another *Rocky* sequel, his left eye bruised and
swollen. She had no idea she'd hit him that hard. Poor
guy. "Did I do that to your eye?" Her words came
out muffled by her hand.

"I've had worse." He reached out, pulled her fingers off her mouth and brought them to his lips.

Heather tensed reflexively, but didn't have the heart
to sock him again. Besides, his lips were incredibly
warm—warm and firm, and rough around the edges.
The way she liked her men.

She swallowed. Her thoughts were taking a dangerously un-Marsha-like turn. In his light suit and tie,
dark thick hair combed back, skin barely shadowed
from his just-shaved beard, sexy mouth curved in a
smile, he could cure frigidity just by making eye contact. In her quest to devastate him as Marsha, Heather
had forgotten how Jack could devastate on his own.
She'd be lucky if her legs continued to prop her up
for the entire evening.

Jack's gaze left her face and travelled down over her outfit; his smile sagged, his good eye twitched. He blinked hard and smiled harder, determinedly stoic, like a kid who'd just been presented with a megadose of nasty medicine. Without a word, he handed her a corsage of exquisite pink sweetheart roses, which clashed so dreadfully with her outfit, she could barely hold back a near-hysterical snort of laughter.

"What a lovely corsage; I'll put it on right away." She fumbled with the pins, struggling to keep Marsha's composure intact, feeling like a nerdy prom date. Jack stepped forward to help, bringing his scent closer, still warm in the air-conditioned room. His knuckles rested lightly on her chest as he guided the pins through the fabric and flowers. Heather gave up breathing; she was sure the rest of her body had already shut down operations. Good thing, or she might indulge the near-uncontrollable urge to wrap herself around his body and cling for the rest of eternity.

"There we are." Jack's right hand still cupped the corsage; his left moved to her shoulder. His gaze glued itself to hers, deliberately sensual, obviously calculating. "I'm glad you're coming with me tonight, Marsha."

He bent forward so slowly she couldn't be sure he had moved until his face was mere inches from hers. She gave a wistful sigh for what she'd be missing, jumpstarted her body back to functioning, and moved her hand to the rosebuds. When would he learn?

"These are so pretty, thank you." She shoved the corsage toward his hand with what would look like an affectionate pat.

"Ungh." Jack jerked his hand away and put a finger in his mouth.

"Oh, gosh, I'm sorry, did I prick you?" She forced her eyes to show concern, instead of envy for his finger as they wanted to. "I have some Band-Aids in a box under the sink behind the—"

"No, no, it's fine. No problem."

He glanced around the apartment; his gaze came to rest on the painting she'd stayed up until four a.m. finishing. Dread seeped through Heather's system. She should have covered the canvas. Jack walked a few paces closer, hands in his pockets, studying her work.

The painting was a blotchy, boiling confusion of colors, reflecting her mood of the previous evening. Passionate reds conflicted with cool icy blues, stomped over flat dull browns almost took over the canvas except for a tight white border that managed to confine them. Everything she'd felt about their date, right out in the open for him to see.

Heather pushed away the dread. He wouldn't see it. What was she worried about? Men had the emotional perception of canned peas. To him it was an amateur-looking mess.

Jack turned his head toward her, brows lifted, his stare intense, quizzical. "Did you paint this last night by any chance? After our date?"

Her eyes widened. Could this be a sign of intelligent life? Had some members of the gender evolved beyond legumes after all? Her mouth opened to speak brilliantly and produced something along the lines of, "Y'huh."

He nodded. They stood silently, looking at each

other. A hundred Marsha-phrases appropriate to the occasion swept through Heather's brain. Unfortunately, she could only stand there inappropriately, trying to interpret his gaze, hoping her own stare hid what she was thinking as effectively. Was it possible someone like Marsha could bring out human traits in men? Had Heather been missing all this simply because she was the victim of a certain arrangement of DNA? Or could Jack be one in a million? She'd dare to hope if she weren't so afraid there wasn't any. He was a man on a mission: to keep his chin off the streets of New York by inviting it into her bedroom.

He took a step closer. The calculating look had left his eyes, replaced by confusion that might have been convincing if she hadn't known about the Big Picture. "Do you see what's happening here?"

Yes. You're trying to talk your way into my bed. "We're about to go to your parents' house?"

"I cooked a leg of lamb last night."

"Ah. Well." She nodded rapidly, wondering when Rod Serling would appear and explain all this to an invisible audience. "That is something."

"Marsha." He glanced rather desperately toward the window as if he hoped it would prompt him on how to continue. "Last night something happened that affected us both. Something I can't really define…"

Heather took a step back, summoning Marsha's ironclad defenses against the opposite gender. *Mayday, mayday. Incoming bull-manure. Commence evasive maneuvers.* "You mean when I punched you in the nose?"

He didn't crack a smile; if anything he looked more

off-balance. "Don't you see? We both went home and had to—"

"What do you do with all that food?"

"What?" His right eye narrowed incredulously to match the left. Heather allowed herself to breathe more normally. Evasive maneuver complete. Subject diverted.

"A whole leg of lamb for one person...that's a lot of meat." She smiled tightly, wondering why her brain allowed her mouth to say "lot of meat" in front of the most desirable man on the planet.

He continued to give her that intense, questioning stare. Then he sighed and closed his eyes for a full second in an extended blink. Heather had a feeling he was suppressing the urge to give a manly yell and punch the wall. Was he furious she'd sidestepped his come-on again? Or frustrated at his failed attempt to communicate honestly?

When he opened his eye-and-a-half, the sensual, calculating look had returned. Marsha caught Heather's disappointment and threw it out the window. Anyone in Jack Fortunato's current position would have to be guilty until proven innocent. No matter how well he played the sincere lover, he could only convince her he was genuine by abandoning the phony seduction attempts.

Jack grinned and moved to escort Heather to the door. "Let's just say having a lot of meat has never been a problem for me, Marsha."

"Oh, really, Jack?" Heather plastered a sweet smile onto Marsha's face and preceded him out the door. "When I come across too much, I hack it in pieces and run them through the grinder until there's not a single fiber left intact.''

Jack's cocky grin faded; his Adam's apple leapt above his collar in an abrupt swallow.

Heather pulled the door shut behind him. *Okay, mister, you're on.* Marsha was more than ready for the evening.

5

"HERE WE ARE, parking place and everything." Jack pulled up opposite a row of brownstones, each with flower-filled window boxes and iron railings running alongside the front steps. "We're a little early. We'll surprise them."

Heather almost laughed. Surprise them? They'd suffer cardiac arrest. Marsha wasn't exactly Jack's usual squeeze. Even if he'd tried to warn his family, Heather doubted they'd be prepared. Ms. Gouber defied description.

"My sister Stellie will be there, and her husband, R. James." Jack wiped his forehead and adjusted the collar of his polo shirt.

He'd seemed nervous during the entire ride to Brooklyn. In abstract, the nice family evening must have seemed a brilliant way to further his standings in the bet. But Heather would guess that faced with reality, he was having second or third thoughts. With Marsha by his side, he risked losing his stud reputation in front of his nearest and dearest.

"My brother Roger will be there too, though Stephanie can't make it tonight."

"Aha." Heather suppressed a smile. She and Stephanie had agreed the strain of the evening would be considerable without the added temptation to giggle together over every new bizarre aspect.

"Then there's Grandpa Giacomo..." Jack put the car in reverse and turned to back into the parking space. "Uncle Tony, and Aunt—Damn!"

"Aunt Damn?"

"Aunt Mary." He scowled. "I forgot, it's her birthday. That means the twins will be here, too, with their four kids."

"Is that bad?" She could guess. Six more people to watch him carry out the charade of desiring Marsha's company. Bad.

"No, no. Of course not." Jack backed the car into the parking place, pulled forward, then shifted into reverse once more and checked his rearview mirror. "Just more of a crowd than I expected. I wanted Mom and Dad to get to know you a little."

Heather jerked her eyes to his face. Not a trace of insincerity in his voice. Not a sign of guilt or remorse over the way he was using his family to get to her. Maybe Marsha should turn up the heat a little.

"Jack, may I be frank for a moment?"

"I'd rather you stayed Marsha, but if you want to be Frank..." He grinned at her rolling-eyed expression. "Sorry, go ahead."

"Women would come back from the dead to go out with you. A blind date is one thing, but why do you want to see someone like me again?"

For a split second, his features assumed the look she'd predicted: wary, trapped, near-apoplectic. Then, unexpectedly, his expression cleared, became warm and natural. "Because you're funny, and smart, and interesting. And to be honest..." he reached out and slowly traced her lips with his thumb, "...your mouth looks like it would taste good."

Heather swallowed and glued her tongue to the back of her teeth to keep it from emerging to explore his skin. *Marsha, help.*

His thumb gently parted her lips. He started a slow lean forward, cupped her chin and pulled her face to meet his. Heather beat back a cry of anguish. He was going to make her fend him off *again?* The guy deserved an A-plus for persistence. She wasn't sure how much more she could take.

Luckily, Marsha remained unmoved. She put her hands on Jack's thigh as if to stop herself unbalancing toward him, smiled pleasantly into his face, and leaned her weight on his leg.

The pressure transferred down to his foot, depressed the accelerator, and sent the car rolling backwards into an embrace with the bumper behind them, triggering an ear-blasting siren alarm.

Heather regretfully yanked her hands back from the hard strength of his thigh and clapped them to her ears. "Oh, gosh, I'm so sorry," she yelled.

Jack jerked the car into gear and dragged it forward. "So much for surprise," he yelled back. "My family will be out in droves to get a peek at you."

"Why?" Heather shouted. "You never bring women over?"

"What?"

"Women." Heather pointed to herself, then the house. "Bring them here, ever, you?"

"Once in a while," he bellowed. He put the gear in neutral and switched off the motor. "But, I told them you were...uh..."

"A Plain Jane?"

"No!" The car alarm stopped; the word came out a deafening shout into the sudden silence. Jack turned toward Heather, face tense with concern, eyes earnest. "No. I don't think of you that way. I said you were different from the—"

"Hey, Jack! You going to keep her in there all day or let us meet her?" A tall, slender woman stood on the front steps, hands on her hips. Her nearly-black hair was pulled back into a pony tail that frizzed out of control behind her head like a giant mushroom cloud; her pronounced nose jutted out from under dark eyes and brows, over full lips. Everything about her was large, but she managed to be beautiful, in an exotic, almost masculine way.

"That's my extremely no-nonsense sister, Stellie. I think you'll like her."

"I'm sure I will." Heather pushed open the car door and got out, wincing at the blast of heat that melded her suit's polyester fibers to her skin. She walked toward Stellie, hand outstretched, smiling for all Marsha was worth.

Stellie took her hand in a warm clasp. "Hey, bro." She spoke to her brother with her eyes on Heather's face. "You weren't kidding when you said she was different. Look at this." She grinned an enormous scarlet-lipped grin and pumped Heather's hand. "You can't imagine how sick we were of the plastic women he brought home. Glad to see he finally got real. Welcome, Marsha."

Heather returned the handshake and smile, a little disoriented. Women seldom greeted her with that kind of warm effusiveness. They either assumed she was after their men, dismissed her as brainless, or avoided her out of some weird competitive impulse. If Stellie's reaction was anything to go by, Marsha would be the hit of the party.

"What the heck happened to you?" Stellie gave her brother a hug and a raised-eyebrow stare. "Get fresh a few times too often?"

Heather tightened her lips to hide their smile. A bad start for Jack. He was counting on his family to convince Marsha he was just another boy-next-door.

Jack slid Heather a sheepish glance. "Actually, I—"

"Giacomo, Marsha, *benvenuto,* welcome!" A tiny, comfortably plump woman emerged from the house and stood at the top of the front steps. "Eh, Giacomo, what happen'? You get some man jealous for his woman?"

Heather allowed herself the smile. Jack looked as if he suddenly longed to visit another continent.

Mrs. Fortunato beckoned to Heather without waiting for Jack's reply. "*Vieni, vieni,* come here. Let me get a look at this." She grabbed Marsha's arm and peered up into her face with black lively eyes. "Ah, Giacomo, you gotta winner here. Lotta character in those eyes, lotta heart in that smile. *Si, bene.* You finally bring Mama a real woman. Come in, come in, Marsha. Let's see how good you can eat."

She half-escorted, half-dragged Heather into the house. Heather glanced back and caught Jack's grin of relief. Attention had been diverted away from his predatory habits. Marsha had been invited into the fold. Now he only had to ride out the evening and launch his attack later, on a victim mellowed by Chianti and hospitality. Or so he thought.

Heather grinned back at him, fully prepared for battle, and stepped through the foyer. The Fortunato house was blessedly cool, cluttered, but clean, and boasted lived-in comfort that made Heather want to curl up in a corner with a book for days on end. The living room was overfurnished with enormous upholstered chairs, each occupied by its own dark, heavyset, TV-watching male, and overdecorated with paintings, photographs and porcelain figurines. A complex assortment of appetizing smells floated through the air, dominated by herb-infused tomato and garlic. Four children of various mobile ages raced in from another room, screaming and laughing, then raced out again.

"Hey, Vinnie." Mrs. Fortunato shouted over the kids' noise and the on-air babble of baseball announcers. "Marsha's here, *la donna di Giacomo.*"

The men turned. Five sets of dull, TV-glazed eyes widened and stared at Marsha with astonishment, then blinked and crinkled into polite, welcoming smiles. All except for Roger, who shook his head rapidly and stared again, like a cartoon character doing a double take, mouth hanging open until he glanced at his brother and snapped it shut.

Heather beamed at all of them, from the very-ancient Grandpa Fortunato through the youngest, who must be the father of the squealing quartet. Their reaction thrilled her. Not a leering glance in the place. No chance of dull flirtations, straying hands or wives running for their husbands' firearms. Marsha was a lucky woman.

The children ran screaming back into the room and collapsed on top of each other in a wriggling mass of arms, legs and hysteria. The largest man, clearly Jack's father, rose from his lounger with obvious effort, as if he were leaving part of his body behind him.

"Dad must think you're something special if he leaves The Chair." Jack whispered the words into her hair, his chest close to her shoulder, hand touching her arm. She stood there, trapped into inaction by Heather's urge to melt against him and Marsha's to let her elbow make immediate and violent contact with his abdominal wall.

"Hey! You little monkeys pipe down there." Mr. Fortunato swatted the nearest child's behind with agility that belied his slow rise from the chair. He advanced, hand outstretched, deep set intelligent eyes narrowed curiously. "Marsha, eh? You give him that shiner?"

"Uh...yes." She shook his hand, wondering if she should have called him sir. "It was an accident."

"I bet he deserve it. How long you know this guy?" He gave his son an affectionate whack.

"Just two days."

"Two days, eh? That's two days too long for a nice girl like you." He leaned forward confidentially, still holding her hand. "Take my advice. Dump him on his ass. He's no good for women. No good." He turned and went back to his chair, playfully swatting another juvenile rear on the way. Heather swallowed a giggle. She had a feeling the exchange would be the extent of their contact for the evening.

The warm male body tensed perceptibly behind

her. "Dad has some…exaggerated ideas about my previous relationships."

"Really?" Heather swung around to face him and folded her arms across her chest to indicate Marsha expected further clarification. "How so?"

Jack look startled for a second, then shoved his hands in his pockets and exhaled through pursed lips. Heather allowed herself an invisible smirk of satisfaction. Gotcha.

"Well, he seems to think I…that is, that I—"

"Subscribe to the Babe of the Month Club?" Heather raised Marsha's thick eyebrows and blinked like a judgmental school marm.

"Something like that." He grinned sheepishly. "But he's wrong, I promise."

"I see." She lowered one eyebrow into a skeptical glare. "Only the Every-Other-Month plan?"

"No, Marsha. Not for a long time." He smiled as if she were the only person in the room and took a step closer. "Especially not since I met you."

Heather put her hands to her chest as if overcome with emotion. "Two whole days off? I'm beyond flattered."

He shook his head and reached down for her hands. "You know what I mean."

Heather made Marsha return his intimate smile. "I think I really do, Jack."

A little boy dashed by behind her. Heather leaned back slightly to intercept him. He spun off Marsha's rear and sent her lurching forward to land heavily on Jack's foot.

"Oh, I'm so sorry." Heather clapped her hands over her mouth in mock-horror to hide her giggle.

Like those smiling clown punching bags, Jack just kept popping back up for more. She had to admire his determination. "Is your foot okay?"

"'S fine." He tried to smile, body stiff in obvious pain. "Didn't hurt at all."

"I'm so glad." She pushed her glasses up her nose and smiled radiantly. "You were telling me about your experimental forays into chastity…"

He gave a tight smile. "Actually, I think I'll skip—"

"Giacomo! You didn't introduce her to everyone? You didn't ask her to sit down? *Mio dio,* who taught you those manners?" Jack's mother came in from the kitchen trailed by Stellie and three warmly-smiling women who must be Aunt Mary and her twin daughters, holding trays of champagne glasses and plates loaded with antipasti. The four children emerged from their tangle on the living room floor to run, screaming, out of the room again. "Marsha, pardon this chaos. You must think we're savages."

"Please don't apologize—it's wonderful." Heather accepted a glass of champagne from Aunt Mary, who went on with her daughters and Mrs. Fortunato to make the rounds of the room. "At my parents' house you can hear dust hitting the floor—or you could if Mom allowed any in the house."

Stellie erupted into loud laughter. "Sounds like Jack's place—he's the clean sheep of the family. Have you been over there yet?"

Heather shook her head. Nor would she be going any time soon. Jack was hard enough to resist when she could keep him off-balance. On his own turf he'd be deadly.

A masculine arm slid around her waist to the small of her back. Heather started to move away, but caught Stellie's eyes on her and decided to spare Jack the embarrassment this once. Plenty of time for revenge later.

"I hope she'll come over soon," he said. "I want to cook for her."

"Cook?" Stellie's sharp gaze shot to her brother, then bounced back and forth between him and Marsha. "How long have you known each other?"

"Since yesterday." Jack gave Marsha's thick waist a little squeeze. Heather tensed, hoping the padding felt natural, and wondering if she should find another excuse to stamp on his foot. She didn't relish being unveiled here.

"Yesterday." Stellie's eyes discontinued their strobe action; a smile spread over her face. "It hits you that way sometimes. R. James and I knew we wanted to get married after our third date."

Jack's arm fell away. He seemed to have a sudden urgent need to clear his throat repeatedly. Heather tried to choke down her laughter, but came up with an undignified splutter she hoped sounded like a sneeze. Stellie had unwittingly accomplished Marsha's goal of fending Jack off, albeit more creatively than stamping on his foot. Apparently Jack wasn't quite ready to take Marsha for a stroll down the aisle.

"Hel-loooo, Marsha. I'm Stephanie's boyfriend, Roger." Roger came up and shook her hand, apparently recovered from the shock of seeing her, eyes brimming with mischief. "I confess I was dying of curiosity to meet you. Jack hasn't brought a woman over in quite a long time. You must be someone really…special.'' His mouth twitched.

Heather narrowed her eyes, warning him to be careful. He buried his nose in his champagne glass, jaw clenched against the obvious need to snicker.

"What do you do, Marsha?" Stellie smoothed the awkward moment with her question, unaware she'd just created another. Roger would probably burst a blood vessel when he heard Marsha's chosen profession. Heather opened her mouth to change the subject.

"Marsha's a beautician." Jack made the announcement in a firm voice, without a trace of irony, as if he were daring them to laugh.

Roger's body convulsed; he sprayed a mouthful of champagne back into his glass and received an elbow to the ribs from his sister.

"How nice," Stellie said. "Where do you work? I'll stop by sometime and see you."

Where did she work? Heather smiled brightly, mind spinning in panic. "I…uh, actually I'm more of a freelance beautician at the moment."

Roger went rigid, stifled a whimper and shuffled away, apparently unable to take any more.

Stellie nodded politely. "Just starting out?"

"Y'huh." Heather clutched her champagne as if she were trying to squeeze the liquid through the glass. This was not a comfortable moment.

"Everyone starts somewhere." Stellie put a friendly hand on Heather's shoulder. "If you need someone to practice on, I'm happy to—"

"Okay, everybody listen up." Jack's mother raised her glass and surveyed the room. Stellie, Heather and Jack swung around, probably equally grateful for the

rescue from their conversation. "I gotta announcement. Everybody find a seat and pay attention."

Jack guided Heather over to a crimson sofa draped
in scarves and sat as close beside her as Marsha's
large rear would allow.

"First, Happy Birthday to Aunt Mary." The group
cheered and toasted Aunt Mary, who beamed, bowed
and turned beet red. "Second, something very special.
Finally, finally, finally, Stellie and R. James are gonna
make Vinnie and me grandparents in February."

A split second of silence was followed by a giant
roar of approval. Jack shot off the couch and enveloped Stellie in a tremendous, rocking bear hug from
which only the frizz of her pony tail emerged. The
rest of the family followed, pounded R. James on the
back and joined the brother-sister embrace.

Jack threw his head back for a whoop of joy, then
kissed the top of Stellie's head and squeezed her until
she was breathless, laughing, pleading for release. He
let her go; his eyes met Heather's over the rejoicing
bodies. She smiled and raised her glass, moved by the
family's uninhibited celebration. News that big in her
family rated a paternal nod and a plastic-surgery-
restricted maternal smile, maybe a pat on the hand.

Jack extracted himself from the familial tangle,
moved back to the couch and pulled her to her feet.
"Cheers, Marsha." He retrieved his champagne and
clinked his glass to hers. "Sorry to desert you. Stellie
and R. James have wanted this for so long. It's been
hard on all of us."

Heather sipped her champagne and looked up into
his face. Even with the nasty bruise, his eyes were
boyish, electrically alive, his color high, his breath

still coming fast. He swallowed his champagne and laughed, as if his exuberance refused to be contained and escaped when he wasn't paying attention.

Tears gathered unexpectedly in Heather's eyes, threatening to wash skin-colored paths through the orange on her face. To say the evening hadn't turned out as she expected was like saying the edge of the universe was pretty far away. This man cared deeply for his family, took their happiness and sorrow as his own, wasn't embarrassed to show love or joy.

A slow, familiar ache grew in her heart until she felt she'd disappear into it, like a body into quicksand. She wasn't sure what hurt more: that Heather didn't have this kind of love in her life, or that she'd been able to glimpse it only through Marsha.

"Okay, *mia famiglia,* into the dining room everybody." Mrs. Fortunato herded her still-jubilant clan to the dining room where a feast awaited that could have fed Heather's family for two weeks. "*Mangiamo.* Let's eat!"

Heather took her place between Jack and R. James, so aware of Jack's presence beside her she might as well have been sitting in his lap. He turned toward her, winked his good eye, and gave a smile that left her feeling just-kissed. She managed a smile in return and reluctantly identified another awareness.

Heather Brannen, aka Marsha Gouber, was starting to want to lose the bet.

"*Ciao,* Marsha." Mrs. Fortunato surprised Heather with a warm hug. "Tell Giacomo to bring you again soon. I love a woman who can eat."

"Nobody who's tasted your cooking could worry

about calories.'' Heather patted Marsha's bulging stomach, feeling like her own wasn't far behind.

''*Brava. Arrivederci, Giacomo.* You bring this woman back soon. She fits in our family just right.''

''Bye, Mom.'' Jack gave his mother an embrace that had Heather thick-throated again. When she took leave of her own mom, she got a tiny tight Queen's wave on the way down her parents' immaculately edged front path. She blinked furiously. What the hell was the matter with her tonight? She had the emotional balance of a two-year-old.

Jack escorted her down the steps to his car and settled her in. Heather gave one last wave to Mrs. Fortunato, leaned back against the headrest and sighed. It had been a perfect family occasion, something dreamed up by Norman Rockwell. Everyone ate until movement became practically impossible. The married twin cousin took her sleepy kids home. Jack's mother put on Mario Lanza records and the rest of the family gathered in the living room for coffee and conversation that gradually dwindled into contentment.

Sometime during the music, Jack reached over and took Marsha's hand, occasionally running his fingers lightly over hers. By that time, even Marsha was so completely absorbed in the spell of the evening, she'd been unable to summon any anti-pass weaponry. They sat there for what seemed like hours, side by side on the sofa, Heather's every sense completely sated.

Heather sighed again, buckled her seatbelt, and stretched. ''I don't know when I've had such a good time. Your family is so wonderful.''

"And yours isn't?" He pulled the car out onto the street.

"Let's just say we don't spend a lot of time rejoicing in our 'family-ness.'"

He glanced at her in concern. "Sounds like a lonely existence."

"I don't mind so much any more." Heather stared out at the grimy cityscape, wondering why that sounded so sad. "My childhood, however, was a study in isolation."

"This may sound completely nuts to you, but I had a lonely childhood, too." He smiled in response to her look of disbelief. "I wasn't that close to Roger and Stellie growing up. I was older, more serious…tidy." He chuckled. "They were carefree, sloppy and silly together. Then…" He looked over his shoulder and changed lanes to avoid a stopped car.

"Then what?" She held her breath, certain he was about to confide in Marsha, and certain he didn't make confiding an everyday habit.

"It's hard to put this without sounding egotistical, but I had a tough time at school, because…" He grimaced.

Understanding and sympathy flooded Heather's body. "Because of your looks."

He glanced at her in surprise. Obviously he hadn't expected Marsha to comprehend the curse that went along with a pretty face. But Heather knew every nuance of everything he'd felt. Always the center of flatterers' attention, avoided by others who might have been friends, but who didn't want to wait in line or be counted among the flatterers.

She stirred in her seat, a rush of adrenaline making

stillness impossible. "I know how…that is, I can *imagine* how you felt. Kind of like a glow-in-the-dark minnow in a shark pool."

"Yes." He nodded, shifted into a higher gear.

Yes. The thrill accelerated through her, a mixture of energy and euphoric relief. He knew. He could understand more than anyone she'd ever met. "Like no matter what you did, no one changed their opinion of you because they only had an opinion of your looks, not of you."

"Yes." He slapped the steering wheel; the car went faster. "Yes."

Yes. Yes. The floodgates burst. "Never allowing anyone too close in case they wanted you only to advance their social standing. Never allowing anyone true intimacy because they might be after bathroom wall graffiti instead of your heart."

"Yes. Yes." The car sped down Henry Street, flying past cars, dodging pedestrians, nearly taking off into the sky. *"Yes."*

She turned toward him, heart racing, straining against the seat belt to lean closer. "That's why today was so special for me, Jack. You brought me to meet your family as if you really want to get to know me. Most guys take one look and all they want is to get me in the sack."

The car screeched to a stop for a red light and bounced them forward, then back. Jack turned toward her, his look frankly quizzical.

Heather's stomach acquired extra gravity and sank down toward the Earth's core. She'd been so caught up in the moment of true connection, of the mutual empathy she'd been starved for her whole life, she'd forgotten who she really was tonight. Marsha Looks-Like-Goober-Sounds-Like-Gou-*bear*. The realization practically crushed her. He hadn't shared his soul with Heather; he'd shared it with Marsha. "I...mean they take one look and want me in a burlap sack," she whispered.

Jack shook his head. The light changed to green; he accelerated to a reasonable speed. "This is probably out of line, Marsha, but you seem to have some grossly exaggerated idea that you're unattractive. Honestly, it couldn't matter less to me what you look like. I enjoy being with you more than any of the so-called beautiful women I've dated." He reached over and squeezed her hand. "I just wanted you to know that."

"Thank you." Her voice came out in an emotional zigzag.

They drove the rest of the way to Greenwich Village in silence. Inside Heather's brain, however, the noise was so loud it drowned out any hope of drawing rational conclusions. Yesterday, she could easily have ignored that comment. But after seeing Jack in the new light his family cast today, she was terribly tempted to believe him.

She let her wig-encased head lean against the window with a thump. How ironic that a man would find it easier to get past her looks when she dressed down than when she dressed up. Jack had just given what Heather craved all her life—to Marsha. If she took her get-up off now, he'd probably throw her out of the car and back over her. To search for inner beauty in someone plain was deemed noble. To search where beauty already existed on the surface? Most people thought it a waste of time. Heather would strike out where Marsha had scored.

Jack pulled the car into a space several blocks from her apartment. "I thought I'd park here so we can walk some. I'm not ready to let go of you yet."

They walked down Bleeker Street toward Seventh Avenue. A light evening breeze danced over them, sweeping away the heat still rising from the sidewalk. Crowds strolled alongside, singles and couples peeling off occasionally to duck into restaurants or one of the late-night markets displaying produce outside the store. Someone passing out leaflets for massage therapy shoved one into Heather's hand. Here, in the vastness of Manhattan, she felt part of a community—of people escaping hot, cramped apartments to revel in the cooling city nightlife.

A group of teenage girls walked by, caught sight of Jack and burst into squeals and giggles. A knockout in a next-to-nothing red minidress smiled provocatively. Two well-dressed perfectly coiffed women nudged each other and ogled him as they passed. Jack reached for Marsha's hand, smiled down at her and drew her closer. Heather gaped back, warmth spreading through her. With every babe in the city ready to drop for him, he wanted to be with Marsha. Her opinion of Jack was changing fast.

They turned a corner and approached her building. Heather shrunk her steps, willing time to slow to sloth speed so she could treasure every remaining instant in Jack's company tonight. Who knew when the pressures of the bet would reassert themselves and he'd revert to his transparent attempts to score with Marsha?

She turned to peek at him and put her brain on super-alert to memorize every detail. The strength and grace of his saunter; the warmth of his fingers; the way his eyes crinkled exactly like the rest of the Fortunato family when he smiled at her; the way his mouth looked as it descended to—

She had no time to jerk away. Maybe she didn't want to. Jack kissed her with perfect aim on Marsha's orange-y lips. A long kiss. A potent kiss. A kiss that didn't leave her any room for backing out. Marsha might be the intended recipient, but Heather took over and let Jack Fortunato kiss her; responded without thought to consequences; immersed herself in the desire racing through her.

"Yeah. You go, girl."

A chorus of applause and whistles broke into her consciousness. She swung around and faced a group of kids, probably high school students, apparently enjoying the evening's performance. One very-artsy girl focussed her camera and took a picture of what must be a zombie haze of lust and confusion on Heather's face.

She blinked at the flash and shook her head. Photography. François. The bet. She had to stop this.

"Ignore them." The deep male whisper behind her sent replay shivers through her body. "Let's go."

"Where—" Her deep female whisper sounded like it belonged to a lovesick amphibian. How could she have let him kiss her? Surprise attack notwithstanding, Marsha had to keep him at a good deal more than lip's length at all times. Heather cleared her throat and tried again. "Where do you think we're going?"

"To your apartment. I want to kiss you again.

Without the audience.'' His voice, low and close to her ear, resonated with sincerity, not a discernible trace of the macho-man-on-the-make tone that left her cold.

Heather closed her eyes for an endless second, trying to ignore the magnetic pull of his body behind her, and marshalled her alter ego's stoic resistance. Marsha couldn't fail her now. ''I can't invite you up. I have to go…somewhere.'' She rolled her eyes. *Nice one, Marsha.*

''Where?'' He turned her toward him, eyebrow raised into a can't-wait-to-hear-this-one expression.

Heather's mouth opened to deliver a confident response. Unfortunately, she had no idea where Marsha would have to go on a Sunday evening.

''Kiss her again.'' The student's shout kicked Heather's brain back into functioning.

''I have a class.''

''Oh?'' Jack's eyebrow arched further into skepticism. ''What are you taking?''

Panic erased her creativity. She looked desperately around for an idea. Her hand sent a signal to her brain which registered an object in her fingers. She glanced down and crumpled the leaflet to obscure the writing from Jack's view. ''Massage. I have my massage therapy class. It's extra credit for my beautician degree.''

''Massage class.'' His mouth tightened into a disbelieving line.

''Yes.'' Heather pasted an extra-earnest look on Marsha's face, while she gave herself a series of painful mental smacks. *Massage?* Why hadn't she said something more believably Marsha-ish? Like macramé or bootmaking?

"Okay." Jack's tight mouth stretched into a sly smile. "I'll let you go on one condition."

"What's that?" She eyed him warily. Whatever his condition, it was bound to make winning the bet that much harder.

"You let me come over Saturday night."

She tried not to look too pleased. That was it? Not nearly as bad as she expected. On Saturday she'd be six days removed from the magic of this evening. Six days to forget his kiss, to bury her growing suspicion that there was much more to Jack Fortunato than macho predator. And six days closer to the end of Marsha's bizarre three-week adventure.

"I'll bring dinner." He took a step closer and fixed her with his deep gaze. "And you can give me a full-body massage for dessert."

6

"ROGER, it's me." Jack squeezed the cordless phone between his chin and shoulder and stepped over the rim of the tub.

"What the hell is that noise? Where are you calling from, the shower?"

"Uh. Yeah." He steeled himself and moved forward. The icy stream hit his chest and ran down his body. He yelled, half-expecting steam to start rising off his groin.

Roger gave a shout of laughter. "A cold one! Guess that answers my question about your date."

"Rog, I need help."

"Oh, boy. What's cooking?"

"Veal stew, braised endives, tomatoes *Provençales, foccacio* with—"

"Jack, I meant what's happening? What's going on?"

"Oh." Jack contemplated the gooseflesh on his abdomen. What *was* going on? That's what he hoped Roger could help him figure out. He'd kissed Marsha out of pure friendship, affection even, prepared for the clay smell of makeup and the tight pucker of disinterested lips. Instead, her enticing seaside-and-lavender scent hypnotized him, her mouth opened willingly, her passion ignited his to a degree that still made movement uncomfortable.

"I had a good time with her. I even thought we were getting somewhere. Then, brrr, the glacial freeze-off. I'm actually taking this shower to warm up."

Roger tsk-tsked. "I figured you'd hit a home run tonight. You guys seemed totally in tune with each other."

"That's what's so frustrating. I think we are. When I'm with her, I feel energized, and challenged. I can talk to her more easily than any woman I've dated before, about things I've told no one else. She even seems to understand. When I kissed her tonight, man, it was like—"

"Uh, Jack?"

"What?" Jack yanked his arm back down to his side, unaware he'd been illustrating his point with grand wet gestures through the shower spray.

"This isn't about the bet anymore, is it?"

Jack froze, temporarily numbed in his body and mind. He mentally replayed his rambling speech about Marsha and realized he hadn't once mentioned the bet. He hadn't even thought about the kids and how much they needed him. Roger was right. After that one tantalizing glimpse of what it could be like to get close to Marsha, he'd been genuinely upset by her abrupt withdrawal.

Great. That's all he needed.

"Just my luck." He leaned forward to ice his chaotic brain in the frigid water, then remembered the phone at his ear and jerked back. "Stuck on the one woman I've encountered who thinks I have all the charm of Godzilla."

"Hmm. Maybe she's just scared of you."

"No." Jack shook his head. "No woman could kiss like that and be afraid."

"Worry not, brother mine. In my heart of hearts I feel this will work itself out. Give it a couple of weeks. In the meantime, how about a little perverse psychology?" He chuckled. "Perverse psychology. I gotta remember that one."

"Uh-huh." Jack turned his back to the spray, his front sufficiently cooled. "Go ahead, I'm all ears."

"Okay, she holds out on you and makes you nuts, right? So, simple, simple, you do the same to her."

"You mean back off?" Jack frowned. Getting through to Marsha today had been a miracle after all his foiled attempts. What good would retreating do? "I don't see how—"

"When's your next date?"

"Saturday. She's supposed to practice on me for her massage therapy class." A vivid picture popped into his mind of Marsha's hands slowly caressing his entire body. She had very sexy hands—long, slender fingers that looked soft and strong. He groaned and turned his front to the water again.

"Massage therapy class?" Roger's voice rose, as if he were trying very hard not to laugh.

Jack bristled. "This isn't funny, Roger."

"Sorry, sorry. Look, here's what you gotta do. Call her up Friday—tell her you can't make it, you're not sure when you can reschedule. Make up some reason—believable but suspicious. Tell her you'll call soon, nothing more specific, and no chitchat. If my guess is right, which of course it is, within a week you'll need to lay in a hefty supply of condoms."

Jack frowned harder. He hated games involving someone he cared about. And he might as well admit he cared about Marsha. But if the alternative to Roger's plan was grovelling and whining to her about how she wasn't letting him close enough…

Jack twisted off the faucet and stepped out of the tub. No way. He liked to think of himself as a sensitive twenty-first-century kind of guy, but he wouldn't stoop to wimphood. Maybe Roger's idea would work. At least it spared Jack further injury against the brick wall of Marsha's resistance.

He wrapped a towel around his waist and nodded. "I'll try it for a week. If it doesn't fly, I still have time to win the bet before the three weeks are up. I owe the kids that much."

"Brilliant decision." Roger cleared his throat. "So, uh…you think you'll want to see Marsha after the three weeks?"

"Probably, why?"

"Oh, nothing. It's great. Great. Look, I gotta go call Stephanie. Good luck."

Jack clicked off the phone and laughed. His feelings for Marsha obviously surprised Roger as much as they surprised him. He hadn't felt this giddy over a female since Katie Vankowski kissed him under the jungle gym in seventh grade. Come to think of it, Katie had looked a little like Marsha. Maybe he was subconsciously turned on by the Seventies.

He grabbed the towel from his waist and began to dry his arms and chest, bellowing out an admittedly off-key version of "Afternoon Delight." Roger's plan would work. Jack should have figured it out himself. When he pressed hard for seduction, Marsha balked. Tonight, when he'd been attentive and natural, she'd been much more responsive. Put that effect on a larger scale and she might just come around. He could even win the bet in the process and make some kids very happy campers. After that, he could relax around Marsha, and explore his feelings in a more leisurely manner.

He draped the towel over the rack, making sure the ends hung evenly. Just when he'd decided even expensively gift-wrapped women weren't worth the trouble, along came one in plain brown paper who threatened to take possession of his heart. He grinned at his reflection. Beautiful women had gotten him nothing but a lot of wasted, lonely years. If he never saw another one again it would be way, way too soon.

"NO, NO, NO." Heather jabbed the eject button on her VCR and yanked out the tape. "Give me the next one, Steph. There's got to be one 'How-To' video that doesn't equate massage with foreplay. I told the video store guy I wanted technical instruction, but the bozo was too busy bragging about his own personalized sexual services to listen."

"Another offer you could barely refuse." Stephanie handed over the last tape from the stack Heather had rented. "How did you put the guy off this time?"

"I told him I was a cookbook author and invited him up to test samples from *One Hundred Uses for a Dead Anchovy,* and *Love Thy Organ Meats.*" She rolled her eyes. "I should have gone as Marsha. She's my hero. She can do anything."

Heather put the new tape in the machine and sat on the floor. Funny how often during the past week she craved the invisibility and invincibility of Marsha. The chance to leave herself, to explore a different human experience. Harmless fun, as long as she didn't start enjoying Marsha's life more than her own.

Heather watched hopefully as the video's opening credits rolled, over lush orchestral music. Or maybe Heather longed for Marsha because Marsha reminded her of Jack, and how taken he'd seemed with Ms. Gouber by the end of their last date. Heather had relived that kiss over and over like a hyper-romantic adolescent, complete with stomach-fluttering shivers. She'd been kissed many times, but the experience had never lived up to its cinematic promise. Wet lips, squishy lips, biting lips, too much tongue, too-wide mouth—something always kept her from being carried away to paradise.

When Jack kissed her, she not only visited Paradise, but toured extensively and picked out a nice little cottage for her return trips.

The video credits ended; a model-gorgeous woman in a flowing caftan appeared on the screen and smiled. "Hi, I'm Krystal Shandelier." Her voice was a husky invitation. "Grab your most specialest partner, relax, and let our instructors open new, sensual doors, just for the two of you—through the art of full..." her tongue ran over her lips, "body..." she tossed her hair and made eyes at the camera, "massage."

Heather groaned and popped the tape out. "Forget the instruction. I'll have to improvise tomorrow."

"Give it up, Heather. You were an idiot to agree to this massage thing in the first place." Stephanie rose from the floor and glided toward the kitchen. "Mind if I make some tea?"

"Go ahead." Heather let the tape clatter into its case. Stephanie was right. But having to face Jack with her mind half-destroyed by his kiss, Heather had only wanted to escape back to sanity. Agreeing to the massage seemed easiest at the time. Nothing whatsoever to do with a desire to get her hands on that incredible man and stroke him until she died of ecstasy.

"Where's your tea? I can't imagine how you thought caressing his entire body would avoid getting sexual."

"Second shelf over the sink, under the package of apricots. This was not my idea. He trapped me into it." She scooched over to the sofa so her back rested against it. Okay, so the highly charged picture of Jack's skin under her fingers might have influenced her decision to agree. Maybe a little. But not much more than, say, World War Two influenced history.

"So call him and tell him you broke all your fingers. Teapot?"

"Under the sink behind the scouring pads." She could call off the massage date. A simple solution. But the part of her that had become involved beyond just winning the bet couldn't bear to cut Marsha's association with Jack any shorter than it was doomed to be. In her completely false getup, she'd never felt so natural or accepted. "Marsha can pull this off. I'm sure of it."

"Ha. Maybe *she* can. What about you? What about him? What if he turns on his back mid-massage and you discover he's a submarine with a serious periscope problem?"

Heather let her head drop back on the sofa cushion, trying not to moan at the thought of Jack being aroused by her touch.

"Then what?" Stephanie insisted. "You're out of cookies."

"Out of...oh, cookies." Heather surfaced from her naval fantasies. "Tippy top shelf. Box of Oreos."

"How do you get it down?"

"The periscope?"

"The cookies. Are you sure you're not dying to get your hands on him?"

Of course I'm dying to get my hands on him. "I've told you a zillion times I won't do more than a quick rubdown. Open the bottom drawer a little and step on it—you can reach the cookies."

"Has he kissed you?"

And how. "Marsha held him off divinely."

Stephanie's upper body appeared around the corner of the cabinet. "How did Heather do?"

Heather turned toward her friend. One of Stephanie's eyebrows flew up. Heather sat up straight and wiped what was probably a dreamy smile off her lips. "Okay, so it was great. Incredible even. Honestly, I don't know how Marsha resists him."

Stephanie rolled her eyes over a smile and disappeared again. "Maybe she's gay."

"No, not Marsha. She's straight on, guarded, really tough. I like her."

"I see." Stephanie reappeared, carrying a teacup and the package of cookies. "Any other personalities you'd like to introduce me to, Sybil?"

The phone rang. Heather picked up a blue cotton jacket and grabbed the receiver underneath.

"Marsha, Jack. Have I caught you at a bad time?"

"No, not at all." She lowered her voice to Marsha's deep roar and frowned. He sounded strange. Not at all like a man who'd shared a devastating kiss with the woman on the other end of the line. She pointed meaningfully to the receiver. Stephanie nodded.

"Listen, uh, about tomorrow night..."

Heather's stomach flipped, then sank to the bottom of her body. He was going to cancel.

"The contractors need me late at the restaurant."

End of massage date. She should be relieved her lack of skill and experience wouldn't be exposed. She should be glad her studio wouldn't be jeopardized further by the sensual contact. Glad she wouldn't get to see him half-naked, wouldn't get to touch his skin, stroke the muscle beneath, feast her hands on the male length and breadth of him. Yeah. Whoopee. Party time. "Some other night?"

"I'm pretty busy for the next week or so. I'll call you some time."

Heather pulled an anguished face at Stephanie. Marsha was being dumped. "Jack?"

"Yeah?" The syllable was infused with a chilling combination of forced heartiness and an obvious desperate desire to be off the phone.

"Never mind. Talk to you later." Heather replaced the phone, folded her hands carefully in her lap, and stared at them as if they could give her some clue what had caused Jack's about-face.

"He cancelled?"

"I think Marsha just got the old heave-ho." Heather put her thumbs together. *Here's the church.*

"You're kidding! What about the bet?"

"I guess he got tired of being fended off." She barely recognized her flat voice; barely tolerated the numbing disappointment. She extended her index fingers and touched the tips together. *Here's the steeple.* "Maybe Marsha overdid it."

"Hmm. You could have a point there."

"François will be happy at least. *Diablo's* chin is

his." And the studio was that much more certainly hers. So where exactly was her joy and exultation?

Open the doors. She opened her hands. Her smooth palms stared back. Empty. Cavernous. She didn't realize she'd forgotten to turn her fingers inside to make all the little churchgoers until she saw they were missing. She didn't realize she'd fallen for Jack Fortunato with a giant thud until he backed away. Now she felt as empty as the Church of the Missing Digits.

How could he do this? He and Marsha had connected on a deep and important level. They'd been real friends last weekend, and with the kiss, they'd gone beyond friends. He couldn't throw that away. Unless...

Hope rose through her. Maybe he did feel something for her, and those feelings scared him. Maybe Marsha's insistent coldness had discouraged him, not from pursuing the bet, but from making his heart any more vulnerable to her. Heather laced her fingers into a wriggling, enthusiastic congregation. Maybe Marsha could become a little more available and find out.

She disbanded her church and sat bolt upright. *Vive le massage.* But not only a massage. An out-of-state massage, coupled with a lovely seaside atmosphere, Marsha's charming company, and further glimpses of a woman named Heather.

"Stephanie, can I use your house in Connecticut next weekend?"

"Whatever you're thinking, forget it." Stephanie opened her mouth, preparing to allow an Oreo total entry.

"I want to spend some time near the studio. Since Jack will definitely lose the bet now, I might as well start planning what I'll do with the place."

Stephanie rolled her eyes; the Oreo made a return trip to her saucer. "I don't suppose a certain Mr. Fortunato who happens to live in the next town could have anything to do with this sudden longing for Connecticut."

"It's very possible."

Stephanie grinned. "You're falling for him."

"It's very possible." Heather held up her hand to stop Stephanie's triumphant cheer. "But I'm not going to sit here and let him dump me because he thinks I'm not interested."

"He doesn't even know who you are." Stephanie spoke through a mouthful of the newly reintroduced cookie.

"Then I have to start showing him." Heather jumped up and put on a CD of Beethoven's Seventh Symphony. She grabbed her palette, squeezed several colors onto it, and selected a brush. In anticipation of Jack's introduction to Heather, she had to make herself impossible to live without. "If I can make him really like me, he might be willing to stick around when Heather finally emerges."

"I don't know…"

"It worked in *Tootsie*."

"Can't you wait until the bet expires? If François drops in one more time to ask how you're doing, I'll take a swan dive off the *Arc de Triomphe*."

Heather made a long, energetic stripe of electric-blue down the side of the canvas and crossed it with scarlet. "I know. He's been bugging me too. But I can't risk waiting that long. A man like Jack won't exactly be short of other offers." She imagined a battalion of beautiful women clawing for his attention and added a crazed black zigzag across the painting.

"Okay, okay. If you want the house, it's yours."

Heather spun around and regarded her friend suspiciously. "Since when do you give in so easily?"

Stephanie looked back in wide-eyed, Oreo-munching innocence. "Who am I to stand in the way of true love between two people so intent on deceiving each other? And speaking of deception, remember not to tell Jack it's my house. I don't want Roger to know about the Chrissman big bucks quite yet."

"You've got a deal." Heather fought to keep from doing the Charleston all over her apartment. Beethoven acknowledged her victory with a few crashing chords. She'd call Jack tomorrow. If her theory about his true feelings proved correct, he'd jump at the chance to see her over the weekend. Marsha and Jack could have two days together in charming, bucolic Southport. Two days to get Jack to fall so hard for her that when the padding came off, he'd want to continue the relationship.

She fanned yellow over the top of her canvas. Bright, hopeful yellow. She wouldn't let him make love to her until the three weeks were over. François deserved that much, and so did her future career. But as of this moment, Marsha's days of staunch resistance were on the way out.

"COME ON IN—Damn you, you little annoyance."

Heather pushed open the door to Stephanie's apartment and eased Marsha's bulk inside. Her friend bent over a white-clothed table, swearing at a colorful arrangement of miniature vegetables.

"Uh-oh." Heather walked toward the table. "Time to spank the baby zucchini?"

"I can't get the darn carrots to nestle properly. All food these days has to nestle. You off?"

"As soon as I get the keys, yes." She tried to sound like a reasonable, normal adult, but she felt like a kid expecting the Easter bunny. The longest week of her life had finally come to an end. Jack would meet her in Connecticut this afternoon. They'd stroll through the town, sit by the harbor, have a leisurely dinner together. After that, if all went as planned, Marsha would finally get to give him that spellbinding, lust-inducing massage, though she'd have to stop short of total seduction for another week.

"They're on the metal dish next to the door. I typed out directions too, on the yellow sheet under them. You'll need to turn on the air-conditioning right away. Control is in the living room near the front door. Oh lord, this squash has a blemish."

"Thanks, Stephanie. I don't need directions. I'll just take the keys."

"Good luck." Stephanie raised her head and studied Heather carefully. "You're not as orange as usual. And that dress is nearly attractive."

Heather smoothed her full flowery skirt. "I thought I'd phase Marsha out gradually so the eventual unveiling isn't such a shock."

"Good idea. He'll probably—" A loud pounding at the door and the peal of the phone interrupted her. Stephanie rolled her eyes. "I'll get the phone. The door is François for the millionth time. Good thing you're here—you can give the eyewitness report."

Heather opened the door and prepared for a Marsha bellow. "My goodness, I don't know when I've seen such an attractive gentleman. Can I help you, sir?"

"*Pardon?*" He squinted suspiciously. "*Excusez-*

moi, Madame, but I do not think I have had the *plaisir.''*

Heather laughed. ''It's me, François.''

''Sacre bleu, ce n'est pas possible.'' François's face stretched in astonishment, then wrinkled into delight. *''Mademoiselle Gouber,* I presume?''

''In the flesh—or padding in this case.''

He walked around her, cackling in satisfaction, then grabbed her shoulders and kissed her on both cheeks. ''All these months I know you and here I did not know you! You are the actress *magnifique!* The chin of *Diablo* will be mine.'' He slumped dramatically into a chair. ''In just the nick of time, yes? Today, François, brilliant photographer, he is asked to shoot a birthday party for ten-year-olds. Dressed as the clown.'' He raised mournful black eyes to Heather, looking like a vulnerable if somewhat wrinkled ten-year-old himself. ''You will save me from this, no?''

Heather's heart swelled in pity. Not even a sometimes horse's rear should be subjected to such an indignity. ''Yes, François, Marsha will save you.''

''Ah, bon. Now listen. Stephanie told to me you do this not only for my chin, but to get money for a studio.''

Heather shot a killer glare at Stephanie whose back was turned as she chatted on the phone. François put a finger across his lips and shook his head. ''No no, I tricked it out from her. Now! *Attention!* If the bet does not work, François, he will get you the money another way. You deserve the best, *ma cherie.* With your talent, you will be the wow for Connecticut.'' He drew his little body up and nodded. ''François has spoken.''

Heather's swollen heart added another inch or two; she rushed over to François to kneel, take his hands, and thank him worshipfully. Unfortunately, she miscalculated Marsha's extended dimensions. Her padded rear boinged off the sofa on its way to kneeling and catapulted her, face first, into François's lap.

"No, no!" He pushed her away. "You do not need to thank me. Just remember to say it is from François you learn the brilliant artistry to put you on the top."

Heather chuckled and smiled affectionately at her boss. Few people ever glimpsed the loyalty and generosity that lurked under his self-absorbed exterior. She owed it to him to remain strong this weekend, even while she subjected Fate to extra doses of temptation. "I'll remember, François."

"You're kidding!" Stephanie's hitherto whispered phone conversation crescendoed into outrage. "Whose side are you on?"

François and Heather exchanged glances, then shrugs.

"I don't want to hear any more." Stephanie slammed down the receiver. "The little traitor."

"What is it?" Heather asked.

"Get this." Stephanie plonked balled fists on her hips. "Jack cancelled your massage date because Roger told him if he backed off, you'd come running. Right into his bed."

Heather's body went rigid. "What?"

Stephanie folded her arms across her chest. "Chicken-lipped, goat-brained, double-crossing... *man*." She spat the last word out as if it were the worst insult she could think of. The phone rang. No one moved.

Heather sank into a chair, her mind on overdrive.

"It's a game to him. He's still playing the game. I thought—" She looked helplessly at Stephanie, then François, who squinted at her as if she'd just started speaking Sanskrit. The phone rang again.

Heather narrowed her eyes. Anger started low in her body, like the boiling fire under a rocket at the end of countdown. Three, two, one...blastoff. She launched herself out of her chair and began pacing Stephanie's apartment. "He was using me. That ego-driven, testosterone-ridden clumsy oilbag motor-mouth."

Stephanie's eyebrows shot up. "Ooh, good one."

"*Excusez-moi,* but was Mr. Fortunato not *supposed* to use you, Heather?" François made a wide gesture with both hands and turned his head rapidly back and forth between the steaming women. "Was that not the point?"

The phone rang again. Stephanie picked it up one inch and dropped it back into its cradle. "Bye, Roger, you Judas. See if I ever trust you again."

"How could I have been so stupid?" Heather whirled around at the end of a pace. "How could I have thought any male in his prime capable of normal human feelings?"

Stephanie began pacing on the other side of the room. "I never should have told Roger about the bet. I thought he would help us."

Heather swung Marsha around again and nearly sent Stephanie's baby vegetables into orbit. What an idiot she'd been. She imagined Jack felt something for her simply because she wanted him to feel something for her. Every sign of his increasing interest in Marsha could just as easily be interpreted as another more devious effort to win the bet. Once he saw overt sexual offers wouldn't work, he'd resorted to being more "natural." If at first you don't succeed, try, try, try 'til she's on her back with her legs waving in the breeze.

She covered the room again in long stomping strides, hands clenched, allowing the rage and hurt full rein. "He never saw Marsha as anything but a chin protector. How could I have thought otherwise?"

"Why would Roger try to mess up the bet?" Stephanie threw her hands into the air and let them slap down to her sides. "I can't think of any reason, except that he has cheese for brains."

"All men have cheese for brains."

"Moldy cheese."

"With bugs."

They turned and glared at François. His mouth dropped open; he looked back and forth between them. "I am thinking I will go back to my apartment now."

He crept out and closed the door. Heather grabbed her purse and the keys to Stephanie's house in Southport. Jack thought Marsha would come running? Then she would. But not with open arms. With closed fists. And brass knuckles. And mace.

"What are you doing? You're not going up there now, are you?"

Heather spun around to face her friend, one hand on the doorknob, brain boiling with righteous indignation, breath coming fast. "Right now Jack thinks he's got me right where he wants me. Well, he's going to find out if he wants me where he wants me, he'll have to change where he wants me, because I'm not planning to be anywhere near where he wants."

Stephanie frowned. "Could you repeat the part about—"

"Okay, forget that. But I'll tell you one thing." Heather yanked opened the door, pushed Marsha through, and turned back for one more try.

"Jack Fortunato is in for the massage of his life."

7

JACK PULLED HIS CAR INTO the driveway of the huge columned mansion belonging to Marsha's friend. Beside him, Marsha sat, stiff and still, like a flagpole in winter.

"Here we are." He forced himself to sound cheerful. No response beyond a tiny frigid nod.

He got out and turned to stare exasperatedly across Southport Harbor. A breeze brought the scent of the sea and freshly mowed lawns. Yachts and sailboats bobbed serenely in the tiny finger of Long Island Sound; a golf course stretched up the slight rise beyond. Land of the free, home of the brave, and refuge of the tax-sheltered. Whoever Marsha's friend was, she didn't need to cut coupons. Maybe he should try to seduce *her* for the kids' camp money. Even if she were eighty, it would be easier than sweet-talking Ms. Gouber into some display of affection.

He grimaced at the peaceful summer evening, lips tight, stomach tighter. Disaster. The day he'd looked forward to all week long, planned in every detail, fantasized every aspect: disaster. From the moment she opened the door, Marsha displayed the receptive warmth of a cranky mongoose. During dinner, instead of the edgy intimate chatter-about-nothing couples indulged in when they knew they would end the evening entwined and rapturous, he and Marsha exchanged stilted phrases around the clanking of silverware, as if dining with detested relatives.

He sighed. When Marsha invited him to spend time with her this weekend, he'd been so sure Roger's plan had worked. So sure the admittedly underhanded attempt to jar her into awareness of feelings for him had been a smashing success.

He slammed his door shut. Not even close. Ms. Frosty had added several more layers of ice to her ice. If he hadn't felt her heat when he kissed her last weekend, the heat that had haunted him all week long, he'd think she was frozen to her epicenter. Why had she bothered to invite him here this weekend? So she could watch him lose his mind?

He walked around the car to open her door, but she bounded out before he got there. He followed her up the front walk, gritting his teeth. Her agility constantly amazed him. Nothing even jiggled when she walked, in spite of her generous size. She must work out like a maniac. The thought of her lush body, firm under his hands, increased his irritation. If he had to take one more cold shower, his anatomy wouldn't bother resuming functions. He couldn't blame it. To keep bunny going for the carrot, you had to give him a taste once in a while.

Marsha reached the front door and turned around. In the soft evening light, her features were nearly beautiful; her skin tone nearly natural. Even her clothes flattered her better today, though he wished she'd at least undo a few buttons of the high neckline. He shoved his hands in his pockets like a sullen schoolboy to hide yet another wave of arousal. Dumb bunny wouldn't give up the hunt even when the carrot wore the welcoming smile of an executioner.

Marsha cleared her throat and looked down at her fingernails as if they were cue cards. Jack set his jaw, and braced himself for the abrupt goodnight. He took a slow step backward, eyes on the stone stoop, already leaving. Not only would his chin become public property, but this woman he'd truly come to care for would be out of his life forever. Sick disappointment twisted in his stomach. Whatever Ms. Gouber wanted out of her time on this earth, it didn't include him. He swung his foot back for another step.

"Would you like to come in, Jack?"

His head jerked up at the same instant he realized his foot had run out of stoop. He lurched backwards, waving his arms like a berserk windmill in an attempt to regain his balance.

Marsha's hand shot out and caught his belt buckle, exerting enough pull, coupled with his wild efforts, to stabilize him. He looked down at the top of her head, adrenaline firing through his body. She wanted him to come in?

Marsha kept her hand on his belt and cleared her throat again. "I still...uh, owe you that massage."

The burst of adrenaline became a roaring geyser. What the hell game was she playing? Why treat him like contaminated waste all evening and now act like she couldn't wait to play Pat the Bunny?

She snuck a nervous glance up at him, then dropped her eyes again. Her hand released his buckle and fell down to hang awkwardly at her side. Jack's stomach untwisted. The entire picture snapped into brilliant, focussed clarity. How could he not have figured it out before? He wanted to smack himself on the forehead. She wanted him. She'd planned this. She'd been scared to death all evening.

Of course, Marsha was a virgin.

A lump rose in his throat; his heart nearly exploded from tenderness. He took her face in his hands and touched a kiss to her forehead, then one more, slowly and carefully, on each cheek. She cared for him. She cared for him enough to give him a gift she'd given no other man.

"Thank you, Marsha," he whispered reverently.

She eyed him a little strangely and pulled her face away from his hands. "Uh...no problem. I appreciate the chance to practice my technique."

He blinked at her choice of words, then remembered she was talking about massage and nodded, aware he was smiling like a gooey greeting card coverboy. *Back off, Jack. Let her set the pace—it's her first time.* He schooled his features to mute the glow resulting from his discovery. This was her moment; he'd help her through gently and lovingly, show her what pleasure there could be in making love. He'd let her think she'd seduced him this evening. She couldn't know she'd seduced him from the night of their first date.

Marsha unlocked the front door and led the way into the house. A marble foyer greeted them, displaying its immense crystal chandelier with a touch of arrogance. A gigantic sunken living room, more artsy than comfortable, lay beyond the entrance room. Elegant antique furniture lorded over enough oriental rugs to fill a Turkish bazaar. To the left, a dramatic spiral staircase with a wrought iron banister introduced the second floor; to the right, an endless hallway housed room after room down its length.

Jack looked around and gave a long whistle. "Glad

I don't have to clean this place. I bet they need a riding vacuum cleaner.''

Marsha closed the door behind them and hovered nervously, arms wrapped around her chest. Jack could practically feel the waves of tension radiating from her body.

"Would you like a drink?" She cracked a minuscule smile and gestured down the hallway. "The kitchen's that way, in the next hemisphere."

"Should I get the car or can we walk?"

She smiled and led the way. Jack couldn't stop grinning to save his life. Given the chance, he could probably dance up the wall like Fred Astaire. Marsha's words were the first sign of good humor she'd shown all evening. Worry over how to offer herself must have deflated her personality like a failed soufflé. The woman he knew had started to come back.

The sight of the immense, almost futuristic kitchen distracted him temporarily. Two sinks on opposite sides of the room. Two dishwashers. Professional range. Three ovens and a microwave. Built-in refrigerator. Counter space enough for Rhode Island. "Wow. You could do some serious cooking here."

"Kitchen envy?" Marsha reached up to a glass-fronted cabinet and pulled down two cut crystal tumblers. "What would you like? It would be shorter to list what she doesn't have."

"Cognac, please. This house wouldn't belong to Stephanie's friend with ties to the Chrissman Foundation, would it?"

"It would." She put back the tumblers and poured cognac into two giant snifters.

Jack nodded and accepted his drink. He'd heard a lot about the Chrissman family from his gossipy neighbors. Filthy get-out-of-my-way rich, with a daughter who'd ducked it all to live on bread and water somewhere in Manhattan. Though she'd obviously kept this place for some reason—maybe the dog needed a summer cottage.

He inhaled over the exquisite brandy and extended his glass. "Cheers, Marsha. Here's to a lovely evening."

She clinked his glass, mumbled something he didn't catch, and downed half the booze with a loud gulp. His heart ached. He wanted to take her in his arms and whisper that everything would be okay—more than okay. Making love to her would be a slice of unadulterated ecstasy. But this was her show. Her timing. Her moves. Easier on her if he kept up the small talk. He sipped his cognac and savored the rich taste. "You know, I've always heard the alcohol in—"

"Where do you want to do it?" Marsha tossed back the rest of the brandy and rolled up her sleeves.

Jack choked down his next swallow and carefully lowered his glass to the counter before the shock waves reached his hand and he snapped the slender stem. In all his sexually active years, he'd never had an invitation phrased quite that way. Poor Marsha; she was obviously panicking. He walked over to the brandy bottle and refilled her glass. She needed plenty of help to relax. "You know the house—pick your favorite acre."

"Okay." She thought for a moment. "Go back to the entrance hall, up the stairs, left and into the third room on the right. Bed's in the middle of that room so I can walk around you. I, uh, haven't bought my special, uh, massage type…bed thing yet. You go ahead. I'll be up in a sec.''

''Okay.'' He downed the rest of his brandy. Maybe he should give her an opening at some point later on, in case she wanted to back down. She was so nervous she could barely form a sentence. ''I'll be waiting.''

He found the room, hyper-decorated in teal and salmon, with matching everything and enough pillows on the bed to prop up an elephant. The room was chilly, too, as if the air had been turned down too low. He flung the pillows onto the loveseat, stripped to his boxers, lay on his stomach on the bed, and waited.

And waited.

He raised himself on one arm and strained for any sound in the hallway indicating Marsha's approach. Nothing but the hum of the by-now unnecessary air-conditioner. Was she making herself over for seduction or heaving into the commode from terror? If the former, he'd be happy to wait; if the latter, he couldn't bear for her to be alone. He swung his chilled legs onto the floor. Better to risk ruining the surprise than leave her miserable by herself. He tiptoed out into the hallway and listened once again.

Her impossibly light step sounded on the marble staircase. He shot back into the room and dove onto the bed seconds before her knock at the door.

''Come in.'' His body tensed with expectation. Would she be resplendent in black silk? Coy in white cotton? Daring in red velvet? He raised his head. She appeared in the doorway and came toward him, carrying a basket containing a towel and a bottle of massage oil. He put on a smile, trying to hide his disappointment. Not a single change, other than the strong

odor of nail polish. Had she broken a nail? Didn't
that make women crazy? He wouldn't have expected
Marsha to mind, but maybe tonight she did.

"All set?" She put the basket down and approached him rather primly. Not like a woman about
to seduce her man. More like a nurse about to proffer
a bedpan.

"Ready when you are." He put his head down,
facing her, on the only pillow he'd allowed to stay
on the bed, and relaxed his muscles in anticipation of
her touch.

She picked up the bottle of oil and poised it over
his back. "Here we go."

An icy stream of liquid sprayed over his back and
legs. His entire body lifted off the bed and bounced
back down; he gave an outraged yell.

Marsha gasped. "Oh, gosh, I'm sorry." Her deep
tone shook, as if she were a heartbeat away from
tears. "I forgot to heat the lotion."

"S'okay." He forced his breath to slow, fought to
keep from shivering in the cold room. The last thing
he wanted was to discourage her. "No problem. Just
a little chilly. I'll warm up as soon as you start."

"Okay." She settled herself beside him; the smell
of nail polish made him wrinkle his nose. Ghastly
stuff. She must have used a whole bottle on that nail.

She reached out her hands. Jack drew in a breath.
Her touch would be ecstasy. Soft. Strong. Stroking,
kneading, sensual enough to drive him to—

"Ungh." His body jerked uncontrollably. Rough.
Beyond rough. Sandpaper. Beyond sandpaper.
Ground glass. Her hands continued to rasp away at
his back. He clenched his teeth. This was going to be
the longest massage of his life. His skin would be

hanging in ribbons off his body. How could anyone with hands that beautiful have a touch that coarse?

His brows drew down. Freezing room. Cold oil. A sudden need to use nail polish. Rough hands. He shot out his arm, grabbed her wrist and pulled her over on him to examine her fingers. Tiny sprinkles of sand covered her fingertips, cemented into glistening stripes of clear nail polish.

Jack let go her wrist and grabbed her shoulders. "What the hell is going on?"

"Why don't you tell me?" Her eyes narrowed into brown slits, chilling him further.

"Because I have absolutely no idea." He resisted the urge to shake her. He'd been prepared for the gentle, tender deflowering of the first women he'd ever cared for this deeply and she'd been studying Practical Jokes to Amaze Your Family and Friends.

"I thought you wanted to seduce me. I thought maybe it was your first…time." The words left his lips and hung above his head, reforming into a giant, red, flashing "idiot" sign. His reading of her intent had made sense when it nestled safely in his brain. Out in the open, the plan was clearly ludicrous.

"You thought I was still a virgin?" She pushed away from him, off the bed, and set herself defiantly, hands on her hips. "Why, because I'm not attractive?"

Jack stared, incredulous. "Why is everything always about looks? I told you, I'm attracted to you the way you are. I've been preyed on by beautiful women all my life—the entire breed makes me want to retch on sight."

Marsha flinched. Jack cursed himself for bringing up his extensive history—the last thing she'd want to hear in her current crisis of confidence. "I don't find you at all unattractive. I thought you were a virgin because you've been sending more stop and go signals than a miswired traffic light. I take it I was wrong."

"Dead wrong. I haven't been a virgin since disco died the first time."

Jack tried to hide a full-body wince. The idea that Marsha had been with other men burned a smoking path through his ego. Damn. He'd been wildly flattered by the idea that she'd waited all these years for someone like him. Obviously he was operating on the wrong assumptions. "Okay, it was a ridiculous thought."

"It certainly was."

"Then answer this—Why did you make every effort to ensure I had the most unpleasant evening of my life?"

"Because you deserve it."

"Even Charles Manson doesn't deserve this. What the hell did I do?"

"You broke our date last week so I'd come slobbering after you and you could get into my knee-highs."

Jack's jaw dropped. How the hell did she know about that?

Roger. His rage ignited. His dear brother. Soon to be fitted for cement flippers and taken out for scuba lessons. Roger told Stephanie. Stephanie told Marsha.

A warning bell clanged in his head. If Stephanie and Marsha exchanged those kinds of confidences concerning him, Marsha might know about the bet.

Perversely, hope trickled through the cracks in his anger. If Marsha had joined forces with Stephanie to be sure he lost the bet, she'd have a pretty compelling reason to resist his advances. Hadn't she said she was a photographer? Maybe she was a friend of François's, trying to help François get his chin.

The hope flowed faster. Maybe the kiss he'd gotten out of her last Sunday was the real thing after all. Maybe her subsequent chill resulted from getting back on track to win the wager. Maybe she was angry now because she'd hoped he really liked her and after hearing Roger's plan, she believed he wanted her only for camp tuition.

He closed his still-gaping mouth, trying to keep the excitement off his face. So now what? Did he bring up the bet to clear the air? "Try honesty first," as his mom always said? What if Stephanie *had* stayed clammed up as she promised, and Marsha knew nothing about the setup? If he told her now, she'd have twice as much to be angry about. He'd be hard pressed to convince her his desire to make love had nothing to do with the bet any more.

Marsha stood watching him, indignation barely covering her vulnerability, a touch of sadness. Some unfamiliar emotion deep inside him stirred to life. Forget telling her. The bet should die a miserable secret death.

Through Marsha he had regained respect for himself; she'd reminded him he was worth more than the pretty stud everyone took him for. Nothing was worth the risk of losing her. He'd find money for the kids another way, out of his own wallet if he had to—his chin would survive stardom. Marsha deserved more from him than a committment to his own ego.

He got off the bed and took Marsha's shoulders again, affectionately this time, smiling his satisfaction. She gave back a consummate glare that in grade school would be known as the "hairy eyeball."

"I don't blame you for being angry, Marsha. But honestly, I've never met a woman I wanted more, or one who wanted me less."

She frowned. "Which one am I?"

"Which one what?"

"The more woman or the less one?"

"Both. I want you more, you want me less." He squeezed her shoulders. "You see?"

She gave a tiny grudging smile. "More or less."

He pulled her closer, close enough so that he could kiss her simply by bending his head, which he had every intention of doing as soon as the mess had been cleared up. "I don't usually play head games, but I was desperate." His voice cracked like a Swiss yodeler's; he cleared his throat. "You're like no one I've ever met. I feel like a new man around you. I'm...I'm—"

He snapped his mouth shut to trap the words trying to escape his tongue. *I'm in love with you.* Absurd. He'd known her two weeks, and spent most of that time feeling like a factory reject. Love took much longer to grow. Love took give and take. Two to tango. For better or worse. In sickness and—

"You're what?"

He heard the surrender in her voice, caught the trace of hopefulness in her face. His whole being swelled with unapologetic male territorial triumph. She was his. "I'm...going to kiss you until the nail polish melts off your fingers."

"Ohh—"

He cut the syllable short with his lips, took her hands, wrapped her arms around his neck. She was driving him insane. Her heat, her response, ten times more than the week before. Ten times the need, ten times the emotion.

He pressed his aroused length against her firm rounded belly. "Can you feel how much I want you?" he whispered.

She froze. "Uh. Yes. Of course. Yes, I can." Her head thumped forward onto his chest and stayed there.

He slowly withdrew his lower body from the contact. She was uncomfortable. Maybe she wasn't a virgin, but she must not have a great deal of experience with men. He put his hand up to stroke her hair, gently, softly. He could relax her that way. He was in no hurry.

"Does that feel good?" He made a mental note to ask her to cut down on hairspray—the stuff made the strands feel so artificial.

She stiffened. "Does what feel good?"

"Stroking your hair like this."

"Oh. That. Yes. Good." Her gruff voice dropped to a low tremor. "Terrific."

Something was wrong. He tipped her head back; her look of anguish shocked him. "Sweetheart, what is it?"

She shook her head. "Just kiss me again," she whispered.

He hesitated, his erotic charge disoriented by confused tenderness, then leaned forward and gave her a slow, sweet, lingering kiss that was so exquisite his entire body ached in awe of it. He drew back, staring. How could any woman make him feel so much from one kiss? Marsha stared back. They froze that way, gazing into each other's eyes, breathing suspended.

Then, with an explosive mutual rush of desire, they came together, lips and tongues meeting and seeking, hands exploring.

"Marsha," he could barely pant the word out, "God, I want you. I want—"

"Stop!"

François's voice boomed into the room. Jack jerked his head toward the sound; his heart threatened to pound its way out of his chest.

"François," Marsha gasped. "What the hell are you doing here?"

"Stop!" He wagged his finger violently side to side. "There must be no more of this! No! Nothing!"

8

HEATHER'S OPEN MOUTH remained frozen in horror. François. François was there. *Don't panic.* She glanced over at Jack. He turned from her to the French traitor and back, his face increasingly speculative. Of course he'd realize now the bet had been a setup. He'd be furious.

Terrific. Just when she'd truly started to believe he cared for Marsha, any chance of things working out with Heather would be lost.

"François," she tried to make her deep voice pleasant, but ended up sounding dementedly sugary, "perhaps you could tell me exactly what you are trying to—"

"I will tell you! I go to see Stephanie. She takes a call from Roger. While they fight, I see a note to you with directions to this house. Stephanie, she does the bad acting when I ask why you come here. *Alors!* François, he knows something is not right." He jabbed the side of his grey head with a long, large-knuckled finger. "He uses his brain, puts the two with the two, and *voila!* You are caught fooling with my chin."

Heather put her face in her hands and nearly broke her glasses. How did she ever get in such an absurd situation? A woman dressed as another woman, half in love with a man half in love with the woman she

pretended to be, who had just heard him admit that
the woman she really was made him want to retch.
Add a crackpot Frenchman who had apparently lost
track of the fact that his association with Marsha was
supposed to be non-existent, and you had—

Heather gave a short laugh that sounded more like
a cry for help. What the hell did you have? Extreme
chaos at the very least. She felt like the Other Woman
in her own love affair.

"Why don't you think Marsha and I should be together?"

Jack's voice didn't sound as angry as Heather expected. She peeked at him through her fingers. He
stood calmly in his boxers, hands on his hips, mag-
nificent chest bared to the lucky world. Not at all
apoplectic. Could he possibly not have figured out the
bet was rigged? She put her hands down and gave
François an urgent don't-make-this-worse-than-you-
already-have glare.

"Why don't I think you and—" François swivelled
his head back and forth between them like a child
who just figured out his parents caught him in a lie.
He frowned and fingered his ascot.

Heather sighed. "Look, let's just—"

"Because," François held up his hand, his voice
quiet and sincere, "I do not wish you to hurt my
friend…Marsha. I think she is carrying the torches
for you. Women like her, they love a man forever.
Men like you, they use women to line the birdcage."

Jack's eyes narrowed. "What makes you think I'm
like that?"

"Look at you." François gestured up and down.
"*Mon Dieu,* you put the Greek Gods to shame."

"What does that have to do with it?" Heather and Jack snapped the words out in tandem.

Heather smiled sheepishly at Jack's amused, raised-eyebrow expression. She'd momentarily forgotten herself. Marsha thought looks were important. He smiled back, his eyes warm, slightly devilish, as if he were enjoying himself. Whatever the hell he found to enjoy in this mess, she wished he'd share it with the rest of the class.

Jack turned back to François. "What makes you think I'm not carrying a perfectly honorable torch myself?"

"You, too?" François' eyes shot to an impressive width. "*Oh, la la,* thank God I am here. It is worse than I thought."

Jack frowned. "I thought you said you wanted me to—"

"François! Where the hell are you?"

The shout came from somewhere downstairs. Heather let her head drop back into her hands, more careful of her glasses this time. Stephanie. Welcome to Nightmare Central.

"*Ici, ma petite.*" François shouted out the door. "I have just saved my chin from the mortal danger. You will be very happy."

"I'm nothing like happy." Stephanie appeared in the doorway, flushed and out of breath. "I'm sorry, Hea—Marsha, I came tearing after him as soon as I found he'd bolted with the directions. He must have driven here at the speed of light."

"*Ah, oui!* The laws of physics can not hold back the man in pursuit of—"

"Enough, François." Stephanie grabbed him by

the arm and started pulling him toward the door. "Come downstairs. We're going back to New York."

"Stephanie?" A male voice boomed up the stairway. "Are you here?"

"Roger!" Stephanie gasped. "How on earth did you—"

"I followed you. Stephanie, you can't keep avoiding me. We have to talk. I did it because you said they belonged togeth—" Roger appeared in the doorway and froze at the sight of the equally frozen gathering. "Who didn't invite me to the party?"

Jack chuckled. This time Stephanie's head made the trip down into her hands. For once François was speechless.

"Well, isn't this special." Heather gave a hysterical hiccup, halfway between laughter and lunacy. Add further to the mix a man in love with her best friend who had no idea the house he stood in represented only a tiny fraction of her net worth.

"You're looking lovely as always, Marsha. So are you, Jack." Roger looked his semi-nude brother up and down. "Bugs Bunny boxers I gave you in the wash?"

"I hate to ruin everyone's fun, but I'd like to speak to Marsha alone." Jack crossed to Heather and took her arm.

His hand was warm through the cotton of her dress; she wished for short sleeves so he could touch her skin. Probably her last chance to have that kind of contact. After the little talk he wanted, no doubt about the rigged bet, he'd probably bounce Marsha down the marble staircase. Even if he wanted to talk about something else, Heather had to confess about the setup. The escapade had gone on long enough. If he had real feelings for Marsha, she had to let him down gently, then disappear forever.

Roger looked around as if he finally noticed his surroundings. "This place is unbelievable. Who the heck lives here?"

"Let's go downstairs, Roger." Stephanie put her hand gently against his chest. "We have to talk, too."

"And what about *moi?*"

Stephanie gave François a sideways glare. "You can go outside and sit in the doggy pool."

She dragged him out the door; Roger followed, still looking around in awe.

"The *dog* has a pool?" His voice drifted in as Jack closed the door.

"So." Jack crossed over to his clothes, which he must have flung onto the loveseat in anticipation of her massage. His splendid near-nakedness began disappearing into his pants and shirt.

Heather stifled a moan of protest. "So?"

"You want to confess first or should I?" He pulled his polo shirt over his head, looking for one muscle-defining freeze-frame moment like the studly guy in the exercise machine ads.

Heather determinedly looked away from the brain-scrambling sight and considered the options. She'd probably fare better if she went first. That way, she'd be offering the truth freely, instead of appearing trapped into it by his confession.

"I'll go first."

"Shoot."

"In the Seventies, François was one of the hottest tickets in fashion photography. Unfortunately, in an industry noted for temperamental behavior, his was the temperamental-ist, which eventually got him booted out.''

''Right on his bell bottoms?''

''Uh-huh.'' Heather laughed nervously, hoping Jack's mood would stay pleasant when he heard what she had to say. ''Now that fashion has gone retro, he has the chance to make a comeback. Holden House is running ads for *Diablo* cologne that—''

''I know, I know, my chin.'' He fingered it ruefully.

''So Stephanie came up with the idea of the bet.''

''Which you were supposed to make sure I'd lose.''

Heather nodded. ''The shoot would also get me the money I need for a studio of my own, here in town.''

He shook his head, grinning. ''Who would have thought two sweet, lovely women capable of such vicious, ugly deceit?''

''You're not angry.'' Heather stared at him in astonishment.

''Are you kidding?'' He walked over and stood close, still smiling, the heat of his body even more seductive than usual in the chilly room. ''I'm ecstatic.''

''You like being lied to?'' She tipped her head up to look at him, fighting the urge to part her lips dreamily and invite another kiss.

''If it means winning the bet is the only reason you avoided me, yes.'' He took her hands and pulled her as close as her padded stomach would allow. ''Was it?''

''Was what?'' She leaned her head in to touch his chest and closed her eyes, absorbing every delicious sensation his nearness provoked.

''Did you keep your distance only to win the bet?''

He raised her chin with gentle hands and lowered his face until their lips were nearly touching.

"I'm afraid so," she whispered.

"Don't be afraid, Marsha." He moved slowly forward to kiss her.

Heather's real stomach contracted into a tight knot. *Marsha, Marsha, Marsha.* Why was everything always about Marsha? Damn the stupid woman for always butting into Heather's ecstasy. She moved her head back from the kiss. "This isn't going to work, Jack."

"What?" He took hold of her shoulders, kept her from pulling away. "I've never known anything that worked even half this well."

Heather set her brain on overdrive. She had to convince Jack that Marsha didn't want him, and at the same time find out if there was any post-Marsha hope for Heather. "Right now I'm a novelty to you; a woman who doesn't look like every man in the world's fantasy. But what about next month or next year? You walk down the street and turn around some time, you'll see the street strewn with women's prostrate bodies, worshipping your footprints. How long will you be happy with me?"

"Why the hell would I want someone else when I care so much for you? How often do I have to tell you? I grew up—I don't want supermodels. I don't even remember the last time I was turned on by a beautiful—wait, yes I do."

Heather cringed. Bad enough to be jealous of Marsha, without having to hear about someone else.

"It was the day I made the bet. She was coming out of Stephanie's apartment building. God, was she gorgeous. Thick wavy blonde hair, some sort of pink dress. Man. I went nuts. I even dreamed about her. But since I met you, I haven't given her or any woman like her a thought. If I saw her now, I swear she'd do nothing for me. I've changed. Even if you and I don't work out, she isn't at all what I want anymore.''

Heather nodded, every muscle in her body straining to keep herself from crying out over the pain of his words. As soon as she got home, she'd burn that pink sundress and move to Tibet. He didn't want Heather. He wanted Marsha.

Heather pulled away, her only thought to get away from him, drive home, and see that Marsha met a terrible and painful death. Then Heather would have the rest of her ruined life to grieve and get wrinkly.

She took a deep breath. ''I'm sorry, Jack, but you're way ahead of me. You're very sexy and I'm very attracted to you, but that's it. I'm sorry. I don't want to hurt you.''

She tried to give a condescending smile to let him see how little he mattered. If she remotely succeeded, it would be the performance of the century.

''You're dumping me.'' He looked so stupefied she would have given in to sick laughter, except that the amusement center of her brain had been permanently destroyed. And she was so crazy about him that the idea of causing him any pain made her want to stay Marsha forever.

''I'm sorry, Jack. I should go.''

He pushed both hands through his hair and exhaled as if he'd been holding his breath since he walked in the room. ''Look. Just do one thing for me.''

Anything, I'll do anything. Empire State building? I'll jump. Moon rocks? They're yours. "Yes?"

"Take a week and think this over." He reached out, traced the line of her cheekbone down to the corner of her mouth, and cupped her chin. "Then go out with me one more time."

She hesitated. Her response should be a loud, no-nonsense negative. Marsha needed to disappear quickly and mercilessly to avoid the pain her continued existence would perpetuate for both of them.

"Just once more." He leaned forward before she could stop him, eased a slow, gentle kiss onto her mouth.

Her resolve crumpled like a house under an avalanche. She sighed, all at once exhilarated and exasperated by her inability to resist this man. "Okay, Jack. Once more," she whispered.

He kissed her again, fiercely this time, and drew back. Triumph, hope, pain and fear all took turns controlling his features. And something that looked an awful lot stronger than affection.

"Marsha." His voice was a husky whisper. "Marsha. I...I..."

He gathered her hands in his, brought them to his lips. His eyes held hers with an intensity of purpose that jumpstarted her heart into crazy, fantastic, near-panic. He was going to say it. He couldn't say it. He had to be stopped. She'd be lost, drowned, ship-wrecked, ravaged, looted, pillag—

"Marsha, I—"

"Whaaaat?" The roar came from downstairs, so loud it penetrated the thick wooden door of the bedroom and bounced around the salmon and teal interior.

Heather and Jack jumped simultaneously and stared at the door. Apparently Roger just found out who owned the house. Heather exhaled in giant relief, and winced at the same time. Thank goodness Jack would never tell Marsha he loved her; Heather couldn't stand that kind of irony.

"We better go see if everyone's okay." She walked as quickly toward the exit as her wobbly legs would allow, grateful for the easy escape, but feeling as if her heart had been fed through a pasta machine. In a moment of hormonally-induced insanity, she'd agreed to see Jack Fortunato once more. Now she saw quite sanely that Jack and Marsha could never be together again. Because if he ever told Marsha that he loved her, Heather would have no choice but to look directly into his eyes, and tell him the honest, heart-stopping truth.

I love you too, Jack.

BLACK. MARS BLACK. Mars black and Titanium white. Angular shapes. Jagged edges. A swath of anguished, blood-crimson punctured by a vicious streak of black lightning.

Perfect.

Heather laid her brush down and admired the painting. One of her best. No wonder all those geniuses led miserable lives. Misery bolstered creativity.

She pulled out a length of plastic wrap and covered the blobs of paint left on her pallet.

Tomorrow she'd have to call Jack and break their last date. Make it clear Marsha never wanted to see him again. Ever. No point dragging out the pain any longer. Easier on them both to make this temporary separation permanent.

Heather took her brush into the bathroom and washed it in the sink. She'd call him today, but she was busy today. Too many things to do, like…well, lots and lots of things. No time. She'd call tomorrow.

Or maybe the next day.

The door buzzer rang; she dragged herself over to the intercom. Stephanie answered her dismal, "Yes?" and Heather buzzed her up.

"Hi." Stephanie shuffled into the apartment, pale and disheveled, and headed straight for the kitchen. "Oreos."

Sympathy found the one place in Heather's mood not occupied by heartbreak. "Roger?"

"Hates me." Stephanie emerged cradling the package and plopped herself down on Heather's futon. "Jack?"

"Hates me." Heather pushed off a pile of books and sank down next to her friend. "Loves Marsha."

"Bad." Stephanie shoved a cookie into her mouth and sighed.

"Yeah." Heather sighed too. "Bad."

They both sighed again and lapsed into silence except for the slot-machine regularity of Stephanie's Oreo consumption.

Heather gazed at the elaborate molding running around the top of her walls, wondering if she should try counting the zillion or so segments. Just for excitement. If Jack had shown the slightest interest; if she'd sensed the smallest regret in his voice when he renounced the vision he'd cherished of Heather in her pink sundress, she'd have some hope. Something to cling to. But hearing herself labeled a childish fantasy—something to grow out of, to recognize as worthless...his words had been too cutting, inflicted too savage a hurt for her to recover. What had started as a playful adventure had ended in tragedy for both her and Jack. Only Marsha remained unscathed.

Heather twisted her face into a sneer of loathing.

Bitch.

A knock sounded at the door. *"Allo? Allo? François ici.* Let me to come in."

The women turned their heads toward each other and exchanged one more sigh. Heather pushed herself up and opened the door. "Hi, François. How did you get in the building?"

"Bonjour, bonjour. I come in with someone who has the key. Ah, Stephanie is here, too." He brandished a bouquet of yellow lilies, ripped off the paper and divided the flowers into two bunches. *"Pour toi."* He gave one bunch to Heather, one to Stephanie. *"Et pour toi.* Now. François, he will perform the cheering up."

"Thanks, François. You don't have to—"

"Non, non. For me it is the pleasure. Now, Heather. To you I say that you must go to this man Jack and lose the bet *immediatement,* before he finds someone else."

"What?" Heather gaped at him. "What about your chin?"

"What is my chin compared to your happiness, *ma petite?* Compared to *l'amour?* Nothing! Rudolfo is back from Milan; his chin is second best, but I will make the supreme sacrifice. So! I will get my brilliant

career back, you will get your studio, and *voilà*." He
beamed and struck an absurd pose, like a drunken
fencer. "François, he has made the happy ending."

Heather's heart indulged in a brief warm fuzzy moment before it resumed its painful boycott of pleasure.
So. What she'd always wanted would be hers now.
Her own studio. Her new life. How had she ever
thought she'd find total fulfillment in four walls and
a high mortgage? Fulfillment had a whole new description now. Tall, dark, and unavailable.

"Thank you, François. I wish it could be so easy.
He doesn't want me. He wants Marsha."

François stared at her as if he thought she might
need special education. "Who is Marsha?"

Heather shot a look at Stephanie, who paused with
her next Oreo halfway to her mouth. Was he losing
his *marbres?*

"Marsha," Stephanie said. "You know, the dis-
count version of Heather."

"I know nothing of this Marsha. I know only
Heather."

"François, would you like to lie down?" Heather
laid her flowers on the desk and put her arm around
his thin shoulders, genuinely alarmed. "I can get you
some tea if you'd like."

"Ha! You think I am old before my time, eh? No.
I tell you now. Jack and François are the same. We
know only Heather. We love only Heather. Marsha,
she is nothing. She does not exist. You say to me
always, 'the looks, they do not matter.' Yet now, you
tell me when Heather's looks are gone, she becomes
someone else? No! You are you. Marsha is you.
Stephanie is Stephanie, rich or poor. These Fortunato

men, they love you.'' He gave a tremendous nod and
folded his arms across his chest as if he'd just solved
any and all remaining mysteries of the universe.

Stephanie sat up straighter, put down her cookie.
''He does have a point.''

''Of course I have the point!'' François flung out
his arms and nearly socked Heather in the nose. ''And
you mope in this apartment with the paints and the
Oreos. You should be right now in the beds of these
men, singing for joy. You have what everyone wants.
L'amour.'' He drew the vowel out, grinning.
''*L'amooour.* The rest of the problems, they are just
the technical difficulties. And *now!*'' He shot one finger up toward the ceiling. ''I must go. Already I am
getting the calls from other clients. This afternoon I
have a date with a beautiful woman who wishes a
portrait taken by me. Perhaps I shall get more in the
bargain.'' He waggled his eyebrows and swept out
the door, leaving the scent of wine and chemicals lingering in the room.

Heather and Stephanie swiveled their heads and
looked at each other cautiously. A spark lit Stephanie's eye. Heather smiled for the first time all week.
Hope revisited her attitude. She did have one more
play to try and make Jack see through Heather's appearance, to the woman he'd fallen for, the woman
he called Marsha. One more chance.

She smacked her fist into her palm. ''I'm going to
fight for that man.''

''I'm with you.'' Stephanie stood up. ''I hereby
announce a formal declaration of siege on the brothers
Fortunato.''

''Hear hear.'' Heather extended her hand and

Stephanie gave it a vigorous shake. "Roger first. I'll go with you. We'll need his help."

"Why?" Stephanie laughed, eyes shining with excitement.

"Because I have to find his brother."

"You or Marsha?"

"Me." Heather drew herself up dramatically. "Jack Fortunato is about to encounter Heather Brannen once again."

9

JACK SURVEYED the interior of *La Cucina del Cor* with a small charge of satisfaction. Gone were the red-checked tablecloths, dark carpet and straw-covered bottles of Chianti. Gone were the plastic flowers, the wooden flowers, the ceramic flowers, all the borderline tacky decorations his parents had contributed to the restaurant.

Now, the floor was warm and rustic in brick-colored tile; the decor cozy, but with touches of chic that brought the place into the new century. Jack was pleased. He'd be more pleased if time hadn't just about completely stopped. The days were oozing by, gooey second after gooey second. He had a date with Marsha tomorrow, Friday. He had to make it count. Saturday the restaurant would re-open; he could no longer spend every waking hour as he wanted to: trying to convince Marsha they belonged together.

In the meantime, he'd been quietly losing his sanity. He'd already made dinner for everyone in his neighborhood and contributed meal after meal to the local soup kitchen. Something had to give. And that something had to be Marsha. When she told him she felt nothing for him, his life had flashed before his eyes. A lot of his past turned out to be entertaining, but none of it counted if she wouldn't consider sharing his future.

He opened the door to the street and turned out the light, sending the room behind him into a gloomy reflection of the summer storm outside. One step into the wind and rain, and he turned around. The paperwork for the City Kids in Camp grant from Stephanie's Foundation, bless her—he'd left it on the kitchen counter. He strode to the back, grabbed the papers, came back into the restaurant, and almost yelled from surprise. A woman, standing in the dim glow.

"Sorry." She put her hands out toward him. "I didn't mean to scare you."

His jaw fell. *Her*. The woman from outside Stephanie's apartment. Same dress. Same hair. Same...*oh, man*...everything. How did she...how could she—

"I know you're not open." Her voice was pure and feminine, very slightly husky, melodious. She took a step forward, watching him intently. "Some guy was pestering me. I got scared, and...I thought maybe I could hide here, for a minute, until he's gone." She fidgeted nervously with the strap of a small shoulder bag.

Jack stood frozen, gaping like the village idiot, drinking in the sight of her. She'd evidently gotten caught in the sudden downpour without an umbrella. Rain soaked her tousled blonde hair, glistened on the smooth, perfect lines of her cheekbones and forehead; a single drop hesitated, then rolled reluctantly off her nose. The dress clung to her slender body; its dampness made her nipples visibly hard under the rose-colored cloth.

Major, major hard-on.

He cursed himself. What the hell was the matter with him? He finally found someone he really cared for in Marsha, just finished telling her in all sincerity, that women like this did nothing for him, and now at his first sighting, he'd gone into testosterone over-drive.

He clenched his jaw. No. Not his first sighting. He'd seen dozens of beautiful women since he started dating Marsha; they *had* done nothing for him. This one did something powerful. This one sang a siren song that had him half-shipwrecked before he'd even spoken to her. Worse, on hearing some guy had been bothering her, for one crazed second, he'd wanted to charge out on a white stallion, hunt the jerk down, and run him through with a rusty blade.

Ridiculous. He had more control over himself than that. And he'd seen enough helpless female acts to spot a phony a mile away. She might be nervous, might have encountered some weirdo, but Jack didn't sense any real fear.

"I'll get you a towel so you can dry your...self." He gestured to her body, and backed away, afraid if he turned sideways, her effect on him would be sil-houetted in the light coming through the doorway be-hind him. He grabbed a towel from the kitchen and walked back toward her.

She'd turned to examine a picture on the restaurant wall. At his approach, she gave a closed-lip smile and took the towel. "Thanks. I was probably silly to panic, but when my usual routine didn't scare him off, I got nervous." She tipped her head back and massaged the towel over her wet hair.

"Routine?" His eyes travelled over her. God, she was perfect. With her head back and her elbows up, her body arched slightly. Small breasts pushed out, her back curved in an inviting sweep, her perfect rear extended as if begging for attention. Her entire being radiated sensual innocence, a combination so intoxicating he was having trouble breathing.

"My routine—to get rid of unwanted attention." She gave him a quick once-over. "You must have one too, the way you look."

Jack pulled himself out of his moronic stupor. "I usually ignore them. Occasionally I have to become engaged. Once I developed something highly contagious."

"And that works? I guess women aren't as persistent as men." She gave him another close-mouthed smile and started drying her arms. "I usually make up some horrible hobby. I told this guy about my moth and caterpillar collection, and mentioned what an important source of protein they are in a balanced diet."

"I think that would dissuade me pretty efficiently." He gave a convincing chuckle to hide his internal agony of confusion.

How could he be half in love with Marsha and still wonder what this woman would do if he gave in to his urge to taste the rain on her mouth? Had he been kidding himself all these years that he was more than the macho stud he appeared to be? Was he incapable of real emotional depth? Would he always flit from beautiful woman to beautiful woman until he was too old to keep it up? They'd have no use for him then. He'd spend the rest of his days in a dumpster, eating dog food, and telling stories of his old conquests to the pigeons.

"Unfortunately, this guy thought moth-eating sounded great." The towel moved to her chest, down her body; she lifted one leg, dried her ankle, her calf, her knee, her thigh...

Jack turned away. He was not a well man. He needed to cook.

"There." She held the towel out to him. "Thank you very much."

"Not at all." He took the towel and held out his hand, wondering if there were fresh herbs and cheese anywhere in the kitchen. "Jack Fortunato."

"Heather Brannen." She clasped his hand in a firm shake. "Glad to meet you, and thanks for the refuge...Jack."

His name came out like an invitation she couldn't help making. He looked into her eyes, clear blue even in the dimly lit room. Lively eyes carrying humor, attraction, and a touch of anxious worry. His body reacted by familiar instinct, as if they'd been intimate several times, and the sight of her brought back passionate memories.

Jack sent the order to his hand to let go of hers. If he wanted any chance of remaining on his rocker, he either had to make love or pasta.

His hand finally obeyed. *Get a grip, Jack.* This woman was sheer fantasy. He had his ever-after reality in Marsha. He was pretty sure he loved Marsha, pretty sure someday he'd want to spend his life with her. This woman had to be a lights-out, half a deck, no marbles airhead like all the others. Ten minutes in her company would prove that beyond any doubt, reasonable or otherwise.

"Would you do me a favor?" She put a hand to the back of her neck.

"What's that?" He gave a smug smile. Here it

comes. *Would ya help me out of mah wet, wet dress? Ah have always depended on the kahndness of—*

"Could you check to see if that guy is gone?" She adjusted the catch of her necklace. "He gave me the heebie-jeebies."

"Sure." He walked over to the window, rolling his eyes. She was probably undressing right now behind him. Contrary to what she might think, that kind of aggressiveness turned Jack off. Granted, he might pass out at the sight of her naked body, but he wouldn't be taking advantage of her offer. "What does he look like?"

"Short, heavy-ish, dark glasses, trench coat, baseball cap, long, dull brown hair."

Jack suppressed a snort of laughter. Trench coat. Right. Not much imagination, this one.

He gave a cursory glance out the window. "No, I don't—"

His scalp prickled. Outrage bloomed. Right there, just as she described him. The creep actually stood across the street, staring at the restaurant. Without a second's hesitation, Jack strode over to the door.

"Where are you going?"

"I'm going to beat the crap out of him."

"No, Jack." She rushed over and clung to his arm. "Don't. He, uh…he might be armed."

Jack pushed her hand away. "I'll disarm him, then beat the crap out of him."

"Jack." She grabbed him with her other hand.

"I'll teach that pervert to bother you." He pulled free again, his breath coming fast, his only thought to pulverize the idiot who'd frightened her.

"Jack." She caught his shirt. "He's gone. He ran away."

Jack searched the street again. She was right. No pervert. He turned back to her. She stood close, still hanging on to his shirt, eyes glowing. He could have sworn she was happy. Why, he had no idea. Maybe she didn't have the brains to be otherwise. "Why did you hold me back? I wanted to make sure he wouldn't bother you again."

"I...didn't want you to get hurt." She looked down at the shirttail she held in her hand, then opened her fingers slowly, almost reluctantly, just until the fabric fell away. They stared, motionless, down at the shirt for a long, chemically intense second.

Then Heather raised her head. Jack met her gaze, stared into those clear blue eyes. Sensual heat jolted through him, scrambled his ability to think, filled his body with giddy lightness, a touch of awe, and something deeper. Something only one woman had so far been able to stir in him.

"Heather."

"Yes?" Her lips parted; her breath came in with a tiny gasp.

"I need to make pasta. Do you want some?"

He heard the words come out of his mouth and gave himself a mental kick in the head. What kind of warped person had he become? He was considering becoming engaged, for crying out loud. Now he'd purposely chosen to spend more time with a woman who couldn't look at him without turning his lap into one of the great pyramids. He'd even imagined for one brain-dead instant that after fifteen minutes in her company, he had serious feelings for her.

"Thank you. I am hungry." She gave that curious half-smile again, as if she were afraid to part her lips. Maybe she had ugly brown teeth. He smiled, feeling somewhat relieved. That was it. No human could be that perfect. She had no depth and she had ugly teeth.

He escorted her into the kitchen where she perched on a stool. He tried to calm his chaotic mind with a list of the equipment he needed. Pot, chef's knife, linguine, ricotta salata, cherry tomatoes, fresh basil, garlic, olive oil, iron underwear...

"You were sweet to go after that guy for me. I've encountered plenty of creeps, but I've never had Sir Galahad handy before."

"All in a day's work." He filled the pasta pot with water, indulging in a private smirk of satisfaction. Typical. Cooing over some knight-in-shining-armor fantasy. Though granted, he had helped fuel the vision by going off half-crazed after her tormentor, like a besotted thug. He couldn't explain his protective impulse.

Heather pulled her wet skirt up off her thighs and waved the hem gently to dry it, showing occasional glimpses of heaven underneath. Jack swallowed and lugged the pasta pot over to the stove. His attraction, however, any man could explain in an instant.

"Do you ever get tired of being so good-looking?"

Jack turned to her in astonishment. Her tone had been matter-of-fact; she returned his questioning look placidly, didn't appear coy or conniving. She wanted a real answer. To his surprise, he was eager to supply one.

"'Handsome is as handsome does,' my mom used to say." He grabbed two cloves of garlic and smashed them with his knife to loosen the skin. "I try not to think about it."

"Oh, is that how you do it?"

"Yes. Brooding over something I can't change is—"

"I meant is that how you peel garlic."

"Oh. Yes." He chopped the cloves with machine gun rapidity, embarrassingly aware he was showing off. "How do you deal with it?"

"I usually try to pick the skin off with my fingers."

"No, how do you deal with being…attractive." He almost laughed at the understatement. The woman was stunning; she was perfect; she was pure, heart-stopping, lust-inducing, sexual TNT.

"Oh, that." She rolled her eyes.

Jack stopped chopping, curious to hear her answer. Most of the beautiful women he dated had, like him, been treated differently all their lives: revered, scorned, worshipped, detested. But most bought into the idea that their looks somehow made them superior, more desirable as whole people. He suspected that's why none of them had taken the trouble to develop personalities. Ms. Heather was doubtless about to rattle off a long tale of social successes.

"When I was a kid, I did everything I could to be like everyone else." She gave another lips-together smile to hide those horrible teeth. "I acted like a tomboy. I wore no makeup, ignored fashion trends and refused to go to make-out parties."

Jack let his knife fall to the table; he even stopped peeking under the hem of her still-fluttering skirt. When would she do something he expected? "Go on."

"I hung out with the least popular kids at school— at first for the principle, then because I found most of them a lot more interesting than the so-called 'cool kids.' I didn't try out for Juliet. I let someone else be homecoming queen. I didn't date anyone. Basically, I tried not to let my looks trap me into a personality I didn't have.'' She took a long breath. ''What about you?''

Jack stared, trying to digest the words he'd just heard out of her sexy mouth. Intelligent words. Sensitive words. Words that cut right to the heart of who he'd tried to be.

He pulled up a stool opposite her, practically shaking with impatience to share what he'd been through with someone who would really understand. ''I always hated the way I look. Hated how people reacted, the instant judgements they made. I got tired of trying to convince people they were wrong about me before I even had the chance to be anyone.''

Her blue eyes rested on him calmly, peacefully. Again, the odd sense of déjà vu tingled through his body. He couldn't shake the feeling he'd known this woman longer than an hour. Was this what his married friends meant when they said they felt they'd known their spouses all their lives? Was this woman destined for him?

He dismissed the thought. Not possible. Not after he'd found someone like Marsha. These feelings were the result of some temporary emotional short-circuit—the shock of seeing her haunting image brought to life.

He leaned forward, arms on his thighs. ''Eventually, I gave up and played the woman-eating, self-serving side of beef everyone thought I was.''

She nodded. Her dress fell back over her knees. ''I understand, Jack. I don't blame you. I get tired of fighting too. That's why—well, I met a guy a few weeks ago... He's the first man who ever wanted me for who I am, not what I look like.''

"Are you in love with him?'' The question tumbled out of his lips, before rational thought could censure it. Behind him, the pasta water started to hiss. He sat rigid on the stool, not able to suppress the ridiculous and irrational feeling her answer would define the rest of his life.

She looked at him intently, eyes gone dark with emotion. "Yes.''

Jack stood and exhaled an internal scream of frustration. He was jealous. Wildly jealous. Of what? He barely knew the woman. He was supposed to be in love too. With Marsha.

"What about you, are you seeing anyone?'' She tipped her head to one side; her still-damp hair tumbled across her shoulder.

He nodded dumbly, dumped linguine into the now-boiling water, and set about robotically halving cherry tomatoes.

"How long have you been going out?''

"Only a few weeks.'' He pulled off a stem and sliced so hard his knife made a gash in the new butcher block countertop. Already Marsha seemed far away. How could he betray her like this?

Heather picked up a cherry tomato and bit into it. He glanced over and caught a glimpse of even, white teeth. Great. Ms. Temptation didn't even have the courtesy to exhibit a single physical flaw.

"Are things serious between you two?''

"I thought so.''

Her brow drew down in concern. "Something happened.''

Jack mixed the garlic, cheese and tomatoes in a

small bowl. His ego didn't want this happily-in-love woman to know Marsha might dump him. The rest of him didn't want to keep anything back from her, didn't want to retard the burgeoning intimacy between them.

"I think she's getting...cold feet." His voice came out low and husky.

Heather slid her hand up his arm in what was doubtless supposed to be a comforting gesture. Only it made him a good deal less than comfortable.

"I'm sorry. That must hurt."

"It does." He turned his lower body away so she wouldn't see exactly how much. At her touch, the need to become sexually acquainted increased to a tidal wave of primal masculine urges.

He set himself to control the reaction. Wanting her, he understood. But where the hell had this wrenching tenderness come from? This consuming need to know every aspect of her mind? To learn every part of her, from her toes to her hair to her daily vitamin routine? Did she feel the same? Could he risk finding out? Could he stand to live out his natural life if he didn't?

Nope.

He took a slow, calculated step closer. "But the strangest part..."

Her blue, blue eyes widened, with surprise, pleasure, welcome. "The strangest part?"

He took another step, fixing her with a gaze he allowed to contain all his hunger and all his turmoil over the as-yet undefined feelings. "Is that I'm not as sure about her as I used to be. All of a sudden."

Her breath caught in her throat. "Jack." She laid a shaky hand against his chest. "You're boiling over."

"I know," he breathed. "I can't help myself."

"No, I mean the linguine."

The spluttering hiss of water meeting flame almost drowned out her words. Jack sprang back to lower the heat under the pot. The tidal wave receded slightly, but still hovered in the back of his consciousness, waiting its chance to sweep him away again. He needed reinforcement.

"Would you like some wine?" He made a beeline to the cellar, not waiting for her answer. He definitely needed a drink. He had to rid himself of the insane notion that he was in imminent danger of falling in love with this woman—or worse, that he'd already fallen, the day he saw her outside Stephanie's apartment.

He came back with the bottle and poured two healthy doses. Medicinal purposes.

Heather accepted her glass and raised it, tipping her head back to look at him. "Here's to love, Jack. Here's to love's power to triumph." She shook back her hair, put the glass to her lips, and took a sip, all without taking her gaze from his.

The wave rolled in again. Her eyes held him, pulled him in until he stood nearly between those long, luscious legs, closer than he'd ever been, yet still miles from understanding what drew him.

"Triumph over what?" He could barely get the words out.

"The unexpected."

"Are you the unexpected, Heather?" he whispered.

"Yes," she whispered back. "Yes, I am. Let love triumph over me."

"I'm trying." He felt like weeping. "God, I'm really, really trying."

"Promise me." She clutched his shirt and pulled him forward. "Promise me you'll never forget how much you love Marsha. No matter what happens."

"Yes." He hadn't a clue what she was saying. Only that she'd invaded his being and taken over completely. That her body lay open to him, that her mouth was inches away, that her scent enveloped him, familiar and strange all at once, exciting and fresh, but as if he'd always known it.

He put his hand to the back of her neck, drew her up, brought his lips down to—

Heather turned her head; his kiss landed platonically on her cheek. She smiled apologetically. "Your timing's off, Jack."

"You turned your face away."

"No, I meant this isn't the time."

He insisted his brain return to sanity; it obeyed him grudgingly. "I'm sorry. I went a little out of my mind."

"Me, too." Her full lips stretched into their cheated smile; her eyes shone with what looked like joy. "But it was nice."

Jack turned, picked up a chef's knife and chopped the hell out of some fresh basil.

Nice? Nice? What was so damn nice about it? He'd just made a fool out of himself over the most desirable woman in history when he was supposed to be making plans to convince Marsha to give him another chance. Now he'd have this erection for the next three weeks. There wasn't a single "nice" thing about it.

"I should go." She slipped off the stool and stood awkwardly. "I'm glad to have had this time with you, Jack."

She was leaving. The end. Of course. It had to be.

His brain immediately started planning a nine-course formal dinner for eighteen. "I scared you off."

"No, it wasn't you." She came forward, raised up on tiptoe, and kissed him on the cheek. "It's just not our time yet, Jack."

"Yet?" He clung to an absurd irrational hope. Maybe he could move somewhere bigamy was legal.

"I think we might have another chance."

He watched her leave, his hand on the chef's knife, the linguine bubbling on the range behind him.

Gone.

After one short chance meeting, Heather Brannen resonated through his soul as if she belonged there. And now she was gone.

Damn.

He replayed every minute of their encounter, trying to weld every detail into his permanent memory. The way she arched her body drying her hair; the way she clung to him to keep him from going after the threatening stranger; the way she spoke straight to his heart about her own childhood, the way she'd begged him not to forget how much he loved—

Marsha.

She made him promise not to forget his love for Marsha. Jack went over their entire conversation again, straining to remember words, details, clenching the knife until his hand shook. No. He was sure. Beyond any doubt.

He'd never mentioned Marsha by name.

10

"IT WAS AMAZING, Stephanie." Heather paced from one end of her apartment to the other as if powered by a small motor, phone clenched tightly to her ear. She'd come back so high from seeing Jack that she actually tidied her apartment. She'd probably never find anything again, but at least she had great pacing room. "Everything went ten times better than I even hoped."

"No kidding. You don't think he recognized you?"

"No. I was careful about my voice, and made sure I didn't smile. I also wore different perfume. I think I got away with it."

"For now." Stephanie's tone held a note of warning.

"Of course for now. I'll tell him soon, I promise. I just want him to realize he can have the same strong feelings for Heather as he does for Marsha."

"So what's the verdict so far?"

"Good." Heather laughed, unable to control her excitement, and did her best attempt at a pirouette. "I think he really liked me. You should have seen the way he wanted to punch Roger's lights out. Thank him for me, by the way. He makes a great pervert."

"I'll tell him you said so," Stephanie said drily. "I'm glad things went well, Heather. But the longer you wait to tell him, the harder it will be to convince him you're sincere.''

"I know, I know." Irritation swept through Heather. The most irritating of all irritations: the one that comes from hearing an unwelcome truth.

"Trust me, I just lived it. Thank God Roger decided to give me another chance."

"Another chance?" Heather rolled her eyes. "He asked you to marry him."

"Yeah." Stephanie sighed rapturously. "So don't you blow it. We could have a double wedding."

"One more 'accidental' meeting. Then I'll be sure."

Stephanie made a sound of exasperation. "Your trouble is, you think more of Marsha than you do of yourself. Why can't you believe someone might love you the way you are?"

Heather flopped down onto the couch and stared miserably out the window at the pedestrians and traffic, her pacing motor suddenly out of gas. "Because no one ever has."

"I understand." Stephanie's tone softened. "I went through the same thing trying to hide my money. But trust me on this one. You have to explain about Marsha next time you see Jack."

"Okay, okay. Next time I see him." A taxi drew up in front of her building. The passenger door opened. A man's trousered leg appeared, followed by a dark head, an impressive torso... Heather gasped. "Jack! Here. Now. Omigod."

She punched off the phone, bolted off the futon and stood rigid, eyes stretched to their limit, brain synapses firing at top capacity; she could almost hear their electric crackle in her skull. What was she going to do?

Her buzzer rang. She gave a whimper of panic and stared at the intercom.

If she opened the door as Marsha, she'd perpetuate the deception. Jack deserved better than that. Worse, the sight of Marsha might make him decide to commit to her. Then what chance would Heather stand after the Great Unveiling?

But if she opened the door as Heather, in what he thought was Marsha's apartment, he'd figure out the lie immediately. He'd be furious before she even had the chance to explain that falling in love with him was the last thing she expected when she agreed to the bet. That is, the second to last thing. The very last thing she expected was that Jack would fall in love with Marsha.

The buzzer rang repeatedly. Heather walked over to the intercom, quivering hand outstretched, leaning back as if she were about to touch something diseased. She took a deep breath and pushed the "talk" button, not quite brave enough to buzz him in yet. Muffled sounds of impatient shuffling came through the monitor. Heather made her decision.

"Yes?" she boomed.

"Marsha, it's Jack."

"Can you give me a minute? I'm just out of the shower." She let go of the intercom, not waiting for his response, and dashed to the bathroom. She'd become Marsha just for a few minutes, then gently explain the deception before she revealed herself and her feelings for him. That way he'd have a little warning, a little time to adjust to the change.

Hands shaking, she popped in the brown contacts,

yanked on the padding, and frantically coiled her hair to go under the wig, all the while cursing like a sailor.

A knock came at her door. "Marsha."

"Just a minute!" The cursing surpassed even the most inspired sailor. Someone must have come into the building and let Jack in. No time for the orange foundation. Heather pulled the wig onto her head and ran to her closet. No time for all the ugly high-necked button-y stuff. She'd be taking the disguise off anyway, soon enough.

She grabbed a terry robe and wrapped it snugly around Marsha's bulk, heart going for the world's speed record.

"Marsha." The door shook under the latest pounding.

"On my way." He sounded a tad overwrought. She couldn't help being a little pleased. Maybe Heather had unsettled him enough that he'd come running to Marsha for reassurance. She did a last check in the bathroom mirror, dashed toward the front, remembered her glasses at the last second, jammed them on her nose and opened the door. "Hello, Ja—"

He brushed past her into the apartment and turned to face her, hands on his hips, a black scowl settled on his face. "What the damn hell is going on?"

"What do you mean?" Heather closed the door behind her and sank against it. This didn't seem like a bid for reassurance. Something had gone wrong with her plan.

"Who the hell is that damn woman?"

"Uh..." Heather did some speedy calculating, since playing ignorant wouldn't cut it much longer. How had he connected Marsha with Heather? Had he seen through her disguise?

Jack took a step forward, anger seething from every amazing inch of him. Heather grabbed on to the doorknob behind her for moral support. Judging from the high ''hell'' and ''damn'' count in his sentences, she'd better tread very carefully.

''Which damn woman would that be?'' she asked sweetly.

He took a deep breath and stared at the ceiling as if the plaster would instruct him on whether to strangle her now or later. ''The damn woman who came into my restaurant today and knew your name even though I never told her.''

''Oh, *that* damn woman.'' Heather's attempt to affix a pleasant smile to Marsha's face failed miserably. *Nice little oversight, Heather dear.* Apparently her confession would come sooner rather than later.

''Well?'' He looked at her closely for the first time. His brows drew down so far they almost covered his eyes. ''You look different, Marsha.''

''I...haven't put my makeup on yet.'' She wrapped the robe tighter around Marsha's body and pushed her glasses up farther on her nose. Sooner rather than later, but not this sooner. She needed time to ease into the subject.

Jack took another step closer, eyes going up and down her body. Not a nice step. Not a nice look. A stalking, tiger-on-the-prowl step. A calculating how-many-bites-would-she-make look. ''Very different, Marsha.''

She pushed past him into the middle of the room. ''We need to talk, Jack.''

''We certainly do, *Marsha*.'' He swung around to face her. ''For starters, I'd like to know why your rear end has migrated to the front of your body.''

She looked down and gasped. Marsha's lush derriere protruded in all its glory, right under her navel. Heather nearly choked on her own breath. "Damn" and "hell" no longer suited. Most states had outlawed the words she wanted to use. Her own idiocy had cheated her out of a chance to explain this the way she wanted.

"I've never seen buttocks in quite that place, Marsha dear. You should consult a doctor—as soon as you tell me what fun you've been having at my expense so I can share the many chuckles."

"Jack, please." Heather took the wig and glasses off and tossed them on her desk. She stepped out of the padding and kicked it up onto a chair. "I was going to—"

"Well, well." He came forward and grabbed her chin, turning her face side to side, examining her as if she were a pig at the state fair. "Now you look a little more familiar."

He dropped her chin contemptuously, but she couldn't look away. The passion in his eyes, even though it was anger that burned there, mesmerized her. God she loved this man; would go to any length to show she hadn't meant to hurt him.

"Let down your hair." He uttered the command through lips thinned by rage. The muscles in his face set, became rigid, like marble sculpture. He cemented his fists to his hips, biceps and triceps flexed and visible under the short sleeves of his shirt. His legs spread slightly, feet planted on her rug as if he expected a battering ram to the stomach at any moment. Only the chest and stomach of this livid statue moved, expanded and contracted quickly, powerfully, with his breathing. The smell of his aftershave mixed with the faint spicy whiff of the basil he'd been chopping when she left his restaurant.

Inexplicably, Heather's body reacted with a flood of sensual electricity. Great. Turned on by this incredibly sexy, furious man, ordering her around with all the tenderness of a robot. Next she'd be on her knees, begging for a spanking.

"Let down your hair," he ordered again. "I want to see you."

Heather put her hands up and pulled out the pins, tossed her head to free the blonde mass. Jack's eyes darkened; his mouth opened for a slow inhale. She stared at him incredulously. Unless every ounce of her female intuition had malfunctioned, he was as turned on as she was. She flushed; her breathing ratcheted up another notch.

"Take out the contacts and come back here."

Heather walked into the bathroom, removed the contacts with trembling hands, and walked back into the room calmly, not at all as if her insides screamed for sexual satisfaction. Not at all as if she might lose the love of her life if she made even one false move.

She stood in front of him, in her underwear and bathrobe, feeling more naked than she'd ever felt in her life. Marsha had provided distance, protection from Heather's true feelings. With the farce revealed, she faced Jack alone and painfully vulnerable for the first time.

Jack stared down at her. A muscle jerked in his face. He swallowed. Exhaled.

"Damn you."

He grabbed her shoulders, pulled her to him, kissed her with all the frustration and anger she didn't blame him for feeling. His need for her was as strong as his

need to hurt her. He wouldn't listen to reason until
his fury had abated. Until that time she could only
hang in there and hope she wouldn't have to dial
9-1-1.

She clung to him, wanting to be patient, stoic, to
nurture him through his shock and pain. But one of
his hands gripped her head to keep his mouth on hers;
the other pressed her body tight against him. Passion
exploded through her, sent her Florence Nightingale
fantasy out the window. She wound her arms around
his neck, matched his desire, gave herself over to the
wild need to be ravished.

Then, suddenly, she stood alone in the middle of
her tidy room. Jack was striding over to the window,
hands on his hips again, breathing audible, his stiff
back effectively communicating a still-angry message.

"I understand…" His speech was as stiff as his
back, as if the words were being pulled out of him
with a huge pair of pliers. "I understand why you
started, why you became Marsha."

"I wanted to win the bet." She grimaced wearily.
The bet. What a stupid, juvenile idea. But how could
they have possibly seen what was coming? How
could they possibly have known? How could anyone
have known? Who knew?

"But then why…" he turned around, his eyes full
of hurt and rage, "when I was obviously falling
for…her, why didn't you stop?"

Heather winced. "Her," not "you." Not Heather,
Marsha. Any words of love she might have wanted
to say lodged in her throat behind a giant lump of
misery. She felt like laughing, screaming and crying
all at once, maybe throwing a few blunt objects

through the window. He might want to drag Heather into bed, but when the topic changed to forever, only Marsha would do.

"Why didn't you tell me? Was my chin so important you could justify sacrificing my heart to it?"

She swallowed hard, and managed to make a small sound. She had to say something. She couldn't let him stand there and bleed. "I was going to tell you soon. In fact, I planned to put Marsha away forever, but you showed up today, and I panicked. When I realized you were serious, at Stephanie's house, I knew I couldn't take it any further."

"At Stephanie's house?" His eyes narrowed. "Seems to me I made it clear I was more than a little interested before then."

"I thought you were still trying to win the bet."

"Oh, come on." He gestured exasperatedly. "You can't sense sincerity when it smacks you in the face? What did you want me to do, get down on my knees and propose?"

Heather's misery cracked and allowed in a trickle of annoyance. "How could I know you were sincere? I'd only just met you. For all I knew you were a total manipulative slimeball."

"How ironic. I never wondered about you until now."

"Jack." She walked over to him. "This is ridiculous. I don't want to fight with you."

He nodded, not meeting her eyes, and moved toward the door. "I don't want to fight, either. I'm sorry things turned out this way."

Heather's stomach contracted in panic. That was it? Everything over? Just like that? "You're going to chuck everything you felt for Marsha just because she turned out to look like me? After all your speeches about how looks aren't important?''

"Apparently I mis-speeched." He walked the rest of the way to the door. "Goodbye Marsha—Heather—whoever the hell you are."

"I'm both of them." Heather thumped herself earnestly on the chest. "I'm me."

The concept hit her with a jarring thud, suddenly and absurdly obvious. Stephanie had tried to tell her; François had tried to tell her. Why had she fought believing in herself for so long? Why had she persisted in separating Heather from Marsha; being jealous of Marsha; hating Marsha? The old brown cow hadn't a thing to offer that Heather didn't have, too. "I'm Marsha, Jack."

"No. Marsha was sweet, kind, and supportive. You strike me as manipulative and shallow, and—" He broke off with a confused expression.

"Listen to me. I...am...Marsha." *You idiot.* She still wanted to laugh and scream and cry all at once, only now she wanted to throw the blunt objects at him instead of through the window. Her brain spun with the dizzying final clarity of it all. He'd fallen in love with *her.* That kind of feeling didn't change this fast. She just had to make him stay around long enough to mentally merge Marsha and Heather into one woman.

"No. You're not Marsha. I'm sorry." He opened her door.

Heather stomped after him, resisting the urge to allow her fists pummelling time on his thick head. "Why do you think I went to your restaurant today?"

"I have no idea." He paused, one hand on her

door. "To amuse yourself at my expense? Make me lose my mind? Waste pasta?"

"I went so when Marsha disappeared you'd realize you still had me."

He lifted his hands, fingers tensed, as if he were on the verge of violence. "I don't even know who you are."

"Then why don't you find out who I am?" She almost shouted the words to his retreating back. "Why don't you stick around and find out?"

He half turned. "How do you propose I do that? Conduct an informational interview?"

"Make love to me." She blurted the words out before she knew her own intention. As soon as they left her lips she knew she'd chosen the right path. If she and Jack could recapture the passion, they'd have a chance at restoring the true essence of what bound them together.

Jack turned the rest of the way toward her and stood, frozen, in the doorway. "What did you say?"

"I want you." Wild excitement tumbled through her, heated her body. She loosened the ties to her robe, let it fall open slightly.

"You're crazy," he whispered hoarsely.

"Make love to me, Jack." She lifted her shoulders so the material fell away and halfway down her back.

His eyes burned over her body. She sensed his hesitation, sensed his desire, sensed the conflict inside him. Something had to push him over the edge. Something had to tip the balance in her favor. Something.

She let the robe slip to the ground, arched her back in a seductress's challenge and lifted her chin.

"I dare you."

His eyes widened; his breath rushed in; his jaw clamped. He took one heavy step toward her, then stopped, as if defeated by the weight of indecision.

Heather held her breath. He had to come to her. He had to. This might be their last chance. She ran her hands slowly up her thighs, stopped them just under her bra. "I dare you, Jack...I dare you."

His eyes narrowed to dark, hungry slits; his hand shot straight out, caught the door and slammed it shut behind him.

"*Oh* gosh." Heather gasped the words under her breath. Jack was gone. Disappeared. No more. In his place, a wild ravenous animal, charging toward her with all the civilized gentility of a tiger intent on reducing its prey to bloodied shreds.

Hallelujah.

She braced herself for the impact; he swept her into his arms, strode over to her bathroom, kicked the door open, and growled in frustration. He moved to the next door.

"Closet, Jack."

"Where's the damn bedroom?"

"No bedroom—it's a studio."

"Where do you sleep?"

"On the futon, over there. You have to lift the—"

"To hell with it." He strode over to the futon, kicked the folded comforter off onto the floor, knelt, and laid her on top of it. He straightened, fixed her with a savage gaze, and yanked his shirt off over his head.

Heather lay back and watched him. His head emerged from the neck of his shirt, his hair rumpled in a way that made him look like the vengeful outlaw hero from a wild west movie. Her breathing accelerated; her body warmed, every inch open and receptive to whatever this man who owned her heart wanted to dish out. She had no doubt his vengeance would be swift, but hardly terrible. That kind of punishment she'd stand in line for.

His hands flew to his jeans—unbuttoned, unzipped; he lunged forward. Heather cried out, expecting his full weight on her body. He caught himself, suspended on his hands so that he lay over her, eyes shot through with anger and arousal. He glanced down at her bra and panties as if he thought them beneath contempt.

"Take those off."

She nodded, unhooked the front closure of her bra, let it fall open, slid her panties down and off and lay back again, deliberately docile, electric with heart-thudding anticipation, a tinge of unfounded fear heightening her excitement.

He looked her body over, still supported on his arms, not a tremor apparent.

"You're perfect." He said the words through gritted teeth, as if he meant to taunt her with them. His eyes returned to hers; he lowered himself slowly. A quiver of expectation ran over her skin; she could feel the heat of his body as he approached. Her legs parted instinctively; she ran her hands over the solid muscles of the arms tented over her. His weight settled onto her. The hard length of his erection, hot through his boxers, pressed down between her legs. He rested there, powerful, immobile.

Move. She lay still, looked into his eyes, felt the in and out of his breath match the near-panting pace of hers. He didn't move, looked down at her with a lazy, infuriating grin, daring her to be the first to admit weakness, to break under his torture. She closed her eyes, her body tensed, struggled against the paralysis her pride tried to impose on it. *Move, damn you.*

He'd win. She felt helpless against the need for him. Almost imperceptibly, almost against her will, her hips began to rock up against him. A moan escaped her. Another. Her back arched. She reached up, grabbed his shoulders, tried to force his weight into action. *Move. Move. Move.*

"Jack." She gasped the word out, lifted her hips in rhythm, all pretense at control gone. "Jack." She wrapped her legs around his, rocked up against the hard shaft pressed deep against her. "Move, you ass. *Move!*"

He chuckled, low and deep in his throat. "No."

Heather grunted in frustration, a primal animal sound she barely recognized. She moved her hands to his hips, tried to rock him against her, tried again, again, again. Her breath came wilder, faster. Her head thrashed; her cries grew more frequent. Again, again, rocking up against this stubborn, pigheaded self-righteous, arrogant S.O.B. she loved with every atom of her being. Again, again, again.

The frenzy quieted; certainty took its place. She climbed steeper, higher, arched up and up for one suspended endless moment—then fire rippled through her body; her climax pulsated against his pressure, left her breathless and charged with pleasure. She opened her eyes, breath coming in small gasps as the aftershocks continued.

Jack stared, mouth hanging open, eyes gone completely black, his body rigid. He swallowed and blinked. "Ho-ly sh—"

She grabbed his head down, kissed his mouth with

the driving force of the passion still overwhelming her. His chest lowered onto her, he pushed down his boxers. His hard length surged free against her belly; his hand searched between her legs, found her, he thrust inside, thrust again, then lay still.

"Jack, no." She arched her hips up to take him in deeper, body clamoring for the rhythm to resume. He couldn't play this waiting game again; she'd seen the desperate need in his eyes.

He pulled out of her, moved off to grab his jeans.

"What—" She spoke through her panic, then saw the condom he took from his wallet and breathed a giant sigh of relief. "Oh, thank God. I thought you—"

"Put it on." He knelt, straddling her legs, and held it out to her.

She managed somehow, hands trembling, excitement mounting again. There'd be time enough ahead for tenderness; for their love to be expressed. Right now, she needed to help him through his anger and betrayal until he could find his way to her again.

He lay over her, raised up on his elbows, and began thrusting into her, hard and slow, watching her face. "You hurt me."

"I know, Jack. I didn't mean to." She met his eyes, half longing to comfort him, half-crazed by the feel of him inside her.

He increased the pace, a little harder, a little faster. "You should have told me."

"I know. I know. I tried. I mean I wanted to. I mean—"

"You should have." Harder, faster. His breath came more rapidly, less air in each breath. With each push, his head bent toward her, his abdomen flexed into washboard perfection. "You owed it to me…you owed me…you—oh man, Heather." He fell onto her again, slid his hands under her back, crushed her to him, kissed her wildly, pushing, rocking hard and sweet until he strained and straightened, whispered her name, and pulsed into her.

The apartment air-conditioning came on, A car horn blared outside. A man shouted unintelligible words. A bus motor revved, roared and faded.

Heather added a long, unapologetically blissful sigh to the sounds making their way back into her consciousness. A sappy, sated grin wanted to curve her mouth. She let it. Her hand wanted to caress a long path up Jack's back, to bury itself into his thick dark hair. She let that happen, too. This wasn't the time to deny herself anything. Not when she'd just discovered physical and emotional fulfillment with enough explosive power to start World War Three.

Above her, the man who had made her current bliss possible lay still, not quite relaxed, his face still turned away; his breathing beating her own luxuriant pace by several breaths a minute.

Her brows lowered. Someone was tense. Not a good sign. "Jack?"

He grunted.

Her brows lowered further. She poked him in the ribs. "Jack."

He turned his head, gave her a swift smile and a swifter kiss on the cheek, lifted off her and started rummaging for his clothes.

"I take it we won't be basking in an extended afterglow." Heather struggled to her feet, trying to calm her threatening panic. Nothing foreboding about his lack of tenderness, right? Nothing to do with his feelings for her, or lack thereof, right? Guys always wanted a little separation after sex. Right? Didn't they? *Help.*

According to her plan, he should be so overcome by their lovemaking, his distrust and disgust would magically vanish. All thoughts of Marsha should have found their way down the proverbial drain by now, replaced with a burning desire to confess eternal and undying ever-after love for Heather. According to her plan.

Except that Jack had not been given an advance copy for review.

"You wanted me to make love to you." He pulled on his jeans, watching her with a dull, remote expression that made her want to knock on his skull and scream at him to wake up. "I obliged. But I can't stay."

"Why?" She made fists of her hands, tensed every muscle, trying to balance on this teetering pinnacle where things made sense, where the love she'd finally found wasn't about to be ripped away. "Why can't you stay?"

"There's no reason to." He took two strides to the center of the room, bent to retrieve her bathrobe and tossed it to her.

Heather caught the robe by reflex and shoved her arms into the sleeves, too numbed by shock to experience the pain she must be feeling. Apparently the overwhelmingly glorious magic of their union had been a solo experience. His anger hadn't abated at all. She still hadn't made him understand.

She geared up for another attempt. "Jack, listen. Marsha was supposed to be a harmless prank, a creative way to get your stubborn chin on camera. That's it. I would have laid down my life savings you couldn't even bring yourself to kiss her, let alone sleep with her. Falling for her wasn't even a consideration.''

''Why?'' He pulled his shirt on, still staring at her with those chilling, matter-of-fact eyes.

''Because I thought you were the same shallow jerk you think I am now. I didn't believe anyone with looks like yours could be anything else.'' She tugged the robe tightly around her, hating the pleading, desperate sound in her voice, but unable to regard the end of their relationship with as much ennui as he seemed to feel. Thank God she never told him how deeply she felt about him. This level of humiliation was plenty. ''I was wrong about you. Why can't you admit that possibility about me?''

''Because you got to see me for who I really am, then came to like me. I came to like you before I saw who you really are.''

Heather shook her head. *Like?* She loved him. Their relationship couldn't possibly end over padding, a wig and glasses. Shouldn't love rise above such technicalities? ''The only difference is the way I look. The *only* difference.''

''I'm sorry, Heather.'' He finished dressing and crossed over to her front door. ''You are a very desirable woman. But you're not half as beautiful to me as Marsha.''

Heather recoiled. Once again her looks had cheated her out of any chance at happiness—with someone who should have known better. Jack couldn't see past her appearance any farther than the worst of them. He hadn't really loved Marsha. He only loved the fact that she didn't look like Heather. "You're in love with a fantasy, Jack."

He nodded slowly, looked her up and down as if he wanted to forget every detail as quickly as possible. "So I discovered. Goodbye."

He opened the door and walked out.

Heather stared incredulously at the door closing behind him. A mistake. This was all a mistake. Any second he'd come back in and admit he'd made a mistake. She heard the elevator doors open. Shut. No. He wasn't on that elevator. He'd changed his mind. He was still standing out in the hall. She rushed forward and flung open the door.

He wasn't there.

She whirled and rushed over to the window. He'd change his mind on the ground floor. She saw him step out into the street, hail a taxi. Hail another. And another. Her mouth twisted in an agonized smile. Still couldn't get a cab worth a damn.

He'd get discouraged and come back up. Or, she could go down and help him. Make one last attempt to—

A cab stopped. Jack got inside. Heather leaned against the window, feeling its uncaring coolness on her heated forehead. The cab merged into the traffic, turned onto Thirteenth street and disappeared.

He was gone.

11

JACK'S CAB PULLED TO A STOP in front of Stephanie's apartment building. He struggled out, stuffed two twenty-dollar bills into the astonished driver's hand, hightailed it into the building's lobby, and pushed Stephanie's buzzer impatiently. He needed to talk to Roger. He'd gone almost halfway to Roger's apartment in Queens before he remembered his brother would be spending the day with Stephanie, to celebrate their reconciliation and engagement.

He pushed the buzzer again. They had to be there. If he didn't spill to someone soon, he'd start trying to braise the hallway carpet. How could he not have seen that Marsha was Heather? That Heather was Marsha? How could he have been so blind? So clueless?

He shook his head. He didn't see because he didn't want to see. He didn't want to know Marsha wasn't real. He wanted desperately to believe in her, couldn't bear to think she might turn out to be an illusion— worse than an illusion, a joke, played on him at his most vulnerable point.

He punched the button again. Where the hell were Roger and Stephanie? Probably going at it on the living room floor. Just where he'd been barely an hour ago. He shouldn't have made love to Heather. Especially after she'd made it clear the whole charade was just an amusing pastime that had taken a small detour for the worse.

He'd listened, waited patiently, then not so patiently, then writhing in agony, as she argued the finer points of the escapade, always trying to show it wasn't her fault—trying to show he was wrong to be so furious. Nowhere in the conversation had she admitted to even the slightest degree of affection. Now that he thought about it, Marsha hadn't ever confessed any deep passion either.

He let his head thump against the wall. Marsha. What a joke. He had to stop thinking about her. He had to stop thinking about both of them, and conquer this hopeless anger and frustration. He'd rarely been this furious with anyone, let alone someone he desired. And he'd never combined that fury with sex.

He clenched his fists against the cool wood next to his head. But, man, it had been wildly exciting. She was perfect. She'd abandoned herself so completely to her body's need. Why couldn't her heart need him like that?

He pounded the buzzer again. *Come on.*

In that minute or so after his mind-blowing climax, when he'd wanted most to hang on to his rage, the truth had come to him in an almost unbearable rush: He loved her. In spite of her deception; in spite of her lack of understanding, her lack of remorse. He loved her, even though he continued, out of sheer self-protection, to insist she and Marsha had nothing in common except the technicality of being the same person. At that point, he'd wanted only to escape as fast as possible.

He loved her. He wanted her to love him. He was a complete moron.

A woman came into the lobby. He turned and gave her a distracted smile. Her eyes widened in astonishment, then narrowed to sultry slits. Jack sighed. Was he now sentenced to a lifetime of pouty-lipped offers from strangers? Forever denied what he craved most just after he found it? His heart ached for Marsha—Heather. Whichever.

"Allow me," the woman crooned, and fit her key into the lock as if it were the beginning of a sex act.

Jack suppressed eye-rolling distaste and nodded his thanks.

She crowded him onto the elevator, bringing a dense cloud of over-sweet perfume with her. She punched the button to her floor and turned provocatively. "What can I get you, gorgeous?"

"Fourth floor, please."

She pressed the button. To his horror, she reached down for the hem of her dress and started waving it up and down, as if her underwear needed fresh air. She leaned forward so her breasts practically jumped out of her bra. "Ever done anything really, really fun in an elevator?"

Jack opened his mouth for the usual put-off, when a picture flashed into his mind. Heather, perched on a stool in the restaurant, flapping the wet hem of her dress.

I met a guy a few weeks ago... He's the first man who ever wanted me for who I am, not what I look like.

Uncertainty began to tear away Jack's torment. Had she meant him? Of course. Of course she had. Because he'd fallen for her when she looked like Marsha?

Are you in love with him? He'd asked in a state of

wild jealousy. Now it turned out he'd been jealous of himself. *Are you in love with him?*

Yes.

Jack's eyes widened. His breath began coming faster.

"Ooooh." The woman flapped harder. "I can tell you're as ready as I am."

He stared at her, barely registering her presence, going over the restaurant encounter with every ounce of his concentration. What else had Heather said? She made him promise never to forget how much he loved Marsha. No matter what happened.

She wanted him to keep loving her, no matter who she was. Crazed excitement began racing through his system. Heather loved him. Marsha loved him. They both loved him. He gave a short laugh.

The woman oozed forward another step. "Want to push the alarm button and…get acquainted?"

He grinned, his mind full of Heather. "I'd love to. You know, elevators are great places to find extoplasmostic larvae, and I might need some help."

"Exto—what?" The woman's eyes turned wary.

"Extoplasmostic larvae. The minute babies of the Quangdofilous bacterial beetle, my specialty. Ah! Such a fascinating dusty little world they inhabit." He babbled the words happily, feeling like he'd conquered Mt. Everest and stood at its peak, surveying the beauty of the rest of his life spread out before him. Heather loved him.

"Uh…here's my stop." The woman edged toward the door. "Maybe some other time."

Jack got down on his hands and knees and began to inspect the floor. "If you're sure you won't join me…"

She stepped off the elevator, mumbling something about a colossal waste. The doors shut behind her.

Jack sprang to his feet and paced impatiently until the elevator reached Stephanie's floor. He burst out, raced to her door and pounded mercilessly.

A long minute later, Stephanie opened the door, mussed and cranky-looking in a long robe. Her brows raised. "What are you doing here? Where's Heath...uh—"

"Heather's over at Marsha's place."

Stephanie's brows crashed back down. "Still Marsha? I thought she was—"

Jack pushed past her into the apartment. Roger came sleepily out of the bedroom, wearing a pair of boxers with red hearts on them. "What's up?"

The sight of Roger triggered something in Jack's brain. He advanced on his brother. "You knew about Marsha, didn't you? You knew and didn't tell me."

Roger backed up, hands raised in surrender. "Steph made me promise. She insisted you guys were made for each other. What do I know?" He sent her a glowing smile. "I do what I'm told."

"You set us up?" Jack turned to Stephanie, mouth hanging open incredulously. "This whole thing was a matchmaking ploy?"

Stephanie indulged in an irritatingly smug grin. "I could have just traded the chin shoot for the cash you needed. But you and Heather had a lot in common, and I just had a feeling..."

"You had a feeling." Jack shook his head and laughed. He couldn't help it. No two people had ever been brought together in a stranger way. He'd been trying to put one over on Marsha. Heather had been putting one over on him. Stephanie on Heather...

Like a picture that turns out to be picture within another picture, and so on and so on.

"So what's going on with the lady in question?" Roger asked. "Where is she?"

"I need your help. Both of you." Jack held out his hands, aware he was beaming with more wattage than the whole of Las Vegas. "I'm going to ask Marsha out on her very last date."

HEATHER SAT ON HER SOFA, staring out into the street with tired, unmoving, unblinking, dry-as-hell miserable eyes. She had to look at something. The view of her life going down the toilet was not inspiring. She supposed she still half hoped to see Jack's cab coming back around the corner. So far nothing. Merely five or six hours had passed. There was still time to wait. She'd probably die of dehydration in a few days anyway.

Not that anyone would notice. Or care.

She'd tried everything to make Jack understand she hadn't meant to hurt him. Nothing worked. Maybe he didn't want it to.

So much for forgive and forget. So much for love conquers all. So much for happily frigging ever after. Something about Heather made them all run away, screaming for the Marshas of the world.

The phone rang. She moved her eyes and stared at it dully. Phone. Whoopee. She had no one in her life she wanted to speak to. Ever again.

Second ring. She twisted her face into a speculative scowl. On the other hand, maybe she could derive some comfort from another human voice. As long as it wasn't Stephanie. Stephanie was happy. Stephanie was engaged. She hated Stephanie.

Third ring. One more and the machine would pick up. Let it. The machine could talk to them. The machine hadn't had its heart impaled on a skewer.

Fourth ring. The machine picked up. It was Stephanie. She did sound happy. She wanted Heather to call the minute—no, the *second* she came back. She wanted Heather to come over right away, dressed as Marsha, so François could photograph her.

Yeah, right. Heather snorted and turned away. Like she'd really want this chapter of her life documented for posterity. She stared dismally at the street. A car went by. Another. A lady walking her dog. Then nothing.

The air in her apartment began to thicken; the walls sagged and closed in. Heather jumped to her feet. She had to get out. Go for a walk. Clear her mind.

She slumped back onto the couch and let her head loll on the cushions. And have to fend off every man in New York? No, thanks. Not in the mood.

She was trapped. Quicksanded. Her life wasn't even worth its whirl down the porcelain bowl.

Her eyes shot open. But Marsha could walk anywhere with total impunity. Marsha could bring her the relief she needed. Heather jumped back off the couch and headed to her bathroom. Thank God for Marsha—her only true friend.

Half an hour later, Heather emerged triumphantly, padding, wig, contacts and glasses in place; high-necked multi-button armor on; orange foundation and horrific makeup applied.

She blew Marsha an affectionate kiss in her full-length mirror, and spent ten aggravating minutes trying to find her keys, buried in all the neatness. That done, she sailed out of the apartment, down the elevator and out onto the sidewalk.

The air outside had cooled considerably, a good thing for her man-made-fiber outfit. A breeze blew across the street, bringing a faint whiff of hot dogs from the cart on the corner. Heather struck out toward Seventh Avenue, feeling a tiny bit more human. She had gone only a few steps when she heard feet pounding the pavement behind her.

"Miss. Oh, Miiiiiss."

She turned around at the sound of the nasal whine, and gasped in involuntary horror. Marsha's perfect mate, in all his questionably masculine glory. Too-short, too-tight black and white checked polyester pants, white socks glowing shamelessly above blue lace-up sneakers. The belt of his pants rode halfway up to his chest, displaying the mid-sized paunch underneath to advantage. Blue ink had oozed from a pen to stain the pocket of his white not-at-all-cotton shirt. His hair had been slicked back except for a stubborn cowlick which stood up, Alfalfa-style, on the top of his head. Predictably, tape held together the broken bridge of his coke-bottle glasses.

Heather could only gape. Was this the type of man the Marshas of the world were prey to?

She chastised herself immediately. Had she learned nothing from her experience? Lurking under the geeky exterior might be the heart of a soulmate. Forget she just lost the only one she'd ever want. "Yes?"

"Hi. Uh, hi. I, um, couldn't help noticing you, you're so beautiful and everything. I was wondering if you'd, uh, like to go out with me."

Heather forced Marsha to smile politely, to cover the mad giggle bubbling up inside her. Not the suavest come-on, but endearing—and at least she could still laugh. "Thanks, but I don't really—"

"Please." He produced a bouquet of wilted daisies from behind his back.

"How sweet." Heather smiled at the bedraggled bouquet, genuinely touched.

"Please...Marsha."

Heather stiffened. Marsha? Only Stephanie, Roger and François knew about Marsha.

And—

Heather peered closely into the man's face. Her mouth dropped open. Her heart began doing a hot Latin number in her chest. "Jack."

"Who?" His face twisted in exaggerated confusion. "I'm Freddy. Freddy Fingleding, your classmate from Vodeedo High. Don't you remember me?" He pushed his glasses up onto his nose and grinned goofily.

Joy built a crazy pressure through Heather's body until she was afraid it would blow Marsha's wig off the top of her head. Jack. It was Jack. He'd come back to her.

"Gosh, Marsha, I sure would like to take you out to dinner. To some really swanky place—like Beef 'n' Beef...'n' More Beef. Would you like to go with me, Marsha? Would you? Huh?"

"Oh, Freddy." Heather gazed up at him. "I'd love to."

He reached out both hands and cupped her face, drew it toward him and kissed her. Heather melted into him as far as their combined padding would allow, returned his kiss with all the love she hadn't yet been able to express.

When they drew apart, both pairs of glasses had

been knocked askew. Jack sported a smear of orange makeup across his face; Marsha's wig felt decidedly off-center.

Heather didn't care. He'd never looked so handsome. She'd never felt so beautiful in her life. "What made you come back?"

"You." His voice lowered to its usual pitch; he smiled a real smile. "Both of you. I finally heard what you'd been telling me all along."

"That I didn't ever mean to hurt you?" She practically sobbed her relief at finally being able to explain.

"That, and—"

"That I would have told you about Marsha sooner if I hadn't been so sure you wouldn't want me?"

He touched her cheek tenderly. "That, and—"

"That making love with you was the most incredible experience of my life?"

He laughed. "And—"

"That I...love you?" She said the words carefully, as if they were fragile; her mind, body and time itself stopped to wait for his response.

"Yeah." His smile grew. "That I love you."

Heather gave a hiccuping sob of laughter. He loved her. Not Marsha. Not some idealized vision—but her.

He pulled her close again. Their glasses met and parried. Heather's padding started to itch. The wig slipped another inch.

"Jack," Heather murmured against his mouth. "I think Marsha and Freddy have a dinner date at Beef Central. We don't want to keep them."

"No." Jack lifted the edge of Marsha's wig and planted a line of leisurely kisses down Heather's hairline. "While they're off getting acquainted, what do you say we go back up to your apartment and do the same?''

''My thought exactly, though we may want to double date again some time in the future.'' Her voice came out an ecstatic whisper. Nothing in her life had ever felt this right, this wonderful. She and Marsha had both found their perfect mates.

She took Jack's arm; they headed toward the entrance to Heather's building. An elderly couple strolling along stared rudely. The woman gave a snort of laughter. ''Look at those two, Herman. Are they made for each other, or what?''

''Yeesh.'' The man coughed and gestured with his cane. ''They're gonna have one set of homely kids.''

Jack smiled at Heather and winked. ''What do you think?''

Heather laughed, her heart near-bursting with happiness. ''For their sake, I certainly hope so.''

Return to the charm of the Regency era with

GEORGETTE HEYER,

creator of the modern Regency genre.

Enjoy six romantic collector's editions with forewords
by some of today's bestselling romance authors,

**Nora Roberts, Mary Jo Putney,
Jo Beverley, Mary Balogh,
Theresa Medeiros and Kasey Michaels.**

Frederica
On sale February 2000

The Nonesuch
On sale March 2000

The Convenient Marriage
On sale April 2000

Cousin Kate
On sale May 2000

The Talisman Ring
On sale June 2000

The Corinthian
On sale July 2000

Available at your favorite retail outlet.

HARLEQUIN®
Makes any time special ™

Visit us at www.romance.net

PHGHGEN

Back by popular demand are

DEBBIE MACOMBER's

Hard Luck, Alaska, is a town that needs women! And the O'Halloran brothers are just the fellows to fly them in.

Starting in March 2000 this beloved series returns in special 2-in-1 collector's editions:

MAIL-ORDER MARRIAGES, featuring
Brides for Brothers and *The Marriage Risk*
On sale March 2000

FAMILY MEN, featuring
Daddy's Little Helper and *Because of the Baby*
On sale July 2000

THE LAST TWO BACHELORS, featuring
Falling for Him and *Ending in Marriage*
On sale August 2000

Collect and enjoy each MIDNIGHT SONS story!

Available at your favorite retail outlet.

HARLEQUIN®
Makes any time special ™

HEART OF THE WEST

Every Man Has His Price!

Lost Springs Ranch was famous for turning young mavericks into good men. So word that the ranch was in financial trouble sent a herd of loyal bachelors stampeding back to Wyoming to put themselves on the auction block!

July 1999	*Husband for Hire* Susan Wiggs	January 2000	*The Rancher and* *the Rich Girl* Heather MacAllister
August	*Courting Callie* Lynn Erickson	February	*Shane's Last Stand* Ruth Jean Dale
September	*Bachelor Father* Vicki Lewis Thompson	March	*A Baby by Chance* Cathy Gillen Thacker
October	*His Bodyguard* Muriel Jensen	April	*The Perfect Solution* Day Leclaire
November	*It Takes a Cowboy* Gina Wilkins	May	*Rent-a-Dad* Judy Christenberry
December	*Hitched by Christmas* Jule McBride	June	*Best Man in Wyoming* Margot Dalton

HARLEQUIN®
Makes any time special™

Visit us at www.romance.net

PHHOWGEN

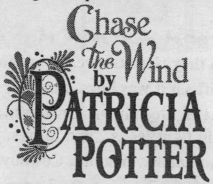
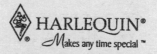

HARLEQUIN
Duets

When they were twelve, it was horses.

At fifteen it was boys…and horses.

**At eighteen it was cowboys…
in tight jeans…and horses.**

And *now*…look out, Cowboy!

Talented **Carrie Alexander** brings you

The Cowgirl Club

three smartly funny stories about love
between three most improbable couples.

April 2000 **Custom-Built Cowboy**
July 2000 **Counterfeit Cowboy**
October 2000 **Keepsake Cowboy**

Available at your favorite retail outlet.

HARLEQUIN®
Makes any time special.™

Visit us at www.romance.net

HDTCC